T0165359

PARIS
OF
TROY

By Chris A. Detherage

iUniverse, Inc.

New York   Bloomington

PARIS OF TROY

iUniverse books may be ordered through booksellers or by contacting:

iUniverse
1663 Liberty Drive
Bloomington, IN 47403
www.iuniverse.com
1-800-Authors (1-800-288-4677)

Because of the dynamic nature of the Internet, any Web addresses or links contained in this book may have changed since publication and may no longer be valid. This is a work of fiction. All of the characters, names, incidents, organizations, and dialogue in this novel are either the products of the author's imagination or are used fictitiously.

ISBN: 978-1-4502-3166-4 (pbk)
ISBN: 978-1-4502-3168-8 (ebk)

Printed in the United States of America
iUniverse rev. date: 5/24/10

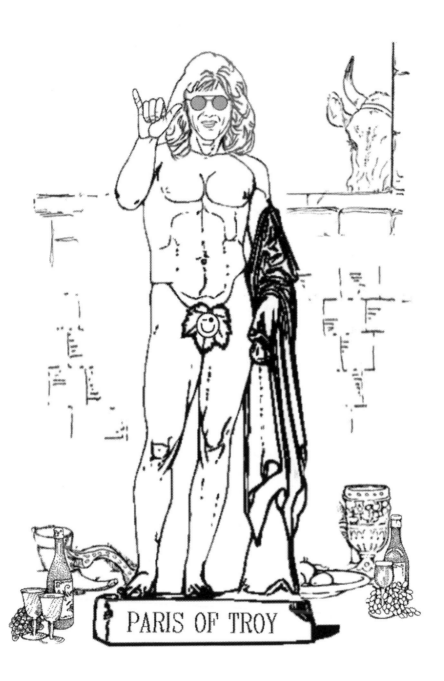

PARIS OF TROY

Chapter One

Because of their ability to cure the clap, I used to think that doctors, especially expensive, discreet ones, could heal just about anything. I was wrong, unfortunately, because I've recently learned that when it comes to serious battlefield wounds, there isn't a heck of a lot they can do for you.

The doctor studies my wound closely and frowns. He looks more like a disappointed fortuneteller than a confident physician.

"I'm afraid you don't have much time left," he says, very apologetically. "Maybe today, perhaps tomorrow."

He's talking about my death, of course, and normally, his prognosis would scare me enough to start praying for divine forgiveness and intervention, but right now, there's no need for such drastic action. That's because I know my dear wife, Oenone the Nymph, is on her way to save me with her magic and she'll get here maybe today, surely tomorrow. Then, after she has healed my wound, we will return to our farm on Mount Ida and live there in happiness, just like we should have done all along, you know, before I screwed everything up for us.

So, until Oenone arrives, I have to lay here in this hospital room and suffer for all the mistakes I have made since leaving her. And brother, I do mean suffer. My body bears two painful wounds that are equal in magnitude to the terrible sins I have committed. One is profoundly psychological and the other is embarrassingly physical.

1

Both hurt like fuck. You see, I suffer spiritually from the guilt I feel for causing so much death and destruction. Because of my careless lust, thousands of innocent people have died in a horrible war that has raged on now for ten years. There isn't a family in Troy that hasn't lost a loved one in the fighting, including mine. Little wonder then that everybody hates me and are, no doubt, glad I lay suffering. Who can blame them? And I'm sure they're amused by the location of physical wound. Heck, they're probably falling down about it because get this: I have a poisoned arrow sticking out of my testicles. No shit, I was shot there a few days ago by Hercules' toady sidekick, Philoctetes.

In the fucking balls, for god's sakes!

I mean, what kind of guy shoots another guy in the nuts?

A really sick one, you'll agree.

And let me ask you something else. Is there a worse place for a man to be wounded in? Fuck no there isn't! That's especially true when you're a guy like me because I've always been the type who tended to let the little head do all my thinking. It's what helped start this stupid war. And it's what has always gotten me into trouble. No big secret there. Just ask anyone and I'm sure they will tell you that I was wounded in exactly the right place. Poetic justice, they'd probably call it. And I'm not inclined to disagree with them either. I got what I deserved, I guess. But what I don't deserve is all the blame they have heaped on me for starting this damned war because, you see, the truth is, there's a whole host of others just as guilty for starting it as I am. And, oddly enough, some of these people still visit me throughout the day. They come in, acting all innocent and shit, to see if I am still among the quick because, as the old saying goes, death opens a thousand doors for the living.

Helen, my beautiful partner in crime, usually pops in at least twice a day to check on me. But she does so more out of concern for her future than for my suffering because she knows that her fate will be in question if I die. She doesn't love me and probably never did. She just wants to go back home to Sparta so she can start whoring around again. Good luck! I know that won't happen because my father, King Priam,

2

will never let her go. He'll hang on to Helen even if it means Troy will burn for it. Dad visits me too. He sits in a chair next to my bed and prattles on and on about the war. I usually ignore him when he does, because, believe me, nothing causes one to lose interest in king and country like an arrow in the balls does. Anyway, he's got my death all figured out; he intends to marry Helen to my brother Deiphobus so he can continue to thumb his nose at the Greeks from Troy's walls. And that's exactly why Deiphobus shows up every now and then because the sooner I quit breathing, the sooner he gets to have Helen as a bride and becomes next in line to the crown. It's what the bastard has always coveted. Well, he can have the whole black, bloody business, for all I care, and command of the Trojan Army too. That should make that duty-bound, flag waving, son-of-a-bitch Aeneas happy because he'll finally get an army commander who enjoys playing soldier as much as he does. God, how Aeneas drives me crazy with his military bullshit! Like clockwork, he marches into my room every morning and pesters me about army crap until I feel like my brain is going to explode. But he isn't anywhere near the pest my loony, fortunetelling sister is. Cassandra's been predicting Troy's demise ever since I stepped foot in the place and since that doesn't seem likely to happen now, she's had to content herself with forecasting my death instead. Sis usually swings by once a day to see if her latest fantasy has come true. She wants me to die and she wants me to die now so that she can finally run around telling folks, "See? I told you so!" Well, fuck the bitch; I intend to stay alive just to spite her. The only faces I still care to see belong to General Cadmus and my sister Polyxena. Together, we almost ended this damned war. But that doesn't matter now. All that matters is that Oenone comes to rescue me before it's too late.

The room I lie in is a dark and dreary place. That's because a single, small window severely restricts the amount of sunlight that can enter it and so, oil lamps must be hung around me in order to provide the doctor with enough illumination to see and care for my wound. When the wind blows through the narrow slit, it causes the flames in the lamps to flicker and suddenly, the walls around me are filled with a multitude of dark, dancing shadows that never cease to fill me with a sense of dread. Brave, I am not. When the shadows appear, as they are doing right now, I usually close my eyes to them. If I am lucky, I will drift off to sleep. If I am not, then I will lie here and remember.

This morning, I am not lucky.

I remember. I remember....

Like most guys, my earliest memory is of my mother's breasts. How big and round and nourishing they were. I remember clinging to them with my tiny hands and sucking on them with my tiny lips but most of all, I remember the warmth they provided me. Then, all at once, I remember being torn from mother's bosom by a pair of rough hands and the warmth was gone. After that, everything seemed cold — the earth I lay on, the stars in the night sky and the wind that howled around me. One by one, a strange assortment of animals appeared around me. I looked at each and wondered if they were my new mothers. And then the rough hands appeared again with the sunlight and I remember being warm again.

I am, of course, talking about the time I was abandoned on the slopes of Mount Ida as an infant. Can you believe that shit? I still have a hard time believing that my parents would so callously abandon me to my death but that's exactly what they did. And that's also the type of parents I had: callous. And if that wasn't bad enough, they were also very superstitious. That's how I ended up with a one way ticket to Mount Ida. You see, one night, while my mother was pregnant with me, she had a dream in which she was giving birth to a flaming torch that would someday set the entire city of Troy on fire and burn it to ash. If you ask me, I think my mother was suffering from a severe case of heartburn — she always did like to smother her food with too much pepper and garlic — but, unfortunately for me, nobody thought of that. Instead, my father summoned the soothsayer Aesacus to interpret my mother's dream.

And, by the by, let me tell you a little something about royal soothsayers — they're always looking for a reason to justify their cushy gigs. That's why you'll never hear one of them attribute anything to the simple workings of nature. With them, everything's always the will of the gods. And, of course, lo and behold, they're the only ones who can interpret that will. How fucking convenient for everyone!

Little wonder then, that Aesacus declared my mother was about to give birth to a son who would cause disaster to Troy. Duh! What did folks think the idiot was gonna say? Take some bicarbonate and try to squeeze out a good, long fart? No fucking way! And so, soon after I was born, momma and poppa sent for Agelaus, the court's Royal Baby Killer, and ordered him to take me to Mount Ida and abandon my ass on its windy slopes. Agelaus did as he was instructed but when he returned the next day to recover my remains; he found that I was still alive and kicking. How I survived, I don't know. Probably just dumb luck. But nevertheless, survive I did. It also helped that Agelaus was a farmer because, as everyone knows, farmers are always in need of a helping hand, and in me, he saw a chance of obtaining free labor for years. So, instead of leaving me out another night to die like he was supposed to do, he bundled me up into a purse — hence the name Paris — and carried me down to his farm at the base of Mount Ida.

Okay, you see the kind of shit I had to deal with here? I was screwed from the get-go. I mean, I'm born and before I could get properly settled in, I'm dumped in the middle of Bumfuck Nowhere like an unwanted dog. Try reconciling that one for the rest of your life. I'm telling you it can't be done. Little wonder then that I was so screwed up and made so many mistakes. Who fucking wouldn't? So don't blame me. Blame my lousy parents.

Anyway, as I have just said, Agelaus became my overseer and his farm became my workplace. I grew up tending his flocks of sheep and herds of cattle on the slopes of Mount Ida. I had escaped death but the one thing I could not escape was the royal blood that flowed through my veins. Centuries of noble breeding had combined in me to produce a very handsome, intelligent and energetic youth, all of which are definitely not the sort of traits that one usually finds in a farmer. That's because farming, on the whole, tends to be extremely boring and, as a result, farmers tend to be a dull lot. I mean, mostly, all they do is sit around watching the animals eat, fuck and shit, and when they're not busy doing that, they stare up at the sky and wonder if it's going to rain on their ass. Believe me, farming definitely wasn't the occupation for a blueblood like me. That's why I was always restless as a child and would do just about anything to alleviate the mind-boggling boredom of my days. Luckily, Agelaus alertly noticed this and instead of bitching about it like most bosses would have done, he sought constructive ways of tempering my restlessness. That's how I got an education and became a crack shot with a bow. One day, when I was eight or nine, Agelaus suddenly showed up with a towel-head tutor named Omarr whom he had hired to teach me how to read and write. And, to insure I didn't waste his money, Agelaus also handed me a beautiful bow and a quiver full of arrows. The deal was, I could play with the bow only after I had mastered all of Omarr's lessons. It should come as no shock when I tell you it took me only a few months to learn to read and write. I mean, what boy can't wait to get his hands on a weapon of mass destruction? Come on! So off I went, joyfully killing all sorts of animals with my new toy — rodents, birds, deer, squirrels, etc. — just about anything that looked like it could be penetrated with an arrow, except the livestock, of course, although, believe me, I was tempted. And let me tell you, I eventually got so good with the bow that I could hit a fly in the ass at a hundred cubits! I'm not kidding, I really could. I actually proved it one night when I was ten, although, I must admit, not by shooting something as small as a fly, but by shooting something a whole lot bigger and deadlier — cattle thieves. Almost the same thing though. Both are big pests to cattle herders.

It happened like this: one night, while I lay dozing underneath a tree, I heard the warning sound of snapping twigs. Suspecting that a bear or a wolf might be lurking nearby, I swiveled around slowly and saw the dark outlines of about five...no, wait...twenty...yeah...twenty men standing amongst the cattle not more than thirty cubits away. Rustlers! I couldn't believe my eyes and for a moment, I simply froze. I didn't know what to do. I was only ten years old for god sakes! But as the rustlers began to lead the cattle away, my mind cleared, and suddenly,

I knew exactly what I needed to do. Silently laying an arrow on the bridge of my bow, I slowly drew back the string and notch; taking aim at the nearest man, I let the arrow fly. I knew the second it left my bow that it was on target. And it was! Catching the man squarely in the neck, I watched as he desperately clawed at the protruding arrow and staggered agonizingly towards his comrades. Then he dropped to the ground like a stone. The men around him immediately shouted at each other in alarm and began scurrying all about the place in complete confusion. A lot of good it did them! I quickly sprang to my feet and, on a dead run, I took aim and loosed my arrows one by one, until all thirty rustlers were dead. Fuckers never had a chance, I tell you. How terrifying I must have looked as I silently darted around them loosing death each time I did. Murder? Maybe. Fun? You bet it was. Exhilarating too! And that's exactly the state of mind Agelaus found me in the next morning.

Looking around at all the dead bodies, Agelaus asked me what happened.

"I killed the shit out of them!" I shouted, proudly puffing out my tiny chest as I did.

"Rustlers?" Agelaus asked.

Obviously, he wasn't what you'd call real quick. It's a trait most farmers share.

"Yes, rustlers," I answered, "And look, each one has an arrow in the neck. Ain't I a great shot?"

Even then, I loved tooting my own horn!

Agelaus looked at me in a way that he had never done before and said, "Yes, kid, you are a great shot."

"Damn straight I am!" I yelled with glee. "Shouldn't I get a reward?"

And that's how I got the name of Alexander. Agelaus gave it to me as a cheap reward and also probably just to shut me up. It means "protector" or something cool like that. I'm not really sure exactly. Anyway, it's a damn sight better than Paris. Unfortunately, it wasn't much of a reward though, mainly because the only people who ever called me Alexander were Agelaus, Helen, Menelaus and Deidameia. Everyone else stuck with my baby name. That has always annoyed me a little.

Anyway, after that, I was a bit of a celebrity. Word quickly got around to the other farmers about my deadly skill. Why, I couldn't walk through the local market without being stared at. Of course, being starved for attention, I absolutely loved it! You should have seen me. My chest was puffed out boldly, my neck was erect, and my lips were formed in a haughty smirk that said: lookout, I'm a man killer. How splendid I must have looked!

Unfortunately, the only bad thing about being a celebrity is that it doesn't last forever. And that's especially true in a farming community. It wasn't long before it seemed everyone forgot about my deed. That's mainly because my ass was back up on the mountain tending Agelaus' herds. Out of sight, out of mind, I guess you could say. And it didn't help matters that I now had nothing to do except watch the animals perform their daily biological functions. I mean, since I was clearly such a dead shot with a bow, there was no use in me honing my skills any further. Why should I? So my days were filled with boredom again. I had absolutely nothing to do. At night, I prayed for another encounter with rustlers. Heck, I even herded my cattle into valleys that were known to be infested with cattle thieves. It didn't work though. I couldn't pay the bastards to steal my cattle. I'm not sure if this was because if they were afraid of my reputation or just being stuck up. Your guess is as good as mine. Anyway, I eventually gave up and took my cattle back home.

Fortunately, Agelaus came to my rescue once again and found me something new to focus my energy on. He got me a lyre and I took to the musical instrument like I took to the bow. I would spend whole days strumming on it and composing songs. And, just like the bow, I got good with the lyre. Damned good! How do I know? Well, let me tell you something, cattle just love music and, more to the point, they love being sung to. I know this because they used to form a circle around me when I played and sang. It's the only time I saw them register a thought other than grass and ass. And if I could charm the world's dumbest creature like that, little wonder then that I could charm the knickers off any female who listened to me play. I'm not kidding. Ask the women of Mount Ida and they'll tell you they couldn't get half way through one of my songs without losing complete control of their passions. Old women, young girls, wives and sweethearts used to flock to my pastures just to hear my music and get crazy.

And that's how I discovered the best diversion of all: sex.

Picture this: I'm sitting under a tree innocently strumming my lyre. A tiny sliver of cloth barely covers my manhood. The lyre rests on my naked, glistening thigh. A farmer and his wife come wandering by. The farmer hears my music and gives me a disgusting look. He smells of last week's cow shit. The wife, however, looks over at me wistfully and smiles. Suddenly, she decides to pick some nearby flowers and tells her husband to go on ahead without her. He grunts, spits on a rock and continues on his way. Before the dunderhead disappears over the next hill, the wife is pressed so close against me that the sliver of cloth falls to the ground.

That's the way it was for me.

It was like shooting fish in a barrel.

Pretty soon, I had so many women chasing after me that I had to start writing them down in a black book just to keep track. Ask any playboy worth his salt and he'll tell you the hardest part about seducing women is the scheduling. So it was for me.

"Hi, Paris, baby," a girl would teasingly flirt. "Doing anything this afternoon?"

"I'm sorry, darling," I'd answer, "I'm busy."

She'd make a pouty lip, pretending to be upset.

I'd open my black book, find an empty date and say, "How about next Tuesday afternoon?"

Suddenly, she'd be happy again and nod her head in agreement.

And I'd write: Do Dora, Tuesday afternoon.

I was in pussy heaven.

There was only one hitch though.

Well, two actually — husbands and boyfriends.

Seems they didn't like me giving private concerts to their wives and girlfriends. As a matter of fact, they downright hated it. Now, I know I said that farmers are dumb and all — and they are — but, occasionally, one of them would wise up enough to figure out their better half wasn't outside picking flowers. That's why I always did the dirty with one foot in my robe. Believe me, no one can get dressed faster on the fly than I can.

I called it the Mount Ida Quickstep.

And friend, let me tell you, I was fast. I could outrun a deer if my life depended on it and there were many occasions that it actually did. Looking back on it now, I can't remember a time over sixteen in which there wasn't some jealous farmer or another who didn't want to wring my neck. That's also, by the way, when I discovered what a great big coward I am. Believe me, it's one thing to shoot sixty rustlers with arrows from about fifty cubits away but it's another thing altogether to fight a man face to face. Especially face to face with a damned farmer. Suckers tended to be a lot tougher than me. Helen once said that I had a body made for love and not war — fitter for Venus than Mars, I think she actually said — and she was right. So, there was no way in Hades I was about to go toe to toe with a damned farmer. It would have been committing suicide. Besides, I didn't have the guts for it either. Nothing could freeze my blood and fill me with sickening dread than the threat of bodily harm could. I panicked every time my health was in danger and my first thought was always to run away as fast as I possibly could. Call me a coward if you want, and I won't deny it, but, at least, I was a healthy coward and, to me, that's what mattered most.

As my age increased, so did the number of my lovers. I guess you could say I became something of a sex addict. By the time I was eighteen, I was making love to at least two or three women a day. No wonder then, that I gained the reputation of being something of a shiftless, lady's man. I always thought that was a bit unfair though. Was it my fault so many women wanted me? Who could blame me for taking advantage of my situation? And I've always thought it funny that people condemned me alone for doing so. I mean, why not condemn all the ladies that happily gave themselves to me? I didn't force them to do anything. They did it willingly. What was I supposed to do? Say no? Fat chance! So, I did what any hot-blooded, young man would do — I screwed their brains out. And what about the husbands and sweethearts of the women I ravished? Shouldn't they blame themselves for failing to maintain their partner's sexual interests? Damn straight they should. And besides, while we are still on the subject, is there any wonder I became addicted to sex? I mean, having no real parents, I grew up starved for affection. Sex filled that void. It's the only human warmth I ever experienced. So cut me some slack for being so damned horny for it all the time.

Anyway, the thing about a bad reputation is that it's almost impossible to get rid of. You can't work it off — trust me, I know — nor can you do much of anything to convince folks otherwise. Once you get a bad rap, it seems to stay with you forever. Ironically, I learned this when I fell in love with Oenone and pledged to give up other women for good.

One morning, while I was down by the creek washing up in preparation for the day's activities — I think I had three women scheduled for that day, I'm not sure — I suddenly noticed this beautiful woman bathing downstream not more than a stone's throw away. Being somewhat of a natural pervert — all sex addicts are — I quickly ducked into some nearby reeds so that I could spy on her undetected. Let me tell you, she was drop dead gorgeous and, without a doubt, the most beautiful woman I had ever seen up to that point. From my hiding place, I studied her up close. Her breasts were firm and large, so much so, that they seemed a bit out of proportion with her slender frame. Each breast was tipped with a large, brown nipple. She had dark, almond shaped eyes that perfectly matched her light brown skin. Her legs were short and shapely. She was not a tall girl, maybe six inches shorter than me, and her hips, like her breasts, were ample. Her nose was long and straight and situated above a pair of firm, red lips.

Her hair was as black as a raven's feather and hung loosely down to the small of her back.

I squatted in the reeds and gaped silently while she slowly washed herself with small handfuls of water. I followed each drop as they slowly rolled down the contours of her body and imagined my tongue doing the same thing. Soon, Mr. Happy was rock hard and I could not resist stroking him. So there I was, hiding in the bushes, staring at the naked beauty, cranking away lustfully like some lonely sailor at sea, when, all of a sudden, she turned in my direction and said, "Paris, are you having fun?"

Imagine my surprise, multiply it by ten, and you won't even be close.

And, let me tell you, it's hard to keep your dignity when you get caught doing something like that! What do you say? I'm sorry? Excuse me? I had an itch? Believe me, there is absolutely nothing you can say that makes any sense so I didn't bother to answer her. I just stood there frozen in mid-stroke and gasped.

And then something really truly amazing happened.

She turned so that I could get a better look at her wonderful body!

Really, she did!

I'm talking full frontal, eye-popping, nudity here. You know, the best kind.

I couldn't believe it — or her. She wasn't the least bit annoyed or embarrassed by my presence. As a matter of fact, she seemed to welcome it.

"Do you like what you see?" she asked and smiled seductively.

Like? That would be putting it mildly. More like love. Or lust. I never could tell the difference between the two, you know. Anyway, whatever it was, I wanted her bad.

Unable to control myself any longer, I stepped out of the reeds and boldly waded towards her. She watched me advance with a provocative smile on her lips that seemed to say, "Come closer if you dare." Of course, this only served to increase my passion further and I swear, by the time I got close to her, my mouth was absolutely watering.

For a moment, we stood in the middle of the creek, maintaining salacious eye contact, savoring the moment. Then she looked away almost nonchalantly and said, "Too bad you are busy with your girlfriends today because I'd ask you to spend it with me if you weren't."

And that's when I did it. That's the moment I gave up other women. Snap! Just like that! That's how bad I wanted her.

Retrieving the black book from the pocket of my robe, I held it before her for a long second and said, "This is the book I use to keep track of my girlfriends."

She rolled her eyes, signaling that she wasn't very impressed.

But that was not my intention.

With a quick flip of my wrist, I sent the book flying into the air. She followed its flight with her eyes and watched it hit the water a short distance away. Then, as the book slowly began to sink beneath the rippling waves, she turned back towards me with a look of wonderment on her face that quickly changed to appreciation that, in turn, quickly changed to pure lust. I don't have to tell you which look I liked the best.

Two snaps later, our bodies collided with more passion than I had ever known before. It was like an explosion of wet flesh. Before I knew it, I was out of my robe and my manhood was buried deep between her wet thighs. She wrapped her legs around my hips and, as the water sloshed all over us, I screwed her in joyful abandon. Then something strange happened — she started screwing me! You see, incredible as it may seem, the women of Mount Ida never really fucked me; they preferred that I did all the work. Typical boring farm girls, you might say. But with Oenone, it was very different. She knew what she wanted and what's better, she knew exactly what I wanted. Suddenly, I became aware that she was on top of me and was rapidly riding my dick with her hips. I floated in the shallow water as she did, with my head back and eyes shut, enjoying every moment of it and just when I thought nothing could get any better — it did. Easing herself off of me, she slowly began sliding down my body, kissing it softly as she went until she reached my thighs. Slipping in between them, she took my cock in her mouth and began to make tight, little circles around it with her tongue, first in one direction and then the other. Then a bunch of things started happening all at once.

Wonderful things!

Scary things!

Fun things!

With each bob of her head, my toes curled tighter and tighter, my eyeballs turned over in their sockets about five times and my body twitched wildly out of control. My only thought was to cum as quickly as possible because I was pretty sure I'd lose my mind if she continued on much longer. Luckily, I did. Cum, that is. Never before or since have I experienced such a mind-blowing climax. It felt like a hundred volcanoes erupted in my dick all at once. I'm sure the gods all the way up in Olympus heard me scream as it did.

I was impressed by Oenone's lovemaking skills to say the least.

When I had recovered enough strength to speak, I looked at her and mumbled, "Where'd...how'd...you learn to do that thing with your mouth?"

"Faunus the Satyr taught me," she proudly confessed.

Of course! Satyrs! You know — those creatures that are half goat and half man. Mount Ida was thick with the hairy bastards. Sometimes, I used to hear them late at night. They loved to play the pipes and dance in the moonlight. I'd lie awake and listen to their wonderful melodies. They loved women too. It's like they lived for nooky. They were always bird-dogging around Ida for a hot piece of ass and since I was doing the same thing, it's funny that I never bumped into any of them. Still, I guess if I ever do, I owe them a bit of thanks because Oenone sure knew what she was doing.

Anyway, ask any guy about his first blowjob and he'll tell you that it was a life changing experience. So it was with me. For the first time in my life, I was totally in love.

Or lust.

Like I said before, I never could tell the difference.

"What's your name?" I asked, caressing her softly.

"Oenone the Nymph," she answered, again quite proudly.

"Well, Oenone the Nymph, I love you," I joyfully proclaimed.

"We'll see," she replied nonchalantly.

Now, I probably should have taken that as a warning but I was never one to think too deeply about anything — especially when it came to sex and females — and so I shrugged it off. All I wanted was to spend more time with her and, luckily, that's what she wanted too. We were inseparable after that. I quit farming altogether so I could constantly be by Oenone's side. During the day, we often hunted the mountain glens together, me with my bow and her with a meshed net. She showed me where the wild beasts hid their young. Every evening, we dined on tender roast meat and every night, we made love for hours and hours on beds of soft grass and leaves. During those sessions, Oenone taught me the fine art of lovemaking. She even had names for the various sexual positions we made love in. There was The Monkey, The Swing, The Tortoise, The Dog, The Foot Yoke, The Knot of Fame, so many, as a matter of fact, that she could have filled an entire book with them. She also showed me how to perform cunnilingus and I quickly discovered that nothing made her reach an orgasm faster than that did. God, how I loved the sounds that she made while I munched away in her private garden! I don't know who enjoyed it the most. Afterwards, she would reward my efforts by making me a special cookie. Like all good Nymphs, Oenone knew every useful herb and root there was. Using poppy seeds as the main ingredient, she would bake me some cookies that, when consumed with wine, opened my brain to all sorts of psychedelic images. Believe me, Zeus himself never saw the wonderful shit I saw after eating Oenone's treats. All in all, it was a wild time, to say the least, and I was head over heels in lust, or love.

"I love you," I'd say to Oenone in complete contentment.

"Prove it," she'd always answer.

So one day, I actually did. Taking out my trusty, little pocketknife, I went into a nearby forest and carved "Oenone" on the trunks of about a hundred beech-trees. I specifically chose that type of tree because, having carved shit on them before, I knew that as the tree grew in size, so would my carvings. Oenone knew it too.

"Rise up and grow straight with my glory!" Oenone cried at the trees when she saw my handiwork.

Then she kissed me and said, "Thank you, my love, thank you."

And that's precisely when our relationship started to change.

Little did I know all the trouble my romantic gesture would lead to because, if I did, believe me, I wouldn't have done it. As every guy eventually learns, once you start openly demonstrating your love to a woman, there's just no end to it. That's because a woman grows to expect it and if you don't keep doing it, then doggone it, you just don't love them anymore. And if you combine that with a bad reputation like I had, well, it's a vicious cycle in which there's just no escape.

"Like them?" I asked, gazing proudly at the carvings.

"Yes, I do," she said, snuggling up against me. "But if you really loved me, you'll build me a hut to live in."

"A hut?" I asked, surprised.

"Yes, a hut," she quickly answered.

"Why on earth would I want to do something silly like that?" I asked.

I couldn't understand it. We seemed so happy living outdoors. We were free to go wherever we wanted, anytime we wanted. Why would we want to give that up for a stinking hut?

"To show that you are ready to settle down with me," she answered, stepping away from me.

That's when it began to dawn on me how much trouble I was in.

"I've just spent the last four hours carving your name on a bunch of fucking trees. Isn't that enough? Look! I've got blisters on my fingers."

I held my fingers up so she could see them. I figured injuring myself would be more than enough to show her how much I cared.

Shows you how dumb I was.

She pushed my hand away angrily and shouted, "I knew it! You don't really love me! My father warned me about you. He said that you were lighter than dry leaves and would fly away from me in the shifting wind."

Ah, yes, her father Cebron! In case you don't know, he's the thousandth son of Titan's Oceanus and Tethys, and the god of the Kebren River. While that might sound cool and all, let me tell you, it ain't. That's because the Kebren is a minor tributary of the Scamander, a major river on the Trojan plain. Cebron always hated being the god of a minor river. "Why can't I have a bigger river?" he'd constantly whine. "All I got is this tiny cesspool that Paris' cows piss in everyday." Believe me, life's a bitch when you're the thousandth son to anyone. Anyway, because of my cows, the piss-smelling bastard hated me almost as much as he hated his unimportant river and he was constantly bringing up my sordid past in an effort to convince Oenone that she should break up with me.

You see the position I was in?

I had no choice but to build Oenone a fucking hut!

So I did.

It wasn't much of a going concern actually. Just a simple thing made of wood, mud and thatch. The floor was strewn with straw. It took me about an hour to build. You could have coughed and blown it over.

I hated it.

Oenone loved it.

For two days anyway!

"Paris, our hut is awfully little," she mused aloud one morning.

"That's why it's called a hut. It's supposed to be little," I answered sarcastically.

"Well, there isn't enough room for my things," she explained.

"What things?" I quickly pointed out. "All you own are some herbs and a mesh net."

"Well, I was thinking about getting a spindle, you know, so I could make us some clothes and doilies."

"Doilies?" I had never heard of such a thing before.

"To put on our furniture," she explained.

"What furniture?" I asked, looking around the empty hut in confusion.

"I was thinking about getting some furniture too."

I stood quietly for a second, trying to think of something good to say, and when I couldn't, I decided to do what most guys do in my predicament — I pleaded my ass off.

"Ah, pookey, baby, darling, doodle pants, please, come on, please, let's just keep everything the way it is, okay?"

"No, Paris, it's not okay," she quickly snapped. "Our relationship needs to grow, we need to grow. That's why you need to build us a house to live in."

"A house!" I cried.

I definitely knew what that was.

"Yes, just like the one my sister lives in."

"You sister is a kook!" I blurted angrily.

Really, she was. Her name was Asterope and, outside of my sister Cassandra, she was, without a doubt, the dingiest broad I ever met. You see, she had a thing for snakes. Whenever she would see one, she'd run over and stomp on it like the snake was a bug or something. It was the strangest thing I ever saw and if you ask me, I figure she did it because she was afraid of men. I think the snakes were just a substitute for a man's penis. That's why I was always careful to cover my crotch whenever Asterope was around.

"No, she's not!" Oenone shouted, furious. "She's a very warm hearted girl!"

Yeah, right. Ask any cold blooded snake.

"And, you know what?" Oenone continued. "She warned me about you!"

Oh, shit, not that again. Here it comes, thinks I.

"She said that there is less weight in you than there is in an ear of grain. She asked me why I trusted my seeds to sand and why I plow the shore...."

"Alright, alright!" I interrupted. "I get it. Enough already! I'll build you a stupid house!"

Oenone's face quickly lit up with a happy sparkle. Overwhelmed with emotion, she threw her arms around me and gave me a big hug.

"Oh, you will? You will?" she said in my ear.

Like I had a choice!

"Yes," I said glumly.

"Oh, thank you, thank you, thank you!" she shouted while smothering my face with kisses.

I was just about to reach up under her skirt to reap my reward for being such a good boy when she said, "Let's make it a big house, with three rooms, you know, one to entertain guests in and one to cook in and a bedroom and...wait, no, let's make it four, because I'll need a place to put the spindle in."

Suddenly, I didn't feel like doing any reward reaping. I felt more like stabbing myself in the eye with a dull stick. But I didn't. I ended up building Oenone a house instead. It took me about two months of hard work to do it. I was always in motion during that time. I worked and worked and worked. I even broke my leg in the middle of its construction.

"Oh, what a shame," I said, looking down at my injured leg, "now I won't able to work on the house for a very long time. Guess I'll just have to take it easy until my leg heals."

Of course, I was secretly gladdened by my injury. I saw it as a perfect excuse to get out of all the work I had been doing. Visions danced across my mind of me lying around comfortably while Oenone took care of my every need, blowjobs included. Yes, sir, I was one happy cripple alright.

For a day, anyway.

Oenone studied me and my leg warily for a moment and said, "Don't worry, baby, you'll be as good as new tomorrow."

"But my leg's broken!" I protested. "I can't stand on it! There's no way I can work! I need months of rest! Maybe even a full year!"

Oenone smiled knowingly, turned and suddenly darted inside our hut. When she came back out, I noticed that she was holding a bag of roots and herbs in her hand. Pouring the contents into a large bowl and adding some water, I watched in dread as she stirred the mixture into a thick green paste.

Applying the concoction to the injured portion of my leg, she said, "Honey, I can cure any kind of wound there is. Tomorrow, you'll be just fine."

And I'll be damned if she wasn't right. The next day, my leg was completely healed. It's like the injury never occurred! And so, I had to go back to work on that stupid house. Let me tell you, sometimes it was a pain in the ass to have a Nymph for a girlfriend, although, right now, with an arrow sticking out of my balls, I consider it to be more of a blessing.

Anyway, like I said, I built the house in two months. When it was done, I figured I'd never have to prove my love to Oenone ever again. I mean, there it was in stone, brick and wood for everyone to see. The house was a shrine to our love and a testament to my commitment. That's the way I viewed it anyway. Unfortunately, Oenone didn't. To her, there was something missing. Heck, with her, there was *always* something missing. I swear, I could never make that woman happy no matter how hard I tried. And believe me, I tried everything.

Two weeks after the house was built, I went into the kitchen to get a bite to eat only to discover that we were out of meat.

Turning to Oenone, I said, "I think we need to do some hunting, we're out of food."

"We're not going to go hunting anymore," she answered bluntly.

"Why not?" I asked, dumbfounded.

"Because we have a house to keep now," she replied. "We can't leave it and go off gallivanting around the countryside like hungry wolves anymore. We have to stay here and care for our home."

I tried to get a grip. Apparently, I had built a house that I was going to starve to death in! That's never good news.

"How are we going to eat then?" I asked, hoping that she knew some way to magically produce food. With nymphs, you never knew.

"You need to ask Agelaus for some cattle," she directed. "I'm sure he'll give us part of his herd. He owes you something for all those years you worked for him."

I don't have to tell you how that idea sounded to me. Not only did the thought of becoming a farmer again sicken me, I was pretty sure Agelaus would laugh in my face. We hadn't exactly parted on the best of terms, you see. When I announced to him that I intended to quit farming so I could live the high life with a Water Nymph, he told me, point blank, that I was making a huge mistake. Says you, I answered angrily before storming off in a huff. How could I ask Agelaus for cattle after that? And that's exactly why I asked him. As I said before, I was fairly confident that he'd say no, so what did I have to lose? I figured he'd tell me to get lost and then I'd be filling my belly with roasted deer meat before nightfall. A sure deal, I thought.

"So you want to return to farming again, do you?" Agelaus asked with a sharp tone of sarcasm in his voice.

"Yes," I answered, trying to sound like I really meant it.

Agelaus scratched his beard and eyed me closely for a long moment.

Hurry up and say no, I thought impatiently to myself, so I can get something to eat. My stomach was growling something awful.

"Well, okay then, how about fifty head?" Agelaus suddenly said.

You could have knocked me over with a feather!

"Oh, ah, well, I don't know," I backpedaled nervously, "that seems way too generous."

"Nonsense, fifty is a good number," Agelaus quickly countered. "I'll even throw in Cronus."

Now, I was totally befuddled. Cronus was Agelaus' prized bull and the jewel of my Agelaus' eye. He loved that bull more than anything. I never dreamed he'd ever willingly part with the beast.

"I can't let you do that. It's way too much," I said. And then, just to jog his memory, I added, "Especially after the terrible way I treated you and all. Don't you remember how rude and selfish I was? I wouldn't blame you if you said no."

While I awaited his answer, I desperately repeated over and over again in my mind, please say no…please say no…please say no.

Instead, the bastard smiled, slapped me on the shoulder, and said, "Ah, it's okay, boy, we all make mistakes."

Don't I know it, I mumbled glumly.

"There's just one thing I want you to do," Agelaus continued.

Hang myself? I hoped he'd say.

"I want you to marry that girl," Agelaus said.

And that's exactly when everything faded to black.

I fainted.

Whether I did so from lack of food or from the dreaded m-word, I don't know. All I know is that when I woke up five minutes later, I was soaking wet. Agelaus was standing over me holding an empty bucket. It was empty because he had poured water on my face in an effort to revive me. I looked up at Agelaus and saw that he was grinning from ear to ear. That's when it hit me: Agelaus was playing the same goddamned game I was! He didn't really want to give me any of his cattle anymore then I wanted the damned things, and just like me, he was just looking for a respectable excuse to get out of the deal. You see, he figured I'd refuse to get married and then he'd be able to tell folks he turned me down because I wouldn't make an honest woman out of Oenone. That would be enough to keep public opinion firmly in his corner since, for some strange reason, farmers tend to put a lot of stock into marriage.

Anyway, like mine, Agelaus' stratagem backfired. I mean, there was just no way in Hades I could decline his offer. What would I say to Oenone if I did? I'm sorry but Agelaus wouldn't give me any cattle because I refused to marry you? I don't have to tell you how well that would have went over! Like it or not, I was fairly stuck.

"So are you going to marry that girl or not?" Agelaus asked, confident of my answer.

"Yes, I guess I will," I answered weakly.

That certainly took the wind out of Agelaus' sails! At first, he looked shocked. Then he looked sick.

I wasn't having a very good day either. I went from being hungry, to being a farmer, to being married. Ain't that the way life works though? I mean, one second, you're happily screwing your brains out without a care in the world and then, in the next, someone or something comes along and changes everything until, suddenly, you find yourself caught up in things you never imagined possible.

Story of my life!

Oenone and I were married a couple of weeks later. It was a lavish affair in which it seemed everybody and their cousin was invited. There were tears everywhere. Oenone was crying because she was so happy. Oenone's father and sister were crying because they weren't. Agelaus was crying because he was about to lose Cronus. I was crying because I was going to be a farmer again. The local women were crying because my concerts were over for good. The only ones who weren't weeping were the men of the community. I swear, I've never seen the bastards so happy. Some of them were actually doing back flips in celebration!

We spent our honeymoon inside our new home and when it was over, I had a pregnant wife on my hands. I swear, when it rains, it pours, doesn't it?

"Are you sure?" I asked Oenone when she told me the news of her pregnancy. I was hoping it might be indigestion or something.

"Yes, I'm sure," she answered. "Now get to work building a baby's room."

And that was that. I spent the remainder of her pregnancy remodeling the house. I had to knock down walls to add new ones and, once I got the roof up, Oenone made me paint the child's room — first blue, then white, then pink, then yellow, then blue again. She never could make up her mind. After that, my ass was busy collecting baby furniture. I must have went to a kahbillion flea markets during her pregnancy and there wasn't a day that passed in which I didn't find myself hauling something up the slopes of Mount Ida to put in that damned room. I don't think a boy has ever been born with more stuff.

Nor do I think a boy's been born that has cried as much either.

We named him Corythus and, believe me, the child certainly had a healthy set of pipes on him. His wailings could have deafened a Siren and what's worse, he went at it morning, noon and night.

Here's how he sounded on a good day: Waaahhhhhhhh, waaahhhhhhh, waahhhhhhh, waahhhhhhhh, waaahhhhhhh!

Here's how he sounded on a bad day: Waaaaaaaaaaaaaaaaaa aaaaaaaaaaaaaaaaaaahhhhhhhhhhhhhhhhhhh!

Imagine listening to either one for about twenty hours a day and you'll know why my right eyelid still twitches nervously when I'm anywhere near a baby.

Oenone and I were at a loss on how to stop the kid from crying. She couldn't find a root or berry that would calm the child and all I could come up with was to abandon the baby on the slopes of Ida. I mean, it was pretty clear that the child didn't like his situation with us, so it seemed like a good idea all the way around. But, of course, Oenone wouldn't agree, and so, for the next five months, we didn't get more than four hours sleep a day. During that time, we were never fully awake or fully asleep. And I don't have to tell you what that does to a marriage. Sex went right out the window after the first month, which, as any sex addict will tell you, is tantamount to a death sentence. Luckily, I had the cows to look after, so, I always had a convenient excuse to sneak off somewhere for some alone time with Mr. Happy. It's how I maintained my sanity during that period. Who hasn't?

Okay, now, I know this next part is gonna be a little hard to believe but, I swear, it actually happened.

At least, I think it did.

One morning, after a particularly long, lonely, sleepless night with junior, I decided to move the herd to the north side of Mount Ida so I could put as much distance between me and the wailing brat as possible. Finding a secluded glen to release the cattle into, I immediately laid down under a nearby tree in order to catch up on some much needed masturbation and sleep. Just as I was getting into the first, I became aware of a buzzing sound near my ear. Thinking that it was a fly, I waved my free hand across my face to make it go away. Only it didn't. The buzzing seemed to get louder than ever. Annoyed, I rapidly began waving both hands across my face in a desperate attempt to drive the creature away. As I did, I suddenly felt my left hand strike something about the size of a hummingbird and immediately heard a tiny voice yell, "Shiiiiiiiit!"

Having never heard a hummingbird cuss before, I opened my eyes and glanced around quickly. Everything appeared to be normal except for the tiny guy standing next to me. I was so startled, I nearly broke something standing up. Wide eyed, I stared down at the tiny man in wonderment. He appeared to be about six inches tall. Yep, six inches. On top of that, he also had a pair of little wings protruding from both sides of his golden hat and sandals. That's what made the buzzing noise.

Rubbing his shoulder painfully, the little guy shouted, "Why'd you do that for!"

"I'm sorry," I answered, "I thought you were a fly."

"Do I look like a fucking fly to you, you stupid pud-puller!" the man yelled. For a little guy, he sure was sassy.

"No," I answered and then, not exactly sure what he looked like, I asked, "What...who...are you?"

He rolled his eyes at me indignantly and said, "I swear, don't they teach you hicks anything? I'm Hermes."

Having never been very big into religion, the name failed to ring a bell and so, I could only stare down at him with a blank expression on my face.

"You know, Hermes, Messenger of the Gods!" he shouted. "Surely, you've heard of me?"

I shook my head no and shrugged my shoulders.

Once again, the tiny fellow rolled his eyes in disgust, then, mostly to himself, he said, "I told Zeus this was a bad idea."

"Zeus?" I quickly asked.

"Yeah, Zeus," he answered. "You do know who Zeus is, don't you?"

"Sure, I do," I fired back. I wasn't *that* stupid.

"Well, slop them hogs and let's have us a hoedown!" he sarcastically yelled. "The jerk jockey knows something after all!"

Had I not been so thoroughly amazed by his presence, I probably would have mashed the tiny guy into pulp right then and there for being such a smart ass. Instead, I leaned down and studied him closely.

"Is this a dream or something?" I asked.

Hermes put his hand to his forehead and rubbed it impatiently. "Yeah…sure…whatever…who cares…let's just get this over with… yes, you're right, genius, this is a dream. You fell asleep while you were choking your chicken and now, in this dream, you get to judge a sexy beauty contest."

"Wow, I never had a cool dream like this before," I said in wonderment. "A beauty contest?"

"Yeah, a really fun beauty contest between three Immortal Goddesses," Hermes explained, as if to a child. "You get to choose which one is the most beautiful by awarding her a pretty golden apple. Doesn't that sound fun? Wanna do it? Huh? Huh? What do you say?"

"Sure!" I quickly agreed.

Okay, I know exactly what you are thinking here: nobody in their right mind would ever agree to judge a beauty contest between goddesses because, as any dunderhead will tell you, no matter how fair you try to be, you're just gonna end up pissing off the losers. And that ain't healthy. So, in my defense, all I can say is that I really thought I was dreaming. Not for one second did I think any of it was real. I mean, who hasn't had an erotic dream or two? I had them all the time. That's why I was so careless and, well, downright stupid.

"Great!" snapped Hermes and, in a flash, he was gone. A solid gold apple rested in the place where he had been standing. Picking the apple up, I studied it closely and noticed there was some writing running along its side. Turning it slowly, I read the inscription out loud to myself. "For the fairest one," I said in a faint voice.

"That'll be me," a female voice suddenly announced.

"No way, sister," another female voice immediately protested.

"You both know it's me!" a different female chimed in.

Startled, I turned around quickly and found myself facing three of the hottest babes imaginable. Everything about them was perfect. I guess that's why they're called goddesses. And such goddesses! I gaped at them as they slowly sashayed towards me; their naked, lithe bodies swaying gently with each step, and I thought, well, Paris, old boy, this is without a doubt the best wet dream you've ever had!

And then, it got better.

First, Hera came towards me, tall and stately, staring proudly into my eyes. The effect she had on me was simply breathtaking: beautifully firm, round breasts, shining long black hair, piercing brown eyes, perfect skin and body — little wonder she is the queen of all gods. I was in awe and lust at the same time. Behind Hera came graceful Athena. Her beauty instantly caused me to take a deep breath: she had a slim white neck and shoulders, below which hung two large, ample breasts; a slim waist supported by firm hips and shapely long legs; unbound light brown hair flying softly in the wind, mysterious, flashing gray eyes, and a pair of ruby red lips that seemed to be curled into a knowing smile. I could not help but smile back at her. Next came exotic Aphrodite. She was simply the nastiest looking woman I had ever set eyes on and I don't have to tell you how appealing that was to me. Lust was written all over Aphrodite — from her beautiful, long blond hair that hung wildly down to her small waist, to her large, wanton blue eyes, between her open, luscious pink lips, on her soft, pale skin, around her big, round breasts, over her glistening hips and down her shapely legs.

The goddesses stopped several feet in front of me and paused there for a moment so I could ogle them closer, which I did with gusto, until the thought hit me that since this was my dream, I should have fun in it. So, I ordered them to walk around some more, because, you see, when I judge a beauty contest, I prefer to see a bunch of bouncing breasts and wobbling buttocks as I do.

Obligingly, they paraded around some more, bouncing and wobbling wonderfully, until I got the bright idea to ask each what my reward would be should I declare her a winner. Of course, I was expecting some sort of sexual reward, you know, something along the line of a blowjob or an all day romp in the hay, so it's not hard to imagine my disappointment when Hera promised to make me lord of all Asia and Greece, or when Athena offered to give me wisdom and knowledge. Who gives a crap about those things when you haven't been laid in months? It was my dream and, goddamnit, I wanted to get hot and nasty in it! I needed sex! I craved sex! I swear, I was so damned horny, I'd have humped ugly Medusa herself if she would have showed up. And that's exactly why I ended up choosing Aphrodite. She came towards me with a seductive look on her beautiful face that would have given a blind man a hard-on and said, "Choose me, Aphrodite, and forget harsh wars and cares of state. Take my beauty and leave the scepter and the torch of wisdom. What does love know about learning and wars?"

Now you're talking, sister, thinks I.

"Take me," she murmured seductively, "and I will give you the love of the most beautiful woman in the world."

Judge's interpretation: Choose me, baby, and I'll fuck your brains out.

"Yes, sirree, bob!" shouts I eagerly. "I choose Aphrodite!"

Okay, just for the record, I want to say that I actually thought Aphrodite was offering herself to me sexually. Can you blame me? She was, without a doubt, the most beautiful woman I had ever seen and so, it wasn't hard for my fevered mind to interpret her words in the manner that I did. Not for a second did I think she was talking about a third party. So cut me some slack.

Thinking that I was finally going to get laid, I ran over to Aphrodite and wrapped my arms around her. Hera and Athena stared daggers at me as I did. Like I gave a rat's ass what they thought! All I cared about was getting my reward.

Aphrodite pulled me into her naked body ecstatically and whispered, "Thank you, Paris, from now on I will be forever by your side."

"Side? No, baby, I want you in front of me," I said lustfully, lining up our lips for a kiss.

Some kiss.

I kissed empty space.

Aphrodite disappeared just before our lips could meet. The other two goddesses were gone as well. And so was that stupid apple.

Puff! Just like that, the dream was over.

Disappointed, I rounded up the cattle and trudged back home sporting a big erection under my robe.

"Where have you been?" Oenone asked angrily, meeting me in the door of our house. For once, the baby was asleep.

I flashed my most winning smile, pointed down at my still-excited member and said, "Honey, we need to have sex."

Oenone immediately shook her head no and said, "No way. I haven't slept in thirty-six hours. Put that disgusting thing away right now!"

"But baby," I pleaded, "if we don't have sex pretty soon, I think I'm gonna lose my mind."

"Lose your mind? What do you know about losing your mind?" she snapped. "I have to stay here all day and listen to our child cry while you sneak away somewhere and do god-knows-what. Don't you dare talk to me about losing your mind, buster! I'm gonna lose my mind if I don't get some sleep!"

"I'm serious, baby," I said, "I had the weirdest dream today. I dreamed that I judged a beauty contest between Hera, Athena and Aphrodite."

Suddenly, Oenone's face changed. She looked more concerned than angry. Matters of religion always had that kind of effect on her. "Go on," she said firmly.

"Well," I explained, "they were naked and then they each promised me a reward if I choose them. Hera promised me power, Athena promised me wisdom and Aphrodite promised to give me her love."

Oenone folded her arms across her chest and looked at me skeptically. "Aphrodite Acidalia promised to give you her love?"

"Yep," I proudly declared.

"Her love? Aphrodite said that exactly?" she demanded.

"Yeah, kinda," I replied, less sure.

"That doesn't sound like Aphrodite because she's married to Hephaestus and she's seeing Ares and Apollo on the side. Why on earth would she want you?"

"Because I'm good in bed?" I answered, hoping it would jog her memory enough for us to stop wasting time and start getting busy.

"Yeah, right," she sarcastically snapped. "What exactly did she say?"

"Well, ah, she said that if I chose her, she'd, ah, give me the love of the most beautiful woman in the world," I stammered.

Oenone stared at me gravely for a moment and then, in a voice thick with dread, asked, "Which one of the goddesses did you choose?"

"Aphrodite, because I am so damned horny," I replied, feeling confident that I had finally made my case for having sex.

"You big dolt!" Oenone erupted. "Aphrodite wasn't talking about herself and it wasn't a fucking dream!"

"Sure it was a dream!" I yelled back. "There was even a itty bitty guy in it with wings who said his name was Herman or Harry or something like that. He told me it was a dream. And Aphrodite…"

"Hermes, you fucking idiot," Oenone interrupted, "and how could you dream about something you don't even know about? Up until today, you never even heard the name Hermes before, nor did you know that Hera is a goddess representing power, or Athena represents wisdom or Aphrodite represents love. How could you have dreamed any of those things? Don't you realize what you've done?"

"No," I answered, totally bewildered.

"I'll tell you what you've done, buster," she explained, "you've tempted the gods, that's what you've done. And right about now, I'm sure Hera and Athena are very angry with you and busy plotting some sort of revenge and I'm also sure that Aphrodite is equally as busy arranging things so that you can be with another woman. And no matter what you do, you can't do anything to stop them."

And then Oenone started to cry.

Big time crying!

I'm talking messy wet, snot down the nose crying, you know, the really scary kind.

I stared at her in shock for a few minutes and then said, "Ah come on, don't cry, baby. It wasn't real and besides, even if it was, how do you know Aphrodite wasn't talking about you. You are by far the most beautiful woman in the world."

For a heartbreaking second, Oenone didn't respond. Then she wiped her tear-swollen eyes and said, "Thanks, but why would Aphrodite promise you something you already have? No, she was definitely talking about another woman."

And then she buried her face in her hands and sobbed some more.

Suddenly, I didn't feel horny anymore.

Maybe it's because I was already totally screwed.

Chapter Two

"Does it hurt?" my father, King Priam, asks in his scratchy voice.

He's talking about the arrow sticking out of my dick, of course.

I turn my head and flash him a quick what-do-you-think look.

"It looks like it hurts," he says.

No shit.

I close my eyes and turn my head away from him, hoping that he will go away and pester somebody else. But I know he won't. I've learned that no matter how much I ignore him, he'll just sit there jabbering on and on like he did yesterday and the day before that.

"The Greeks are quiet today," he says.

And like yesterday and the day before, I could care less what the Greeks are doing. Believe me, when you have an arrow poking out of your balls, you're pretty much only concerned about one thing. Well, maybe two.

"They're building something big down on the beach," he adds.

They can build themselves silly for all I care.

"Maybe they're building new ships to go home in," my father continues to prattle.

That's a pretty good guess since we destroyed most of their ships during the last battle but, on the other hand, with that crafty son-of-a-bitch Odysseus running things, you never know. Anyway, whatever they're doing, I still don't give a shit.

For some reason, my father grows suddenly silent. All I can hear is the sound of his heavy breathing. As the quiet continues to grow, my pain-wracked brain begins to wonder why my father has finally shut up. Is he about to leave? Has he gone to sleep? Curious, I glance over at him for an answer and see that he appears to be in deep thought about something. Knowing that he will eventually tell me what's on his mind, I close my eyes again and enjoy the silence.

Unfortunately, I don't get to enjoy it for very long.

My father sighs heavily and says, "Antenor and Panthous are again advising me to return Helen back to the Greeks. What do you think?"

Immediately, I open my eyes and stare at him. He has a truly sincere, pleading look on his face. I can tell that he desperately wants me to advise him otherwise. It's the only reason he asked me. He wants me to tell him what he needs to hear. He wants me to tell him that this horrible war was justified. He wants me to ease his conscience. Only I can't. Not now. Having spent the last three days languishing on death's doorstep, I've finally come to realize how stupid this war has been.

I nod at him earnestly and say, "I think you should return Helen back to the Greeks. It'll put an end to this stupid war once and for all."

At first, my father looks stunned, then, almost in a flash, anger sweeps across his aged face. He sits bolt upright in his chair and yells, "Stupid war?"

"Yes, stupid!" I holler back. If he doesn't like it, he can hit the fucking door.

Unable to contain his emotions, he stands up and points a trembling finger at me. "Have you forgotten about what the Greeks did to my sister Hesione?" he shouts.

Like I could ever forget that! It's a dead horse my father loves to beat over and over again.

It happened nearly a generation ago, when that big thug Hercules suddenly showed up outside Troy's gates claiming that he had just ridded the city of a sea monster and demanding tribute for his services. That's the way Hercules operated. He roamed around the countryside strong-arming folks out of money by claiming to have killed imaginary monsters for them. Of course, nobody ever saw the monsters he claimed to kill but it didn't matter much since everybody knew Hercules was a homicidal maniac — he actually slaughtered his own family with his bare hands — and folks figured it was probably safer just to give the lunatic what he wanted. Unfortunately, Troy's king, my grandfather Laomedon, chose to do the opposite and so, in no uncertain terms, he told Hercules to beat it. It's not hard to imagine how Hercules took that. Returning a week later with six ships and seven hundred drunken Greeks, Hercules found a weak spot in the city's walls and soon, Troy's streets were filled with lots of grieving widows. During the carnage, Hercules killed my grandfather and captured my aunt Hesione, whom he gave to his buddy King Telamon as a war prize. Telamon promptly carted her off to his home in Salamis, Greece where he made her his bride and Queen. Not a bad deal if you ask me, given the circumstances and all, but my father, quite understandably, thought otherwise. When dad became King of Troy, he sent his buddy Antenor off to Greece to demand Hesione's return. The Greeks responded by laughing their asses off at my father's demands. Needless to say, Antenor returned home empty handed. My father never forgot or forgave the insult. And that's the real reason this stupid war continues to go on. Tit for tat. My father refuses to give Helen to the Greeks because they refused to return Hesione back to him. It's just that simple. And that fucking stupid.

"Well, I haven't forgotten!" my father rages on. "The Greeks kidnapped my sister and refused to give her back! They even laughed at me!"

Yeah, yeah, yeah, I think, rolling my eyes towards the heavens. Same old story, I've heard it all before.

"Well, they can sit out on that stinking beach and rot, for all I care!!" he roars. "Serves the bastard's right! I'll never return Helen back to them! Who's laughing now!"

The stupidity continues.

"And if you die," my father adds, "I'll marry Helen to your brother Deiphobus. That'll show them!"

Oh, yeah, that'll show them all right, thinks I, that'll show everybody that you are completely out of your fucking mind. Anyway, do whatever you want to do, I don't care, just go away and leave me alone.

"If only I was young again!" my father rants. "Then I'd show the Greeks how to fight. Just like I did on the Sangarius River in Phrygia. I fought as an allied soldier then and…"

I stick my fingers in both ears and squeeze my eyes shut so I can't hear my father talk anymore. It doesn't help much though. I can still hear him faintly droning on and on.

"That's when I carved a bloody path through the enemy with my sword," my father raves on.

Frustrated by my fingers' inability to silence him, I grab my pillow and wrap it around my face. Using the palms of my hands, I press the sides of the pillow hard against my ears and lie as quiet as a stone. My world immediately becomes muffled, dark and warm. I call it my happy place. In it, my father's voice seems far away and I feel alone at last. I exhale hard against the pillow, hoping that the words he planted in my head will exit from my mouth along with my breath. It's how I maintain my happy place — nothing comes in and everything bad goes out.

For I don't know how long, I keep breathing into my pillow until my father's words are gone. Eventually, most of them are. Only a few of the more troubling remain. No matter how hard I try, I just can't quit thinking about my father's intention to marry Helen to my brother Deiphobus after I am gone. Oh, don't get me wrong, it's not that I am worried the war will continue because of their marriage. Like I mentioned before, I've pretty much ended it. Nor is it because I still have strong feelings for Helen. Believe me, I lost what little affection I felt for her a long time ago. No, I'm troubled because I have always hated my brother with a purple passion and the thought of him someday becoming King of Troy while holding Helen in his arms sickens me almost as much as the poisoned arrow has. In my opinion, Deiphobus doesn't deserve either prize. As a matter of fact, Deiphobus doesn't deserve shit. That's because Deiphobus is, without a doubt, the biggest weasel you're ever likely to meet, bar none, including me. And I'm the god's own original weasel! But I was never weasel enough to try to kill my own brothers. That's where Deiphobus tops me. You see, he's as much responsible for Hector's death as Achilles is and, what's worse — at least, to me it is — the treacherous fuck damned near killed me once. Of course, I suppose you could make the argument that when Deiphobus tried to kill me, he didn't know I was his brother, but still, you can't dispute the fact that the bastard tried.

It all began the morning my father's soldiers came to take Cronus away.

They showed up four days after the dream I had of the beauty contest. They rapped on the front door of my house and announced that they had come to take my bull away. Just like that! They didn't bother trying to explain why they were taking my bull away or attempt to offer me any kind of a payment for it. That's the problem with soldiers. They're not big into details. They just show up and do whatever it is they're supposed to do without much of an explanation. Naturally, that can be downright confusing to a simple civilian like me, so it's not hard to imagine my state of mind when I opened the door.

"Why?" I immediately asked the soldier standing in front of me.

"Why what?" he answered back.

"Why are you taking my bull away?" I asked again.

The soldier frowned at me and turned to the other soldiers standing behind him for an answer. There were ten of them altogether and, up to that moment, I had never seen a more terrifying collection of men in my life. They were dressed in short purple kilts and their bodies were protected by bronze helmets, breastplates, ankle guards and greaves. Each man was armed with a long thrusting spear and a short sword. A large wooden shield covered in bronze rested across each of their backsides like capes.

"Sarge!" the soldier yelled. "This guy wants to know why we are taking his bull."

"Orders!" the Sergeant shouted from in back of the crowd. He was one of those military types that have always filled me with dread: square face, cold eyes, no neck, enormous torso, massive legs, standing straight and steady. You know, the kind of man that eats rocks for breakfast.

The soldier turned back to me, shrugged his shoulders helplessly and said, "Orders."

"Orders?" I asked.

"Yeah, orders," the soldier answered.

I guess he expected me to say, "Oh, well, in that case, please, go right ahead and take my prize bull away," but, being a stupid civilian in need of a little more information, I couldn't resist the urge to rush out the door and confront the Sergeant.

Bad idea!

I didn't get more than three steps out the door before I found myself facing a deadly row of spear tips.

"Stop right there, Sonny," ordered the Sergeant.

Like I could go any further!

"You best just turn around and go back inside your house," he continued.

Now, I'm not a brave man, especially when I am surrounded by men who look like they would rather kill and eat me more than anything else, but I just couldn't let the soldiers take Cronus away without making an attempt to stop them. Agelaus would never let me hear the end of it if I did. So I summoned what little courage I had and said, "What gives you the right to take my bull away?"

Immediately, the soldiers stiffened and I heard one of them say, "Want us to stick him now, Sarge?"

"Nah, hold on a sec, boys," the Sergeant said, studying me closely. "This civilian poses an interesting question. What gives us the right to take his bull away? Hmmmm, I suppose I could state the obvious and say that our spears and swords gives us that right, but then, we would need to ask ourselves whether might makes right."

The soldiers glanced at one another slyly and began giggling under their helmets. Clearly, the Sergeant was toying with me for their entertainment. I was much too frightened to laugh along with them. Besides, I never did enjoy military humor much anyway. That's because I was always a bit leery of guys who think it's funny to stab other guys in the guts with sharp objects until they die.

"And I would be the last person in the world to ever say that might gives us that right," the Sergeant proclaimed, all tongue-in-cheek like. "So where does that leave us? I guess it leaves us with the order from King Priam commanding us to take away this man's bull and, as his loyal soldiers, we have no choice but to carry those orders out cause, if we don't, then society will break down and anarchy will reign, and I know that this here civilian wouldn't want that to happen."

The soldiers chuckled amongst themselves some more. Then, one of them stuck the point of his spear in my face and said, "Well, civilian, you don't want society to break down do you?"

"No," I said meekly, tilting my head away from the spear tip.

"I didn't think so," the Sergeant said with a sarcastic sneer. "Let him go, boys."

The soldiers laughed loudly and lowered their spears. As they were walking away, I asked, "Isn't there anything I can do to keep my bull?"

The Sergeant paused for a moment and said, "Well, I guess you could try to win the creature back."

"Win him back?" I asked cautiously, wondering if he was making another joke.

"Yes, win him back," the Sergeant explained. "In five days, your bull is going to be first prize at the funeral games King Priam intends to hold for his dead cousin. If you want him back, all you have to do is go to Troy and beat some of the best athletes in the world. That should be easy for a fine young man like you."

The soldiers laughed again. Obviously, they didn't believe I was up to the task.

Ignoring their snickers, I asked, "What kind of games?"

"Ah, well, let's see, I think there's three of them altogether," the sergeant answered, "ah, archery, running and wrestling and...oh, yeah...there'll be lots and lots of cake to eat too. You should like that. Okay, where's your bull?"

The soldiers laughed some more.

Now, you may be surprised to learn that, even as I lead the soldiers to Cronus, my mind was busy planning how to get him back but, I'm telling you, it really was. I figured all I had to do was go to Troy and win a couple of events. Namely, the foot race and archery contest. Given my superior skills in both these areas, it seemed like an easy thing for me to do. Of course, I knew I had no chance of winning the wrestling contest since the only wrestling I had ever done was with the opposite sex but I wasn't overly concerned about that because, as the soldiers were leading Cronus away, the Sergeant assured me that winning two of the three events would be enough to get Cronus back.

There was only one thing I never figured on.

The old ball and chain.

After the soldiers were gone, I bolted into the house to gather a cloak, some food and my bow. Since it was my intention to follow the soldiers all the way to Troy, I was in a hurry to collect those things and be out the door as quickly as possible. While I was in the kitchen loading up a knapsack with a shepherd's ration of bread and cheese, Oenone suddenly appeared behind me holding our baby and asked what I was doing. She looked as bedraggled as an abandoned puppy and I could barely hear what she was saying over the child's constant crying.

"The...the...soldiers came this morning and took Cronus away," I said, almost out of breath. "I'm going to Troy to win the bull back."

Waaahhhhhhhh, waaahhhhhhhh, waahhhhhhhh, waahhhhhhhh, waaahhhhhhhh!

"You're going where?" she asked in voice loud enough to be heard over the wailing. When you are the parents of a colic baby, you get used to talking that way.

Waaahhhhhhhh, waaahhhhhhh, waahhhhhhh, waahhhhhhhh, waaahhhhhhh!

"Troy. I've got to win Cronus back!" I answered in an equally loud voice.

Waaahhhhhhhh, waaahhhhhhh, waahhhhhhh, waahhhhhhhh, waaahhhhhhh!

"Wait, wait, wait!" Oenone said, confused. "Tell me what's going on!"

Waaahhhhhhhh, waaahhhhhhh, waahhhhhhh, waahhhhhhhh, waaahhhhhhh!

I closed the knapsack, turned around and said, "Well, this morning, the King's soldiers came to take Cronus away. In five days, the bull is going to be a prize at funeral games the King is going to hold in Troy. I'm going there to compete in them and win Cronus back. It should be easy to win because…"

Waaahhhhhhhh, waaahhhhhhh, waahhhhhhh, waahhhhhhhh, waaahhhhhhh!

"No, no, no!" Oenone suddenly interrupted, shaking her head adamantly. "You're not going anywhere, buster. You're gonna stay right here and help me take care of this baby!"

Waaahhhhhhhh, waaahhhhhhh, waahhhhhhh, waahhhhhhhh, waaahhhhhhh!

"Honey! I've got to get Cronus back!" I yelled, half pleading, half demanding.

Waaahhhhhhhh, waaahhhhhhh, waahhhhhhh, waahhhhhhhh, waaahhhhhhh!

"I don't care!" Oenone fired back. "You're not leaving me alone with our baby! We'll get another bull!"

Waaahhhhhhhh, waaahhhhhhh, waahhhhhhh, waahhhhhhhh, waaahhhhhhh!

Now I wanted to cry.

"Honey, there isn't another bull in the world like Cronus. I've got to get him back!" I explained loudly.

Waaahhhhhhhh, waaahhhhhhh, waahhhhhhh, waahhhhhhhh, waaahhhhhhh!

"No way, mister! You're not going anywhere! Here, take the baby. I need to get some rest!" Oenone said, offering the child to me.

Waaahhhhhhhh, waaahhhhhhh, waahhhhhhh, waahhhhhhhh, waaahhhhhhh!

I backed away from them both warily and said, "I'm sorry, but I've got to go right now! I don't want to lose the soldier's trail! I'll be back in about ten or eleven days!"

Waaahhhhhhhh, waaahhhhhhh, waahhhhhhh, waahhhhhhhh, waaahhhhhhh!

Oenone pulled the baby back into her breast and her face actually turned purple.

Then red.

"You bastard!" she exploded with rage.

Suddenly, the baby quit crying. Go figure.

"I know what this is all about!" she hissed. "You're off to seek the prize Aphrodite promised, aren't you?"

Of course, I was shocked. I didn't know how to respond. Believe me, at that moment, Aphrodite's promise was about the last thing I had on my mind.

I opened my mouth once or twice to say something in my defense but I couldn't get a single word out of it. That's because Oenone was still busy yelling her fool head off.

"Well, you go right ahead, you sorry bastard!" she screamed. "I always knew that you would abandon me someday. I just never dreamed that you would abandon your child also. My father and sister were right about you — you are a goddamned lowlife. Well, you go ahead and fuck your dirty little whore. See if I care. And don't come crawling back to me afterwards. I don't care how miserable you are!"

I listened to her tirade and thought: I can't stand this anymore. I'm tired of the way you're always bossing me around. I'm sick of your mistrust. What have I ever done to make you not trust me? Nothing! All I've ever done since we have met is kiss your ass and try to make you happy. And what do I get for my efforts? Not a fucking thing except distrust and scorn. You know what? Fuck you! And fuck your piss-smelling father and your wacko sister too!

Fortunately, I had enough sense not to say that to her out loud. For once in my life, I took the high road and, looking back on it now, I'm awfully glad I did. What I said instead was: I'm sorry, honey, but I've got to go. I love you and I'll be back as soon as I can. I even tried to give her a hug as I said those things but she pushed me away. Still, I know that my last words affected her deeply because I saw tiny teardrops form in the corner of her eyes. That's why I know she will come to my rescue now and heal my wound despite of what she said. I have no doubt that she still loves me. It was in her eyes the day I left.

I bolted out of the house about three seconds later and was quickly on my way. Luckily, the soldier's trail wasn't hard to find or follow because Cronus couldn't walk more than a hundred cubits at a time without taking a huge dump. I swear, I don't think an animal has ever lived that has managed to produce as much poop as that big white lunkhead has, but, on the other hand, I don't think one has produced a finer herd of children either, and that's exactly why I was so desperate to get him back. I was counting pretty heavily on making a small fortune selling Cronus' offspring to the local farmers.

I followed the soldiers as closely as I could without being detected. Our first day's march took us as far as the Scamander River and on the second day we headed west, following a trail that closely skirted the river's edge. We remained on that track for the next two days, always keeping the river on our right and the sun scorched stony hills to our left. The going was easy enough throughout the journey and, what with all the beautiful scenery, fresh air, sense of freedom and the confidence I had in winning Cronus back, I felt downright giddy as I trekked along.

On the fourth day, the soldiers topped a large hill and I noticed one of them point to something off in the distance. When I got to the same spot, I looked in the direction the soldier indicated and saw a height crowned with a fortified citadel not more than two leagues away. It was Troy, of course, and, I'm telling you, I've never seen a more imposing place. Guarded by a double band of stout walls, the city was split into two distinct sections: a stone citadel situated on a promontory that stood about forty cubits above the surrounding plain and a lower city that sat directly below the towering stronghold. The citadel itself wasn't actually all that big, maybe five acres in total size, but its massive stone walls gave it an almost impregnable look. From my perch, I estimated that the walls were about eleven cubits high and more than five cubits thick, not a bad guess, as I discovered later that day. Three massive fortified limestone gates controlled traffic in and out of the citadel: the South Gate, the East Gate, and the dominating Northeast Bastion Gate. Tiny specks of soldiers walked slowly along the narrow walkway that ran on top of the citadel's walls and gates. From there, they could look down on the city below and see just about everything that was happening inside it. That's because the lower city was so thickly crowded, its buildings pushed right up against the citadel's walls. Altogether, I'd estimate that there were nearly a thousand structures of various shapes and sizes crammed into the lower city's space of about seventy-five acres. To a country boy like me, the city looked like a stuffy and uncomfortable place to live and its only appealing quality appeared to lie in its well-laid network of cobble stone streets and avenues. An outer wall surrounded the bulging city like a fat man's belt. It was smaller than the citadel's wall, perhaps only five cubits high and two thick, and much weaker, being primarily constructed out of simple mud brick. Four weakly fortified gates controlled access to the town, one on the east side, one on the west and two in the south. Outside the city's gates, a broad, level plain stretched down to the ocean almost a half a league away. Vast fields of wheat, barley and lentils grew on the plain and a small harbor of sorts existed on the shoreline. In the bay beyond, fleets of fishing boats and trading vessels could be seen drifting peacefully on the rolling waves.

Realizing that the journey was almost over, the soldiers picked up their pace and so did I. Unfortunately for the soldiers, however, Cronus did not share in their eagerness to reach Troy and so, they were forced to slow down after a short distance and proceed at a speed more to the beast's liking. Not me though. I kept running faster and faster until I eventually caught up with the soldiers. At first, the troopers appeared to be shocked by my sudden appearance, which is understandable, but after it dawned on them that I had been on their tail all along, they couldn't help but be somewhat curious as to my purpose.

"Where are you going?" one of the soldiers yelled as I ran by.

"To eat some cake!" I shouted back, smiling and waving over my shoulder as I did.

They laughed and waved back.

Cronus took a shit.

A short time later, I came to the ford on the Scamander River and crossed it along with a large group of local farmers. Figuring that farmers were the same everywhere, I didn't try to strike up a conversation with any of them, as I wasn't the least bit interested in talking about the weather or hearing about the latest bean harvest. Besides, I'm not too sure I could have carried on a conversation with anyone amidst all the fantastic sights and sounds that soon greeted me in Troy.

I entered the city through one of the lower city's south gates and walked through its bustling, crowded streets in total wonderment. Every building and plaza seemed to be jam packed with people. Of course, I'd never seen anything like it in my life; goods, livestock and produce were everywhere in abundance, the sounds of bartering and laughter filled my ears, and I never imagined there were so many gold and silver coins in the world. Everyone I saw seemed to have their pockets or purses loaded with the stuff. The clothes they wore were colorful and in the cosmopolitan style: merchants in full-length wool or linen robes, tied in at the waist by cords and dyed in a multitude of bright colors; they were busy selling their wares to an almost endless stream of prospective buyers who crowded around their booths and, much to my delight, I quickly noticed that most of the merchant's patrons were women.

And, by Zeus, what beauties they were!

Troy's bazaars were certainly places to see smoky dark eyes, silky black hair, and soft brown skin. Most of the women wore pleated dresses decorated with little gold or silver disks while a flirtatious few preferred to sashay about the place wearing transparent silk shirts that barely concealed their breasts. I don't have to tell you which style I preferred the most! Anyway, all of the women wore makeup of some sort: dark gray eye shadow on the upper and lower lids, cherry red painted lips, cheeks decorated with little red circles and ears rimmed with scarlet. I also noticed there wasn't an ear lobe without an earring attached to it or a neck devoid of a necklace. The overall effect the woman had on me was absolutely mesmerizing to say the least and that's the reason I almost got trampled to death by a herd of onrushing horses.

Yep, horses.

That's the other thing I should tell you about Troy — the city was crazy in love with horses. Its citizens actually believed their horses were a gift from Zeus and so, they treated the creatures like honored houseguests. Believe it or not, my sister-in-law Andromache actually fed her horses grain mixed with wine and once, a Trojan officer actually decided to fight the Greeks on foot one day in order to keep his horse from missing mealtime! How crazy is that? Pretty darn crazy if you ask me. Heck, I never gave Cronus anything other than a nice pat on the head and he was worth fifty horses! Anyway, there were stables all over Troy and that's why the city had such well-organized streets — so folks could enjoy riding their horses about the place at just about any speed they wanted. I discovered that the hard way while I was standing in the middle of one of those streets gawking at some nearby females. I was so smitten by their beauty that I failed to heed one of Troy's most familiar refrains: Make way for the horses! Before I knew it, I found myself facing an onrushing horde of galloping horses. There was no chance to turn or duck, so I was left with little choice but to stand there like a helpless fool while fear, mingled with panic and despair, gripped me. So this is how it ends, thinks I, if I don't die, I'll surely be maimed for life. Luckily for me, just as I was almost under the horse's hooves, the lead rider recognized my peril and had the good grace to lean forward and offer me his hand. How I caught it only Zeus knows, but I did, and with a mighty leap, I swung myself up behind him and wrapped my arms tightly around his waist. I'd have kissed him too, if I hadn't been so damned scared.

"New to the city?" he yelled over his should at me.

"Yeah," I shouted back.

"Thought so," he answered.

I glanced around for a moment and saw that we were leading a troop of mounted soldiers up the main thoroughfare that led to the citadel.

"Where are we going?" I yelled.

"We're not going anywhere. I'm dropping you off as soon as I can find a good place to stop," he shouted back.

I'm all for that, thinks I, the sooner the better too.

Oh, don't get me wrong. I was very thankful to be alive but, the truth is, I've never liked being on horseback all that much. To me, it always seemed like a good way to get my neck broken and so, like anything dangerous to my health, I always avoided it whenever I could.

I suppose we rode on for another five minutes or so. I don't really know. When it's your first time on a galloping horse, time tends to go by fast, so it seemed like only a few minutes before we finally arrived at the citadel's South Gate. There, the man reined up and the horse glided to a stop. The rest of the troopers thundered on through the gate.

Thankful that things were finally standing still again, I quickly jumped to the ground and looked up at the man. He was about my age, strongly built, with luscious blonde hair that fell well past his shoulders. He had a handsome face that seemed a bit out of place for a soldier, with beautiful blue eyes and a jutting chin.

"What's your name?" I asked.

"Aeneas," he answered.

"Well, thank you, Aeneas, for saving my life," says I.

"No need to thank me. Thank the gods instead. You can do it right over there," Aeneas said, pointing to a line of six stone pedestals on which the clay images of several Trojan gods were perched.

I looked over at them and said, "I will."

Of course, I never did. Like I said before, I was never that big into religion.

Aeneas smiled broadly down at me, gave his horse a slight nudge with his heels and rode off through the gate without saying another word.

I stood there for a while after he left, happy to be in one piece, refusing to buy the sacrifices the priests offered, and wondered where I should go next. Since the crowd around the citadel's South Gate was made up of a bunch of unattractive soldiers and public officials, I decided to walk back down to the lower city where things were much more to my liking. I was just at the point of heading that way when I suddenly heard a familiar voice behind me say, "You know, that damned bull of yours sure does crap a lot."

Turning around quickly, I found myself facing the Sergeant once again. He met my eyes with a friendly nod and grin.

I smiled back broadly and said, "Thank god he does because I sure had one easy trail to follow."

The Sergeant laughed amicably. "I suppose you're here to compete in tomorrow's games?" he asked.

I nodded my head yes and said, "You told me it's the only way I can get my bull back."

The Sergeant pondered my words while he stepped a bit closer and then announced his verdict. "Well, kid," he said, "I wish you luck and all, but remember, I also told you that you'll be going up against the best athletes in the world and...."

"I can beat them," I interrupted. God, how I loved to brag! Believe me, nobody was ever prouder of me than me.

For a brief moment, the Sergeant seemed to be taken aback by my confidence, then he raised an amused eyebrow and said, "You're a cocksure little bastard, aren't you? Okay then, well, here's some advice, keep your eye on Deiphobus. He's the man to beat. You'll be able to spot him easy cause he'll be strutting around like a goddamned peacock. Beat him and you'll get your bull back."

"Okay, I will and thanks for the advice," I said and then I asked him where the games were going to be held.

The Sergeant pointed off to the west and said, "The Sports Arena is just outside the lower city's western gate. The games should start shortly after sun up tomorrow."

Having nothing else to say or ask him, I thanked him once again for his help and said goodbye. He nodded and waved goodbye but, as I was turning away, he suddenly stopped me.

"Hold on a sec, kid," he said.

I turned back around and saw that he appeared to be thinking about something. He studied me closely for a second, walked several steps off to the side, looked at me again, then walked back and asked, "Are you really that good of an athlete?"

"I'm pretty sure I am," I replied.

"You think you can beat that shithead Deiphobus?" he asked.

"Yeah, I do," I answered firmly.

"Are you confident enough for me to bet a whole month's pay on it?" he asked.

I looked at him impatiently and said, "Look, I wouldn't have come all this way if I thought I was going to lose."

The Sergeant scratched his beard and looked at me quizzically. It appeared as if he was trying to make up his mind whether or not to bet on me. Finally, he did.

"Okay, kid," he said, "I'll put my money on you. I figure the odds on you winning should be about a thousand to one. If you win, I'll make a goddamned fortune."

"Well, then, I guess this time tomorrow, you're gonna be a goddamned rich man," I answered, grinning smartly.

The Sergeant looked delighted and gave me another one of his thunderous shoulder slaps. "Now you're talking!" he shouted. "My name's Pandarus, you're Paris, right?"

"Yeah," I answered.

"Well, Paris, do you have a place to stay for the night?"

"No, I was planning to curl up in an alley somewhere or something like that," I admitted.

"Oh, that won't do," Pandarus said, shaking his head adamantly. "Now that I'll have my money riding on you, I need to make sure you get a good night's rest. Wanna stay in the barracks?"

I accepted, and followed him into the citadel. As I said before, the fortress wasn't all that big, so it's no surprise that the place was packed tighter than a sack of sand. I surveyed it as I followed Pandarus' hulking form through the crowded inferno that swirled around us. There were about twenty-five buildings crammed together inside the citadel's walls where, according to Pandarus, the royal family and their servants lived. The royal palace stood by itself near the center of the citadel; it was a lavish, multi-pillared, two story affair that was absolutely teaming with all kinds of soldiers, officials and aristocrats. A tight row of private mansions, servant quarters, storehouses, workshops, stables surrounded the palace. The military barracks Pandarus took me stood near the South Gate. It was a sturdy, two-story building, with a roof supported by several large columns of stone. The place was home to about three hundred soldiers of the Imperial Guard. Inside, there was a main hall and kitchen area downstairs where the men ate and socialized. At night, or when not on duty or whatnot, they slept upstairs on tiny cots.

Now, I don't know if you've ever visited an army barracks before, but, if you have, I think you'll agree that they're not the most pleasant smelling places in the world. As I followed Pandarus up the stairs, my senses were assailed by a nasty odor that can only be compared to a pile of sweaty clothes — a really big pile of sweaty clothes. I swear, the smell was strong enough to make a pig vomit.

"Damn," I said, pinching my nose shut. "This place smells horrible."

Pandarus smiled knowingly and said, "Welcome to the army, kid. Smells like shit, doesn't it? Believe it or not, you actually get used to it after a while."

I had my doubts.

We walked in silence down the row of cots filled with sleeping soldiers until an empty one finally appeared. Raising his hand, Pandarus signaled me to stop and said, "This one's yours."

I stepped past him and silently sat down on the cot like an obedient houseguest.

As I got situated, Pandarus said, "I'm the watch commander tonight, so I'll wake you up in the morning."

I glanced around anxiously at my surroundings for a moment and said, "Are you sure it's okay if I sleep here?" Of course, what I really meant was: do you think it's safe for me to sleep here? I mean, I was surrounded by a rough looking group of men and me, being pretty and dainty, well, it seemed like an awfully dangerous place to spend the night in.

Pandarus deduced my true meaning and said, "Don't worry, as long as you don't sleep on your stomach or prance around the place naked, you should be okay."

It's not hard to guess how much naked prancing I did that night or what position I slept in, nor is it difficult to figure out how much sleep I got either. Besides being afraid that one of the soldiers would wake up at any moment and make me his love doll, I couldn't get used to the smell and noise of my surroundings. I never imagined men snored, farted, coughed or belched as much as I heard them do that night. It sounded like one long constant roar. I tried going to my happy place but wasn't able to. The human symphony around me was far too great for that. The only sleep I got that night came shortly before sunrise, after all of the soldiers had awakened and gone downstairs to eat breakfast. Finally, the place became quiet enough for me to sleep in and, as I did, I had a strange dream. Well, I guess it wasn't that strange, especially after the one I had of the beauty contest and all, but still, it was pretty amazing. In the dream, Aphrodite appeared next to my cot.

She was as beautiful as ever, except, this time, unfortunately, she was fully dressed.

"Hello, Paris," she said.

"I'm not talking to you," I instantly snapped.

"Oh, why not?" she playfully pouted.

"Because last time you got me all hot and bothered and then disappeared," I replied angrily.

Believe me, when it comes to sex, I have a wicked memory.

"Oh, I'm sorry, baby," she answered. "Can you ever forgive me?"

I stated the obvious. "Well, I guess I could if you finish what you started."

She gave me one of her dazzling smiles and patted my cheek affectionately. "I'm sorry, honey, but we don't have time for that right now because in a few moments you are going to wake up."

"Fuck that, baby, I don't want to wake up," I protested.

"Oh, but you must, darling," she said. "Today's your big day. Today's the day you become a prince."

"Screw that too," I said. "Come on, baby, take your clothes off and lie down on top of me."

"I don't think that's a good idea," she answered in Pandarus' deep voice.

Yep, in Pandarus's voice.

Try putting those two things together!

Shocked, I opened my eyes and saw that the big lug was standing over me.

"And you'd better get rid of that too," he said, pointing down at something in the middle of the cot. "It'll get you into a lot of trouble around here."

I glanced quickly down to where he was pointing and saw that I was sporting a gigantic erection. I swear, it looked like there was miniature pup tent in the middle of my bed. Embarrassed, I instantly sat up on the opposite side of the cot with my back turned towards him and tucked the monster away.

He laughed and said, "Looks like you're ready for the contest."

Before I had a chance to tell him about my dream and what I was ready for, Pandarus ordered me to gather my things and follow him. I quickly grabbed my stuff and fell in behind him, weaving this way and that through the crowd of soldiers until we reached the South Gate. There, Pandarus stopped for a moment, reached inside a bag, took out a biscuit and tossed it to me.

"Thanks," I said, taking a bite of the biscuit, "why the hurry?"

"I didn't want the other guys cutting in on my action," he said. "That would lower the odds."

"Makes sense to me," says I, over a mouth full of biscuit. "Are we headed to the Sports Arena?"

"Yes, we are," he said brightly. "Follow me."

Even now, after all the blood and death I've witnessed since, I can still close my eyes and see what that wonderful morning looked like. The streets outside the arena were packed with a multitude of carriages, the excited crowd streaming into the stadium shoulder to shoulder, the women looking more beautiful than ever as the men carefully guided them along, the bookies standing off to the side, calling out bets and the vendors selling refreshments, some shouting, "Wine, get your wine here!"; the soldiers maintaining order in each entrance, warning the crowd to slow down and not to push, assuring it that there were enough seats for everyone, and the children laughing or chattering gaily with their parents as they entered the arena.

And I can still see the stadium itself even though it's long since been destroyed by the war; the dew on the great green field glistening in the early morning sun, the pavilion encircling it, richly adorned in brightly colored flags and decorations, its seats slowly filling up with spectators. The luxurious Royal Box located in the middle of the pavilion, where my family sat, being prepared for their arrival by a small army of servants. The referees standing in the middle of the field looking serious and the athletes silently milling about the turf, some of them stretching their muscles in anticipation of the day's events, others standing blank faced, watching the crowd gather. And what athletes! I've never seen a finer collection of men in my life. All appeared to be strong limbed and agile; they sauntered easily about the field completely naked, their bodies, like the dew, glistening in the sun's rays. As Pandarus and I entered the field, a few of them glanced towards me, no doubt, sizing me up.

"You still think you can beat them?" Pandarus asked, looking back at them.

"Yeah," I said, more to convince myself than him.

"Okay then, I'll go place the bet," he answered. "You go ahead and get ready. Limber up or something. The contest will start when the royal family gets here."

"Which one's Deiphobus?" I asked.

"He's not here yet," Pandarus said over his shoulder. "He's a member of the royal family. He'll get here when they do. Trust me, you'll know the bastard when you see him."

After that, I undressed and wondered around the field trying my best to look like an athlete. I even imitated the stretching exercises they were doing. Well, sorta. Having never done them before, I must have looked a bit silly, if not downright awkward but, if I did, I never noticed. That's because my mind was focused completely on the surrounding crowd. Believe me, it's a might unnerving to be gawked at by thousands of people, especially if it's your first time, which, of course, it was for me. So it shouldn't be at all surprising that I began wishing I was back home in bed, with the covers pulled over my head.

Luckily, my stage fright didn't last very long because a band suddenly began to play and the spectators instantly rose to their feet. The royal family had arrived and everyone's attention was suddenly diverted to them. I turned and faced the Royal Box with the rest of the athletes. We stood at attention while the royal family took their seats. It was the first time I had seen my mother or father since they abandoned me but, of course, I didn't know anything about that, so, to me, they were just a bunch of royal cattle thieves. After the family of rustlers got settled in, a naked young man suddenly came bounding out of the box and onto the field below. Instantly, the crowd exploded with a deafening cheer. In response, the man smiled and raised his arms triumphantly in the air.

That's got to be Deiphobus, I said to myself.

And then, as he strutted around the place like a proud peacock, I became sure it was.

Almost instantly, I hated the self-centered fuck with a purple passion.

Looking back on it now, I guess you could call it sibling rivalry or something like that, which, as any parent will tell you, is about the most natural form of hatred in the world. It's no wonder then that my purpose for winning the contest immediately changed. I wasn't content any longer just to win Cronus back, oh no, now, something deep inside of me said I had to beat that pompous son-of-a-bitch Deiphobus if it was the last thing I ever did.

And, you know, it damned near was.

But I'm getting ahead of myself a bit here.

Anyway, after the royal peacock was done flashing its feathers, the referees signaled for the athletes to come together in the middle of the field. Altogether, I'd say there were about thirty of us. When the referees were satisfied that we were all there, they sat about arranging us into a series of seven orderly ranks. Having never competed in a sporting contest before, or even seen one, I wasn't quite sure what to do, so I was forced to mimic the actions of the men around me. This served me well until I made the mistake of becoming the fifth member of a four-man rank. I swear, sometimes it seems like things are organized in such a way to make you look like a damned fool!

"What the heck are you doing?" the referee snarled.

"Lining up," I answered weakly.

"There are only four men to a rank," the referee said impatiently.

I glanced at the four athletes I had lined up with, flashed them an embarrassed grin, and took a step backwards.

"Not there either!" the referee immediately shouted.

I looked over and saw that I had joined another full rank. The athletes in it shot me an annoyed look.

"Come on, kid, pull your head out of your ass," one of them said, all unfriendly like.

Before I could respond or take another step backwards, the referee quickly grabbed me by the arm like I was a lost child and pulled me to the back of the pack, where he shoved me into my proper place. The crowd burst into laughter as he did and I'm sure the odds on me winning the games immediately became incalculable.

After I was finally situated and the crowd's laughter died down, the head referee shouted out an order and we began marching around the stadium in a very business-like manner. The crowd cheered and waved at us as we walked along. Unable to control myself, I beamed and waved back at them, and I must have looked pretty fine as I did because some of the ladies in the crowd blew kisses at me as I passed in front of them. That was very wonderful, of course, and I remember thinking that being an athlete wasn't without its perks.

After a couple of turns around the arena, we finally came to a stop in front of the Royal Box. Then some trumpets blew a fan fair and a cheer went up as Cronus was lead into the arena by a small group of soldiers. I had a hard time recognizing him at first because he had been washed, buffed and brushed for the occasion. To me, he looked like a big hairy white ball. Anyway, he didn't appear to be very impressed by his situation because he immediately raised his tail and took a huge shit in front of the entire assembly.

Good boy, thinks I.

Then the trumpets blew again and the hubbub died away enough for my father to stand up and make a little speech.

"Fellow countrymen," he said, "welcome to the funeral games to honor the death of my cousin Xuthus."

Fuck you and fuck your cousin, I mumbled under my breath.

"And I bid welcome to this great assembly of athletes," my father continued, "I will reward the champion of these games with this fine bull and let the citizens of Troy crowd around the victor and deck him with garlands."

Keep your lousy garlands, I thought, just give me back my bull, damn you.

"And so, great athletes, compete with honor and strength," my father droned on. "Be swift of foot and sure of aim. Strive to be perfect in every event, just as my cousin Xuthus strove to be in life. So, without further ado, let the games begin!"

Then it was time to compete and the referees immediately set about organizing the first event. As luck would have it, especially for me, the games opened with the wrestling competition. Why was that so fortuitous, you ask? Well, like I said before, I knew there was no way in Hades I could win the wrestling event, unless, of course, my competitors were all female and, even then, my chances of winning were still a bit dodgy, so, I planned to lose as quickly and as painlessly as possible because, you see, in doing so, I figured I'd be conserving all my energy for the other two events. Good strategy, huh? Damn right it was. And healthy too!

In preparation for the wrestling contest, the referees began arranging us according to size and weight. Since I was a little guy, I kept getting pushed further and further back in the line until I found myself standing next to you-know-who. Yep, that's right, I got matched up with Deiphobus. Now, if you think about it, it's not very surprising that we were paired up since we were biological brothers and therefore, almost identical in every detail. The only difference between us was that he appeared to be much stronger while I was by far the better looking. I've always been of the opinion that my brother got the short end of the stick.

For a long moment, we stood there studying each other closely. I'm not sure what was going on inside the dunderhead's mind as we did, but I felt like I was looking at myself in a mirror and, if I hadn't already hated the bastard with a passion, I'd have probably wondered why we looked so much alike. Instead, I couldn't help but be annoyed by our uncanny likeness.

"Are you from the country?" Deiphobus asked, all polite like.

"Yeah," I quickly snapped, "and what's it to you?"

"I was just wondering, that's all," he answered with a friendly smile. "I'm Prince Deiphobus and it's very nice to meet you."

Okay, now, that really pissed me off!

Stringing together a quick comeback, I yelled, "Well, helloooo, Prince Fancy Pants!"

Immediately, several of the athletes and a couple of nearby referees turned to see what the commotion was all about.

Now that I had an audience, I shouted, "Well, well, I, ah, I don't give a flying fuck who you are!"

Instantly, my brother seemed to lose his breath and I thought he'd faint right on the spot. Like most members of royalty, he wasn't used to being addressed in such an insulting manner. Nor were the athletes or referees around us used to seeing a member of their monarchy treated so rudely. It nearly scared the shit out of them! They looked at me all nervous like, their eyes pleading with me to stop.

Fuck that, I was on a roll.

I poked an angry finger in my brother's face and let him have it. "You are nothing but a big sack of... pig snot!" I yelled.

And that's when my brother went plumb dumb crazy.

His head started to twitch something awful and his eyes began rolling around all crazy like in their sockets and his arms started flapping about rapidly and then, just when it looked like he was about to fly away, he stopped, took a deep breath, composed himself, smiled serenely and lunged at me like an enraged tiger.

There wasn't time to run away, but luckily, I didn't need to because the referees were close enough to grab my brother and pull him away before he could lay a single finger on me.

"Get a hold of yourself, Prince Deiphobus!" one of them shouted as they restrained him.

The other referee looked at me and said, "You get a hold of yourself too and apologize."

"I ain't apologizing for shit!" I instantly snapped. "He started it!"

"Did not!" Deiphobus shouted.

"Did too!" I mouthed back.

"Did not!" Deiphobus shouted again.

I shook my head yes and stuck my tongue out at him.

Deiphobus growled, tensed his muscles and tried to lunge at me again but the referees held him firmly in place.

"Come on, Prince Deiphobus, save it for the wrestling match!" one of them yelled as my brother struggled to break free. "You don't want the people to think you are a bad sport."

And that's when it hit me.

As the referees dragged Deiphobus away, I suddenly realized I could use his anger to turn the crowd against him. All I had to do was make him look like a poor sport, which seemed easy enough, and, best of all, with the referees around to restrain him and a large field for me to escape into should he break free, it seemed safe too. That, of course, was the main thing, and once I realized I could strip that prancing peacock of his feathers without running a big risk to life and limb, I didn't hesitate to start plucking.

"That's right, jackass, save it for the match!" I yelled. "I'm going to kick your sorry, pig snot ass!"

Deiphobus flashed me a look of total rage, and once again started struggling with the referees in an attempt to break free, all of which, of course, made me laugh amusingly. It took the refs several minutes to subdue him and after they did, there was a meeting of sorts in the wrestling arena, where it was decided that Deiphobus and I should fight first.

I was so proud of my handiwork that I fairly leapt into the ring.

And then, by god, I about leapt right back out again!

That's because Deiphobus met me in the center of the ring with a look in his eyes that unmistakably said: I'm going to rip your heart out and eat it in front of you, then I'm going to poop it into a bowl and make you eat it and then I'm going to rip your liver out and repeat the whole process all over again.

You see the kind of mindset I was dealing with there?

And that's exactly when I realized I had made a really big mistake. How I kept from losing my nerve and running away right then and there is way beyond me but, believe it or not, for some reason, I didn't. Maybe it was because of the huge crowd that was watching us — trust me, it takes a lot of courage to be a coward in front of thousands of people — but, mainly, I think it was because I heard the referee announce that the first man who became pinned for three seconds would lose the match. Since I planned to be that man, I quickly reasoned that I could stick it out for three seconds.

"Three seconds, right?" I nervously asked the referee.

"Yeah, three seconds," he answered.

"When do you start counting?" I asked.

"As soon as your shoulder makes contact with the ground," he answered.

Had I known what was going to happen next, I'm pretty sure I would have ran away.

You see, lasting three seconds wasn't the problem. Getting to the three seconds was.

After the referee finished issuing his instructions, I retreated into my corner with the intention of flopping down on the ground and curling up into a little ball as soon as the match started.

That was my plan, anyway.

Didn't work out that way though!

That's because Deiphobus was after me before the word "go" could leave the referee's mouth. I swear, I've never seen a peacock move so fast. Of course, I had no choice but to run from him, dodging this way and that, hoping to elude his murderous grasp long enough to find enough time and space to curl up in. So we raced about the ring, both of us screaming our asses off, him in anger, me in fear; around and around we went, how many times, I don't know, but it must have been very amusing to watch us because, I swear, the crowd was positively howling with laughter after the first couple of turns. I could actually hear them laughing above our screams. And I'm damned glad they were so amused because that's why the referee decided to step in and put an end to the outrageous spectacle. As my brother and I completed our sixth turn around the ring, the referee suddenly lurched forward and grabbed my brother by the arm. That gave me time enough to find a nice, safe place to curl up in. And, Jack, let me tell you, curl up, I did! Roly-poly bugs don't roll up into a ball any tighter than I did. You couldn't have pried my arms and legs apart with a crowbar. Believe me, I know, because Deiphobus tried. Well, almost. He was on top of me about a half second later, pulling and pushing, hitting and kicking, desperately trying to get at my throat, no doubt, so that he could choke the shit out of me. But I wouldn't let him. I kept my chin tucked tightly under my arms and legs, while, the whole time, I was pleading with the referee to start his countdown.

Finally, he did.

"One!" the referee shouted in a loud, deliberate voice.

Oh, thank god, it's almost over, thinks I.

"Two!"

Come on, come on, say it, I impatiently pleaded.

"Thr….."

The referee never got to finish the word three because Deiphobus suddenly turned around and punched him so hard in the face that he was immediately knocked unconscious. That's how intent my brother was on killing me. He didn't care who he had to maim in order to do it!

It's not hard to guess what my emotions were as this sank in, along with the knowledge that the one man who could save my life was out cold. I looked over at the referee's limp body and yelled, "Referee man, wake up! Say three! Wake up! Three! Three! Please, wake up!"

"Shut up and fight!" my brother shouted back.

Fuck that.

"Three! Three! Three! Three!" I kept yelling over and over again, hoping the referee would suddenly gain consciousness, remember where he was and stop the fight.

Losing patience with his inability to pry my hands and legs apart, my brother suddenly grabbed a hold of my body and, with a mighty jerk, lifted me up over his head. Now, I don't know if you have ever been manhandled in such a manner, but if you haven't, I'm here to tell you that it's not a very pleasant experience, especially if you're afraid of heights, or, like me, afraid of dying in general.

"Stop it. Put me down!" I pleaded, as I dangled over his head. "It's not fair! You've won! I heard the referee say three!"

"No you didn't," my brother said, looking up at me with an evil sneer on his face.

Before I could convince him that I had, or beg for my life, or even say I was sorry, he sent me flying through the air with a mighty toss of his arms. I screamed for my life, which felt like it ended a couple of seconds later when I made contact with the iron-hard ground. Never before in my misspent life had I experienced so much pain all at once. Upon impact, it felt like every bone in my body cracked simultaneously and my innards tried to squeeze their way out of my throat. I couldn't take a breath of air without experiencing a new degree of pain somewhere in my body. It was all really too much for me to bear. All I could do was lie there, battered and bruised, almost in tears, and plead for my life.

"Stop!" I shrieked, over and over again. "Stop! Stop! Stop! Threeeeeeeeeeee!"

My brother grinned, slapped his hands together in delight and bounded towards me. I closed my eyes and curled up into ball once again. Seconds later, he was on top of me, pounding me with his fists and howling like a demon. I screamed and begged for mercy. I even told him I was sorry for insulting him. I told him I was the big fat snot pig, not him. A lot of good that did though, as my cries only seemed to make him hit me harder.

The crowd, of course, went nuts booing my brother's poor sportsmanship and, although it lifted my spirits a tad to hear that my plan was working, I would have been far happier to see someone rushing to my aid. The nearby referees seemed to be in a quandary about what to do next. Not only was Deiphobus out of his mind and clearly dangerous, but he was also a member of royalty and that alone made them hesitate for a moment. I swear, the things folks are willing to let royalty get away with!

"For god's sakes," I screamed at them, "pull him off before he kills me!"

That seemed to clue the bastards in on my predicament and give them the excuse they needed to come to my aid. Suddenly, I was aware of people running around the ring. I closed my eyes and waited for them to pull Deiphobus off of me. When they finally did, I opened my eyes and saw that they were dragging him away. He glared down at me as they did, yelling something to the effect that he would be back shortly to rip my balls off and shove them down my throat.

Fat chance I was going to stick around and wait for that to happen! Fuck that! Fuck Cronus too! They could have the big shit bag for all I cared! He certainly wasn't worth getting killed or, worse, getting horribly castrated over. All I wanted to do at that point was put as much distance between my balls and Deiphobus as I possibly could. The sooner, the better, too!

I stood up slowly, relieved to find that apart from some nasty scrapes and bruises, I really wasn't in that bad of shape. Eyeing the nearest exit, I was just about to sprint for it when I heard a voice say, "What the fuck was that?"

It was Pandarus.

You know, the guy who had just bet a month's worth of pay on my sorry ass.

And he didn't appear to be to very happy about his investment.

"What the fuck was that?" he asked again. He was obviously talking about my poor wrestling performance.

I pointed a shaking finger towards Deiphobus and said, "Did you see that? He tried to kill me!"

Pandarus shrugged his huge shoulders, looked in Deiphobus' direction and said, "So what? He tries to kill everybody. He's a prince and that's what princes do. No big deal."

If Pandarus was trying to reassure me, he didn't even come close. After all, he was only thinking about his money, while I, on the other hand, had my precious scrotum to think about.

Shooting him a look of utter disbelief, I hollered, "No big deal? Are you kidding me? No big deal? Well, mister, let me tell you, it's a big deal to me, cause I'm the one he's trying to kill and I'm not about to give him a second chance so I'm outta here!"

I turned and began jogging towards the exit.

But I didn't get very far.

Pandarus suddenly came up behind me and savagely grabbed me by the ear, immediately bringing me to a stop.

"Ow, ow, ow, ow, ow," I said, as his fingers painfully bit into my earlobe.

"Now you listen to me, you little pussy," he snarled, "I just bet a lot of money on you to win this here contest and, by god, that's exactly what you are going to do."

"Ow, ow, ow, ow, ow," I replied.

"If you don't," he continued, "you ain't gonna have to worry about Prince Shithead over there killing your ass cause I'll do the job myself. Understand?"

I shook my head yes, of course. What else could I do? He meant it; no doubt about that. And besides, he was pinching my ear something awful. So, anyway, there I was, stuck between two lunatic killers. Win or lose, I was pretty much a dead man. My god, I remember thinking, what have I done to deserve this? All I wanted to do was get my stolen property back. Why am I the one being punished? Why isn't Prince Shithead being punished?

And then, oddly enough, almost on cue, he was.

I was rubbing my ear and generally feeling sorry for myself, with Pandarus lording over me, when a referee suddenly walks up to us and says, "Well, that's it for Deiphobus, he's been suspended from the games for assaulting a referee."

At that, Pandarus smiled broadly and was all over me, assuring me that victory was ours now, and that he would soon be a rich man. I smiled back at him while I got over my surprise and listened to the referee continue: it was fair that Deiphobus got kicked out the games, he said, hitting a referee should never be tolerated, and if it was up to him, Deiphobus would be banned from the stadium too, but since he's a prince and all, he gets to sit in the royal box and watch and what's even more unfair, Deiphobus also gets to crown the champion with garlands just to show that he's not a bad sport.

Of course, I agreed with the referee, frowning and saying it was too bad cause I had really wanted to compete against Deiphobus, but it was probably for the best, since I would have drubbed him in the other two events and that probably would have upset him even more.

It was all bold talk, to be sure, said mainly to appease Pandarus and not at all depictive of how I really felt. The truth is, if I could have sprouted wings at that moment, I'd have flown back to Mount Ida without a wave goodbye; Deiphobus, Pandarus, Cronus and the games, all be damned. But, if there's anything I learned from being a craven coward, it's not to look like one if you can help it, especially if your life depends on it, which mine clearly did at that particular moment, so I smiled at Pandarus and tried to act confident, you know, just so he wouldn't murder me.

Pandarus listened to my comments with a satisfied look on his face, which was good, I guess, because it gave me hope that I might survive after all, then he grabbed my arm and said, "Hey, you want some cake?"

Before I could answer, I found myself being dragged to the south end of the arena, where there were about a half dozen tables absolutely covered with stacks and stacks of cake. I was famished, and while Pandarus stuffed his bag full with the sweet stuff, I attacked a nearby stack with all the gusto of a hungry wolf. About four mouthfuls later, Pandarus grabbed me again and we made our way back to the wrestling arena where we found a comfortable place to sit and watch the other athletes beat the shit out of one another. As we did, Pandarus offered me some of the cake he had stowed away in his bag. I gladly accepted, of course, since, like drinking liquor, eating food has always calmed me down during periods of stress. Anyway, as I ate, Pandarus would nudge me every so often, point to a certain athlete and tell me something about him.

"That's Euphorbus, son of Panthous," he said. "He's an excellent charioteer and good with a spear but not much of an archer or runner. You'll beat him easy, I'm sure."

No doubt, after the wrestling contest, you're as surprised as I was to learn that Pandarus would still think I could beat anybody easy but, believe it or not, he actually did. Evidently, he still believed my silly boastings. I, on the other hand, wasn't as confident as I had once been. My tussle with Deiphobus had given me a big dose of reality and shaken my nerves up something awful. Heck, I wasn't sure I could outrun a peg-legged fat baker in a downhill race. Of course, I couldn't tell Pandarus that, not unless I wanted to die, which I wasn't too keen on doing just then, so I had no choice but to sit there like a good lad and listen to him prattle on.

"Over there's Eurpylus, son of Telephus of Mysia," he said. "He's a real momma's boy, but good with a bow. You'll have to keep an eye on him during the archery competition."

Nervous that I had to keep an eye on anyone, I took another piece of cake from Pandarus' bag and crammed it in my mouth. The piece was so big that my jaws couldn't come together and I had to breathe through my nose as I chewed it. It was at this point that Pandarus noticed I was paying more attention to the cake than to him.

"Are you listening to me!" he abruptly yelled.

I almost choked I was so startled. For several agonizing seconds, I struggled to swallow a half chewed portion of cake until, finally, somehow, mercifully, I managed to get it down. When I could breathe again, I looked at Pandarus and shouted, "Yes, I'm listening to you and for god sakes, please don't yell at me like that!"

Pandarus considered me with those cold eyes of his, which froze my innards, then he turned his attention back to the athletes. "That there's Polites," he said, "Deiphobus' quiet little brother. He isn't as strong as Deiphobus but he's a real fast runner. He's mainly a distance runner but now that his brother is out, he's the guy you'll have to beat in the running contest."

Alarmed that a member of Deiphobus' clan was lurking close by, I measured the distance to the nearest exit and said, "Deiphobus' brother?"

"Yeah, but don't worry, he's not a patch compared to Deiphobus," Pandarus assured me.

That seemed like a bit of good news, but still, just to be on the safe side, I made a quick mental note to stay out of Polites' way.

"That's Melanippus, son of Hicetaeon," Pandarus continued. "He's a good man to have by your side during a fight."

I nodded and took another slice of cake from his bag.

Pointing towards an athlete with very dark skin, Pandarus said, "That's Memnon, Prince of Ethiopia. I don't know much about him except that he's supposed to be a great soldier. We'll have to keep our eye on him and see how he does."

Over a mouthful of cake, I mumbled, Yup.

"That big guy over there is Glaucus, son of Hippolochus the Lycian," Pandarus droned on, "a good wrestler and archer. Not sure how fast he is though."

I nodded again, you know, just to make him think I was listening and grabbed some more cake.

"That big fellow there is Phereclus, son of Tekton," he said. "He's strong because he carries around wooden beams all day. He's a master ship builder. He'll win the wrestling competition easy now that Deiphobus isn't in it."

And so he did. Phereclus was, just as Pandarus said he was, a very strong man, and I'm sure that he would have given Deiphobus a run for his money, which is also to say that Phereclus wouldn't have had any trouble kicking my pansy ass. Luckily, I had been smart enough to avoid that to start out with, and, as I looked at the wounded athletes around me, I realized my decision to scratch the wrestling competition had been a very wise one indeed. I swear, there wasn't an athlete without a serious injury on him of some sort, while, in comparison, all I had on me were a bunch of cake crumbs and a minor bruise or two. While this was just dandy with me, I had enough sense to realize that others would view my cleverness as being somewhat less than sportsmanlike and so, when I joined the other athletes for the running event, I tried to look as inconspicuous as possible. I did this by helping Melanippus to the starting line. He was bruised, bloody and limping terribly, all of which, luckily, presented me with a perfect way to slip past the crowd undetected. And, I did too. Well, almost. Unfortunately, Deiphobus saw through my little masquerade. As I took my place on the starting line, I glanced over at the Royal Box and saw the crazy son-of-a-bitch was staring at me from it with a look on his face of utter fury. Clearly, he had divined my stratagem and was, without a doubt, burning with rage that it had worked. My hair stood upright and, once again, I got the urge to run towards the nearest exit, and I probably would have too, if Pandarus hadn't been standing behind me. So there I was again, like I said before, trapped between two killers, damned if I did, damned if I didn't. It was Paris R.I.P., for sure, time of funeral to be announced momentarily.

And then the referee shouted, "Ready…set… go!"

He said it so fast that I was caught by surprise and, as a consequence, I immediately fell behind the other runners by several steps. Realizing my predicament, I panicked and bounded forward, threading my way through the herd of athletes until I reached its front; there I found Polites leading the pack, just as Pandarus predicted he would. I was so scared, I didn't take time to look over at him as I drew up even, I just went plunging by, as quickly as my legs would carry me, like a man whose life depended on winning, which, of course, mine did. All I could do was race to the finish line and victory — and possibly death at the hands of Deiphobus afterwards later. The crowd was roaring as I forged ahead — at least ten steps ahead of Polites — and then I was across the finish line.

Everything went crazy after that; the crowd went bonkers, and the other athletes surrounded and congratulated me; it was pure pandemonium, and then Pandarus appeared, slapped me on the back and screamed, "By god, boy, you are fast!" Big Phereclus came walking by, smiling and shaking his head in agreement. So did Memnon and Glaucus. Even Polites, my younger brother — although I didn't know he was at the time — came by to tell me he had never seen anyone faster. This was a high compliment to be sure, and since he had obviously, at one time or another, seen Deiphobus run, I couldn't help but feel a little satisfied by it. I say a little because the race left me feeling mostly frightened — a lot frightened, as a matter of fact. I mean, I came within eleven steps of losing my goddamned life! Eleven steps! Believe me, Jack, that's cutting it way too close for my liking. I was shaken, I tell you.

So, after that, I did the only thing I could do.

I ate some more cake.

The more cake, I figured, the better, because its sweet taste made me feel disconnected from all the bad shit that was happening.

It was while I was standing next to the cake table, cramming as much of the sweet stuff in my mouth as I possibly could, with Pandarus at my elbow harping on and on about how rich he was going to be, that someone suddenly touched me on the shoulder. I turned to find a beautiful, black-haired babe with big boobs and dark, alluring almond eyes standing directly behind me. She was dressed in a long, red robe that was tighter than tight had a right to be.

"You certainly are a very interesting fellow," she said, all flirty like.

I just stood there and gaped, praying that a hem would break.

She studied me closely for a long moment, kinda like a butcher studies a side of beef, and then she turned to Pandarus and said, "Well, Sergeant, aren't you going to introduce us? It seems the cat has got his tongue."

Pandarus' face went flush. Then he bowed slightly and said, "Your Highness, I'd like to present Paris, from Mount Ida."

Then to me, he said, "Paris, this is Princess Polyxena, daughter of our great King Priam."

At that, he elbowed me and signaled that I was supposed to bow. But I couldn't. All I could do was stand there and wonder what it would be like to peel that dress off and slide between those luscious thighs of hers.

Okay, I know what you're thinking here: my god, he was ogling his own sister, yuck, how sick! All I can say is that I didn't know Polyxena was my sister at the time and besides, my thoughts weren't any different than those of the other guys standing around us. So cut me some slack.

Embarrassed by my lack of courtly manners, Pandarus immediately began apologizing profusely.

Polyxena listened to him patiently, giggled and said, "That's okay, Sergeant. I like him. He's cute. Perhaps you should bring him by the palace tonight. Maybe I can help him find his tongue."

That took me aback, at first, mainly because I wasn't expecting it, but then I quickly recovered and flashed her the smile that I reserve for women whom I want to fuck.

To my delight, she quickly smiled back. It was obvious that we were of one mind. Then she turned away and as I watched her leave, I boastfully whispered to Pandarus, "She wants me, oh, yeah, she wants me bad."

Pandarus waited until she was a respectful distance away and said, "She wants everybody bad, you clod."

"Huh?" I asked, casting him a look of utter confusion.

He chuckled and said, "She's a fucking nymphomaniac."

"Really?" I asked, looking back at Polyxena in wonderment.

I had never seen a nympho before, I mean, outside of myself, of course.

"Yep," he continued, "and besides half the town, she's also screwed every member of the Imperial Guard."

"Even you?" I asked, almost enviously.

Pandarus nodded, smiled slyly and said, "How do you think I got to be a Sergeant?"

Well, that little hussy, thinks I. Still, I couldn't wait to screw her. That's because I've never been one to turn down a piece of ass just because it has a little wear and tear on it. If I was, I would never have gotten involved with the likes of Helen, or Oenone, or....well, just about every other woman I ever screwed. I mean, hardly any of them were what you'd call a spring virgin when we met, especially Helen. Heck, by the time we met, she'd already pumped out two kids.

Anyway, Pandarus looked at me, then he glanced towards Polyxena, then back to me again and said, "Listen, buster, you ain't screwing nothing ever again unless you win this here next event, got that?"

So there I was once again: the finger of death pointing directly at me. Lose the archery contest and die. It was that simple, and what's worse, there was nothing I could do about it except turn back to the table and starting wolfing down cake like there was no tomorrow, which, given my predicament, was a distinct possibility.

Ten pieces of cake later, the referees announced the archery contest was about to begin.

I could hardly move, my stomach was so bloated with cake, but somehow, I managed to retrieve my bow and arrows in time to join the other athletes for the archery contest. Because I had moved so slowly, I was the last athlete in a line that had formed in front of a row of twelve axes placed one in front of the other. You see, the athlete who could shoot the highest number of arrows through the small holes in the axe heads won the contest. Each athlete was allowed three arrows to accomplish the feat with.

Eurpylus was first in line. He held a fine bow crafted in Messene and looked very confident. As he waved at the crowd cheerfully, I pulled my bow from its leather case, strung it and selected three arrows. Then, Pandarus was at my side asking if I was any good with a bow. I assured him that I was and sarcastically offered to give him a demonstration, you know, by shooting him in the ass or something like that. He declined, of course, and cautiously backed his way into the surrounding crowd until I couldn't see him anymore.

"First archer up!" the referee yelled, and a hush fell over the stadium. I dropped the leather case, while Eurpylus knelt down about four cubits from the row of axes and notched an arrow. Everyone held their breath as he raised his bow and fired. I swear, I went pale as the arrow went flying straight through the axe holes and into the field beyond.

The crowd went nuts, and I felt like I was going to throw up. I never imagined an archery contest could be such a desperate adventure.

Pandarus was right, Eurpylus was the man to beat with a bow. He was good. Real good. He notched the second arrow, fired and got another round of cheers as it made its way cleanly through the row of axes.

Oh god, thinks I, please miss the next shot, please miss, please miss, please, please, please.

And, then, much to my relief, he did. The third arrow was slightly off. It nicked the edge of the sixth axe and went careening somewhere off to the side. The crowd groaned loudly as it did. I smiled, of course, and recovered my breath.

After that, none of the other athletes managed to get more than one arrow through the axe heads, which was just peachy with me. Then, it was my turn. I must have looked like a nervous, pregnant cow as I knelt down before the axes. I mean, I was shaking visibly and my stomach was still bloated from the butt load of cake I had ingested earlier. Anyway, I knew it was three arrows or death, so I swallowed hard and looked around one last time. Polyxena stood up and waved at me from the Royal Box; Deiphobus sat next to her, glaring, and, although Pandarus was nowhere to be seen, I knew he was lurking out there somewhere, waiting to assassinate me if I lost.

There wasn't a whisper as I notched the first arrow. Slowly, I raised the bow and pulled the string back until it rested against my cheek. There, I held it for a split second, aiming carefully, while my bowels rumbled miserably and sweat poured down from my forehead. When I felt my aim was true, I held my breath and let the arrow fly.

Now, let me tell you, normally I would have made that shot without any problem. Heck, I probably could have done it with my eyes closed. But, because I was so nervous when I released it, the shot was slightly off center and the arrow barely cleared the twelfth axe. As a matter of fact, it scraped the side of the last axe as it passed through, it was that close.

And I don't think I have to tell you how frightened that made me feel.

I barely had enough courage left to attempt a second shot but somehow, from somewhere, I mustered just enough. I waited in front of the axes, my guts churning wildly, for the crowd to stop cheering before I picked up my second arrow. When I did, I notched the arrow and tried to settle my mind. It was like trying to settle the wind and, what's worse, my guts felt like they were on the verge of exploding but like before, somehow or another, I managed to find enough strength to fix my eyes on the target and focus.

How I made the second shot, only Zeus knows. But I did; it went whizzing through the axes cleanly this time but, I swear, only by a hair, if that much. Of course, the crowd couldn't see how close the shot was, so it roared forth confidently. I, on the other hand, wasn't so sure, mainly because I knew how close I had come to ending my life.

So there I was, down to one arrow — one arrow to win, one arrow to live — and me, on the verge of having a nervous breakdown. I wiped my brow, looked down at the ominous third arrow and fretted. For how long I did that, I'm not sure, but it must have been a while because a referee eventually appeared by my side to ask me if I was planning to take all day to shoot my last arrow. I asked him if that was possible because, believe me, if I could have taken all day, I would have. Unfortunately, he shook his head no and said I couldn't. I nodded back at him reluctantly and reached down to pick the third arrow up. My hand was shaking so badly, that the referee couldn't help noticing how frightened I was.

"Don't be nervous, son, it's only a game," he said, all reassuring like. "It's not like your life depends on it."

I wanted to start crying and say, yes, yes it does, Mister Referee Man, but I couldn't because Pandarus would have killed me anyway, so there was nothing left to do but notch the arrow and watch my life pass through those stupid axe heads.

Once again, I pulled the string back to my cheek, took careful aim, and, whether I was ready or not, I let it go. Almost immediately, I heard the crowd start screaming as the arrow left my bow and then....

I was lying on my back staring up at the pretty blue sky.

How nice, thinks I, the clouds are so beautiful and fluffy today. Hey, that cloud looks sorta like a sheep and that one over there, well, it looks kinda like a vagina and that one....

Suddenly, Pandarus' grinning face appeared over me, completely obstructing my view of the pretty clouds.

"What, what happened?" I asked.

"We won!" he shouted. "You did it!"

That still didn't explain my present condition.

"What am I doing down here on the ground?" I asked.

"You fainted!" he screamed, slapping on the shoulder.

In case you haven't noticed it yet, I have a tendency to faint during particularly uncomfortable situations. It's a trait that most cowards have and although it can be a bit of an annoyance, I'm here to tell you that it does offer you a wonderful reprieve from any danger you might be facing.

For a moment anyway!

And that moment disappeared when big Phereclus suddenly reached down and hoisted me atop his massive shoulders. From there, I could see everything and everybody in the stadium and, believe me, it was pure pandemonium all around. Everybody in the stadium seemed to be laughing, jumping around and cheering hysterically. I could hardly believe my eyes, nor could I believe that I had won. But I did. And what's weirder, everyone seemed to be thrilled out of their minds about my victory. Even Eurpylus, the man I had beaten, came by to shake my hand, and Melanippus asked me where I had learned to shoot so well. And then Phereclus paraded me around the place on his shoulders, and the cheering re-echoed, while the band banged away, and people tossed flowers at me, and girls blew kisses at me, and...well...it was, without a doubt, the most wonderful thing that ever happened to me.

Then the noise died away a bit, and I saw a small procession of referees, military officials and assorted bigwigs marching towards me. Ahead of them walked Deiphobus carrying a golden garland.

"They're coming to crown you," Phereclus shouted up at me.

I tried to smile and look eager to accept my reward but, the truth is, my stomach was still rumbling something awful and seeing Deiphobus coming my way only upset it more, so I would have been far more pleased if someone would have handed me a seltzer and kindly escorted me out the nearest exit. But, as it was, I was stuck on top of that mountain of a man, with nothing left to do but hope my guts wouldn't explode and to try to look as humble as possible so Deiphobus wouldn't kill me.

And, you know, I almost pulled it off.

Deiphobus approached me very cordially, even though, from the angry look in his eyes, I could tell that he still wanted to wring my neck. I smiled down at him politely as an official in the group murmured something noble about the contest, then the band played a little tune, and as it did, Deiphobus stepped forward to place the garland on my head. I closed my eyes and bent down to accept it.

And that's exactly when I threw up!

And, what's worse, Deiphobus didn't have time to get out of the way!

So I spewed half digested cake all over his pompous ass! It was like a water fountain going off! I couldn't stop myself. I just kept vomiting and vomiting, while, the whole time, he just stood there like a fucking statue, refusing to move a single muscle to get out of the way. I couldn't believe it, nor, from their faces, could anybody else. They stood around us, side-by-side, wide-eyed, with their mouths open in surprise, silently watching me vomit all over their prince. For a good five minutes the spectacle lasted and then, when I was done, I swear, you could have heard a pin drop, it was that quiet.

Deiphobus stood motionless for a moment or two afterwards, then he raised his hands to his face and carefully wiped the vomit from his eyes. When he could see clearly again, he looked at the people around us and smiled gently. For some reason, probably because it was the polite thing to do, they smiled back at him. Then he sighed deeply, as though in resignation, and walked slowly over to a nearby soldier. There, he handed the soldier my garland, and then, much to my horror, he reached down and grasped the soldier's sword.

Believe me, it didn't take a genius to figure out what Deiphobus was going to do with that sword, nor did it take me more than a half second to jump to the ground and start running for the exit. If folks were amazed by how fast I had run during the competition, I'm sure they were doubly amazed by the deer-like speed I displayed getting to that damned exit.

Unfortunately, it didn't do me much good because, when I got to the exit, I found that it was absolutely jammed with people, so much so, that my progress was instantly checked, giving Deiphobus a chance to catch up with me. I watched him approach from over my shoulder and cursed myself for not leaving earlier when I had the chance. Gulping down my fear, I pushed my way through the crowd, pleading with folks to get out of my way, telling them a deranged madman was behind me and generally informing everyone within earshot that I was way too pretty to die.

About half way through the exit, Deiphobus was right behind me, not more than five cubits away, laughing crazily, sword in hand, calling out my name. I was much too busy pushing my way through the crowd to answer him; my heart was pounding like a drum and my damned stomach was aching again. Suddenly, the end of the exit appeared and I could see that the streets beyond it were filled with people. No use running into them, I thought, but to where? I quickly glanced to my right and saw a religious temple about fifty cubits away. Then I remember how Oenone had told me once that they were places of sanctuary, where a person could find refuge and protection in, no matter what their crime was.

Never before or since have I wanted to visit a religious temple so goddamned bad as I did at that particular moment!

"Sanctuary!" I screamed, as I came bounding out of the exit.

"Sanctuary!" I screamed again, running towards the temple door.

"Sanctuary! Sanctuary!" I screamed, as I pulled the door open and ran inside the temple.

Everything was quiet and still inside; the wall lamps flickered dimly on a great room in which a gigantic statue of Zeus stood in the center. There were no priests or priestesses present to run to for protection so I slammed the door shut and ran over to Zeus' statue instead. Believe me, when my life is in danger I can be one religious bastard and so, I hugged Zeus' big toe and started praying to him for help:

Great Zeus, I know we haven't talk much but I've been kinda busy enjoying the world you created, especially the female half of it — good job, by the way — and ahhh...please forgive me of my sins and the many others I'm bound to commit if I survive this mess...speaking of which...please save me from Deiphobus and please don't let me get castrated or harmed in the process and better yet, maybe you should just go ahead and kill Deiphobus because he's really a bad person and he won't be missed by anybody...and ahhh...maybe you should zap him with one of those lightning bolts of yours...you know...make a big show of it...that would show everyone how great you are...and ahhh...if you save me, I promise to sacrifice forty cattle to you...well, maybe twenty, cause it's the breeding season and all...make that ten cause I've still building my cattle business...you understand...and ahhh....

God, how I pleaded, and, of course, I got nothing back but silence — that's prayer for you! Then the door of the temple suddenly swung open and Deiphobus appeared in the doorway.

"Anybody home?" he sarcastically shouted.

I immediately shrieked in fear, let go of Zeus' toe and ran behind his heel. I figured since Zeus was being such a stuck-up prick, his statue might still protect me if I managed to keep it between Deiphobus and me. I know that sounds a bit silly but it's the only hope I had at the time.

Deiphobus walked slowly towards me, swinging the sword back and forth. He was grinning fiendishly and there were still tiny bits of dried cake on his face and in his hair. When he got to the statue, he stopped, pointed the sword at me and said, "Bad manners to run away without giving me a chance to crown you." Then he lunged at me but I quickly darted to the opposite side of the statue.

'Sanctuary!" I shouted.

"Never heard of it!" he shouted back.

Around and around the statue we ran, huffing and puffing, our footsteps echoing around the room as we did. For how long it went on, I don't know, but eventually we had to stop in order to catch our breath. It was then that I heard something move in the archway behind me. Turning, I saw a priestess standing in the shadows. She was cloaked in a heavy robe from head to toe and the lower half of her face was hidden behind a flimsy golden veil. At first, I couldn't believe that she was there, then her eyes blinked and I realized that she was real and that there was finally someone in the temple who I could turn to for protection.

Only, I realized it a little too late.

Before I could run over to her, Deiphobus slammed into me, knocking me to the floor. Leaping on top of me, he laughed savagely and placed the tip of the sword under my chin.

"Now I got you," he said. "Ready to die?"

It was a stupid question, to be sure, and one that I flatly refused to answer or even consider. Turning my eyes forlornly to the priestess, I pleaded, "Sanctuary, for god sakes, sanctuary!"

Then a whole bunch of things happened all at once.

The door of the temple burst open and in walked the rest of the royal family. I'm talking King Priam, his wife, Queen Hecuba, their great warrior son Hector, their nympho daughter Polyxena, and the runner, Polites.

And the priestess lowered her veil and walked towards Deiphobus and me as if in a trance.

And Deiphobus began slowly pushing the blade of his sword into my throat.

And I started crying and pleading for my life.

And the priestess started mumbling something crazy about a long lost brother.

And, strangely enough, it was the last thing that caught everybody's attention. Can you believe that shit? I was the one about to be murdered and what was everyone concerned about? The crazy bitch saying things that didn't make any sense!

Deiphobus suddenly appeared startled and looked up at the priestess. The others quickly walked over to her.

"Are you sure, Cassandra?" Polyxena asked the priestess.

"Yes, I'm sure," the she answered firmly. "He is the one who was cast out long ago. He is our lost brother."

Polyxena glanced down at me with a very disappointed look on her face.

Then Cassandra turned to the King and Queen, pointed at me and said, "Mother, father, that man is your son."

For a second, everyone appeared to be dumbfounded. I, of course, didn't have a clue what she was talking about but it didn't matter much, because, whatever it was, it was good enough to stop Deiphobus from killing me and because of that, I quickly figured it would be in my best interest to play along.

Looking up at the King and Queen, I flashed them my best puppy dog eyes and shouted, "Momma, papa!"

Chapter Three

My father is gone.

The room is quiet now.

Thank god!

I wonder if he left while I was asleep. Then I wonder if I was really asleep or just daydreaming. Right now, I can't tell the difference between the two.

The room smells of medicine, ointment, piss and blood. They'll probably have to fumigate the place after I am gone. I open my eyes slightly and notice that the sun is shining through the little window. It's still only morning and I wish it was night. Tonight, I'll wish it was morning because Oenone should be here by then and I'll be saved.

I turn my head and am surprised to see that my mother, Queen Hecuba, is sitting in the chair next to my bed.

She is sitting there wearing the same long, loose, flimsy gown that she has worn everyday for the past month. It is so disheveled, that its low neck line now hangs half way down her right arm. She looks pathetic. Her once beautiful hair is now a mass of tangles and her eyes appear dim and far away. She's been this way ever since Hector's death.

And, oh yeah, one more thing — she's a dog.

I'm not kidding.

She really thinks she's a dog!

What kind of dog, I'm not really sure, but from her deep bark, she sounds like one of those big sheep dogs.

Hector's death really screwed her up.

I can't help but feel sorry for her even though she abandoned me to my death when I was an infant. I also can't help but wonder how she can be so distressed by Hector's death and not mine. Did she go crazy the day Agelaus came and took me away? Nope. Far from it. The way I heard it is that she was proclaimed a hero for putting Troy's interests ahead of hers and a feast was given in her honor. I wonder if she thought about me while she enjoyed her appetizer. Did the image of me lying there all alone on that barren mountainside cross her mind during the main course? If it did, she never told me so. Little wonder then that we were never very close after I came back home. Still, I hate to see her in this terrible condition and since I am leaving soon and we'll probably never see each other again, I tell her it's okay, that I forgive her.

She just sits there, looking at me with those faded brown eyes. What kind of reality she has going on behind them, I dunno.

"Ruff, ruff, ruff!" she barks.

Should I pet or hug her?

"Ruff, ruff, ruff!" she goes again.

Fuck it. I decide it might be best if she leaves now. Her barking is a little more than I can take right now. I fumble for the ball I keep under my pillow for this sort of an occasion and throw it through the door. Instantly, my mother jumps out of the chair and chases the bouncing ball down the hallway. I say goodbye to her and wish her luck as she does.

I'm glad I forgave her. I guess I owed it to her since she saved me from Deiphobus' clutches that day in the temple when that crazy son-of-a-bitch wanted to kill me for soiling his reputation and, well, you know, for barfing all over his ass.

I mean, there I was, in that fucking temple, pinned underneath Deiphobus, with the tip of his sword biting into my neck, calling out to good ole' momma and papa for help, when my nut job sister

Cassandra suddenly looks at Deiphobus and says, "Go ahead and kill him because if he is allowed to live then Troy is doomed. Kill him! Kill the destroyer of Priam's city!"

Cassandra shouldn't have bothered because Deiphobus was already playing fast and loose with his sanity and didn't need encouragement from anyone. He smiled broadly, as if something truly delightful was about to happen, and slowly resumed pushing the blade into my throat. My eyes went wide in terror. God, what pain! It felt like a hot razor was being shoved straight down my neck.

"Stop! Stop! Momma! Papa! Sanctuary!" I shrieked.

Desperately, I tried to kick myself free, but Deiphobus held me firmly to the floor, until, finally, I felt the blade bite into my windpipe and I realized I was nearly done for. Taking a deep gulp of air, thinking it was my last, I quit struggling and waited for the inevitable.

And that's precisely when my momma, the sheep dog, saved my life. Only she wasn't a dog at the time. That was later. At that moment, she was a normal and beautiful woman. Thank Zeus for that.

"Stop!" she shouted. "Better that Troy should fall than that I should lose a son!"

Go figure that one out! I mean, first, she abandons me to protect Troy and then, she saves my ass in spite of Troy. Who can figure the mind of a woman? Certainly not me. I guess that's why I've always been more interested in their bodies.

Anyway, Deiphobus suddenly stopped, frowned, and looked over to our father for further guidance. It was, after all, Priam's decision to make.

I exhaled and wondered what was coming next. Everybody's eyes, including mine, quickly focused on my father's face.

At first, he looked resolved, and I thought I was a goner. Then he glanced over at my mother and seemed to melt.

"Stop," my father said, grudgingly. "Do as your mother says."

Oh, thank you, thank you, thank you, thinks I.

"But father, the prophecy..." Cassandra quickly protested.

Ignoring her, my father shouted, "Goddamnit! I said stop!"

The forcefulness of it startled Deiphobus, so much so, that he immediately tossed the sword to the floor.

"Now get off of him!" my father commanded.

For a moment, Deiphobus glared down at me, as if to say: "Next time I'll kill you quicker!" and then he stood up straight, shook his head in disgust, and stomped towards the door in a heated passion. My father immediately followed him, shouting to the top of his lungs, "Bring me the Royal Baby Killer!" Of course, I didn't know what he meant by that, nor did I care, mainly because I was far too busy thanking my lucky stars.

After my father was gone, Cassandra turned to the others and said, "On this day, Troy's fate has been sealed. Horrors shall be released that are too shameful for my tongue to announce! Poor Troy! If the city only knew what misery was in store of it! O, miserable Troy, you will lose ten thousand dead."

And I'm like; will this bitch ever shut the fuck up?

Luckily, the rest of my family felt the same way as I did. They impatiently nodded at Cassandra as she spoke, you know, kinda like the way folks do to a long-winded preacher when they all have something else better to do, and then, when she was finished with her little sermon, my brothers quietly helped me to my feet.

Cassandra let out a loud, exasperated sigh as they did and mumbled something depressing to my mother and Polyxena about dancing fires and the sounds of armed men. To my relief, they ignored her ranting as well and came to my aid. Polyxena, still looking disappointed, wrapped a pink scarf around my neck to stop the bleeding and my mother planted a kiss on my cheek. Then my brothers carried me out of the temple and placed me in a nearby carriage. I have no clear recollection of the trip to the palace but my neck was still leaking like a sieve when the carriage got there and so, there was a general uproar, and I was hastily carried into a room where I was quickly surrounded by a team of doctors. They removed the scarf from my neck and since I was too weak to speak, all I could do was lie there, bleed and roll my eyes at the doctors in panic.

"Lucky, bastard," I heard one of them say. "Another centimeter and the jugular would have been cut."

"Yeah, lucky bastard," another one said. "Okay, let's stop the bleeding and get him patched up."

Of course, I was all for that. Then I saw a long needle-like object flash by my face, felt a shape piercing pain in my neck and, for the second time that day, I passed out cold.

Sweet, peaceful oblivion!

Believe me, hibernating bears don't sleep as deep as I did then.

I woke up two days later, lying in a warm bed of soft blankets and fluffy pillows. I opened my eyes and looked around until I realized that I was safe and in one piece, then I closed them again and lay there, thoroughly enjoying the fact that I was still alive.

When I opened my eyes again, I looked beyond the bed and saw that I was in a lavishly decorated room, with purple curtains over the windows, silver plated furniture scattered about and rich tapestries on the walls. As I turned my head gawking at everything, I felt a sharp pain in my neck and discovered it was heavily bandaged. It was still throbbing when I settled back down but the pain wasn't enough to ruin my good mood. I had won Cronus back and escaped Deiphobus' murderous clutches. Beyond that, I remembered something about being identified as a long lost son of the monarchy, which, of course, seemed completely ridiculous and so, I didn't believe a single word of it, chalking it up instead as a silly mistake that would, sooner or later, be rectified. Until then, I figured I'd lie there, recover my health and enjoy my pleasant surroundings for as long as I could.

I snuggled against my pillow, and my neck hurt, causing me to cuss Deiphobus loudly, at which a servant of some sort stuck his head in my room, looked at me for a second, and then announced to someone down the hallway that I was awake. After that, there was a great deal of commotion and in comes a small army of servants carrying food, clothes and drink.

"I'm glad you're awake, Your Highness," says an old man with a baldhead. He was apparently the leader of the group. "We've been waiting all morning to serve you. Please don't move much, sir; we'll attend to your needs. Just tell us what you desire."

Now, I don't know if you've ever been treated like royalty, but if you haven't, well, let me tell you, it's a whole lot of fun. I mean, basically, you're fawned over and attended to by people who actually act like it's a big honor to wipe your ass. Not that any of them did, well, actually wipe my ass, but I'm sure they would have if I had asked. I mean, heck, they did just about everything else. They fed me, washed me, and dressed me. I even had a hairdresser and a manicurist come in to fix me up. Anyway, like I just said, it's a ton of fun to be fussed over and, you know, my conscience didn't bother me one bit either. Why should it? I didn't tell anyone I was a prince. That wacko priestess did. And the rest of the royal family believed her. Was it my fault they were so damned dumb? Fuck no, it wasn't. And besides, Prince Deiphobus tried to kill me. I figured that alone justified having a good time at the Royal's expense.

And so I did.

For two more days anyway.

Until Agelaus suddenly showed up.

He came walking into my room just as the stylist was putting the last curler in my hair.

I looked up at him, smiled and yelled, "Boss!"

"Hello, boy," he answered quickly, almost in an embarrassed whisper.

From the look on his face, I could tell that he was nervous about something.

Assuming it was because of the situation, I immediately dismissed the stylist so that I could explain things to him privately.

"Don't worry," I said, grinning up at him. "It's okay. You're not gonna believe this, but everyone around here thinks I'm a prince. Ain't that a hoot and a half?"

Then I laughed.

Only Agelaus didn't laugh with me.

He just stood there looking like someone had just punched him in the gut.

So I quit laughing.

And that's when my cowardly instincts began to kick in. Sensing that something was terribly amiss, I stood up and asked him what was wrong.

He stared at me for a second, rubbed his brow nervously and stammered, "Well, kid, the truth is, ah, you are, ah, well, you are really a prince."

Imagine my surprise, multiply it by a kahbillion, add another kahbillion, and you won't even be close.

I'm sure I went pale with shock, which must have contrasted vividly with the bright red robe I was wearing. If I had known I was going to be so surprised, I probably would have worn a lighter color. Like beige or an eggshell blue or a …well…you get the picture.

"Wha, wha, wha, what?" I stammered back.

"It's the truth," he said. "You see, when you were born, there was this here prophesy that said you would bring doom to Troy, and so I was commanded by King Priam, your real father, to take you to Mount Ida and abandon you there. And so I did."

I almost couldn't believe my ears. It was like listening to a bizarre folk tale.

"Only when I came back the next morning," he continued, "you were still alive, so I took pity on you, and carried you home so you could work the farm with me."

"So you're the Royal Baby Killer!" I shouted, finally realizing why he had suddenly showed up.

"Yes," he answered glumly, "it's my part-time job."

Pissed, I turned away from him abruptly, causing a curler to abruptly fly out of my hair, and said, "Why didn't you tell me about this before?"

"I don't know," he said with a slight sigh. "It just never came up. I mean, you never asked. Didn't you ever wonder who your parents were?"

I must admit I never really did. I just assumed they had something better to do than to mess around with me.

"No," I answered, feeling a bit sorry for myself.

"Well, no use worrying about that now," Agelaus said. "We've got bigger fish to fry."

"What do you mean?" I asked, turning back around.

"Well, for starters, we've got to figure out a way to save our lives," he answered.

I certainly didn't like the sound of that.

"Why would they want to kill us?" says I. "We haven't done anything."

He stared at me coldly for a second. "Dunderhead!" he shouted. "Do you think they are going to ignore the prophecy and let you live? These people are a religious lot. And do you think King Priam is going to forgive me for failing to carry out one of his commands?"

Yes, hopes I.

"Fat chance!" he shouted. "No doubt, the executioner is busy sharpening his axe right now."

So there I was once again: the finger of doom pointing squarely at my ass. I could only imagine how much time I had left to live. Minutes, I figured. I was in a tight spot for sure and there seemed to be no way out this time. After all, I was sitting smack dap in the middle of a palace guarded by a whole shitload of soldiers. No way could I walk out of the place without causing alarm. My only hope seemed to be my mother. She had saved me once and I wondered if she would or could do it again.

While I was busy pondering this, Agelaus started pacing around the room in deep thought. He always did that when he had something difficult to figure out and since our lives were on the line, I'm sure it was the hardest brainwork he ever did.

I quickly began to take the curlers out of my hair. I needed to look good for my dear, sweet, loving mother.

Just as I was pulling the last one out, Agelaus abruptly stopped, swung on his heel, smiled at me broadly and said, "I've got it!"

Before he could tell me what it was he got, a soldier suddenly appeared in the doorway and said, "The king will see you now. Come with me."

You can guess how eager I was to follow the soldier. And I probably wouldn't have either if Agelaus hadn't grabbed me by the arm and pushed me towards the door. I walked along behind the man, listening to the sound of our footsteps, and looking around at the soldiers standing guard along the way. My heart was pounding like a kettledrum. The palace seemed full of people, many of whom stopped and stared at me silently as I walked by. Sweat ran off of me like rain and I wondered why I was in such a tight fix. And then I wondered how I was going to get out of it. And when I realized I couldn't, I cursed the day I had left Oenone to come to Troy.

Agelaus appeared calm though and that gave me a ray of hope. When you're a coward like me, you latch on to anything for strength and so, as we entered the throne room, I walked as closely to him as I possibly could.

The throne room itself was a grand affair. It was a fine, spacious room, adorned with colonnades of hewn stone. A bright red carpet ran down the center of the room's polished marble floor. Huge statues of various gods and heroes stood on either side of the carpet. Overhead, a large balcony was decorated with hundreds of colorful flags. Everything was lit up by dozens of large candelabra. My father's throne sat at the far end of the room. Resting above three tiers of marble steps, it was a large, richly crafted chair of silver and gold. Next to it, on either side, were the smaller thrones of my mother and my older brother Hector, the crown prince.

As I said before, the place was packed with people. The edge of the red carpet was lined with soldiers; all standing at attention, behind them stood a multitude of nobles and court officials, while, overhead, the railings of the balcony were jammed with common citizens. My mother, father and brother sat on their thrones looking very aloof and regal. Standing around them and on the steps below, were members of my immediate family. All together, I had five full brothers and sisters and about forty other half brothers and sisters. I was never quite sure of the latter's exact number, nor do I think anyone else, including my father, was either. Let me tell you, dear old dad was one horny bastard, that's for sure. Anyway, they were all there, leering down at me like an uninvited guest.

The spectators watched in silence as Agelaus and I walked towards the throne. When we reached the steps, we stopped and bowed deeply. While I was bent over, I saw my reflection in the glassy floor and thought, well, here you are in the soup again, Alexander old boy, try not to faint, and then a pair of purple slippers appeared, and the golden hem of a robe.

"Arise," a voice commanded from overhead and when I did, I found myself confronted by a bearded wretch wearing a long, pointed purple hat that perfectly matched his purple slippers.

It was Aesacus.

Remember him? He's that holier-than-thou asshole who interpreted my mother's dream and started all my trouble.

And from the look on his face, I could tell that he was annoyed by my presence, no doubt, because he was the one who had engineered my death to start out with. Believe me, soothsayers don't like it when their advice is ignored. It threatens their livelihood. I mean, what if everyone suddenly went around thinking rationally about things? Aesacus would be fucked, wouldn't he? Little wonder then that the bastard wasn't overjoyed to see me.

Turning quickly to Agelaus, he asked, "Are you the Royal Baby Killer?"

"Yes," Agelaus answered.

"And is this young man the baby you were commanded by our king to kill?" he asked.

"Yes," Agelaus answered.

A loud murmur shot through the crowd.

Aesacus raised his hand for silence. "And is this the young man whose birth threatens the future of Troy?"

"Says you," Agelaus answered.

With that, a tremendous commotion broke out within the crowd; there was jostling, fist shaking, tons of shitty looks and loud calls for our death. The soldiers — bless them all — braced themselves against the angry mob and held it back.

I almost pissed myself, I was so damned scared.

Looking over at Agelaus, I impatiently whispered, "This is your big plan? To get us killed? For god sakes, come up with a better one before they tear us to pieces!"

He stared at me in silence and, for a minute, I wondered if he had gone mad. God knows, I was ready to. But before I could lose it completely, Aesacus once again held his hand up for silence and when the room had settled, he said, "Can you tell the court why you failed to carry out our king's commandment and therefore put the welfare of Troy in jeopardy?"

"Yes, I can," Agelaus answered firmly.

"Then you may address the court," Aesacus said, stepping to the side.

Agelaus took a step forward, and slowly looked at my family, maybe for a full minute, and then he glanced at the crowd around it. They watched him still and silent, no doubt, wondering what he was about to say.

Turning back to the king, he said, "Your Majesty, I did as you commanded. I took the infant to Mount Ida and abandoned it there. However, when I returned five days later, I found a mother bear suckling the infant. Believing it was the will of the gods that the baby should survive, I gathered him into my arms and took him home, naming him Paris and rearing him as my own beloved son."

I swear, it got so quiet, you could have heard an ant fart.

All I could do is look over at Agelaus and marvel. So that's your plan, thinks I, using their silly superstitions against them. I swear, the simple bastard could be one clever son-of-a-bitch when he wanted to be.

Priam appeared astonished.

Mother looked pleased.

My father glanced over at my mother, who nodded approvingly, and then turned back to Agelaus.

"A bear?" my father asked.

"Yes, Your Majesty, a bear," Agelaus answered.

"For five days?" my father queried.

"Yes, my lord, for five days," Agelaus answered.

My father looked over at Aesacus sharply and said, "What say you?"

Aesacus fidgeted about uncomfortably for a second or two and said, "Well, ah, well, I don't know, Your Majesty, I, ah, I guess I should consult the stars or, ah, offer a sacrifice to the gods or...."

"Oh, fuck that shit!" my father impatiently interrupted. "It's clear what they will say. Just look at what a fine young man he is. And the fact that a bear kept him alive proves that your prophecy was wrong. How could such a fine young man like him possibly be a threat to Troy?"

Yeah, motherfucker, I thought, answer that.

Of course, he couldn't. I mean, not without looking at goat's liver or something silly like that first.

My father knew that too and so, losing patience with Aesacus, he stood up, looked at the assembly and said, "What says Troy?"

And, do you know, in one voice, the crowd shouted that I should be allowed to live! Can you believe that shit?

And, do you know, my father proclaimed me prince and second in line to the throne right then and there! Amazing, isn't it?

And, do you know, everyone got so worked up that the dimwits rushed out afterwards and built me a house inside the Citadel to live in!

Goes to show you: The bigger the lie, the more likely people are to believe it.

Go figure.

Chapter Four

"Go figure what, honey?" Helen asks.

She is sitting at the edge of my bed looking as radiant as ever. How long she's been there, I don't know.

"Oh, nothing, darling," I answer. "I must have been talking in my sleep."

We still call each other honey and darling and a bunch of other sweet things like that. It's all part of the act. We don't really love each other and probably never did but since folks have been outside killing themselves for us, we like to keep up appearances for their sake.

Her long hair is golden and curly and I long to reach over and touch it. Her body is perfect, her breasts are large and firm and although Helen's been nothing but trouble, I still long to fuck her. As a matter of fact, I'd screw her right now if I didn't have this goddamned arrow sticking out of my dick. I still want her. I can't help myself. That's the problem with being a sex addict. It's hard to say no, especially when they shove it in your face. And, it doesn't matter how dangerous it is either. It's almost like you got no choice. You have to do it.

Anyway.

She sits on the chair casually, with her long shapely legs stretching outwards in opposite directions while she winds a strand of yellow hair around her finger over and over again. She always plays with her hair when she is nervous about something.

"What's wrong, baby?" I ask.

She stops twirling the strand of hair around her finger, releases it, improves her posture a tad and says, "I was just thinking about my future, that's all."

See there? She's as self-centered as ever. I mean, I'm the one who's dying and she's worried about her future! You see the kind of shit I have had to put up with all these years? Believe me, Helen is one selfish bitch. I've never known her to think about anyone else but herself. Don't believe me? Well, get this: she deserted her nine-year-old daughter Hermione just so she could be with me in Troy. She dang sure did. And, friend, if that ain't selfish then I don't know what is.

"Oh, Alexander, Alexander, Alexander," she moans loudly. "What am I going to do? Whatever will become of me?"

I stare at her in astonishment and wonder if she even knows that I'm in a considerable amount of pain.

"Do you know that your father intends to marry me to Deiphobus when you die?" she asks.

I almost feel sorry for Deiphobus.

Suddenly, her eyes narrow menacingly and she says, "Well, if your father forces me to marry him, I'll kill Deiphobus with his own sword!"

I know she doesn't really mean it. Helen doesn't have it in her to kill anybody. Well, not directly, face to face, in cold blood, anyway. Oh, she might hide Deiphobus' sword so he can't defend himself in an emergency but as far as doing the deed herself, she just doesn't have the guts for it.

Helen knows this too and calms down.

"Oh, Alexander," she sighs again. "All I want to do is go back home to Sparta. I miss my child and the rest of my family. I miss the decorated halls of my palace and I miss talking to women of my own age."

Well, boo-fucking-hoo! So what? I miss being able to take a leak or walk or sit up straight or fuck. So, excuse me if I don't cry you a goddamned river right now.

She turns and stares at the window longingly. "But most of all I miss Menelaus," she says. "He was a good husband and he loved me so."

Oh, god, now I'm really going to cry! Or scream! Menelaus a good husband! Ha! Good god almighty, but the bitch is laying it on thick now! I can't believe she just said that! I guess she's forgotten that Menelaus and I were best friends once. It's true, we were, and let me tell you something else; Menelaus was a fucking pig of a husband! Believe me, I know, because I personally saw the way he treated her. Love her? Yeah, sure he did, but only as a trophy. You see, the truth is, that's all Helen ever was to him — just a prize to be shown off. Do you know he actually made her strip naked and stand up on a table during a royal banquet once just so his buddies could admire his prize? Yep, he did. And that's not all. Why, he even made wax casts of her breasts so that he could make drinking cups from them! And what's worse, he had the balls to pass them out to his friends! I swear, there isn't a king in Greece that doesn't have his very own boob-shaped goblet to drink his wine out of. Now, if that's something a loving husband does, then someone drag in a table and heat me up some wax! See what I mean about Menelaus? Take my word of it; the fucker was as bad as me. The only thing he really loved was drinking booze and screwing other women. In those two areas, he was absolutely the best. Bar none. Little wonder then that we became fast friends.

We met shortly after I became a prince.

And let me tell you something about being a prince. It's simply wonderful. As I've mentioned before, you get treated like you're some kind of god. And, although that sounds pretty cool — which it is — that's also when the trouble begins. At least it was for me. You see, after awhile, I actually began to feel like I was god. I felt different than the rest of mankind. I felt above them. I felt better than them. I felt as if there was nothing I couldn't do and, because of that, my behavior knew no limits. And that's eventually what got me into trouble. It all started the day I refused to go home.

"Are you sure you don't want to go back to Mount Ida with me?" Agelaus asked.

We were standing in front of the house Troy's citizens were building for me. Located inside the citadel between the homes of my brother Hector and my father, it was a fine two-story affair with a high vaulted bedroom that promised to be the perfect place to entertain chicks in.

"Nah," I answered, shaking my head slightly. "I'd better stay here a while. I don't think it would look very good if I leave right now. I mean, they're building me a house and all. It just wouldn't be polite."

He looked at me steadily. "You know, if you stay here, you'll just get yourself into trouble."

Agelaus was right, of course. He knew me better than I knew myself.

"I'll be okay. You go on and take Cronus home," I said. "I'll be home directly, after all the hubbub dies down. Tell Oenone that I'll be home in a couple of weeks."

He scratched his ear and studied me closely for a moment. Then he smiled skeptically and said goodbye. I gave him a polite nod, patted him on the shoulder, and watched him walk away in silence.

Okay, I know, I should have left with Agelaus right then and there, and went back home to Oenone. Believe me, I wish I would have because, if I had, then a whole bunch of folks would be alive today and I wouldn't have this fucking arrow sticking out of my dick. But I didn't, mainly because I liked being a prince, and after my house was built, well, honestly, I forgot all about going back to Oenone altogether because, you see, that's when the parties began. Or, maybe I should say, that's when the party began, because that's exactly what it felt like — one great big wild party. It started the day my house was completed and ended the day my father sent me packing to Greece. I spent the months in between getting drunk and screwing my brains out. It was a sex addict's dream come true, for sure. That's because chicks absolutely adore princes. I'm not kidding. They go crazy over them and you don't even have to get them drunk to get their knickers off. Try pulling that one off on your first date. I promise you, if you're not a prince, it can't be done. So anyway, it wasn't long before my house was full of babes looking to score with the new prince. Of course, none of them knew I was married and I didn't see any reason to tell them. I mean, I didn't want to break their hearts. Besides, I don't think it would have made any difference, because, like I said, they go bonkers around a prince and lose complete control.

That's how I got them to compete in the Miss Nude Troy Beauty Pageant. Sure did. I held the event in my backyard and it was attended by fifty women competitors and a whole host of drunken spectators. Some chick named Wilma won mainly because she had a huge set of knockers and answered the judge's question by stating that her favorite sexual position was "any position a man wants to do me in." I mean, who can resist a woman with such charms?

Then there was Let's Get Drunk and Get Naked Day, followed by a little something I called "Grease Nude Female Wrestling Night." Both were a lot of fun and, in my opinion, it fostered goodwill, sisterhood, togetherness and a whole bunch of sexual fantasies that are still with me today.

Unfortunately, my two neighbors didn't share my opinion.

It wasn't long before my brother Hector started complaining. He was always in his backyard lifting weights, doing pushups or sticking something with his spear which, by the way, is kind of a shame, because he had a real hot wife named Andromache. He should have been inside sticking it to her instead, if you know what I mean.

"Paris, appalling Paris!" he'd yelled over at me from his backyard. "Our prince of beauty - mad for women, you lure them all to ruin! Leave those poor women alone!"

"What's that?" I'd yell back, pretending I couldn't hear him above the din of the party. "You have a little dick?"

"No, I said leave those women alone!" the idiot would scream back.

"Huh?" I'd respond again, putting a hand to my ear. "You like to get fucked in the ass by a herd of donkeys?"

"No! No! Listen to me!" He'd shout back and then slowly yell, "I... said...leave...those...girls...alone!"

Once again, I'd shake my head as if I couldn't hear him and shout, "You fuck like a seven-year-old?"

By then, my guests were positively rolling on the ground with laughter, even the guards on the walls overhead were dying. Hector, the twit, never once got the joke but my father did and he would always step in to save his favorite son.

"Paris, you idler, who wallows in the fat of the land!" my father would chime in from his backyard.

He was always back there too, barbequing. And the funny thing is, he had the balls to yell that at me while barbequing the fat, juicy parts of a cow. The fucking hypocrite!

"Listen to Hector!" dad would continue to whine. "He's the best of all my sons! Just ask your mother!"

And the dumbest, I'd think, just ask anybody.

Anyway, eventually, I got so sick of their constant bitching that I moved my party indoors and, do you know, that's when things really got out of hand because that's when I came up with the bright idea of turning my house into a tavern. But not just any old run-of-the-mill tavern, mind you! No, sir! Mine was totally unique. You see, mine featured live music and, best of all, nude dancing girls! I came up with the idea one night while watching a couple of naked chicks dance on top of my dining room table. I guess you could call it an epiphany of sorts. And since my tavern was the first one in history to provide this exquisite form of male entertainment, you can safely credit me with inventing the business.

I named my place "Paris' Dollhouse" for obvious reasons but because it was located next to the royal palace, folks quickly nicknamed it "Paris' Pussy Palace". I don't have to tell you how well that went over with my father and brother. Anyway, I staffed it with local chicks that worked in four-hour shifts. Of course, I did all the interviewing and hiring, which, let me tell you, was the best part of the gig. The girls would come in, and I'd ask them their name, then I'd ask them to show me their groceries and then, if I liked them, I audition them by having them dance around a bit, and then, if I really liked them, I audition them a little further by having them perform a lap dance on my face. Brrrrrrrrrrrr! Best-damned job I ever had!

In business, they say location is everything and since my tavern was located inside the citadel, its clientele was the rich and powerful, you know, folks with very deep pockets, and so, it wasn't long before I was rolling in the dough. God, what a haul I made! I charged one golden coin just to step foot through the door and two silver ones for a single goblet of wine. The dancers worked for tips and they made so much money that I didn't have to pay them one red cent to perform. I swear, every night, my girls went home with their purses crammed full of gold rings, necklaces, jewels, and coins. I even saw a few of them leave with expensive ceremonial swords stuffed into their belts! Believe me, it was the best of times for all concerned. And fun too. So much fun, that my sister Polyxena actually became a dancer. And, let me tell you, Sis took to stripping like a duck does to water.

"Now, don't be nervous when you go out there," I said to her backstage just before her first performance. "The place is packed with horny, drunk guys just waiting to see you dance."

"Good!" she eagerly answered. "Can I start getting naked now?"

"No, no, no," I quickly answered, "wait until you are onstage."

The only overhead I had was the cost of wine, which, by the way, I watered down to make a profit, and the salary of the service staff, you know, waitresses, bartenders, musicians and bouncers. Of them, the bouncers were probably the most important since the house rule was "look but don't touch" — excluding lap dances, of course — and the only way I could keep the customers from pawing my girls for free was to hire some burly guys to stand around and encourage them not to do it. At first, I hired a bunch of local thugs from the surrounding town but that didn't work out too well because they proved harder to control than the customers.

Surprisingly enough, the problem was solved one day when good 'ole Sergeant Pandarus suddenly walked through the front door. Did

I say Sergeant Pandarus? Sorry. I should have said, Captain Pandarus, Commander of the Royal Guard, instead. You see, the bastard managed to buy himself an officer's commission and a title with the money he had won on me. Hilarious ain't it? Anyway, when he came in, he sniffed around the place for a minute or two, smelled a profit and immediately wanted in on the action.

"I'm sorry," I said, "but I don't need a business partner or an investor. I'm doing pretty well on my own."

"Surely, there is something I can help you with," he quickly asked in an insistent manner that left me with distinct impression that he wasn't about to take no for an answer.

"Well," I said grudgingly, "I am having a problem with bouncers. They cost too much and I'm having a hard time controlling them."

He pondered this quietly for a moment until a foxy grin slowly crossed his face. "Well, well…" he said, "seems like I can help you out after all. Since I am Commander of the Royal Guard, and seeing how your place is inside the citadel, well, then, technically, I guess I am responsible for its security. I see no reason why I shouldn't assign soldiers to maintain order in the place."

I couldn't help but laugh, his reasoning was so clever.

He chuckled along with me for a second, and then he got serious again and said, "For five percent of each night's profits, of course."

How could I refuse such an offer? I mean, not only was I sorta getting free labor, I was also getting someone to manage it for me. And for what? Five percent of the profits? Chickenfeed really.

"Of course," I agreed, smiling keenly as we shook hands to seal the deal.

After that, guarding my tavern became the soldier's favorite assignment. It sure beat the shit out of standing guard on a cold, lonely wall all night long. Not only did they get to ogle the dancers during their watch, they also got to manhandle a blueblood every now and then. I'm not completely sure which one they liked doing the most because both put a big fat smile on their faces. Anyway, it doesn't matter, my problem was solved.

Unfortunately, another one immediately popped up in its place.

I blame myself for this one. In addition to asking the girls their names during the interview, I should have also asked them a little something about their prior employment. If I had, I would have discovered that a large number of them were prostitutes in Troy's Temple of Aphrodite. Now, I know this doesn't really sound like much of problem, especially for a nasty little devil like me, and, believe me, it wasn't, but, for the men of Troy, it dang sure was. You see, because the prostitutes were all busy working for me, the Temple quickly became a pretty lonely place for the men of the city to worship in. And that wasn't good. Especially, for the horny married guys. So it wasn't long before a bunch of them banded together and marched up to my place in protest.

I was busy auditioning a beautiful brunette when they arrived. A security soldier knocked on my bedroom door and said that there was a group of men standing outside the tavern, yelling something about religious rights and a bunch of other stuff that didn't make a whole lot of sense. At first, I couldn't respond, mainly because the brunette had my face in a leg lock, but when the audition was over with, I quickly got dressed and went outside to see what the hubbub was all about.

"Excuse me," I said all friendly like, "but I think you got the wrong house. My father's house is next door."

Nobody moved.

Then the leader of the group, an ugly fucker with a wedding band on his finger, stomped up to me and said, "Give us back our whores."

And I said, "I ain't got your whores."

And he said, "Yes, you do! And we intend to protest outside your tavern until you restore our religious freedoms."

That left me totally lost, of course. I never could make sense out of religious folks.

"Freedoms? Whores?" I asked confusingly. "What the heck are you talking about?"

"The freedom to worship the Goddess Aphrodite as we see fit," he said impatiently.

"And that's got what to do with me?" I asked, equally as impatient.

"Look," he said, "we know you have our whores inside shaking their titties and dancing all around the place in a very obscene manner, which, by the way, we find very offensive, and we want you to close your tavern so we can get back to the business of worshipping Aphrodite in the proper manner."

I'm not often stumped, but, for the life of me, I couldn't figure out what the guy was talking about and so, I did what any respectable tavern owner would do in that situation.

"Okay," I said calmly.

"Okay, what?" he asked

"Okay, then," I answered.

"Okay, then, what?" he asked impatiently.

"Okay, then," I said, "give me a second, while I step inside and talk to the whores. Stay right where you are."

"Okay," he said.

Now, I don't know what you would have done but I wasn't about to let a bunch of religious pricks spoil my fun. So I stepped inside and talked to the soldiers instead. I asked them to go outside and get rid of the protesters, something, I quickly discovered they were only too happy to do. Like I said before, the soldiers just loved my place and because they did, they were extremely protective of it.

"You want us to ventilate a couple of the bastards?" the sergeant of the guard asked.

"Ventilate?" I asked. I never did understand army lingo either.

"Yeah, ventilate, you know, stick a couple of them with our swords," he answered. "I promise it'll make the others run away pretty fast."

His fellow soldiers made loud grunts of agreement.

"No, no, don't do that," I said. "Just slap 'em upside the head a bit, maybe that'll restore their sanity."

"Can we make them eat dirt and bark like a dog?" another soldier eagerly asked.

"Yeah, that'll be fine too," I said.

About an hour later, a bunch of bruised and humiliated religious protesters limped their way up into the mayor's office — an old fool named Antimachus — demanding that he close my tavern at once and send the prostitutes working there back to the Temple where they belonged. And, you know, he would have too, that is, if I hadn't bribed the shit out of him first. I had to give the fucker all kinds of gifts and a whole piss bucket full of gold just to keep my doors open. Small wonder then that I've never had much respect for politicians since. They're the only bunch I've ever met with character flaws worse than my own. I mean, why don't they just come out and say, "We don't give a shit about the people we are supposed to serve. We've never given a shit about them. We're just here to make money." It's just so damned obvious, ain't it?

Anyway, so there I was, getting filthy rich running a titty tavern, wallowing in sex and booze every night, without much sign of trouble, except, of course, that Temple of Aphrodite crap and my family's constant bitching about my bad behavior, but neither one concerned me very much because I was nestled in too comfortably with my dancing whores to worry about anything. Of course, that was downright stupid of me, and I know this now, but back then I didn't have enough sense to recognize that I was living in a flimsy house of cards that could easily be toppled over by the slightest puff of wind.

And that's exactly when Menelaus blew into town.

He sailed into Troy's tiny harbor one sunny morning aboard a sleek, handsomely decorated war galley.

Now, you can say anything bad about those dirty Greeks you like and I'll agree, but let me tell you, the bastards really know how to build one damn fine boat. Their ships are all built for speed. They are light and lean. Their hulls are narrow, straight and low, to cut down on wind resistance and to ease beaching. They are also beautiful things to look at too. Their hulls are usually decorated with a set of eyes in the bows and images of lions, griffins or snakes. For some reason that I've never been able to figure out, a nasty looking bird's head is always carved in every ship's stem post.

Menelaus' rig was known as a penteconter; a fifty-oared speedster, with twenty-five rowers on each side. Troy's pathetic little navy of outdated tubs had nothing to match it. Little wonder then that Menelaus' sudden appearance provoked a wave of excitement amongst the city's population.

Soon, the harbor was filled with thousands of gawking Trojans, including me. Every one of us was craning our necks to get a look at the famous King of Sparta and his fancy ship. From all the excitement, you'd have thought that the great Zeus himself was dropping in for a visit. And you wouldn't have been far off the mark either because Menelaus and his brother were about as close to gods as any two humans could get.

"Menelaus and Agamemnon, my lords, twin throned, twin sceptered, in twofold power of kings from god."

Those are the words of a song that the bards went around singing. With publicity like that, no wonder the bastard was so popular.

As his ship sailed into the harbor, Menelaus posed on its bow, looking like a fearless adventurer. He stood with his hands on hips, his chest puffed out, one leg propped up on the railing, his distinctive long red hair flying in sea breeze behind his erect head. Bearded and well built, he was wearing a black woolen tunic and a belted kilt with fringed edges and tassels. I doubt there's been a more flamboyant man in this neck of the world since.

Standing just behind Menelaus, were the figures of three women. Yep, three! And such women! They were fine, strapping black haired beauties certainly worth a good long look. They were dressed in flowing sleeveless gowns of black, purple and crimson strips. Winding bands of gold bracelets covered their bare arms. Each wore a tight-fitting bodice that emphasized their full breasts. For a while, excited whispers went around the crowd that one of them was Helen, but then some guy who knew said that Helen had blond hair and so, the girls were probably Menelaus' concubines, Pieris, Tereis and Cnossia. That wasn't what the crowd wanted to hear, of course, since Helen was so famous and all, so they sneered at the man until he shut-up. He was right though. The girls were Menelaus' concubines. He never went anywhere without them. I don't blame him either. Given a choice, I'd rather go to bed with three concubines than with one Helen any night of the week. Anyway, the four of them stood on the bow of that ship like golden statues while the crowd roared with approval. I cheered too, mainly for Menelaus' taste in women, until someone abruptly grabbed me by the arm. It was Hector.

"Are you sober?" he asked with an air of impatience.

Looking at him indignantly, I said, "Why?"

"Because it's our job to welcome King Menelaus into our father's kingdom," he answered.

I'm not sure if I was sober or not, but if I wasn't, well then, I'm sure the prospect of eyeing Menelaus' women up close sure sobered me quickly because soon after that, I found myself standing on the beach beside Menelaus' ship. Hector and I watched in silence as a group of burly seamen lowered a gangplank so the ladies wouldn't have to jump down on the beach. When it was in place, Menelaus and his royal entourage, which consisted of the three concubines, another woman and a man, walked gracefully down it to a tremendous applause.

The King of Sparta was in the house! Can you diiig it!

Strutting over to where we were standing, Menelaus stopped, waited for the applause to die down, and when it had, he raised his hand in greeting and simply said, "Hi, man."

For a moment or two, everybody beamed at him, except, of course, me. In my mind's eye, I was busy undressing and mounting the four women standing behind him. That's what sex addicts like me do. Fuck all that prince shit!

"Hi, man, how's it hanging?" Menelaus said again in an effort to get things moving along.

Okay, since birth, Hector had been trained for ceremonies like this. He knew what to do, what to say and how to act but even so, I don't think he was prepared to greet someone as cool as Menelaus.

As the crowd turned their eyes expectantly towards him, Hector licked his dry lips, squirmed, and, at last, bowed and said, "Hi....er... welcome to Troy...er...Your Majesty...it's hanging...ah...swell."

My brother was so uncool it was funny. The concubines had to cover their mouths to keep from laughing. I pretended to cough. Menelaus looked away.

Fixing his gaze on the city behind us, Menelaus said, "So that's Troy. Wow, man, what a mind-blowing place."

The crowd applauded appreciatively, as if Menelaus had said something deeply profound, and since he wasn't one to let a good applause go by unnoticed, he held up his hand and waved again.

Then, at Hector's insistence, there was the usual boring display of statesmanship between him and Menelaus that involved a great deal of bowing and protestations of love and respect between Sparta and Troy. When they were done, Menelaus asked permission to visit the city for the purpose of observing propitiatory rites at the graves of Lycus and Chimaereus, sons of Prometheus, who were buried there, in order to alleviate the effects of a plague in Sparta. Since this was a common practice, Hector, on behalf of our father, granted him permission to do so. With that, both turned to introduce the members of their respective parties.

Menelaus went first.

Turning to the newest woman in his entourage, he said, "This little honey here is Princess Deidameia, daughter of Lycomedes, King of Scyros. She's just turned eighteen and her father has asked me to introduce her to Priam's court."

Now, I hadn't seen her on the ship when it was pulling into harbor, probably because I was so focused on Menelaus and his concubines but I later learned from another observer that she was indeed there, leaning casually on the railing near the stern. How I missed her, I don't know, as I have never been in the habit of overlooking hot chicks. And brother, let me tell you, Deidameia was certainly the very picture of sexual impudence. She was dressed in a bodice of such thin silk that her plump firm breasts and thin waist were clearly visible underneath.

Her tight, long skirt was split on the sides, revealing a pair of shapely legs when she walked. Outside of that, Deidameia wasn't what you'd call a striking beauty by any means. Especially when compared to the likes of Helen or Oenone or Polyxena anyway. Deidameia was of average height, with a round pug nose, dimpled cheeks, a saucy little smile, shoulder length sandy blonde hair, blue eyes, all of which could only be summed up as being very cute. It was her lewdness, however, that set her apart from other cute girls though. In this department, she more than held her own. Deidameia was living proof of the old adage that it's not what a girl has, but it's how she uses it. And Deidameia sure knew how to use what she had, alright. When she bowed to my brother, she deliberately remained bent over for a long moment so that everyone could get a good look at the outline of her sexy, little ass. Believe me, it was enough to make your mouth water. I know because my brother slobbered something stupid about Scyros and welcomed her to Troy.

Menelaus then introduced the man. "This scruffy seadog here is Captain Phrontis, helmsman of my ship and the best sailor that ever sailed the wine-dark sea."

As Phrontis bowed, my brother complimented him on the beauty of his ship, to which, Phrontis proudly proclaimed, "She's a beauty, all right, and built for speed too. She'll show her ass to anything, wind or no wind."

Oddly enough, Phrontis could have been talking about anyone of Menelaus' concubines as well. And, unfortunately, that was as close to an introduction as they got because, not being members of royalty, Menelaus saw no reason to introduce them.

And so, it was Hector's turn.

Turning to me with an air of trepidation, my brother said, "Your Majesty, I'd like to introduce my brother Paris, second in line to my father's throne."

And that's when the unexpected happened.

Menelaus immediately looked over his shoulder and winked at the girls, causing them to raise their eyebrows and widen their beautiful eyes in excitement.

Then he bounded forward, grabbed my hand and started shaking it hardily.

"Dude!" he exclaimed, "I've…we've…heard so much about you and your totally cool tavern. We can't wait to party in it with you."

I was flabbergasted, to say the least.

So was Hector. He immediately groaned and rolled his eyes towards heaven in disbelief.

Finding my voice, I said, "Sure, yes, sure, ah, Your Highness Majesty Dude, ah, you're welcome to drop by anytime you like. I'd be honored to entertain you. Happy hour is at six."

Still pumping my hand wildly, Menelaus said, "Drop by? No, man, that won't do. We were hoping that you would allow us to shack up with you during our stay in Troy."

I, of course, couldn't figure any of this. The King of Sparta holing up in my nasty little tavern? I was lost. The universe seemed to be spiraling completely out of control. Unsure as to what to do or say, I looked over to Hector for help. He was trained for diplomatic shit, not me.

"Your Majesty," Hector immediately jumped in, "wouldn't you rather stay in my father's palace? I think you would be far more comfortable there."

"Oh, no, no," Menelaus said, shaking his head adamantly. "We'd very much prefer to shack up with your little brother."

Hector looked over at me, shrugged his shoulders helplessly and said, "Of course you can, Your Majesty, if this is what you desire. I'm sure my brother will be only too happy to have you as a guest in his house."

I could only nod my head in agreement.

Now, get this. The truth is, Menelaus' real reason for visiting Troy was to party at my place. Oh, sure, there was a plague in Sparta and all, but that only gave him a convenient excuse to sail across the Aegean to visit my tavern. Menelaus was like that. He was always looking for reasons to go off somewhere to have a good time, dead cousins, dead uncles, things like that. I know this because he personally told me so. Of course, the folks back in Sparta dying of the plague never suspected it. To them, their king was off seeking help from the gods to ease their plight. And if you told them their king was partying his ass off, well, I'm sure they wouldn't believe you. That's how good Menelaus was at covering his tracks. And so, there you are, now you know, Menelaus was a selfish, oversexed, immoral bastard. No wonder we hit it off so well!

And where was Helen during all this? Well, she was back in Sparta minding the roost. By then, she and Menelaus had been married for about nine years. They even had a daughter around that age named Hermione. But their marriage had cooled. Not that it was ever that hot. Maybe it was lukewarm in the beginning, you know, like most marriages are before the partners figure out what big jerks they got themselves hitched to. Like I said before, Helen was just a trophy to Menelaus, something he had won and something he loved showing off to his buddies. To Helen, Menelaus was a way to maintain power in her hometown. You see, after the death of her two maniac brothers, Castor and Polydeuces, Helen's father, King Tyndareus, had little choice but to pass the throne on to his daughter and son-in-law Menelaus, so, no matter how you cut it, Sparta was really more of Helen's home than Menelaus'. That's why leaving it in order to have a good time somewhere else was never a big deal to Menelaus. Nor was it a big deal to anyone else either. That's because Helen actually ran things in Sparta. Of course, she did it discreetly, you know, so as not to tarnish her famous husband's reputation. I mean, Menelaus was, after all, the little brother of Agamemnon, who, as everyone knows, is the big he-dog of Greece. And pissing off Agamemnon isn't a healthy thing to do. Just look at me. I fucked with Menelaus' reputation and now, I've got this arrow sticking out of my dick. See what I mean?

And while we are on the subject of reputations, let me tell you something about Helen: she isn't without her dirty little secrets either.

No, sir, she ain't, not by a long shot. I have it on good authority that Iphigenia, you know, the daughter of Agamemnon and Helen's sister Clytemnestra, was actually Helen's child. I say she *was* Helen's child because, as you probably already know, ten years ago Agamemnon plunged a knife into Iphigenia's heart in order to get some favorable winds from the gods so that his navy could sail over here and kick my ass. Anyway, the story goes that when Helen was twelve, she was abducted by King Theseus of Athens, who kept her for about a year until she was rescued from his clutches by her two brothers and a tough guy named Menestheus, who just happened to be Theseus' rebellious cousin and after the throne of Athens, which, by the way, he got in the process of rescuing Helen. And here's where the story gets good. After Menestheus becomes king and all, he doesn't return Helen to her brothers right away. No, sirree. He keeps her for at about six months. Hmmmm! And when he finally gets around to sending her home, guess what? Helen's about six months pregnant! Dang sure was. Whether the father was Theseus or Menestheus or some lucky stable boy, only Helen knows. So, anyway, three months later, Helen's back in Sparta where she gives birth to Iphigenia and since Helen was so young, and had tons and tons of rich suitors banging on her bedroom door, she decides to give the child to her sister and Agamemnon to raise. Believe me, Helen was never one to put motherhood ahead of personal desire. Anyway, that's why Agamemnon never batted an eye when he sacrificed Iphigenia. She wasn't really his child! And here's the real kicker. You know who told me that story?

Menelaus!

Yep, he sure did.

Goes to show you what good friends we became.

I have to admit though, in the beginning of our friendship, I was pretty nervous hobnobbing around with the likes of Menelaus and his entourage but, you know, I quickly got over it. After a while, I didn't feel nervous at all. I felt exhilarated mainly because I was doing crazy things for once with people of my station who were sex addicts just like me. I can't tell you how good it felt to finally have a bunch of friends like that. We didn't give a shit about anything. I felt as if I was flying to the moon on Pegasus' back or stealing fire from the gods. I felt invincible.

Anyway, after performing the sacrificial rites at the graves of Prometheus' sons, Menelaus and his little band of merrymakers wasted little time making themselves at home in my tavern. My family, of course, was shocked, except, maybe, for my father, who, in his own words, "Didn't want a bunch of dirty Greeks stinking up his palace anyway." Hector muttered something to the effect that our behavior was scandalous and, looking back on it now, I have to agree with him. We were scandalous. Big time scandalous! And we didn't give a tinker's damn what anyone, including my family, said about us. We were too busy having the time of our lives. You should have seen it. Menelaus, Deidameia, Phrontis and the concubines just loved my place. And they were loved back by the tavern's staff. I swear, the musicians never sounded as good, nor did my girls look or dance any better than they did then. I couldn't keep the girls off the stages or out of my royal guests' laps. And that also included my sister Polyxena, who, by the way, went absolutely nuts over Menelaus. Before I knew it, those two were screwing each other's brains out on a level that was almost incomprehensible. They couldn't have stopped if they wanted to, all of which, forced me to entertain the other four girls all by myself. Hey, it was a tough job but someone had to do it! And friend, let me tell you, entertain them over and over and over again I did, sometimes together, sometimes one on one. And best of all, it went on, night after night, for almost a month. It was, just as Hector said, a very scandalous affair indeed. Yet, believe it or not, the most startling event was still to come. I blame myself for it and, just for the record, I want to state that I should have known better and I'm sorry it happened.

Ain't it the way though? I mean, one moment you're riding high on Pegasus' back and the next, fate grabs hold of you and slams your ass back down to the ground. Story of my life!

In this case, fate took the form of an empty wine bottle. Or, I guess I should say, empty wine bottles. It happened the night Menelaus decided to invite his ship's crew, which consisted mainly of rowers, over to the tavern for a good time. While that sounds completely innocent and an excellent example of good leadership, it was also an invitation fraught with danger. You see, the rowers were Phaeacians and, as everyone knows, Phaeacians have hollow legs and tend to drink like fish. So, if you're gonna entertain these hardy fellows, your wine cellar better be up to the task. Unfortunately, mine wasn't. Antheus, the tavern's chief steward, informed me of this around midnight.

Now, I don't have to tell you what kind of condition I was in when he told me the news, as I had been drinking and fornicating for close to eight hours straight, so cut me some slack about what happened next.

I'm not certain how Antheus broke the news to me. However, I do remember that I was lying under the center stage table with Deidameia in my arms at the time. We had just finished a frenzied round of lovemaking, our fifth, I believe, and so, I probably told Antheus pretty fast what he could do with his damnfool problem.

Only it wasn't his problem.

It was mine.

I swear, sometimes, running a titty tavern can be a major pain in the ass!

Anyway, I also recall his concerned face glaring down at me and then a hand seizing me by the ankle, and I was dragged from under the table and over to the bar so the two of us could hold a quick business meeting. All around the tavern, Phaeacians were drinking, clapping to the music and throwing coins at the dancing girls. Menelaus was in the corner booth playing with Polyxena and his concubines. I'm not sure where Phrontis was at but my guess is that he was probably off diddling a dancer somewhere.

Once I was heaved up onto a stool, Antheus looked me in the eye, all scared like, and said, "Sir, we are almost out of wine. You have got to do something!" Obviously, he didn't want to be the one to tell the rowdy Phaeacians there wasn't any more booze left.

Answering him was a mistake as I was in no condition to think straight. I should have just passed out right then and there. Given what happened next, I wish I had. But I didn't. Instead, I made the fateful decision to go next door, to my father's house, and raid his wine cellar. I know it sounds crazy but like I said before, I was drunk as a sailor. The odd thing is that Antheus went along with me. So did Deidameia. Together, the three of us stumbled across the lawn to dad's house. We were stopped briefly near the front door by a guard who waved us on after recognizing my face. After that, there were a series of dark carpeted hallways and rooms in which I got completely turned around. Finally, we came to a long, broad staircase, which we climbed. I'm not sure why we climbed it as the wine cellar was located…well…down in the cellar. But climb it we did. At the top, I told Antheus to stay there and alert us if anyone was coming. He must have argued with me because I remember taking him by the collar and forcibly ordering him to stay put. What his thoughts were as Deidameia and I staggered away can only be guessed at. But I bet they weren't too happy. Anyway, another series of rooms were encountered until finally, in a particularly dark one, we came to the foot of a bed. It was there that my little head told me to take advantage of the situation. So I quickly undid Deidameia's bra with one hand and pulled her down upon the bed with the other (yup, even drunk, I was that smooth). She was all for it, of course, and in no time at all, her legs were wrapped around my hips. As I settled into place, she started moaning and groaning something fierce.

And that's precisely when that I thought I heard a man's voice.

Instantly, I froze in mid-thrust and sensed something was terribly, terribly wrong.

Unfortunately, Deidameia didn't. She passionately pulled me into her with her legs and screamed, "Come on, baby, fuck me real good! You're cock is soooo perfect!"

After that, there was an agonizing second of suspense which seemed to last a lifetime and then, well, all Hades broke loose.

"What the heck's going on down there!" the voice shouted.

Chapter Five

"It's all your fault!" Helen complains with an agitated nod of her head in my direction. "I never wanted any of this to happen."

The audacity of her accusation stirs me from my thoughts and I turn my face to confront her. "Oh, yeah?" I say. "And whose idea was it to sneak over to Kranai and fuck?"

It was Helen's, of course, and just so you know, Kranai is a tiny, rocky island sitting just outside the harbor of Helen's Spartan home. It was the first place Helen and I screwed.

"I had to!" she snaps back with an air of vindication. "You couldn't keep your hands off of me so I thought the best thing to do was to go somewhere private where we could talk."

"Talk? Talk?" The ridicule in my voice is unmistakable. "How could you talk? As I recall, your lips were wrapped around my dick before we were more than five cubits away from the boat dock!"

It's true, they were. And it was also one of the most memorable blowjobs I ever got, mainly because I was rowing a boat when I got it. I'm still amazed I didn't row us off into the Aegean somewhere.

Helen stares at me in disgust for a good, long moment while her breasts heave up and down with every angry breath she takes. God, I want to squeeze them so bad right now. If I could, I'd reach out and pull her into to me. I always enjoyed angry sex with Helen and I have to confess that, sometimes, I purposely pissed her off for that very reason.

Finally, she heaves a heavy sigh, turns around and stares out the window again.

"Did all this really happen?" she mummers half to herself.

"Unfortunately it did," I answer.

"All I want to do is go home," she says quietly.

I know exactly how she feels.

I want to go home too.

And I especially wanted to go home after Antheus' death, almost as much as I do right now. But my father said I had to stick around and make restitution. Then he made me do all sorts of restitution stuff. First, and worse of all, I had to shut down the tavern and I can't begin to tell you what a sad day that was, especially for my dancers. They were absolutely heartbroken by it and the sight of them trudging back to the Temple of Aphrodite was one of the saddest things I ever saw. I felt like a total bastard and it took me two cases of wine to regroup. Then, when I was all sober and shit, I had to give Antheus a big funeral, which, by the way, I was late for. It seems as if I never could get to a funeral on time. I was late for Aesacus' and Hector's funerals as well. Anyway, after I got Antheus' ashes properly taken care of, I had to hold some games in his honor. That proved to be very, very embarrassing personally because I almost killed another athlete when I hit him on the noggin with the discus. I never could throw those stupid things very good and...of course...I was drunk when I threw it.

Little wonder then that I became something of a social pariah after all that. I'm telling you, the folks of Troy avoided me like I had the plague or something. And worse, they started thinking about Aesacus' prophecy again and began wondering if I wasn't a dangerous little shit after all. You should have seen all the crappy looks they gave me whenever I would walk down the street. I wasn't welcome anywhere.

Ironically enough, the only friends I had during that time were Greeks. Menelaus, Deidameia, Phrontis and the concubines remained firmly in my corner, gods bless them for it, and it was Menelaus who finally rescued me from that nightmarish situation.

He's the one that came up with the bright idea for me to go to Pytho so that I could be purified of Antheus' death by the priests there. My father was all for it, of course — anything to get me out of his hair — and so were the people of Troy. They had had enough of me too. The bastards even created a special fund in order to raise enough money to build me a ship with. They called it the "Good Riddance to Paris Fund" or the GRPF for short. There were GRPF drives in every Trojan neighborhood and it wasn't long before enough cash was collected. Anyway, the jokes on them because Captain Phrontis oversaw the construction of the ship, and so, Phereclus, Troy's master shipwright, ended up building me a boat that was not only faster and finer than anything the city's rotten little navy possessed, it was also sturdy enough to keep me safe during a savage storm.

And to make sure I got to Pytho and minded my manners once I was there, Aeneas was assigned by my father to watch over me. You may remember him: he's the guy that saved me from being trampled to death during my first day in Troy, so, I guess he was a pretty good choice. And, coincidentally, believe it or not, he was also my cousin. What are the odds? But best of all, we were from the same place. Aeneas was raised on the slopes of Mt. Ida too, and although he lived on the rich side of the mountain and I was from the poor, we both grew up gazing at the same peak. That counts for something, I guess. Outside of that, Aeneas was a little strange mainly because he went around telling folks the goddess Aphrodite was his mother. Of course, you really can't blame him for believing he was Aphrodite's son since he was told that by his father, Anchises, who should know, and you really can't blame his father for saying that since Anchises had been struck by a bolt of lightning and his brains had gotten scrambled around his head something awful. Anyway, I never told Aeneas about my experience with his so-called mother. I figured having one wacko aboard ship was more than enough. I did, however, let Aeneas paint an image of

Aphrodite on the ship's sail, you know, just to cozy up to him because, at that point, I needed all the friends I could get.

Besides Aeneas, Captain Pandarus and a small detail of soldiers were sent with me as well. Did I say Captain Pandarus? Oh, there I go again! I should have said Sergeant Pandarus instead. You see, being the Commander of the Guard and in charge of the king's security, my father held Pandarus personally responsible for my bungled burglary and so, Pandarus was busted down to sergeant and fined to a point where he was almost broke. I don't have to tell you what kind of mood that put Pandarus in. That's why I tried to stay out of his way as much as I possibly could. I did that by spending the voyage to Pytho aboard Menelaus' ship, where it was safe and the atmosphere was a heck of a lot friendlier.

Speaking of which, Menelaus couldn't wait to leave Troy since all the fun was over and all. It's a testament to our friendship that he stuck around until my boat was built. Of course, the Pytho thing was just an excuse for us to go somewhere else and have a good time.

"You mean we're really not going to Pytho?" I asked.

We were sitting on the beach near his boat, drinking wine and soaking up the sun. The girls were frolicking naked in the water before us.

"Sure, man," he said, "we're going to Pytho, got too, you know, for appearance's sake, but afterwards I figure we'll boogie on over to Sparta. I want you to check out the chicks there. I know you'll really gonna dig them."

Sounded just like what a fellow in my predicament needed.

I took a big gulp of wine and said, "Are they beautiful?"

Menelaus tilted his head towards me, smiled and said, "Dude! Take my word of it, Spartan chicks kick ass and I'm not just saying that because Sparta's my kingdom."

I smiled back and nodded towards the girls, who were busy splashing each other with water. "As beautiful as them?" I asked.

"You betcha," Menelaus answered lustfully. "Bro, you know what they call Spartan chicks?"

"No, what?" I asked.

"Thigh-flashers," he proudly proclaimed.

"Thigh-flashers?" I quickly responded. I didn't know what that meant but I sure liked the sound of it.

"Yeah, man, thigh-flashers," he replied. "You see, Spartan babes like to exercise naked every morning, hence the nickname thigh-flashers, and they do this one particular exercise that involves beating their buttocks with their heels as many times as possible. You should see them go, dude! Anyway, all that exercise really builds up their thigh and ass muscles. I can't wait for you to mount one of them because she's totally gonna be the ride of your life, man."

It's both ironic and prophetic he said that because, of course, the Spartan woman I picked to mount was Helen and, just like he predicted, she's been the ride of my life. Of course, I can't help but shake my head in complete wonderment every time I think about it. Maybe the whole thing was the will of the gods after all. Or maybe it's just because I was so damned stupid. Anyway, whatever the reason, it was Menelaus' idea for us to go to Sparta and because of that, he unwittingly set into motion the tragic events that followed.

We left Troy immediately after my ship had been constructed, supplied and manned. All of Troy turned out to wave goodbye to Menelaus and bid me good riddance. The only person upset to see me go, other than Polyxena, was my sister Cassandra. The dingy bitch stood on the beach yelling, "Where are you going, Paris? You will bring a conflagration back with you. How great the flames are that you are seeking over these waters, you do not know." At least that's how I remember it. I never did listen to anything Cassandra said. Neither did anyone else.

We sailed or oared west towards the setting sun, then south by west, and the temperature got so hot that we stripped down to our loin cloths, female company included, and I got my first taste of life at sea, which, for me, consisted mainly of lounging around the deck with Menelaus, drinking vast amounts of wine and dallying with the girls. I enjoyed myself, for sure, and so did my friends. The rest of the crew went about performing their duties as if we weren't even there. They were a highly skilled bunch of sailors and I could see why Menelaus treated them so well.

After a couple of days, we came to the island of Scyros. You might recall, the island was Deidameia's home and so, we pulled up to the place expecting a big reception. Instead, we were greeted by a royal messenger bearing an order for Deidameia to immediately disembark alone. You see, word had reached Deidameia's daddy, King Lycomedes, of his daughter's scandalous behavior in Troy and, as you might expect, he wasn't exactly beaming with pride over it.

I watched her pack her bags with a heavy heart because, not only was I losing one of the last five friends I had to my name, I was also losing someone whose company I was really beginning to enjoy. You see, sex with Deidameia was great because she was one of those special chicks who could have an orgasm with little or no effort. All it took was a minute or two of regular sex, nothing fancy, except maybe a little dirty talk, and then, BAM! After that, she'd let me do any selfish, perverted thing I could think of. And best of all, especially for a sex addict like me, Deidameia would do it anytime, anywhere. Obviously, I was going to miss her a lot.

Unfortunately, Deidameia was going to miss me too.

When she finally had her things in order, she suddenly turned to me and said, "Give me your hand."

I placed my hand in hers; for a moment she studied it carefully, then she placed it over her heart and said, "Paris, I will always love you and, no matter what happens, I will always keep you here in my heart. Perhaps, after Pytho, you will return to me?"

You may be sure that I was shocked. I had no idea she felt that way. Up until then, we had been fuck- buddies with no strings attached. Oh, sure, I was fond of her because, like I just explained, she was my type of woman but I felt nothing for her I'd call love. Still, if anyone knows what to do in that kind of circumstance, it's me, so I took her into my arms and pledged my love, then I kissed her long and hard, you know, just so she'd believe me. Then, almost on cue, a hatch flew open and the messenger stepped in to drag Deidameia from my arms. I produced a big tear as he did and swore an oath to Deidameia that I would someday return to her embrace. Pretty romantic stuff, you'll agree. Of course, it was all just an act, as I always liked to leave my girlfriends feeling loved because it makes bumping into them afterwards a far less dangerous experience.

After that, there was nothing left to do but set sail for Pytho, so it was all hands on deck, heave ho, that sort of thing, until we were well underway again. I won't weary you about the rest of our voyage except to say that the sun turned my skin a golden brown during it. If you could have seen me standing on the bow of Menelaus' ship, stripped down to my skivvies, my bronze body dripping with sweat, spoutin' sailing lingo, you'd have swore you were looking at a salty pirate. I must have cut a fine figure too because, several times, I caught the concubines giving me something more than their usual glance.

Little wonder then, that I turned heads — male and female — when we finally dropped anchor in the Gulf of Corinth a few days later. In case you don't know, the Gulf, or a portion of it, lies about three leagues south of Pytho and it's the starting point for most visitors wishing to journey there. The place was absolutely jammed with ships. I'd estimate that there were at least a hundred vessels of every type: huge Greek thirty-oared Triacontors, tiny Phoenician trading galleys, tubby Egyptian barges and long Athenian Argos. They were anchored so close together, you could have walked across them to the shoreline from a league out and, if you did, you'd have walked into the biggest tourist trap in the world. I swear, there were merchants everywhere, all looking to make a profit off of the thousands of religious pilgrims who made their way through the port every year. I think the place was called Cirrha or Crisa or something like that. I'll just go with Cirrha. Anyway, prices for everything in Cirrha were about a hundred percent higher than those found anywhere else in the world. On top of that, you had to pay a landing tax just to step foot in the place and then, believe it or not, you had to pay another tax to leave it. The bastards got you coming and going! And, if that wasn't bad enough, the town was as packed with people as the bay was with ships. I'm not kidding when I say you couldn't take a step anywhere without bumping into someone. It's true, you couldn't. And if you tried to beg the other person's pardon for stepping on his foot or something like that, chances are, he wouldn't have understood you. That's because there were at least a dozen different dialects spoken there. Besides every accent of Greek, I also heard Egyptian, Phoenician, Hebrew, Persian and a bunch of others I couldn't even recognize. Believe me, taken as a whole, the place was enough to make you swear off religion forever and swim back home.

But, like I said before, when you are a king or a prince, you get treated vastly different than normal folks, and so, once the peasants of Cirrha caught a glimpse of their betters, they wasted little time welcoming me and Menelaus into their expensive little tourist trap. We were escorted through the streets with great fanfare, which was refreshing, considering our frosty reception on Scyros, and then we were lodged — at our own cost, of course — in a big, beautiful mansion complete with a vast wine cellar and a whole army of servants to take care of us. It was just the place two rich lowlifes like us needed and it wasn't long before the joint looked like Sodom and Gomorrah on a Saturday night.

I don't recall how long we stayed there, as we had a whole smorgasbord of foreign women to work our way through, but I think it took us a week or two or three before we could focus on the task at hand, namely, our pilgrimage to Pytho.

It began the morning after our third going away party. There was a knock on my bedroom door that sounded like a hammer. I immediately sat bolt upright and heard Menelaus' voice yell, "Alexander, wake up, man, time to go to Pytho and get your ass purified." Before I could respond, he was there, next to my bed, staring down at the naked beauties still asleep in it. There were three of them because, you see, ever since the concubines, I had developed a fancy for that number. Anyway, they lay there with their bare bodies gleaming in the early morning sunlight. Who they were or what their names were, I didn't know. We had encountered one another during the excesses of the previous night when proper introductions weren't really necessary.

I watched Menelaus study them while I fumbled with my clothes and wondered why he was so interested. I mean, I'm sure he'd left a bed full of naked women himself. I was just about to ask him when he put his hand to his beard, stroked it gently and, all serious like, said, "Do you know who these women are, dude?"

"No," I answered, "I met them at last night's party."

"Well," he said, "they're all members of Cirrha's upper crust." Menelaus was always more in tuned socially than I was.

Good for them, thinks I, now I won't have to pay for a carriage.

Pointing a finger in turn at each, he said, "That one's the niece of the town's leading merchant, and that one's the sister of local physician and that one....well...that one's the mayor's wife."

I looked at the girls, then at Menelaus, shrugged my shoulders and said, "So I managed to bag some rich pussy, who the fuck cares?"

"Who cares?" says he with a slight chuckle. "Dude, I'll tell you who cares. The mayor is downstairs right now looking for his better half."

I almost gave birth!

Now, if someone can get dressed quicker and run out the back door faster than me, especially when there's an irate husband walking through the front door, I'd really like to meet him. I swear, before Menelaus could bat an eye, I was dressed and shimmying down the nearest drainpipe like a frightened rat.

"Alexander! Where are you going?" he yelled at me from the balcony.

"To Pytho!" I shouted back from the street below. "I'll meet you there."

Menelaus laughed and waved okay.

And that's how my journey to mythical Pytho began.

I was still in a panic as I picked my way through the crowd of pilgrims that jammed the road to the place, but, after a half a league or so, I calmed down enough to notice the area's surrounding beauty, which can only be described as spectacular. Bright green olive and

Cyprus trees on either side walled the road I walked along. The tranquil shade they produced tempted me to lay down under them and nap a while, but since I was still, technically, a man on the run, I thought it best to keep moving. The great, green avenue I continued on cut straight across a wide coastal plain, gradually climbing towards a pocket of forested hills and rocky mountains that combined to form a sort of a protective enclave around Pytho. Of these protrusions, the most noticeable was a towering mass of rock called Mount Parnassus. Its peak was covered in snow and parts of it were cloaked by clouds, giving the mountain, as a whole, a rather inviting and mysterious look. The trek towards it was a tiring one but — and here's the coolest thing about the journey — just when I was at a point of stopping to rest, I turned a corner and, snap, there was Pytho. It was hidden from view in a cleft between a mountain in the east and a high ridge on the west and situated just far enough so its tiring visitors could refresh themselves in the cool streams that flowed all around the place.

I have to admit that I was pretty excited about visiting Pytho, not because I am very religious, which you know I ain't, but because the place was so damned famous. You see, the Greeks believe Pytho is the center of the world and they mark the site with a large conical stone they call the "navel". I've seen the thing and it looks like a large vase turned upside down. The story goes that Zeus released two eagles, one to the west and one to the east, commanding them to fly to the center of the world, and it was at Pytho they met. The Greeks also believe that the navel belongs to Gaia, the goddess of the earth, and for that reason she is worshipped there, although now, I'm told, Apollo is all the rage. Anyway, folks by the butt-load, come from near and far to worship there and since much of that worship involves the exchange of gifts and tithes, especially if you wanted to chat with Gaia's Oracle, Pytho has grown to be one of the wealthiest places on earth.

As I recall, Pytho was not a town at all, but a sacred district made up of rich temples, pavilions and monuments, of which, the most spectacular was the Temple of Gaia. In order to get to the temple, I had to follow a little path known to the locals as the Sacred Way. It's pretty easy to figure out why they named it that, since the pathway is lined with so much wealth and beauty that walking down it becomes a religious experience in itself. That's because, on both sides of the path, all the way up to the temple, there are a multitude of fancy war memorials and statues dedicated to this or that god, goddess, hero or king, all of which are fashioned out of gold, silver, marble or bronze. The sight of all these precious works of art, some twenty cubits high, gleaming in the clear mountain air is simply awe inspiring and, all around me, scores of pilgrims were bawling their eyes out, while others were busy busting their guts praying. But, believe it or not, the best was yet to come. At the end of the trail stands the Temple of Gaia, and believe me, the place is totally spectacular. Huge and stately, decorated with silver and gold leaf, it is a hex-shaped affair, of six by fifteen evenly spaced marble columns supporting a stone roof that is situated over a large inner chamber. It's in there that the Oracle communes with her goddess. I stood and gazed up at it in wonderment and have to admit that it was the most beautiful structure I have ever seen. Covering two acres, it had taken centuries to build, I was told, and since I've also seen the Egyptian Pyramids, I can honestly say they pale in comparison to Gaia's Temple.

A cluster of various sized pavilions surrounds the temple, all stuffed to the roof with brilliant works of art. To give you an idea what one looked like, the Oracle's favorite pavilion was a circular building, constructed entirely out of marble, with twenty columns arranged around an exterior diameter of about fifteen cubits. There were a further ten columns, arranged in a circle, inside the building's interior. The roof above was decorated with gold leaf. Its interior contained a dozen dazzling sculptures of the various gods of Olympus. The statues of Hera, Athena and Aphrodite weren't exactly as I remembered them from my dream, but they were nonetheless beautifully done. In the center of the building, just inside the ten columns, there stood a statue of Gaia all by itself. I remember walking around it in silence, inspecting it closely — god, but Gaia had nice tits — when I suddenly encountered an innocent looking young girl sweeping the floor next to it. She wasn't a beauty by any means, just a simple, plain country girl by the look of her, you know, kinda like the ones I used to screw on Ida.

"Hello," I said politely.

She stopped sweeping, lowered her eyes shyly and, in a soft voice that was almost inaudible, said hello.

"This is a beautiful pavilion isn't it?" I said.

"Yes," she said timidly, "it is my favorite."

Since we were alone, I considered giving her ass a squeeze, for, although she wasn't a beauty by any means, she was close at hand, and that, of course, was the main thing, but, strangely enough, I didn't. That's because something in the back of my mind warned me against it. What it was, I'm not sure, but it felt strong, so, for once, I decided to heed the warning from my big head and move on. I smiled politely, made a slight bow and walked past her thinking, too bad, darling, you've just missed a good time. She nodded her head demurely as I passed by and resumed sweeping.

I was on my way to the next pavilion when I suddenly heard Menelaus shout out my name. Turning around quickly, I saw that he was walking towards me with a stranger by his side. They were followed closely by a small group of men, of whom, Phrontis' face was the only one I recognized.

"I see you're still alive," Menelaus joked as the party drew near.

I nodded my head that I was and said, "Thanks to you."

Menelaus smiled broadly, turned to the man next to him and said, "Your Majesty, this is the dude…er…friend I told you about. This is Prince Alexander of Troy."

The man surveyed me indifferently with a set of cold, gray eyes. As he did, I thought, careful now, Paris, here's a fellow you don't want to be messing around with.

The stranger was a big man who stood at least three inches taller than Menelaus and about six inches more than everyone else, including me. He was also more muscular than Menelaus. From his massive shoulders, I pegged him to be a javelin thrower. A thick stock of black hair fell to his shoulders and an equally dark beard surrounded the lips of his handsome face. He was dressed in a richly decorated tunic and armed with a silver-studded sword that hung from his shoulder by a single ox hide strap. A massive lion skin cloak hung from his shoulders, which, while out of place on someone else, seemed to fit his arrogant manner perfectly. He was certainly not a man you had to look at twice to remember. Believe me, once was enough to last a lifetime, at least it was for me. I don't think I've seen another man, other than Achilles or Thonis, of course, who scared the shit out of me more.

"So this is Paris," the man said, half to himself, half to Menelaus.

Naturally, I was taken aback by this, mainly because the brute called me Paris instead of Alexander but the sword dangling from his shoulder quickly reminded me that the son-of-a-bitch could call me anything he damned well liked and get away with it too. So, I gulped down my anger, not to mention my pride, and tried my best not to look annoyed.

Turning to me, Menelaus said, "Prince Alexander, I'd like to introduce my brother, Anax Agamemnon, Ruler of Mycenae."

Okay. Notice Menelaus called his brother anax? In case you don't know, anax is an old term that means high king in Greek. Menelaus was using it to indicate that his brother was the greatest king in Greece. Little wonder he did too. With Sparta tucked safely away in his back pocket, Agamemnon's domain stretched from the Peloponnese to the islands of the Aegean and as far east as Rhodes. A ruler with a kingdom like that deserves to be called anax, I guess. Still, it shows you what an arrogant bastard Agamemnon was. I mean, to require your own brother to use a formal term like that certainly borders on maniacal don't you agree? You bet it does. And that, by the way, pretty much sums Agamemnon up: he is a maniacal bastard of the highest order. But, like I said before, he wasn't someone to be trifled with, and I knew that from the start, so, without further ado, I bowed humbly and mumbled something stupid about being honored to be in his presence. I'm telling you, Hector himself, with all his fancy diplomatic training, couldn't have done it any better. When I rose, I could see that Agamemnon was comfortable with my performance because he signaled his satisfaction to Menelaus with a quick little nod.

"My great brother has come to see the Oracle," Menelaus continued on eagerly. "We bumped into each other this morning after you left. I've been busy telling him all about you and my trip to Troy ever since."

I have to admit, watching Menelaus kiss his brother's ass was an uncomfortable thing to do. The fact is, outside his brother's company, Menelaus was as cock-sure a man as you'd ever want to meet, but inside it, he was little more than a sniveling little toady. I looked at him as if he had suddenly turned into a stranger.

Menelaus must have noticed my confused gaze because, a few moments later, when his brother was turned around talking to another member of their party, he shot me a look that could only be interpreted as a plea to bear with him; you know, it's the kind of look a child gives his friend when the parents are around. I, of course, understood immediately, since I had my fair share of overbearing family members to deal with too, and so, I nodded back in acknowledgement.

When Agamemnon was done with his little chitchat, he turned and walked away with his nose in the air. Everyone else, including me, followed after him like a pack of hungry puppies. We made our way through the jumble of pavilions until we finally came to the Temple's steps. There, a priest rushed out to greet us. He smiled and bowed respectfully, clapped his hands together, and suddenly, he was joined by a dozen young priestesses. And what a wonderful sight they were! Their heads were crowned with laurels and they wore long white robes that reached down to their bare feet and, although, not more than seven were, what I'd consider bed worthy, I immediately thought I'd died and gone to heaven. They smiled broadly and gave us a cute little curtsey, which, of course, sent happy thoughts rolling down my spine to Mr. Happy.

"These are the Inspired Maidens, Your Majesty," says the Priest, "and they will prepare you to see the Oracle."

The maidens indicated that we should follow them, which, of course, we dutifully did. They led us inside the temple's forecourt where we were met by a scrawny priest and his equally scrawny goat. Compared to the maidens, the priest and goat were quite the gruesome twosome, I assure you.

Okay, now, here's where everything starts getting a little weird so bear with me. You see, believe it or not, before we could gain admission to the Oracle, we had to get permission from that damned goat first because the temple priests believed that, somehow or another, the goat already knew how the Oracle was gonna react to our visit. If the creature shook its body when doused with a bowl of water, well then, that meant everything was just peachy with the Oracle and we could go right in. But if it didn't shake the water off properly or if it did any number of things that goats normally do, you know, like chew, slobber, piss or shit, then, we were totally screwed.

I swear, the stupid things religious folks come up with! You got to love them though. They sure know how to keep us non-believers entertained.

Anyway, we had little choice but to stand there like a pack of idiots and hope the damned goat took a shine to us. While the priest was busy scooping up a bowl of water, I looked around at the circle of Greeks to see if anyone felt as ridiculous as I did, but they seemed totally mesmerized by the ceremony. No surprise there. Take my word for it, Greeks aren't what you'd call deep thinkers. Anyway, when the priest had enough water, he carefully turned back around so as not to spill any of it, then he said some kind of mumble jumble bullshit, which nobody understood, and poured the water all over the animal's backside. For a moment or two, the goat looked up at him in silence, of course, and then, like most animals do when they get wet, it shuddered to shake the water off. Instantly, water went flying everywhere! I swear, there wasn't a member of our party who didn't catch, at least, several droplets of it. The best thing was, since Agamemnon was standing out in front, his fancy clothes took the full brunt of the animal's discharge. As his clothes absorbed the water, Agamemnon looked down at them in disbelief, like he was surprised that the water would dare touch him without his express permission, then, when it became clear it actually had, he raised his head slightly and glared angrily down at the goat. Believe me, it was a comical sight to behold.

And then it got funnier.

Almost apologetically, the goat immediately walked over to Agamemnon and started licking the water off his clothes with its long pink tongue.

"He really likes you," the priest said to Agamemnon, then, bending down to the goat, he scratched its ugly forehead, all affectionate like, and said, "You like King Agamemnon don't you girl? Yes you do. She loves her new friend. Yes she does."

Shows you just how perceptive that stupid goat really was, doesn't it?

Anyway, I had to bite my lip to keep from laughing at the scene. The others cringed and moved closer together as if to shield themselves against an impending explosion.

But instead of blowing his top, Agamemnon pushed the goat away impatiently and said, "Can we please get on with it? I don't have all day. I have a kingdom to run, you know."

And folks to kill and maim, thinks I.

With that, the priest immediately straightened up and nervously muttered, "Oh, yes, Your Majesty, yes, sure, of course, I'm sorry."

Then he turned to the maidens and signaled them to take Agamemnon away as fast as possible.

The maidens didn't say anything; they simply motioned us to follow them, which we did. As we walked towards the Oracle's chamber, the goat bleated loudly. The effect was as if the animal was sad to see Agamemnon go and how I kept from exploding with laughter is beyond me. The goat was still bleating when we entered the chamber's side anteroom and took our seats, then it finally stopped, no doubt because the priest had taken it away for safety's sake. For several moments afterwards, we sat there in expectant silence. Then a maiden with big tits suddenly entered the room and asked which one of us needed to be purified of murder. Of course, she was talking about me, but, the funny thing is, every man jack in the room stood up! I looked over at my companions in amazement and wondered what kind of psychopaths I had gotten myself involved with. The maiden appeared just as amazed as I was, that is, until another maiden with little tits whispered something in her ear. Looking around the room once again, Big Tits said, "Will Prince Alexander of Troy please come with us?" With that, I nudged my way through the crowd and followed the maidens out of the antechamber. I was then led down a short corridor and into a small side room.

Inside, I was surrounded in that room by twelve vestal virgins. I was counting my lucky stars when Big Tits suddenly asked me to take off my clothes.

"What?" I quickly said, thinking, maybe, I had misheard.

"Please take off your clothes so we can perform the ceremony," she replied.

So I did.

And, what's better, so did she.

She stood there naked before me, big hooters and all.

And, wouldn't you know it, I immediately got an erection leering down at 'em!

I'm not kidding, I actually did!

And, believe me, there wasn't a maiden in the room whose eyes weren't focused on Mr. Happy. Still, all I can say is, they must have been firmly committed to their religious vows because not one of them moved a muscle in my direction, except, unfortunately, the naked maiden, who suddenly, and without any warning, picked up a large bucket from the floor and poured its contents all over me.

I instinctively closed my eyes as she did and felt the warm liquid flow down my body. When I opened my eyes again and looked to see what it was she poured all over me, I can't tell you how shocked I became.

It was blood! Dark red, half congealed, fucking, stinking blood!

Whose, or what, I didn't know.

All I knew was, Mr. Happy had disappeared and I was standing in a room full of frigid women, one, of which, was naked and splattered with fucking blood! What kind of fucked-up religious ceremony is this, thinks I? Before I could ask, the naked bitch — she had suddenly gained that status with me — reaches down again, picks up another bucket and pours that one on me too!

Now, if the maidens were expecting me to shudder like that damned goat, they were in for a big disappointment. I had reached my breaking point.

Standing with my eyes firmly closed, I yelled, "Goddamnit! That's fucking enough! This is the Twelfth fucking Century, there has got to be a better way! I'll pay money, say prayers, wear ash cloth, light a candle, anything, just don't dump anymore blood on me!"

"That one was water," the naked bitch answered curtly. "We have to wash the blood off, it's the final part of the ceremony."

I glanced down quickly to see that she had indeed poured water all over me.

"Oh," I relied in a calmer voice. "Well, in that case, keep going." I mean, for the first time since the ceremony began, we seemed to be of the same mind.

Reaching down again, she picked up another bucket full of water and poured it on me. She repeated this process over and over again until I was completely clean. I can't say it was the best bath I ever had, but I can say it was certainly the strangest. When it was over, the naked maiden grabbed one more bucket of water and I watched intently as she washed herself off with it, big titties and all. I, being a gentleman, offered to lend her a hand, but she flatly declined. When she was done, we were both handed towels to dry off with, and once again, I offered to assist her but she shook her head no. Like I said before, I never could understand religious folk.

When we were dressed again, Big Tits looked at me and said, "Now you are absolved of your crime."

Honestly, I have to admit, I didn't feel absolved. As a matter of fact, I felt just as guilty about Antheus' death then, as I do now. I guess it's just as well though. He was a good man and didn't deserve to die that way, accident or not. And no religious ceremony can ever wash that away. Anyway, the important thing was that I had been publicly absolved of his death and so, from that point of view, I guess the ceremony was worth it. Other than that, the whole thing was a stupid waste of time, water and blood.

When I rejoined the others in the anteroom, they were still sitting there in silence. Agamemnon, who wasn't accustomed to waiting on anyone or anything, looked like he was about to explode. Not wanting to set him off, I didn't say anything when I sat back down among them. I did, however, give Menelaus a quick nod, which he understood and returned. For a while, there wasn't a sound in the room, except for the constant tapping of Agamemnon's foot, which, believe me, was far scarier than it was annoying. Finally, Agamemnon couldn't take it any longer. He stood up abruptly, looked at the priest, placed a hand on his sword and roared, "I must set sail to Ithaca before night fall and so, I demand to see the Oracle at once. You've kept me waiting long enough!"

Now, as everyone can tell you, making Agamemnon wait isn't a real healthy thing to do. Just ask Iphigenia — that is, you could, if she was still alive, of course. Agamemnon sacrificed her ten years ago because he grew impatient for his navy to sail to Troy and so, if he would do that to his own daughter, or, I guess I should say, niece, it's not hard to imagine what he would do to that poor priest.

The priest must have sensed what kind of peril he was in because the fellow immediately shrieked and disappeared behind the curtain that separated the anteroom from the Oracle's inner sanctum. Moments later, he returned and, in a nervous voice, said, "I apologize for the long wait, Great King, but the Oracle has been in deep consultation with our Holy Mother Gaia. She will see you, King Menelaus and Prince Alexander now."

For a second, Agamemnon looked surprised, then annoyed, and said, "Why does the Oracle want these two to accompany me?"

I have to admit, I was as surprised as he was that the Oracle wanted to see me too. So was Menelaus. He glanced over at me with raised eyebrows, and I shrugged my shoulders at him to signal I didn't understand either.

The priest fidgeted around nervously for a moment or two — no doubt, he was formulating his reply carefully — and finally said, "Dread King, whose wisdom is boundless, who honors this humble temple with his greatness, the prophesies the Oracle is about to receive concerns the three of you."

Agamemnon flashed the priest a suspicious look and then he turned to me and said, "Do you know anything about this?"

Unable to find the courage to say anything, I meekly shook my head no. Menelaus quickly did the same thing.

Turning back to the priest, Agamemnon sighed impatiently and said, "Okay, then, let's get this crap over with."

My sentiments exactly, thinks I. The sooner I was out of Agamemnon's company, the better.

Without further delay, the curtain was pulled aside to allow us entrance to the Oracle's sanctum. Surprisingly enough, it was a small room actually, not more than four cubits wide and four cubits long. The place was also crowded with all sorts of objects. There was the Navel, of course, which I already told you about, and a statue of Gaia, perfect boobs and all. Next to it, stood a bronze tripod, where the Oracle sat, and to the right of that, the Sacred Laurel grew, it was a scrawny bush that the Greeks thought was, well, sacred. But most peculiar of all, the sanctum had a rocky, earthen floor, across which, a deep crack ran. The Oracle's tripod was situated right over the gash and, from the fissure, there rose a mysterious, sweet smelling vapor. I smelled it the second I stepped foot in the place and I swear, after a couple of whiffs, I felt strangely lightheaded.

The curtain was quickly drawn behind us, so the others couldn't see, and almost immediately after that, the Oracle entered the room.

And you're not gonna believe who she was!

She was the same young girl I had bumped into earlier!

Goes to show you that, sometimes, you never know whose ass you're about to grab. Anyway, she walked into the room wearing a long, white robe just like maidens outside were dressed in and, without a word to anyone, took a seat on top of the tripod. When she was situated, the priest stepped forward and placed a sprig of laurel in her right hand and a small dish of water in her left. Beats me why.

Then it was show time.

And, brother, let me tell you, what a show it was!

For perhaps ten minutes or so, she sat on top of that tripod with her bare feet dangling off of the floor, her body slumped slight over and her eyes gazing down into the little dish. Then, she started swaying back and forth — I figured it was because of the vapors — and just when it seemed she would fall to the floor, her chest suddenly heaved heavily, as if some invisible force had just penetrated her body, and she started to moan loudly.

"Ooooooooh, ahhhhhhhh…yes…yes…yes, oh, god, yes!" she moaned over and over again, while wriggling her bottom around that lucky tripod like a lap dancer after a huge tip.

Okay, okay, I know what you're thinking here: Paris, you sick pervert, you're making that up. And perhaps you're right. It never did take much for my over-sexed imagination to kick in. So, maybe she didn't wriggle around quite that much or moan exactly like that. But, she did moan loudly, and squirm around on that tripod and, I swear, it was all enough to make me want to start humping Gaia's statue right then and there. But, thankfully, almost mercifully, before I could start molesting the nearby artwork, her exertions suddenly came to a stop. Her body jerked violently as if the same invisible force that had initially seized it had just released it and, for a moment or two afterwards, she seemed spent. She just sat there silently with her head down.

In the silence that followed, Menelaus looked over at me as if to say: can you believe that shit? I, of course, couldn't, and shook my head at him in wonder.

And that's exactly when the Oracle lifted her head, looked straight at Agamemnon and said, "The best men of the army must quarrel and then evil will befall your enemy."

God knows what she meant by that but I made a quick mental note not to become Agamemnon's enemy. A lot of good that did! Anyway, Agamemnon seemed satisfied by the Oracle's answer, so, without further ado, he tossed the priest a bag of coins and stormed out of the room. Menelaus quickly followed him. I, however, remained behind. That's because I suddenly remembered the priest had said the Oracle was expecting to receive more than one prophecy and so, I decided to wait for the next revelation.

I stood staring at her silently, noting that her face was flush and her breathing was slow and heavy. My goodness, thinks I, I wished I would have squeezed your ass when I had the chance cause you're a lustful little wench, aren't you?

Now, I swear, what happened next is completely true.

I'm not making it up.

It really happened just like I'm about to tell you.

Believe it or not, the Oracle suddenly sat bolt upright on the tripod, her face twisted with fury, and shouted, "Don't be so disrespectful! How dare you insult me like that! How dare you insult our holy mother like that! Especially in her holy sanctuary! I would never let you squeeze my ass!"

Okay, raise your hand if you've ever had an Oracle read your mind.

Me neither.

I was so shocked that my legs buckled, and I sat down heavily on the holy Naval.

"Get off of that!" she yelled.

I immediately jumped to my feet and stumbled away from the object with only one thought in my head: I'm sorry.

"You bet you are, mister!" she screamed. "And you should be. And you will be. And remember this: When the Greeks build a horse, the Palladium will no longer preserve Troy and the city will perish in flames. Now get out of here! Get out!"

I didn't have to be told a third time. Terrified, I turned around and ran blindly into the curtain, pulling it down off its rings and causing it to fall on top of me. I ran the rest of the way through the temple wrestling with the damned thing. I didn't get free of it until I was outside of the place, and I didn't stop running until I reached the outskirts of Cirrha. I even passed Agamemnon and Menelaus along the way.

"Alexander, stop! Why are you running?" Menelaus yelled as I went careening by.

"I can't stop! I can't think!" I screamed back, "She will hear me! She can hear everything! She's in my head! She's in my heaaaad!"

And that's how I ended my journey to Pytho.

The Oracle rattled me, I can tell you. I guess I deserved it though. I should have been more respectful. And maybe if I would have, she'd explained what the prophecy meant. I still don't have a clue. Oh, I know about the Palladium and all. It's a chunk of wood that fell from heaven one day and, the belief is, as long as it's preserved, Troy is safe. It's out there right now, planted in the center of the citadel. What I don't know is what she meant by the Greeks building a horse. I just can't figure that one out. How can anyone build a fucking horse? Beats me. Anyway, I'm glad Agamemnon and Menelaus didn't stick around to hear it because the bastards would be out there right now, trying to do the trick.

I was so exhausted from the run that I just collapsed on the ship's deck and I didn't stir again until it was well out at sea. Then I gulped down so much wine that I eventually forgot all about the Oracle and the holy scare she had given me. I stayed in that drunken state for the rest of the voyage to Sparta, so I can't tell you much about it. Maybe that's for the best because I do faintly recall a great storm at sea and folks running around me in a terrified state. Luckily, I was much too drunk to care and might have even found the whole experience a bit comical. Goes to show you that cowardice and booze can combine to be a great advantage at times. Thank goodness for that.

Drunk or sober, the trip from Pytho down to Sparta is about seventy leagues by sea, I think, and when it's over, you'll find yourself standing on the ship's deck gazing at an idyllic valley bordered on both sides by two parallel mountain chains. The plain is dotted with numerous thatched-roof stone houses, all of which are surrounded with cultivated fields of olives, grapevines, grain and citrus trees. If you look close enough, you can see the local populace working in them quietly and, if you look really, really close, which I did, you can see that the female half is well worth the trip. You see, Sparta, just as Menelaus said it was, is a land full of beautiful women. Little wonder then, that I couldn't wait to disembark and conduct a closer inspection of the place.

We dropped anchor in the tiny port of Gythion, which is well below the major Spartan port of Helos, because one of Menelaus' palaces was located there. He and Helen also had two other palaces, one in Amyklai and on some hill called Therapne. I never got to visit those two but I was told by Menelaus that they weren't a patch compared to his palace near Gythion. And it was easy to see why. Located on an outcropping of rock that overlooked the port, it was a grand affair that could be called more of a strong hold than a palace. The place had a great, stone citadel encircled by a single wall that was about thirty feet high. To get inside, you had to walk through a narrow entrance that was guarded by a bastion on the right hand. There were lions carved in the limestone over the gateway, which Menelaus said represented his family's crest. Once inside its wooden gates, you walked up a large stone ramp to the citadel. That's where the royal apartments, the treasury, a great meeting hall and the throne room were located. Except for Troy, I've never spent a night in a safer place.

We landed around sundown and, even though it was late in the day, the fuss and noise the people of Gythion made welcoming their King home was tremendous. I have to say Menelaus was certainly a popular ruler. People positively mobbed us on our way up to the palace. As we made our way through the throng, I was a little surprised to see that the people were healthy and happy, given that there was a plague in the land and all.

"The plague's further up north, near Amyklai, and east, near Helos," Menelaus explained after I asked him about it.

And that's the other reason we put in at Gythion. It was healthier.

Inside the citadel, we were met by several of Menelaus' councilors, who gave him a brief update on the kingdom's situation. The plague, they said, hadn't advanced any further and seemed in decline. They attributed it to Menelaus' trip to Troy and thanked him for it. Menelaus looked over at me as they did and winked. I had to clinch my jaw to keep from laughing. When they were done with their little report, Menelaus asked for Helen and their daughter.

"Hesimone is asleep in her room, your highness," one of them answered.

"And our queen is in the temple with her foals," another one chimed in.

Of course, I had no idea what the word foals meant. It was Greek to me — no pun intended — but, from the big smile that suddenly appeared on Menelaus' face, I could see that it meant something pretty exciting.

Grabbing me by the arm, he laughed and said, "Follow me, dude. I'm gonna show you something I promise you're never gonna forget."

And I haven't.

Picture this: a small, round marble, temple covered in vines, lit brilliantly by a large central fire, around which, a dozen naked young females, their skins gleaming with olive oil, some with flowers in their hair, dance around in a religious frenzy, and you'll imagine exactly what I saw.

Now, I've seen women do some strange things in my life — fighting Amazons, a mind reading Oracle and competing goddesses — but the sight of those naked girls, dancing wildly around that fire, certainly ranks right up there as one of the best. And I don't have to tell you how horny the spectacle made me. After about twenty minutes, I had seen enough. Well, I thought, if Menelaus thinks I'm gonna stand up on this wall much longer studying the religious customs of the locals, he's dead wrong.

So I slipped a hand under my kilt and started priming the pump.

After a minute or two, Mr. Happy was...well...fully happy, and I said, "Come on, Menelaus, let's go down there."

He laughed, grabbed my free arm and said, "Hold on, wild man, we can't. They're gonna be at it all night long, it's part of the ceremony, so we can't interrupt, but do you see one you like? I'll fix you up with her tomorrow. Go ahead, dude, pick one."

Disappointed, but still eager, I studied them closely for several moments and finally said, "Yeah, I want that one."

"Which one?" Menelaus asked.

"That one with the blonde hair," I answered, pointing a finger in her direction. "I want her bad."

He laughed again, slapped me on the back and said, "You can't have that one."

"Why not?" I asked.

"Because that one's my wife Helen," he answered.

Well, that certainly took the wind out of Mr. Happy's sails!

For a second, I was surprised, and then embarrassed that I had lusted after my best friend's wife. "Oh, I'm sorry," I said awkwardly, and then, just to change the subject, I bombarded him with a bunch of questions, which he patiently answered one by one. He told me that we were witnessing a rite of passage. The girls, he explained, were dancing their way from childhood to maturity. They started as innocent virgins at sundown, he said, who, by dawn, will be transformed into mature women ready for sex and marriage.

"See all those clothes over there?" he said, pointing.

I looked to the spot near the temple he indicated and saw two different stacks of clothes.

"One stack is the children clothes they wore to the ceremony," he explained, "and the other one's the woman clothes they will put on in the morning after it is over."

"And so the girls are the foals your councilors mentioned?" I asked, nodding my head back towards the temple.

"Yeah, they're called that because they haven't submitted to the yoke of marriage yet," he said.

"And your wife?" I asked.

"Well," he said, with a proud grin, "she's their presiding spirit. She's showing them how to call forth their sexuality."

And that's something, I'm telling you, Helen knew only too well how to do.

She twirled around the temple, her shapely, well-oiled body gleaming in the fire's light. For a while, she slapped out a beat on her bare hips, and then she stopped before the fire and seductively drew her fingers up her glistening thighs and across her stomach, then to her breasts, which she lifted and fondled. Then she fell to her knees before the glowing hearth, arms and thighs spread wide open, shaking her boobs wildly at the dancing flames while chanting something that sounded like, "Lead me to the contest where I will surely toss my blond hair."

Believe me, at that point, it took all my strength not to jump down off that wall and grant Helen her wish. Anyway, from that moment on, I guess you could say I had the hots for her. Can you blame me? I mean, who wouldn't feel that way for a woman with that kind of talent? But, just so you know, even though I felt that way for her, I had far too much respect for Menelaus to do anything about it. He was my best buddy and so, his woman was definitely off limits to me. It's an unwritten rule that pals have. However, that didn't mean I couldn't ogle her indecently.

I whistled loudly and proclaimed, "Wow, Menelaus, you're one lucky dude. Your wife's really hot."

"Ain't she though?" he responded proudly. Then he went on to tell me about how he had won her hand in a contest between the most powerful kings in Greece. And it was easy to see why he was so proud of his achievement. He had beaten a virtual who's who list of Greek heroes for Helen's hand; Odysseus, Diomedes, Menestheus, Aias, Eumelus, Philoctetes, Ajax and Teucer.

"I beat them all," he bragged, "including my brother, and afterwards, Helen's father, King Tyndareus, chose me to marry his daughter. Then the old coot made everyone swear an oath to abide by his choice and to defend me and come to my aid with men and ships should anyone steal Helen or carry her off."

"Do you think any of those guys would really do that, I mean, kidnap her?" I asked.

"No, not really, dude. It'd be way too risky and stupid. My brother would crush them like bugs."

Then, he paused for a moment to reflect on something and finally said, "But with Helen, you never know what's gonna happen."

And that's when he told me the story about how Helen was kidnapped by King Theseus when she was young and how afterwards, she had turned back up in Sparta pregnant.

While Menelaus was talking, I glanced back down at Helen, who was still on her knees before the fire, and I thought, there's a warning in all this, Paris ole' boy. But, before I could figure it out, Menelaus grabbed me by the arm again and said, "Come on, bro, we should go. No use standing up here all night swinging our dicks. Tomorrow evening, there'll be a big feast to celebrate the girl's transformation. You can make your pick then."

"Can I pick three?" I asked keenly.

"You betcha!" Menelaus answered. "More than that if you want."

It's not hard to guess how much sleep I got that night. I just sorta zoned out, giving my mind free rein to imagine all the fun things I was going to do with Helen's latest graduating class of foals. Believe me, it was gonna be great. It was gonna be better than great. It was gonna be fucking awesome. And as I lay there smiling and sporting a record hard-on, I think I fell asleep and started dreaming because Aphrodite suddenly appeared next to my bed and announced the time had come for me to receive my reward. Given my state of mind, it's no surprise that I immediately assumed she was there to finally screw my brains out.

"Perfect timing," I said, pulling the covers away to reveal my erection. "As you can see, I'm all ready for you."

She appeared astonished and then, all of a sudden like, a thick mist rose up around me and I lay there for several moments, coughing and flapping my arms about wildly in an attempt to drive it away. When the mist was finally gone, Aphrodite was nowhere to be seen. It was pretty clear she didn't give a shit about my boner. I was upset by this, as you can imagine, and got ugly.

"You teasing bitch!" I yelled out to her in anger. "I should have chosen Hera instead!"

I can't tell you how long it was after that before I went to sleep for good, but somehow I did, and when I awoke the next morning, I found that I still had an erection and, what's better, there was a maid standing by my bed admiring it. She wasn't especially attractive, but like I said before, she was close at hand, and that's what counts most, so I lunged at her but the nimble little minx avoided my grasp and darted away. That's the other thing about Sparta women — they're incredibly athletic — so it's almost impossible to capture one if they don't want to get caught. I figured that out several minutes later, as I lay on the floor huffing and puffing, having chased the maid around and around the apartment without any success. Of course, after that, I was hornier than ever, and how I made it to the feast that night without bursting into flames beforehand is still a big mystery to me.

I sashayed into the banquet looking classy as shit — a leopard skin cloak, black felt slippers with exaggerated up-turned toes, a gray, tight fitting silk tunic and an equally tight, belted, black kilt with gold tassels — paused for a moment just inside the door, you know, just so folks could get a good look at the prized bull. Believe me, there wasn't a face in the joint, male or female, without an approving look on it, and after I made a quick mental note to thank my tailor, I walked over to where Menelaus and Helen were sitting and bowed deeply.

"Good evening, Your Majesties, I'm honored to be in your presence," I said graciously, but mostly for form's sake.

Menelaus smiled broadly and said, "Rise Prince Alexander of Troy, great friend, and allow me to introduce my queen."

Now, I didn't think it possible, but Helen looked just as good dressed as she did naked. She was wearing a long, white, flowing woolen gown that shimmered brilliantly from the oil it had been treated with and was low cut enough to give any wondering eye a stimulating view of her upper breasts; her bare arms were decorated with winding bands of gold, her beautiful face was framed by long, curly blond hair that fell to the small of her back, she smelled of scented perfume — iris, I think — and her alluring blue eyes were lined with kohl. An arousing sight, I assure you, especially to someone as randy as I was.

Offering me her hand, Helen said, "Welcome to Sparta, Prince Alexander. We are honored to have you as a guest."

Taking her hand in mine, I kissed the back of it gently and thanked her for their hospitality.

And, do you know, she squeezed my hand when I did!

Now, I'm not just talking about an inadvertent squeeze, or even a polite little one. I'm talking about one of those squeezes that unmistakably says: there's more where this comes from, big boy. You know the kind.

Of course, it sent happy thoughts rolling down my spine and, for a second, I considered returning the favor but then, I quickly reminded myself Helen was my best friend's girl, and so, I decided against it. Releasing her hand respectfully, I gave her a polite little bow and turned to Menelaus.

"Sit here, Alexander," Menelaus said, directing me to sit in a chair between them.

"Yes, please," Helen eagerly chimed in while pulling the chair out for me.

So I sat down between them, and after I was settled, they took their seats too, only, as they did, Helen pushed hers right up against mine before plopping down in it. I swear, we were sitting so close together that our arms and legs were actually touching! And I don't have to tell you what that did to me physically. All I will say is, thank god the table was obstructing everybody's view of my lap! Anyway, I sat there as still as a stone, trying hard to control my blood pressure, and I would have succeeded too if Helen hadn't suddenly pushed her boobs into my arm.

"Are you comfortable, Alexander?" she asked.

"Yes…ah…yes, Your Majesty…ah…I am," I muttered while trying to ignore the pressure of her firm breasts and protruding nipples.

She smiled and laughed, no doubt at the sweat she was putting me in, and said, "Good, because I want you to enjoy yourself."

What could I do but grin back at her? The last thing I wanted was to cause trouble between her and me. All I really wanted to do was pick out three of the newly matured girls and give them a graduation present. But it didn't seem like I was going to be able to do that with Helen snuggled so close against me. How could I move away without insulting her? So I was stuck, with nothing left to do but smile like a fool and try to enjoy the meal. Wild boar and beer was on the menu, so I ordered both, but before any of it could come out, I felt a hand touch my knee. Helen's hand! It happened so quickly, I could hardly believe it and her touch instantly brought my dick back to attention right smart. I swear, it's a wonder Mr. Happy didn't poke a hole in the top of the table! Anyway, I let out a surprised squeal, which, luckily, no one heard but Helen, and tried to steady myself by remembering that she was my best friend's girl and host. For five minutes or so, I sat motionless, doing just that, while she played with my leg, until finally, I couldn't stand it any longer, and turned to Menelaus for help.

A lot of good that did!

The idiot was so busy stuffing meat in his mouth and guzzling drink that he was completely oblivious to the world around him.

"Don't worry about him," Helen suddenly whispered in my ear. "The only thing he loves more than his concubines, is his food and drink. He'll be at it for the next hour or so. Then he'll either go to bed or pass out where he sits."

She didn't have to tell me. Having lived with Menelaus for over a month, I knew all about his personal habits. While Menelaus could make love to a woman for hours, he couldn't eat a meal, not even the smallest, without having to take a nap immediately afterwards.

And so it went. While Helen was busy stroking my thigh, Menelaus was equally busy consuming large amounts of meat and wine. Only once did he turn his face to look in our direction. And when he did, he smiled approvingly and asked me to pass the salt. Go figure. But the most astonishing thing is that no one else in the room paid Helen and me the slightest heed either. They were all busy punishing the victuals like a pack of hungry animals! I swear, if you could have seen them, it would have reminded you of a barnyard during feeding time. No wonder my father thought the Greeks were a bunch of pigs!

I did gain a momentary reprieve though when the waiters finally arrived with our meal. Helen discreetly removed her hand while they served us and I probably should have used that opportunity to run for the door, because, immediately after they were gone, she slipped her hand under the table once again, only this time, it wasn't my knee she placed it on!

Okay, let me ask, have you ever tried to eat a meal while a woman played with your cock in public?

I'm telling you, it can't be done, not unless you're really, really hungry, which, unfortunately, I wasn't.

With each stroke of her hand, my eyes crossed more and more until I got double and triple vision, and my mouth began working like a beached catfish gasping for water, and my head started tilting further and further back, and my legs started twitching up and down all crazy like, and my mind went blank, and my toes curled into a tight little ball, and…well…the last thing I remember is my hands clawing desperately at the table top, and looking over at Helen, who smiled and said something that I couldn't hear because my ears were on fire.

And then, I fainted.

Ah, sweet, sweet, oblivion!

I woke up in my room a short time later. My first thoughts were that the whole thing had been a bad dream but my fancy clothes quickly convinced me it wasn't. Then my mind turned to Helen, and even though I hadn't heard what she had said before I passed out, I had seen her lips move, and I realized she had said something containing the word "later".

You know, as in, later tonight.

As in, I'm gonna sneak into your room later tonight.

As in, I'm gonna sneak into your room and fuck your brains out later tonight.

As in, I'm gonna sneak into your room and fuck your brains out later tonight and ruin your friendship with the only friend you have in the world!

Realizing the danger I was in, I bounded off the bed and began pushing furniture against the door. I didn't stop until I felt confident a herd of horny elephants couldn't push it open. Then I dropped to the floor and waited in silence.

Sure enough, a short time later, I heard tiny footsteps coming down the hallway. I listened to them breathlessly as they came to a stop in front of my door. Then the doorknob turned slightly and there was a little push, and another push, and another push, until finally, whoever it was doing the pushing realized the door was blocked and stopped.

Then there was a voice.

Helen's.

"Alexander, are you there?" she whispered.

I curled up into a tiny ball on the floor and chewed my nails.

"Alexander, please open the door," she said.

I wanted to, oh, god, how I wanted to, but I couldn't.

"Alexander, please," she begged.

I couldn't stand it.

"Go away," I whispered back.

"I can't," she said, "I need you to hold me. I need you to make love to me. Please, Alexander, please."

"Don't you see, I can't do that," I pleaded. "Your husband is my best friend. As a matter of fact, he's my only friend. Please don't do this to me."

Then, to my astonishment, she started to sob.

"You don't understand," she said through the tears, "he treats me like dirt. I'm nothing to him but a trophy. Do you know, he once made me take off my clothes in front of his buddies? Can you imagine how bad that made me feel? To be stripped and gloated over like a side of beef?" Her voice shook. "All I want is for someone to love me, if only for one night. Please, Alexander, open the door and take me in your arms."

I felt overwhelmed and was at a loss for words. I knew Menelaus was a pig but, damnit, so was I. And there's the rub. I mean, I couldn't condemn him for being a lout, since I was a one myself, and so I didn't have an excuse to open the door. I know that sounds a might stupid, but us pigs have our own set of piggy rules that we live by. Besides, how did I know she just wasn't using me to get back at him? Women are like that you know, and her next words seemed to confirm it.

"Do you know where he is at right now?" she continued. "He's in bed with his three whores. And I'm all alone."

Sounds like Menelaus, thinks I, the lucky bastard.

Then she laughed sarcastically and said, "Here I am, the most beautiful woman in the world, and I can't get laid."

It was a shame, of course, and a bit ironic, but it wasn't enough to make me start pulling furniture away from the door.

She sobbed some more, which broke my heart, and after her weeping seemed to subside into quick, little sniffs, I gathered my courage one last time and said, "I'm sorry, Helen, but I can't. I just can't."

She didn't answer right off and the silence that followed made me feel uneasy.

"Well," says she at length, "you will!" Then she called me a choice name and stormed away.

I listened to her footsteps fade and breathed a sigh of relief. I had done the right thing, I felt, and I was proud of myself for it. Menelaus didn't know it, and probably would never know it, but I had proved myself worthy of his friendship. And come tomorrow morning, I told myself, everything will have blown over and the two of us can get back to the business of chasing women again.

Of course, I should have known better, because, as always, when things seem to be finally going my way, fate rears its ugly head to screw everything up again.

This time, it was a fucking funeral.

Now, that might not be much by itself, and it ain't, but when your best friend is invited and you aren't, well, that can be a bit of a problem, especially when you're a guest in his home and his wife wants to screw the living shit out of you. Get my drift?

"You're kidding, right?" I immediately asked when Menelaus told me the next morning he was leaving for Crete to attend his grandfather's funeral.

"No, I'm not," Menelaus answered. "My grandfather Catreus died several days ago and I have to go to Crete to pay my respects."

"Okay," I said eagerly, "I'll pack my bag immediately."

After the previous night, leaving seemed like a good idea, the sooner the better too. I hastily began walking around the room collecting my things.

"Oh, I'm sorry, dude," Menelaus said, shaking his head, "but you can't come. I have to go alone."

"Why?" I asked, dropping an arm full of clothes to the floor.

Menelaus looked over his shoulder to see if we were alone and when he was sure we were, he said, "Well, because, after the funeral, I'm gonna hook up with a real hot Cretan princess."

Typical Menelaus!

"So," I said, "I'll keep my mouth shut." I picked the clothes up and started stuffing them into a bag.

Waving his hand to indicate I shouldn't continue packing, he said, "Alexander, listen to me. It's not that at all. You know I trust you, but, you see, she's married and so I have to be very discreet. I don't think she'll be in a giving mood if you are around. That's why you have to stay here."

I looked over at him and gaped. Of course, Menelaus had no idea what he was asking me to do, and I couldn't tell him, so there was only one thing left to do: leave like nobody's business.

I quickly resumed packing and said, "Well, I guess I should return to Troy then. No use hanging around here without you."

"That's nonsense!" Menelaus immediately retorted. "I'll only be gone a week at the most. And Helen will be here to keep you company."

Like I said, the dunderhead had no clue.

"And when I get back," he continued, all heart, "we'll party like it's eleven ninety-nine, I swear."

I had no doubt he was sincere and it was painful for me not to agree but, then again, I knew the dangers and he didn't, so I closed the bag shut and said, "Thanks, buddy, but I really should be going. I'm sorry."

Menelaus considered me for a moment with a hurt look on his face and then said, "You can't go."

"Why?" I asked, throwing the bag over my shoulder.

"Because I can't spare a member of my crew to help you get back to Troy," he explained. "I'll need every man I got to sail to Crete. It's not an easy voyage. And, without someone from my crew to help you, we both know your ship can't make its way back home."

Bad news, for sure, but, nevertheless, true.

"Shit! Shit! Shit!" I immediately exclaimed.

Okay, you see, what I haven't explained is, on the voyage over, Menelaus had provided my ship, which had followed us the whole way, with a pilot and a small crew of experienced seamen. That's because it was originally manned by Aeneas, Pandarus and thirty or so Trojan soldiers, none of whom knew the slightest thing about sailing the ocean. The plan was that they'd learn on the way but, soldiers being soldiers, they'd spent most of the time sleeping and drinking — much like their beloved Prince — and so, Menelaus was right, there was no way we could sail back to Troy on our own.

Bottom line: my ass was stuck in Sparta with Helen.

There was nothing to do but curse some more, which I did with a gusto. I dropped the bag to the floor and cursed my father for not providing me with an experienced crew. And then, as I accompanied Menelaus down to his ship, I cursed my crew for not learning how to sail. And then, as I watched the ship sail away, I cursed myself for going on the voyage in the first place. I wished I had gone back home to Oenone instead. And then, on the way back to the palace, I cursed Helen and the predicament she was putting me in. And then, all of a sudden, I quit cursing altogether. That's because, when I got back to my apartment, I discovered every piece of furniture had been taken out of it except for the room's large, immobile bed. I had nothing left to block the door with! Of course, it was a signal from Helen that our game had started, in earnest too, and it was plain she wouldn't stop until I surrendered to her will.

Now you know why I was so shocked earlier when Helen was spoutin' all that nonsense about her innocence and Menelaus' love. I think you'll agree that both are a bit of a stretch. You'll agree too that Helen's a strange piece of work. I swear, I never could figure out what was going on inside her head. And there's no telling what she's gonna tell everyone when I'm gone. My bet is that she'll tell folks I kidnapped her or raped her or something bad like that. Heck, as much as Helen is into hocus pocus, she might even tell people I deceived her by magically assuming the appearance of Menelaus. I'm not kidding; I wouldn't put it past her. But, no matter what she says, the truth is, before Menelaus' mast dipped below the horizon, her efforts to break my resistance were already well under way.

And, I'm ashamed to admit; it didn't take her very long to accomplish her goal either.

A single day as I recall.

But before you go condemning me and all, let me tell you how she did it first. I think you'll agree that I held out about as long as any normal man would have, and certainly a hell of a lot longer than a pervert like me ever would have. You'll also see that what followed afterwards wasn't entirely my fault either and so, let me resume.

After I stopped cussing, I wasn't sure what I was going to do next; I remember thinking, this is what I get for leaving the farm and prancing around like a prince. I had a hasty notion to grab my bag and head for the safety of my ship, which was still anchored peacefully out in the harbor, and hole up in it until Menelaus returned. I probably would have done it too if Electra, Helen's servant, hadn't suddenly walked into the room and beckoned me to follow her.

"Where are we going?" I asked warily.

"Her majesty requests your presence at the Heraia," she answered.

Okay, in case you don't know, the Heraia is a 'women-only' Olympiad dedicated to the goddess Hera. In it, the women of Sparta race, wrestle, throw the discus and javelin, and jump. While this sounds progressive and all, and it certainly is, there's only one catch: they do it completely nude. I'm talking not a stitch. And do you know what it's like to sit and watch a field-full of beauties doing all those things, especially the wrestling part? Well, all I can say is, it's a wonder I didn't go plumb crazy right then and there, which, I'm sure, was Helen's intention all along.

When I took a seat next to her in the royal pavilion, the games were already well underway and, after a quick survey of the contestants, I instantly knew I was a goner. There were naked women frolicking everywhere, hundreds and hundreds of them. It was a voyeur's dream come true, for sure.

And the way Helen looked didn't help matters either. God, but she was enticing! She sat there in a short ivory dress that left her legs bare almost up to the crotch; and what's better, or, from my perspective, much worse, the dress had a bodice that was made out of transparent silk, and I don't have to tell you what it revealed underneath. No wonder then that I found myself grinning at her like a hungry newborn infant. Helen, for her part, didn't seem to notice, or care. Her Royal Shrewdness just sat there, appearing all aloof and shit, as if I wasn't even there.

When our eyes finally met a short time later, she nodded at me coolly and said, "Oh, I see you're here, Prince Alexander, how nice."

Of course, I knew it was all just an act. I'm not that dumb. But even though I knew Helen was toying with me, it didn't do me any good, because, as you well know, I am morally weak, and the strain of watching all those naked women cavort around the place was just too much for me to handle. In no time at all, I was sitting in my seat, slobbering and twitching like a rabid dog.

Helen noticed my condition, smiled broadly at it, and said, "Are you okay, Prince Alexander? You look nervous. Is there anything I can do for you?"

There were about two dozen answers I could have given her to that, all of which would have gotten me laid in a heartbeat, but I decided not to play her game and say I was just fine and dandy. After that, I forced myself to sit still and smile steadily through the rest of the events. How long I sat there with that silly grin on my face, I don't know, because after a while, everything got messed up in my mind and I sorta went into a trance or shock or something weird like that. I'm telling you, a man can stare at naked women only so long before he loses his wits completely. It happened to me — big time. You see, during the trance, I had a vision of a bullfrog jumping from one lily pad to another, only, they weren't lily pads it was hopping on, they were boobs, hundreds and hundreds of floating boobs, and the whole time, Oenone was standing on the bank, yelling, "Get back here, you horny little toad!" Go figure. Anyway, I didn't snap out of it until a member of the stadium's cleanup crew nudged me.

I immediately looked around at the pavilion and discovered that it was completely empty. The field was deserted too. Needless to say, there wasn't a lily pad…er…titty to be seen anywhere.

"Where…where has everyone gone?" I muttered.

"Home," the cleanup guy answered. "The game's been over for hours."

"Oh," I said, trying my best to sound sane, "well then, yes, of course, good, I guess I should be going home too."

The guy rolled his eyes heavenward and resumed sweeping.

I was still shaking when I got back to my apartment, so much so, that my teeth rattled against the bottle of wine I quickly drained. After that, I jumped into bed and pulled the covers over my head, as I was pretty sure the worst was yet to come.

And I was right too, because shortly after that, Helen quietly entered my room holding a single candle, you know, just so I had enough light to see her naked body through the transparent lingerie she was wearing.

"Do you want me now?" she asked, lowering the candle so I could get a good look at her goodies.

Like I said before, when they shake it in your face, it's almost impossible to say no.

In a flash, I threw off the covers and bounded towards her.

Can you blame me? I mean, I had just spent the day staring at a cloud of naked women and, if that wasn't enough, I had been damned near raped by Helen at the previous night's dinner party, and before that, I had witnessed a bunch of naked chicks dancing around a fire and, on top of all that, Menelaus, the dumb bastard, had practically pushed me into his wife's arms. So, is it surprising that I was unable to control my lust any longer? I think not.

Helen was amazed though.

She shrieked as I took her into my arms and appeared to be surprised that I had surrendered so quickly.

"Don't look so surprised," says I, "I just wanted to make you work for it."

Of course, it was a bold face lie, said mainly for propriety sake. I mean, I had a bad reputation to protect and all.

She answered with a little cry of protest, which only served to bring out the worse in me, and I lifted her up and tossed her on the bed like a sack of grain. She landed like one too, and bounced around a bit afterwards, which, believe me, was a funny thing to watch. When she was finally settled, I decided it was time to get down to business and proceeded to rip her gown off with my teeth.

"Oh, god, yes, yes!" she screamed as I did, then, to my utter amazement, she pulled quickly away and yelled, "No, stop, stop, please stop!"

Now, I don't know what your experience with a woman is, but I wasn't used to a chick changing gears like that, especially one who seemed to be enjoying herself so much, little wonder then, I was so taken aback by her odd behavior that I actually stopped.

"Wait," she said, "not here."

"What?" I answered, unsure as to her meaning.

Looking around the room suspiciously, she whispered, "We can't do it here, somebody might see or hear us."

That's the problem with dating married women — they're always afraid somebody's gonna find out — and so, you have to be prepared to sneak around whenever you do anything with them. I, of course, already knew that, being an experienced adulterer and all, so Helen didn't have to explain matters any further.

"Where?" I quickly whispered back.

"I have a carriage standing by to take us to Kranai," she said.

"Kranai?" I asked.

"It's a tiny little island visible from Gythion, you probably saw it when you sailed into port," she answered.

The image of a rocky little island suddenly entered my mind and I nodded to her that I had.

"Good," she answered, "we can be alone there and not worry about anyone seeing us."

I was all for that, since I was as eager as she was to keep our relationship a secret. This helped make the act we put on during the carriage ride to the harbor very believable to anyone who witnessed it. We sat in opposite seats looking quite regal, as if we were going on an innocent tour of the countryside or something of that nature. It was all nonsense, to be sure, especially at that time of night, but we nevertheless pulled it off quite well I think. We only spoke once during the trip, as I recall, when Helen whispered over to me that our illicit affair was going to last for only one night. I agreed, believing the sooner we got it over with, the better it would be for everyone concerned.

The only fly in our ointment was the boat trip to Kranai. I'm sure the coachmen who watched us row away must have wondered what we were up to. I mean, it's not every night you see a queen and prince float off to god knows where. But, by then, we were both too horny to care. As a matter of fact, like I said before, Helen had her lips wrapped around my dick before the boat was more than a dozen cubits from the dock. And, friend, let me tell you, it's awfully hard to row a boat when a chick's doing something like that to you! No matter how hard I concentrated, I just couldn't keep that silly boat from doing a series of figure eights and loopy-loops, so, back and forth I rowed, over and over again, until finally, during one particularly wide loop, the boat accidentally bumped into that damned island.

We quickly disembarked and made our way to the island's center, where oddly enough, there was a little temple of sorts dedicated to Aphrodite, and then the moon came out from behind the clouds, and I could see Helen's beauty as she spread a little blanket on the ground beside the temple. You may be sure, I was on her before the blanket's corners were properly straightened and soon, the air around us was filled with the passionate sounds of our lovemaking. Unlike my earlier attempt, I made love to her this time in a very deliberate fashion, which, given her hunger for sex, wasn't an easy thing to do, but I'm sure she enjoyed it because, shortly after the end of our first go round, she kissed me softly and begged me to do it to her again just like before. So I did, and after that too, and then, again and again, for hours, until she was finally too exhausted to continue.

Let me tell you, there's nothing more gratifying than satisfying the sexual needs of a spouse, especially if that spouse doesn't belong to you, and by the time our little island adventure was over, I'm proud to admit that Menelaus had one very contented wife. Six hours of sex with ole' Paris will do that for you! Anyway, Helen was certainly a cheerful little soul as we made our way back to the boat and so was I. Not only had I finally got Helen off my back, it looked like Menelaus would be none the wiser and our friendship would remain intact. Yep, I was a very happy fellow indeed. And that should have made me instantly leery because, like I said before, when things seem to be going my way; it's time to watch out.

So, anyway, there we were, happy as newlyweds, laughing about how silly we had been, when, all of a sudden, I saw something that

I'll never forget as long as I live. I saw my ship! It was floating just off shore, Aphrodite-painted sail and all, and, what's worse; Pandarus and a small group of Trojans were standing by my little rowboat. They appeared to be pretty excited about something, and for a moment, I wondered if they were drunk again, but, as we approached, I noticed smudges of blood on their clothes and instinctively knew that disaster was about to happen, or, worse, already had. Instantly, my heart raced and I probably would have run away if Helen hadn't been standing by my side.

"Hello, Paris," Pandarus said in a menacing voice that instantly made my scrotum shrivel.

Struggling to keep my nerve, I said, "Hello, Sergeant Pandarus... what...what brings you out this late at night?"

Pandarus chuckled as if I had said something funny and then he glanced towards the other men and said, "Show him, boys."

I watched in disbelief as the men began pulling diamond rings, gold chains, silver necklaces and an assortment of jewels from their pockets. God, what a haul they had!

"Hey!" Helen suddenly yelled as they did, "those are mine!"

"Were yours!" Pandarus shouted back. "We took them off your hands a few hours ago."

"You did what?" I cried.

"I said we raided the treasury a short time ago, killed a bunch of guards too," he answered. And then he went on, sounding pretty pleased with himself. "I got the idea after watching you paddle around the bay with Helen. I figured since you were kidnapping the Queen, we should go ahead and help ourselves to her treasury as well."

Now, of all the crazy things I ever heard in my life, I swear, that beat them all! And if Pandarus thought I was going to go along with it, well then, he was sadly mistaken. I mean, I might be a lecherous coward and shit, but I'm not a fucking kidnapper. And that gave me the courage I needed to pull rank.

"Men!" I shouted, all regal like, "I command you to return Her Majesty's treasury at once!"

For a long moment, the idiots just stood there gaping at me, then, to the man, they suddenly burst out laughing. It was, without a doubt, one of the most humiliating experiences of my life, especially since Helen was there to witness it and all.

As they laughed, Pandarus stepped towards me, his face worked up with anger, his eyes burning, and said, "Listen to me, Prince Pussy of Troy, out here you don't command shit. You see these men. They're Zeleians. And in Zeleia, I run things. So, from now on, you keep your fucking mouth shut and do as I say. Got that?"

Just in case you don't know, Zeleia is a narrow river valley located south of Mount Ida. It is named after Zeleia the Rock Chucker, who lived in a cave above the valley about a hundred years ago and got rich by not rolling rocks down on people's heads. You see, Zeleia charged passersby a toll to travel through the valley and if they didn't pay it, well then, he rolled rocks down on them until they finally did. That's the sort of neighborhood Pandarus came from and it gives you an idea about the kind of men I was dealing with there.

Anyway, before I could answer, Pandarus bent down close to me, breathed his ass breath in my face, and said, "Besides, you owe me. Because of your drunken antics back in Troy, I lost my position and wealth. You owe me!"

So that's what you're up to, thinks I, you're trying to get back what you lost. Well, it won't do you any good.

Taking a step backwards, I looked at him defiantly and said, "Just where do you think you're gonna spend your new found wealth at? Huh? Greece is out of the question and the minute you step foot in Troy, you'll be arrested and hung for sure."

"Oh, but, you're wrong," Pandarus quickly countered. "Tell him, Aeneas."

My cousin immediately stepped from behind the pack and said, "Pandarus is correct, Paris, you are wrong."

At first, I was surprised that Aeneas was in on the deal, since I credited him with having more brains than that, but I quickly checked myself and said, "How do you figure that?"

"Well, it's like this," he said, "when we get back home, we'll be welcomed as heroes because we will have avenged the wrong the Greeks did to your father when they kidnapped his sister. We are only doing our duty as any loyal Trojan should."

That's Aeneas for you. He was one of those hot-blooded, patriotic bastards who go around starting wars. It's always, god, king, country and buckets of blood with them. What a piece of fucking work!

I looked at him in amazement and said, "And you think stealing another kingdom's gold, especially one Troy is at peace with, is gonna make my father happy?"

He shook his head yes and said, "That and stealing its queen will."

You could have knocked me over with a feather!

The fools were planning to kidnap Helen too!

Utterly fucking amazing!

And that's when the warning I missed with Menelaus suddenly hit me. You remember, the warning I pondered during my conversation with Menelaus in which he told me about the pack he had with the other rulers concerning Helen. You know, the one that said if anyone ever kidnapped Helen, the others would band together to kick the shit out of her kidnapper. Yeah, that one.

Freaking out, I screamed, "Oh, for god's sakes! Do you know what you idiots are starting? You're starting a fucking war! The other kings of Greece have an agreement with Menelaus to come to his aid should any dunderhead be foolish enough to kidnap his wife. I'm warning you all, take Helen to Troy and every army in Greece will follow her there. Is that what you want? A fucking war! Huh?"

"Let them come," Aeneas said, shrugging his shoulders nonchalantly. "Troy's walls are strong enough to stop a dozen armies."

See what I mean about Aeneas? The idea of kidnapping Helen and starting a war was just peachy to him so there was no use arguing the lunacy of it any longer with him. Appalled, I turned to Helen for help. Maybe she had something up her sleeve that could stop the disaster from happening.

And that's precisely when the die was cast.

She looked at me, and I swear to god, said, "That's okay, Alexander, I want to go. I don't want to go back to Menelaus. You know how he treats me. I want to remain by your side and I don't care what happens because of it. Tonight was truly wonderful. A man hasn't made love to me like that since I was eleven years old. Please, Alexander, take me to Troy with you."

I looked at her as if she had suddenly lost her mind. "Are you nuts?" I asked. "You, more than anyone else, know the trouble this thing is gonna cause."

"I don't care," she answered, taking hold of my arm. "I want to stay with you."

"Quit it!" I shouted, pushing her hand away. "We had a deal. One night, remember?"

"But I love you now!" she shouted back.

"No, you don't, you crazy bitch!!" I yelled.

"Oh, stop it!" Pandarus suddenly jumped in. "We don't have time for this. We've got to shove off. You two lovebirds can work it out aboard ship."

Turning on him, I roared, "Oh, yeah? What do you know about shoving off? Or about sailing for that matter? Huh? Not a goddamned thing! Nor does anyone else aboard that hulk! Just how do you think we're going to get back to Troy?"

"Simple," he answered smugly. "We'll just keep heading east until we hit Anatolia. It's a big chunk of land, we can't miss it."

"Oh, okay, genius, and at night, or if it's cloudy, just how are you going to be able to tell east from west when we are in the middle of the goddamned ocean?" I snapped.

He hesitated for a second, no doubt because he had never considered the problem before, then his anger returned and he said, "Look, I warned you to keep your fucking mouth shut."

I was sick of his threats and their harebrained scheme.

"Oh, fuck you!" I howled. "Fuck all of you!"

I woke up a couple of hours later aboard ship with a sore jaw and an aching head. That's what you get when you curse a man the size of a small mountain and make him look like an idiot in front of his buddies. Still, I couldn't help being a little proud of myself that I had. For the first time in my misspent life, I had stood up for myself and, more importantly, I had stood up for a friend.

I don't know which is the bigger shock.

Chapter Six

"Oh, Alexander," Helen sighs heavily. "What am I going to do?"

"Do?" I ask. I mean, where does she want me to start – the war, us, Deiphobus, Priam, Menelaus, her daughter, Sparta? There's just so much.

She doesn't bother to answer. Instead, she abruptly turns away from the window and walks over to my bed. There's a desperate look on her face, like that on a drowning person, thrashing about, searching for something that might save them.

Leaning forward, she takes my hand in hers, and asks if I am in much pain. Her touch is warm and agreeable despite her nervousness.

"Yes," I say, "much."

With her other hand, she strokes my cheek and says, "Poor, darling, I have to go for now, but when I return, I'll bring you something that will take your pain away."

I nod thankfully, close my eyes and focus on her touch. I feel the heat from her perfectly shaped fingers melt into my skin and suddenly remember it was the first thing I felt when I came to after being knocked unconscious by Pandarus.

I awoke, aboard ship, with my head resting in her lap and, just like now, her soft hand was gently stroking my cheek. I've had very few awakenings that were as pleasant.

"Are you okay, darling?" Helen whispered in my ear.

Opening my eyes, I looked up at her beautiful face, and, for a long moment, I thought everything was safe and right, but then, I heard Pandarus' voice nearby and realized it wasn't. And that's when the gravity of the situation set in.

"No, no, I'm not." I answered glumly. "I've just lost my best friend."

Helen shook her head sadly in a make-believe attempt to comfort me and said, "You have me now."

It's not hard to guess how I felt about that! Believe me, I wouldn't have traded Menelaus' friendship for anything in the world, especially not for Helen's. But, of course, by then, it was too late. I was totally fucked.

Looking back on it all, I blame myself for what happened, and for starting all the trouble that followed but, as you can now see, there are others who are equally to blame. Pandarus and Aeneas certainly must claim a lion's share of it. Greed and patriotism are dangerous things, for sure, especially when they combine to start a fucking war. And Helen, for her part, is almost as guilty as they are. She could have put up more resistance, maybe even sacrificed her life, but she went willingly, even knowingly, didn't she? I still haven't been able to figure that one out. I mean, look at what all she gave up. And for what? Me? Ha! I don't have to tell you what a prize I am! Anyway, I guess you can blame Menelaus for her actions and for also leaving the two of us alone together. The dunderhead certainly should have known better. And you can blame the Greeks too, you know, for failing to return my aunt back to my father, or, for even kidnapping her in the first place. But, in the end, I guess the blame rests with me. I can see now how my sexual addiction set everything into motion. If I hadn't been so focused on sex, and acted responsibly instead, and did the right thing, even once, I'm pretty sure this war wouldn't have happened. And so, the Oracle was right — I am sorry for all the trouble I have caused. Very, very fucking sorry! And, speaking of the Oracle, don't try telling me that the whole thing was the will of the gods or shit like that. Cause it wasn't. Anyone who says that is just offering a weak explanation, if not a dumb excuse, for all the tragic events that have occurred. I mean, I've always thought it silly how we humans like to blame the gods or the stars for our guilt. How easy it is for my fellow sinners to explain away their crimes as the machinations of a dark demon, or unhappy god, or far-off twinkling star. Bullshit! Believe me, it was human stupidity and selfishness that started this war and nothing else. I know, because I was one of the selfish, stupid humans that started it.

Anyway, whatever the reason, I was adrift on a ship of fools and in trouble yet again. We were rowing our way east, I presumed. All I could hear was the sounds of the oars striking the water and Pandarus' voice shouting out orders to the crew.

"Ten degrees starboard!" he yelled.

Of course, no one, not even Pandarus himself, had the slightest clue what ten degrees starboard meant. It was just something Pandarus heard Menelaus' sailors yell when they were aboard our ship, and so, he was saying it just to impress everyone.

"Thirty degrees hard to port!" he yelled again. "Put your backs into it, boys!"

Whatever.

Aeneas stood on the stern of the ship, hands on the rudder, steering the ship through the darkness that surrounded us. I could see his black outline just before me.

"Where are we, Aeneas?" Pandarus suddenly walked up and asked. "Are we still heading in the right direction?"

"Fuck if I know," Aeneas answered glumly.

Pandarus exploded, "I thought you were using that big, bright star to guide us east!"

"I was but the damned thing's moved now!" Aeneas yelled back.

"Moved?" Pandarus croaked.

"Yeah, it moved," Aeneas said, pointing a finger up at the wondering star. "At first, it was just above the eastern horizon, but now it's almost directly overhead. See?"

Puzzled, the two of them stared up at the star for a moment. If I hadn't been groggy from prolonged unconsciousness, I'd have probably laughed at them and said something smart like, "I told you so!" Anyway, we were obviously lost and would, no doubt, remain that way while those two knuckleheads were in charge.

"Well," Pandarus says at last, "pick another star and guide on that one."

"Which one?" Aeneas immediately asked, looking around the night sky. "There are billions of them."

"I don't know!" Pandarus replied impatiently. "Just choose one you think is in the east."

"Okay," Aeneas agreed uncomfortably.

And that's exactly how our asses ended up off the coast of Sidon which, in case you don't know, is about two hundred leagues southeast of Troy. Two hundred fucking leagues! In my book, you can't get much more lost than that! All I can figure is, sometime during the first night, Aeneas picked a southern star to steer the ship on, and then, when the sun came up the next morning, he corrected our course and pointed the ship east again. Of course, by then, the damage was done and Aeneas unknowingly steered the ship straight towards Phoenicia.

Mind you, when we arrived off Sidon, I didn't care how lost we were, nor did anyone else. After several days of being at sea, we were staring at dry land again and that's all that mattered. I think it took us about five seconds to beach the ship and jump overboard and another five to reach the city's gates. Unfortunately, the citizens of the city and their king weren't as excited to see us, as we were to see them. Not even close. That's because word of Helen's kidnapping had already reached their ears and they wanted no part of us because of it. That's the thing about being an outlaw on the run — folks tend to be downright inhospitable to you.

"Go away!" King Phaedimus immediately demanded. "You're not welcome here."

"But I'm...Prince Alexander...of Troy," I mumbled while trying to catch my breath from the jog.

"I know who you are and what you have done," he answered angrily.

"You do?" I asked.

"I do," he replied.

"Everything?" I asked.

"Yes, everything," he answered.

"Good, then," I said, scratching my head, "perhaps you can explain it to me cause I'm still a bit confused about a couple of things. You see, I…"

"Great king," Aeneas abruptly interrupted in an effort to keep us on subject. "All we want to do is purchase some fresh supplies and hire a crew to help us get home."

"You'll get neither here," Phaedimus refused flatly.

"Why not?" I asked.

You can be sure he told me, at the top of his lungs too, saying that he wouldn't help us because Agamemnon, who was already on our trail with a thousand ships, wouldn't like it if he did and besides, he said, he wouldn't help us anyway, since I was little more than a brigand.

Well, that startled me, especially the thousand-ship part, and it certainly explained why the king was so disinclined to give us a hand. I mean, if I was in his shoes, I wouldn't want to risk facing Agamemnon's wrath either. I even told him that too, adding, all whiny like, that I really wasn't really a brigand; I was just a victim of circumstances, a poor victim who just wanted to get home, boo-hoo, boo-hoo, poor me, you know, that kind of shit. It didn't do any good though because, when I was done, Phaedimus just looked at me coldly and told us to beat it.

And that's when the real brigand stepped forward.

"A thousand ships, huh?" Pandarus said, all snotty like.

Phaedimus nodded his head yes.

"That means Agamemnon's army numbers about 100,000 men then," Pandarus continued.

The king nodded again.

"Well, there's only one problem with that," Pandarus said. "You see, all those men and ships that Agamemnon has are still hundreds of leagues away, while, on the other hand, my guys are standing right outside the gate there, so it seems to me if you are going to be worried about upsetting anyone, you probably should be worried about upsetting us."

So, there it was: cooperate or die, the Zeleian way. Phaedimus was in a tight spot for sure. One word from Pandarus and his reign was over. Now, in a situation like that, you'd think the king would have cooperated. I know I would have but not Phaedimus. Do you know, he just stood there looking pissed, then he cleared his throat and defiantly spat at Pandarus' feet! It was downright amazing! And it was also the last thing Phaedimus ever did because Pandarus killed him before his spit could melt into the ground. Long live, King Phaedimus! Poor dumb son of a bitch should have taken a bribe. Anyway, it all happened so fast it took my breath away — of course, the murder upset me and I said so.

"Are you fucking mad?" I yelled at Pandarus. "He's a goddamned king!"

"Well, he's a dead goddamned king now, ain't he?" Pandarus snapped back. "Besides, what else could I do? He wasn't going to help us. As a matter of fact, I'll bet the bastard was even planning to turn us over to Agamemnon for a reward."

And then, if that wasn't bad enough, the situation really got out of hand.

Within seconds of the king's death, Pandarus' soldiers came streaming past us, swords drawn, yelling blue bloody murder. I watched in amazement as they ran down the street slashing at everything that moved. I've gone crazy, thinks I; it's the stress I've been through. This can't be actually happening. But it was. Everywhere I looked, murderous Zeleians and terrified citizens were running pell-mell all over the place. I saw one of our soldiers kill a servant woman in cold blood and when I turned away in disgust, I saw another soldier loot an overturned vendor's cart, while his comrade was busy setting fire to a nearby building. It was all just plain nuts, of course, and dangerous too. So dangerous that Helen and I were eventually forced to take refuge in a nearby dress shop.

Once inside, Helen looked around at all the dresses and said, "Oh, Paris, aren't they beautiful?"

"Yeah," I said, glancing nervously outside the window. A Zeleian ran by whirling his sword wildly. Across the street, a family lay in a pool of their own blood.

"I think I'll try this one on," she said calmly.

I glanced at her, then out the window again and then back at her. "Are you crazy?" I asked. "Have you noticed what's going on out there?"

Without lifting her eyes from the dress, Helen said, "Oh, that. Yes, of course, I have, darling. But, honey please understand, I've seen it all before. Happens all the time in Greece and I'm pretty much used to it now. Men are such animals."

I looked at her for a long moment as if she was deranged and then I turned back towards the window. Well, she might be used to it but I damned sure ain't, thinks I. And then, as usual, when my life's in danger, I began searching for a means of escape. Eventually, my eyes fell on the dresses hanging around the shop and a wave of excitement immediately ran through me when I realized they could be a passport to freedom. All we had to do was carry an armful of them to the boat. Anyone who saw us doing it would think that we were simply transporting our loot. And then, once there, we could drop the dresses and disappear into the hills beyond. If we went right then, Pandarus wouldn't notice our absence for hours. That would give us enough time to get safely away. After that, all we had to do was wait for Agamemnon to arrive and then, when we revealed ourselves to him, I'd say I was sorry, tell him the truth, give him Helen and the whole thing would be forgiven. I know that sounds like a stretch now, but, at the time, it sure sounded like a good idea to me.

"Here," I said, handing Helen an arm full of dresses, "Take these and let's get out of here."

Helen looked at the dresses and curled her pretty little nose. "No," she said, "I don't like them."

Frustrated, I pulled the dresses into my chest and said, "Which ones do you like?"

"Well, baby," she said, "I kind of like that red one over there, and that blue one, and that pink one there, and that purple one, and…"

"Take them all!" I shouted impatiently.

"Really?" she said.

"Yes, really," I quickly answered.

"Oh, I don't know, honey, wouldn't that be stealing?" she said, frowning.

Can you believe her? I mean, innocent folks were being butchered outside and she was worried about stealing a few measly dresses! I said it before, and I'll say it again — I never could figure her out.

Reaching into my pocket, I grabbed a handful of golden talents and tossed them down on the floor.

"There," I said, "they're all paid for. Now grab the dresses and let's go."

"Can I get some shoes too?" she asked eagerly.

"Yes, yes, yes!" I impatiently screamed. "Anything! Just hurry up. Pile them on top of the clothes I'm holding."

When we finally emerged from the store, I was holding so many clothes in my arms that I could hardly see where I was going. Anyone who has spent the day shopping with their wife or girlfriend knows exactly what I'm talking about here. Anyway, the streets were still filled with wild Zeleians scampering to and fro, none of whom, fortunately, paid us the slightest heed as we passed. There was only way for us to go. The ship lay about a hundred cubits from the city's gate, which we walked through easy enough. From there, the going got a bit harder, as the sand shifted beneath our feet, causing us to drop a dress here and there. Of course, Helen insisted on stopping as each one fell and picking it up. I cursed every time she did. When we finally reached the ship, I glanced back and saw that we hadn't been followed. By god, we had made it! The moment had come to put as much distance between Pandarus and us as we possibly could. I quickly dropped the clothes I was carrying and directed Helen to do the same.

"No," she said.

She didn't understand, of course.

"Look, baby," I explained, "this is our chance to escape. We can hole up in those hills over there until Agamemnon arrives. Now, come on, let's get going before it's too late."

"No," she said again.

"No?" I asked incredulously. "Why not?"

"Because I want to go to Troy and marry you," she answered.

"Oh, for gods sakes, woman!" I shouted. And then I told her, right sharp, about all the death and destruction a union between us would cause. "Just look over there," I said, pointing towards the burning city, "do you want that to happen to Troy? Haven't we caused enough death and destruction already?"

"I don't care," she said. "I'm not going back to Menelaus."

What could I do? I couldn't make her come with me and I couldn't go alone, although, looking back on it now, I wish I would have tried. It certainly would have saved folks a whole lot of trouble. But, at that moment, I didn't have the guts for it and so, I gave up and did the only thing I could think of doing — I picked the clothes up and climbed aboard. For Helen, Sidon had been a very satisfying shopping adventure, while, for me, it proved to be a lost opportunity, although, I must admit, I was later able to give my mother a couple of the dresses I swiped there as a birthday present.

Anyway, a few hours later, Pandarus appeared on the beach, smiling contently; he and his rascals had almost stripped Sidon bare of its wealth. In addition to that, they also managed to capture a dozen or so beautiful maidens, you know, to make the voyage home a spot more pleasurable. It's no surprise then that the men were in a fine mood as they loaded their ill-gotten gains aboard the ship. Believe me, a Zeleian's downright giddy when he's holding a bagful of loot and an abducted wench; they danced around the deck wildly, holding their bags as closely as the women, until nightfall, and then, they manned the oars and pushed the boat off the beach. All in all, it had been a very bloody day, if not a very lucrative one for the pirates aboard, and although we had managed to replenish our supplies, we failed to hire, or even kidnap, a single experienced sailor. But that didn't seem to worry the crew much, especially after Pandarus announced we'd hug the coast all the way back to Troy. It seemed an easy enough thing to do, I guess, and we probably would have done it too, if we hadn't encountered a storm that very same night.

It hit us sometime around midnight with all the force of a whirlwind. The ship spun round and round in the water as the waves and wind pounded furiously against its hull; I went falling to the deck, with someone stepping on my hand. As I pulled it back in pain, I caught a glimpse of Pandarus, who was busy ordering the men to their oars in an effort to steady the ship. Dutifully, they grinded away with all their strength but most of the time, their oars were in the air, so there was little they could do to stop the ship from spinning wildly out of control. Eventually, the men were forced from their stations by the waves and there was nothing anyone could do except grab hold of something and hang on for dear life. I crawled over to where Helen was lying and tied a rope around the both of us. Then I tied the end of the rope to the ship's mast. After that, we held each other tight and watched in horror as the rest of the crew thrashed about. Two or three of them went spiraling overboard, they kicked and screamed as they went, and Helen began to cry. I, of course, had already given us up for dead. That's because nobody gives up hope faster than a coward does. So, I closed my eyes and buried my face between Helen's splendid breasts. I figured, since I was gonna die, I might as well go out with a big fat smile on my face. I remained like that until the storm finally subsided sometime around sunrise.

For much of the morning afterwards, we lay on the deck recovering our wits. Eventually, Pandarus rose and ordered the men to their stations.

"Which way?" Aeneas asked, manning the rudder.

For a long moment, the two of them studied the sky and the ocean around us. I untied the rope from around my waist, stood up and took a look too. The sea around us was calm again but there wasn't a shred of land to be seen in any direction. And, what's worse, we couldn't see the sun either. It was hidden behind the thick clouds overhead. We couldn't tell east from west any more than we could tell north from south. I won't bore you with a description of my emotions as this became clear, along with the realization that we were lost again — I simply sank back down on the deck in a funk. Our situation was totally hopeless, for sure, and then, believe it or not, it actually got worse.

"Do you see that bird?" Pandarus suddenly said, pointing.

"Yeah," Aeneas answered.

"Follow it," Pandarus directed.

"What?" Aeneas asked.

"Birds fly to land, don't they?" Pandarus reasoned.

"Yeah, I guess they do," Aeneas replied.

"Then follow that bird," Pandarus again directed. "It'll lead us to land."

Okay, now, here's a bit of sailing advice: if you're gonna follow a bird at sea, you'd better know what kind of bird it is you're following.

I know this because the bird Pandarus picked to follow was an Egyptian Grey Heron.

Key word: Egyptian.

And that's exactly where that damned bird led us! Fucking Egypt! It has to be, without a doubt, the stupidest blunders in maritime history. Bar none.

So, after three days of following that stupid bird, there we were, floating off Egypt's Nile Delta. The first thing that struck me about the place was its smell. It smelled like wet mud and stagnate water, which, I guess, is understandable since we were near one of the biggest swamps in the world. Only, we didn't know that at the time, of course.

"Where do you think we are at?" Aeneas asked.

"I dunno," Pandarus answered. "Twenty degrees starboard!"

"What?" Aeneas said.

"I said ten degrees starboard, heave ho, hoist the jib," Pandarus replied impatiently.

Of course, nobody knew what he was talking about, so Aeneas steered the ship a little further on down the coast until a sandy little beach was sighted. We all ran over to the railing to get a good look at it and, since everyone was in favor of sitting foot on dry land as quickly as possible, the decision was immediately made to land there.

The place we landed was called Salt-Pans, which pretty much sums up what it looked like: white sandy flats stretched in directions as far as the eye could see. I've never seen a more monotonous sight in my life. It was damnably hot there too. In almost no time at all, we were drenched in sweat, and so, we quickly stripped down to the lightest of clothing. For the men, that meant loincloths and swords, for the women, under-skirts and shawls. Satisfied that we were properly dressed and equipped, Pandarus decided we should head down the beach in search of civilization. He led the way, of course, while I walked behind the semi-naked ladies, you know, to keep an eye on their…I mean… our assets.

We must have hiked one or two hours, with only a few brief stops to cool off in the surf and drink some water, before we discovered a small path leading off the beach. Pandarus signaled we would follow it, which we did, in single file, and very soon, we found ourselves in another world. Great sand dunes rose up on either side of the track, penning us in like a big snow drifts. Suddenly, the heat became even more oppressive, so much so, that it made the air difficult to breathe. Soon, everyone was huffing and puffing uncomfortably as we trudged along. It's not hard to guess what this did to the cheerfulness of the journey, yet, the worse was still to come.

We were attacked by swarms of blood-sucking gnats!

It was like we were experiencing one of those plague of bugs that the priests conjure up every now and then to show how seriously pissed off their gods are. The air was positively alive with the hungry little bastards. We stumbled along that path slapping every which way at them, and if things weren't bad enough, we had to listen to Pandarus ponder the insect's presence as we did.

"We must be getting close to civilization since there are so many gnats," the idiot reasoned. "I'm sure there's a town or something up ahead. Maybe even a large city. Let's head towards that big swarm over there."

Now, what civilization has to do with the gnat population is still beyond me but Pandarus was positive the two were intimately connected, and so began one of the most arduous treks of my life. How long it lasted, I'm not sure, as I was busy swatting gnats the whole time, but it must have gone on for a while because eventually, our glorious leader started to despair.

"I guess we should head back to the beach," Pandarus reluctantly announced.

"I agree!" I quickly seconded.

I was sick and tired of that desert and those goddamned gnats. I think I had twenty bites on my face, thirty on my arms, and a thousand on my chest, back and legs. It felt like half of the world's population of gnats had just dined on my ass and the scary thing was, I didn't know if I had enough blood left for the other half.

So I started checking my blood pressure and as I was urging the others to do the same, a small boy suddenly came down the trail leading a goat by a rope. He was one of the skinniest kids I've ever seen, all skin and bones, and the goat wasn't in much better shape either. But their poor condition sure didn't affect their ability to run! They took one look at us, and in a blink of an eye, turned around and disappeared up the trail from whence they came.

"After him!" Pandarus immediately shouted.

Without another word, we stampeded along the trail, running as fast as we could to catch up with the boy and get away from those damned gnats. Since I was the fleetest, I soon found myself out ahead, that is, until I suddenly tripped over a rock and fell to the ground. The others bounded past me without a word, which kinda pissed me off, but when I rose to my feet again, I saw why: standing less than a hundred cubits away was one of the most beautiful temples I have ever seen. At first, I couldn't believe my eyes and just stood there silently with others, staring at the thing in total disbelief. I mean, it looked so out of place in that hot, sweaty, gnat-infested desert. As I remember, it was a huge stone building that consisted of thirty finely crafted pillars, all, at least, two cubits wide, it also had a high, vaulted ceiling and a polished marble floor. And, like the pavilions of Pytho, it was crammed full of statues and various works of art. But unlike Pytho, the artwork inside wasn't dedicated to a single god or gods. Amazing enough, they were dedicated to that jerk Hercules!

Go figure.

Apparently, that murderous son of a bitch had passed through there, no doubt, killing enough of the locals during his visit to inspire the survivors to erect a temple in his honor. Believe me, nobody, except maybe that bastard Achilles, could kill folks like Hercules could. He had temples all over the place because of it. Weird, isn't it?

Anyway, in sharp contrast, the temple was also surrounded by a series of shabby, mud huts, where the priests and their fleas lived. The boy lived there too, and so did his goat. I couldn't help but feel sorry for the whole lot — fleas included. The priests emerged from their hovels upon our arrival and seemed about as shocked to see us, as we were to see them. Apparently, they weren't used to folks visiting their temple, which isn't that much of a surprise, given its location and purpose. I mean, who would want to tramp through the desert to pay respect to a homicidal Greek maniac?

Nobody, you'd think.

And that's why this next part is so damned amazing.

You see, nobody would want to visit the place except for a bunch of slaves.

Of which, there were twelve in our party.

Remember those chicks from Sidon? You know, the females Pandarus and his soldiers kidnapped? Yeah, those slave girls. And, if we didn't know about Hercules' temple, they damned sure did, probably because they were from neighboring Phoenicia. And they also knew something else we didn't. They knew they could find sanctuary there. You see, in Egypt, if a slave manages to get to the temple and worship there, he or she receives a sacred mark that grants them freedom. After that, no one can make them do shit. They're totally free!

You can be sure that it took less than a half second for our female captives to run past us and start worshipping Hercules with all their might. Never before or since have I seen a more inspired group of worshippers! They beat the worshippers in Pytho all to Hades. And I don't have to tell you what the sight of all those beautiful, half naked females did to those poor, lonely priests. I swear, the horny bastards ran towards the prostrated women like wild men, elbowing and pushing each other aside. And when they got to where the women were worshipping, they started hollering and hopping around them all crazy like. And it was their caterwauling that attracted the attention of the local warden, a rather nasty looking fellow named Thonis. Don't ask me what he was doing in the area. Maybe he was counting gnats or something. I dunno. But, whatever the reason, he showed up shortly after the hubbub began. And so did his bodyguard, which consisted of about fifty well-armed soldiers in all, none of which looked the least bit happy about all the noise.

Now, in case you don't know, in Egypt, the warden's kinda like the local constable. He goes around the place keeping order and collecting taxes and he doesn't care how many folks he has to kill to do it either, the more the better to him, as it shows the Pharaoh how eager he is to do the job.

Little wonder then that the priests immediately stopped their celebrations and dropped to the ground when Thonis showed up. There wasn't a sound — no laughing, no crying, no clapping, no nothing. And let me tell you, when a bunch of horny guys suddenly get quiet, it can be downright frightening and I have to admit I started getting a bit nervous at this point.

"What's the meaning of all this noise?" Thonis demanded to know from the groveling priests.

One of them, probably the chief priest, rose to his knees and made a long winded statement about how he and his fellow priests were celebrating the initiation of a new group of suppliants into the wonders of the cult of Hercules and how Hercules, greatest of all humans, strong in mind and body, son of the great Zeus, blah, blah, blah, blah, blah…and just when I thought he'd rattle on about that dickweed forever, Thonis looked down at the women and said, "Are you the new converts?"

The priest immediately clammed up so the girls could answer.

"Yes, your honor," says a big titted beauty. She was one of those self-righteous females, you know, the kind that won't go to bed with you until the second date.

"And how did you come to this place?" Thonis asked.

She stood up, pointed an accusing finger over at us, and said, "Those men brought us here against our will, your honor, we are from Sidon."

Shutuuuuup, thinks I.

She didn't, of course.

"They are evil men, your honor," she continued. "They enslaved us after murdering our great king and pillaging our city. They killed many of our fellow citizens and forced us to do all sorts of naughty things aboard their ship."

Thonis and his soldiers glanced over at us with wary eyes and drew their swords.

I shook my head innocently and pointed at my guilty companions.

It didn't do me any good though.

"And, your honor, that man there is Prince Paris of Troy," the back stabbing bitch went on, "and the woman next to him is Queen Helen of Sparta. Paris kidnapped her too. He stole her away after being a welcomed guest in King Menelaus' house. He stole Menelaus' treasury too. Good King Menelaus invited the prince into his home and Paris repaid Menelaus' kindness by raping his queen and stealing his fortune."

Thonis and his soldiers gasped as if they were deeply shocked, and the chief priest made a comment about how utterly despicable my behavior was. His fellow priests immediately agreed, of course, and so did the women huddling amongst them.

The injustice of it left me so dumbfounded that the only thing I could do was gape back at them in horror. Can you blame me? Especially after all the lies and distortions I had just heard? And it's a wonder I've haven't gone completely crazy, as that's the kind of crap I've had to deal with ever since. But the really bad thing is, if I'm remembered for anything, it'll probably be for those falsehoods. Heartbreaking, ain't it? You bet it is.

Anyway, while I was standing there trying to gather my scattered wits, I heard Helen say, "Oh, Alexander, baby, I think you're in a lot of trouble." So, I knew better than to look over to her for help. I turned to Pandarus instead and was disappointed to see that he had a look on his face like he didn't know what to do, and so, I glanced over at Aeneas, who shrugged his shoulders and wished me luck, and that's when I realized I was totally on my own.

I was just about to start crying when Thonis suddenly walked over and said, "Is the woman's accusations true?"

Now, that's a damn tricky question coming from a man like Thonis. You see, bar Achilles, Thonis was the biggest man I've ever seen. He was well over six feet tall and built like Hercules himself. His muscular body was protected from the sun by a cloak made of lion's skins that covered him from neck to his fine leather sandals. He wore a white kilt about his midsection and was armed with a jewel-encrusted sword that hung from his waist by an ox hide belt. He had a black beard, fiery eyes, and an impatient manner that said he didn't put up with any bullshit.

I cleared my throat, took a deep breath and then, all nervous like, said, "Well, your honor, ah...no, they're not...well, kinda, they are...you see, it's very complicated...it's like this...Menelaus was my friend...ah...but he left...and...ah, Helen got horny...and, ah, I was horny too...so we, ah, took a rowboat to, ah, rocky island...then, ah, Pandarus stole the treasury...Aeneas said we'd be heroes...Helen wanted to be my wife...we left in my ship and, ah, kinda got lost...

king of Sidon killed…and I never made a woman do anything nasty in my life…except when she was drunk…and…I was drunk…and… ah…"

Realizing how stupid I sounded, I suddenly stopped, looked Thonis straight in the eyes and cried, "Please, mister, please don't kill me!"

Thonis studied me for a long moment, kinda like a doctor does a mental patient, and finally said, "You and your men will stay here until I can consult with our great Pharaoh on this matter."

I nodded my head eagerly, you know, to let him know I was willing to assist him in anyway, and then I listened closely, for the same reason, as he dictated a message to the Pharaoh. I even helped the writer with some of the spelling.

The message read: A stranger has arrived from Greece, and I suspect he has done a wicked deed from whence he has come. I suspect that he beguiled the wife of the man whose guest he was, he may have carried her away with him, and much treasury also. Compelled by stress of weather, he has now put in here. Are we to let him depart as he came, or seize what he has brought?

I also tried to get Thonis to say I appeared to be a really nice guy but he flatly refused.

After that, we were disarmed and herded into the temple, with Thonis' soldiers keeping a watchful eye on us from all sides, and there I sat, swatting gnats and sweating my ass off, and every now and then a maiden would walk by the temple and stick her tongue out at me. Of course, I was feeling very dejected, and my skin was sunburned something awful, but, at the very least, I was still alive. I also took solace in the fact that Thonis' message to the Pharaoh hadn't included a death sentence, just the confiscation of my property, which was okay with me. The Pharaoh could keep everything for all I cared — Helen, the captive maidens, Menelaus' treasury and the loot from Sidon. I hadn't wanted any of it to start out with.

You can be sure I told Pandarus that too. And since we were so closely guarded by Thonis' men, I felt safe enough to tell him that our miserable situation was also his fault. If he hadn't been so goddamned greedy, I said, none of this would have happened, and that every decision he had made during this journey was a bad one and from now on, he could count me out of his stupid schemes. Given half the chance, I said, I would cut a deal with the Pharaoh and be on my merry way.

That was a mistake, for sure, as my words only set Pandarus' mind to work on escaping. "Keep your eyes and ears open," he whispered to Aeneas, "we've got to figure a way out of here before Paris fucks things up for us."

Aeneas nodded and said, "Maybe at night, when most of the guards are asleep."

Then, Pandarus showed him a small knife he had managed to hide away in the folds of his loincloth and I could see visions of a suicidal escape attempt dancing through his pea brain.

That scared the shit out of me, of course, and I instantly regretted saying anything to him. Since there was no taking my words back, I withdrew from them, and from the rest of the men as well, and tried to remain as visible to the guards as possible so they could see that I was being a good little prisoner. If Pandarus and Aeneas wanted to get themselves killed, it wasn't going to be any of my business.

The only one who seemed to be enjoying our situation was Helen. She was being kept prisoner inside Thonis' tent. Now, another woman might have been frightened to find herself alone with a man like Thonis, but not Helen. That's because she knew men and how to use her beauty to manipulate them. Her rule of thumb has always been: if it's a male and in power, seduce the shit out of it. And that's exactly what the shameless hussy did with Thonis. If you could have seen them walking around the place arm in arm, chattering gleefully, you'd have thought they'd been sweethearts for years. God only knows what they did alone in the tent together at night but judging by how much Thonis kept yawning the next day, I'm pretty sure they weren't sitting around playing Senet, you know, that stupid strategy game Egyptians love to play. Anyway, good riddance, I was glad she was finally out of my hair and wouldn't be around anymore to thwart my plans like she had done in Sidon.

So, I spent the days that followed, milling around that stupid temple, smiling at the guards, pissing on Hercules' statue every time I had to pee, and counting down the hours until the messenger returned with the Pharaoh's response. At night, I slept with one eye open just in case Pandarus and Aeneas tried to escape — not because I was worried they would, but because I wanted to watch the two fools die. I shouldn't have bothered though, as there were always too many guards around us for them to attempt it. Pandarus and Aeneas were dumb but they weren't that dumb. Too bad about that!

Then one morning, about six days after we were taken captive, the messenger that had been dispatched suddenly reappeared and with him, several wagons as well. I craned my neck over the guards' heads to see what it all meant, and from the looks of things, gathered that something exciting was about to happen. Presently, Thonis appeared bearing the Pharaoh's response. He walked into the temple with Helen at his elbow like an obedient wife.

Opening a tiny scroll, Thonis read: Seize the man, be he who he may, that has dealt thus wickedly with his friend, and bring him before me, that I may hear what he will say for himself. Bring the women he is said to have abducted as well so that they may bear witness.

That's all it said.

Now, normally, I would have found a message like that to be somewhat troubling, if not downright scary, but since I felt confident my life still wasn't in any danger, I was eager to get the whole thing over with and so, I accepted it with a relieved little smile. What's more, I think I was so confident that things were finally going to go my way, I might have even signaled over to Pandarus and Aeneas that they were totally fucked now. I don't really recall for sure if I did this or not because, after Thonis finished reading the message, everything sorta went into fast motion. Soldiers and servants started running all around the place loading things into the wagons.

"Isn't it grand, Alexander?" Helen says to me as we climbed aboard one of them. "We're going to get to meet the Pharaoh. I wish I had one of those beautiful dresses you bought for me in Sidon to wear."

I immediately jumped back down to the ground and demanded to be allowed to ride in another wagon. The prospect of traveling to god-knows-where with that two-timing trollop was a little more than I could bear.

"Get back on board," said a soldier rather menacingly. "This is the VIP wagon."

Well, that counts for something, I reasoned, so I reluctantly climbed up next to Helen, and that's how I began my journey to Memphis — a trip I'm pretty sure no other Trojan has ever made, not even the foreign ministers of my father's court. That's because the Egyptian nobility tend to be a snobbish bunch. You see, they just don't think they're better than anyone else — they know it, mainly because they remind themselves of it on a daily basis. And they don't invite outside opinion on the subject either. That's why almost no one gets to go to Memphis. And that's also why I was designated a VIP. You see, only VIPs get invited to Memphis. Everybody else, foreign ministers included, gets routed to some backwater named Heliopolis.

The trip from Salt-Pans to Memphis is about seventy leagues, I suppose, and it's an easy enough journey since much of it goes along the banks of the Nile River. And, let me tell you, I've never seen an uglier river than the Nile. That's because it's so damned muddy and sluggish. I swear, it's so thick and slow, you'd think you could walk across it, and I was told when the wind is just right, you actually can. The Egyptians are downright proud of the Nile though, so much so, they even worship the nasty thing, no doubt because, if it wasn't there, Egypt would be a burned over desert where not even a snake would call home.

Speaking of homes, we encountered quite a few of them along the way. Most were mud fashioned jobs, similar to the ones the priests lived in at Salt-Pans. And just like the priests, the people who lived in them weren't exactly the cleanest or well-fed bunch I've ever seen.

Nor were they the most industrious either. Their idea of farming is to sit in the shade until the river raises enough to water the fields. When the flood is over, they run out to the muddy fields and scatter corn seeds haphazardly about. Then they release herds of pigs into them, you know, to trample the seeds down into the ooze and fertilize them. After that, they go back to their shade trees and wait for the harvest to begin. Little wonder the people are so damned poor. They do have some mighty fine looking pigs though.

And women too!

That's the best thing about Egypt — the women. In my expert opinion, Egyptian women are absolutely beautiful. Oh, they're not Spartan beautiful, or anything like that, but they can hold their own when compared to any other female group I've encountered. The biggest difference is that Egyptian chicks are suntanned and that, in my view, gives them a big edge over the fairer skinned. Egyptian babes get that way because they spend their days wearing nothing but a short little skirt around their hips. Really, they do! It's like they want you to stare at their boobs! And what's better, Egyptian women fuck like rabbits. I know this because the soldiers escorting us were always disappearing with one or two of them every time we stopped to rest. It's a real pity I wasn't able to partake in their hospitality because, believe me, if I hadn't been so closely guarded, I could have fornicated my way to Memphis. But, as it was, I was stuck with Helen, who spent the whole trip mindlessly yammering on and on. She only shut her mouth once, and that's when we passed the pyramids of Giza. Little wonder she did too. I don't know if you've seen 'em but, if you haven't, all I can say is that they are truly breathtaking. Built by some hard-ass named Cheops, I was told each one — there are three of them altogether — took over twenty years and about a kahbillion slaves to build. They stood, more or less, three hundred cubits wide and high, and were built out of polished stones, each, about ten cubits square, and fitted together so tight an ant couldn't squeeze its ass through. The joke is that they were built to bury the Pharaoh and his family in, which goes to show you, just how fucking vain Egypt's royals really are.

Anyway, the only good thing about leaving Giza is that you come to Memphis shortly thereafter. It's about seven leagues between the two I think. I don't remember much about Memphis except rows and rows of mud houses, stone statues and columns on every corner, and topless beauties walking around everywhere. I never got a good look at the place because it was straight to the palace dungeon with my ass, and a couple of days sweating in a hot cell afterwards, while I waited for the Pharaoh to see me.

Helen, of course, got to see the bastard right off. Not that I blame him. Mind you, in my opinion, a Pharaoh who passes up the opportunity to enjoy Helen's company doesn't deserve the title. I do blame her, however, for not trying to get me situated into better quarters. One without rats and a leaky piss bucket would have been just dandy. But, that's Helen for you. She never thought about anyone except herself. And so, I was forced to sit in that nasty cell while Helen and the Pharaoh got better acquainted. Only Zeus, and about three dozen palace servants, knows how well they did that.

As I've said, I was in that cell two days, then, on the third, just as I was settling down to a hardy breakfast of gruel, the door opened, and suddenly Thonis appeared and announced that the Pharaoh was ready to see me. I was a little surprised to see Thonis, as I had thought he was still back in Salt-Pans guarding my ship mates, but, apparently he wasn't, so I gave the gruel to my favorite rat, got up and silently followed the warden down a series of long hallways until we reached the Pharaoh's throne room.

The room was packed with officials, soldiers and whatnot, all of whom stared at us curiously as we walked across its polished marble floor towards the Pharaoh. He was seated at the far end, on a golden throne decorated with all manners of precious jewels. Advisors stood on either side of him; Helen was amongst them and so were the kidnapped maidens, but before I could get a good look at any, Thonis prodded me to bow, which I did, with all the gusto of a repentant man.

"Oh, great Pharaoh, life, health, strength be to you!" cries Thonis. "I bring before you a Trojan prince, so that you may learn from his own mouth why he has come to our shores."

"He doesn't look like a prince," says one of the royal ass-kissers. "Has his clothes been taken from him?"

I was still only wearing a loincloth.

"No, he appears as he arrived," Thonis replied.

"Is it the custom of the Trojans to visit foreign nations wearing nothing but their underwear?" asked another advisor.

Before Thonis could reply, another advisor exclaimed, "Foreigners are such barbarians!"

"Remember Prince Memnon from Ethiopia?" another one immediately chimed in. "He appeared before us wearing nothing but a zebra skin. My god, I thought I was going to faint!"

"And what about that Hebrew emissary Moses?" joins another. "Could you believe how dirty his fingernails were? You could have grown a row of corn in each of them. How disgusting!"

See there? I told you the Egyptians were a pompous lot. You'd have thought, since I was more or less shipwrecked, and their country was hotter than Hades in the summertime, they might have cut me some slack, maybe even felt a little sorry for me, but not those lordly bastards. To them, I was another example of how superior they were to the rest of the world. Of course, I was in no position to convince them otherwise, nor would I have tried if I had been. All I wanted to do was get rid of Helen, her loot, and avert all the trouble they were going to cause. My chance had finally come to do all that and I was ready for it.

"Your majesty," says I, still bowing, "please forgive my appearance but I left my clothes aboard ship and was unable to retrieve them. Had your guards allowed me to do so, I would have dressed appropriately and came bearing gifts as well."

Well, that shut his crones up, right proper, and caught the Pharaoh's attention as well, mainly because it cast doubt on Egypt's hospitality.

The Pharaoh immediately cleared his throat as if he was embarrassed and, in a soft voice, said, "Rise, Royal Prince and welcome to the land of Egypt."

I rose, looked up — and gaped. I'd have bet my dirty loincloth that the man on the throne was actually a woman! He had a long, lean feminine face and a little mouth, without even a hint of hair around it; he also had magnificent brown eyes highlighted in dark mascara, a slender white feminine neck and shoulders, and luxurious black hair tucked up under a tall, pointy crown. He was a she all right, and if he wasn't, well, he was as close to being a woman as any man could get.

Just imagine the possibilities.

Anyway, I was still leering when the Pharaoh said, "Thonis, my Warden of the Nile, informs me that you are the son of the great and wise King Priam of Troy."

"Yes, Great Pharaoh," I answered, returning my focus to the task at hand, "I am Prince Alexander, son of King Priam and second in line to the royal throne."

"And how is it that you have come to our shores, Prince Alexander?" the Pharaoh asked.

"I was driven here by a storm, Divine One," says I.

"And how is it that you have come in possession of Queen Helen of Sparta and these other maidens?" asks the Pharaoh directly.

So there it was: the 54,000 talent question. And you can be sure I had a reply all prepared. I'd spent the night before rehearsing it in front of the rats.

"Well," says I, lowering my eyes, all hang dog like, "I had the misfortune of falling in with some really bad men and I allowed them to led me astray. As a result, Helen and these lovely maidens were taken against their will and their city and treasuries were looted too."

There was an audible gasp from the crowd but I ignored it and continued to confess my sins.

"I realize now how evil our actions have been and truly feel ashamed of them. And although I know it's not much, especially in light of our hideous crimes, but I would like to make restitution if I could..."

I paused for a second, looked straight at Helen, you know, just so I could see her face, and said, "I'd like to hand the Queen of Sparta and the Phoenicians over to Your Highness for safe guarding, along with every bit of the valuables we stole, so that their rightful owners can come to claim them."

I swear, if Helen's eyes could have grown any bigger, they'd have popped out of her head!

That's right, bitch, thinks I, your ass is on its way back to Menelaus!

Then I turned my attention quickly back to the Pharaoh and said, "And if your majesty will be gracious enough to provide me with an experienced pilot to help me sail home, my crew and I will make further amends by sacrificing at the Temple of Zeus every day for the next year. And we will be sure to honor your name while we do."

Now, I'm sure my little confession was about the last thing anyone, included Helen, expected to hear because, for several seconds afterwards, they seemed totally stumped by it and silence reigned. I swear, you could have heard a flea fart. And then, just to add some theatrics to the moment, I dropped to the ground in front of the Pharaoh's tiny feet and kissed them humbly.

(Side note: When arrested and charged with a crime, you should always apologize to everyone involved, talk about God and blame the whole thing on your friends. Works every time. Ask any politician.)

The Pharaoh glanced down at me and then up at his ministers in confusion. For a second, none of them seemed to know what to do, and then they began to whisper back and forth until, finally, one of them nodded his head and whispered something into the Pharaoh's ear. The Pharaoh grunted back in reply and looked back down at me.

"Prince Alexander," the Pharaoh said, "if you had not repented of your crimes, I would have considered avenging your wrongs by putting you to death. You have been truly the lowest of men — after accepting the hospitality of your host and then seducing his wife and plundering his house. Oh, what a wicked deed! But since you now recognize it as such and are repentant of it, I am prepared to forgive you and grant your wishes. I will allow Queen Helen and the maidens to stay here, along with their riches, until their owners come and claim them. I will also give you a pilot to guide you home. Thonis and Helen will accompany you to Salt-Pans to make sure all the valuables you stole are properly accounted for. After that, you have three days to leave my kingdom. I warn you — return all the valuables and depart within the space of that time or you and your men will be treated as enemies. So let it be written, so let it be done!"

A loud round of applause greeted the Pharaoh's announcement, and then everyone dropped to their knees while a scribe stepped forward with a scroll so the Pharaoh could seal the decree with his (or her) signet ring. The Pharaoh shot me an approving look as he (or she) stamped the ring into the hot wax and then, he (or she) stood up and made his (or her) way out of the room, smiling graciously, and swinging his (or her) shapely ass as he (or she) went.

Watching the Pharaoh leave, and reflecting on the decree, which everyone, except Helen, seemed happy about, I couldn't help but be proud of myself for what I had just pulled off. Not only had I averted a war, I had managed to get rid of Helen and salvage my reputation to boot. Needless to say, I couldn't resist grinning over my shoulder at Helen one last time as I was being led away by some servants. She frowned back at me and might have thrown a hissy fit if she hadn't been surrounded by so many adoring officials. I loved it, of course, and soon, I was savoring a hot meal, and clean clothes, and the fact that I had nothing more to fear.

After I was through stuffing myself, Thonis appeared and said we should leave without haste. I agreed even though I had wanted to spend the night in a clean room, figuring instead it was probably best to be on my way before something else could go wrong. Given my knack for trouble, and all I had been through, you can't blame me.

Then, a servant wrapped a cloak around me and escorted me outside to an awaiting wagon. I requested some traveling provisions and was handed a huge flask of wine and a pouch of bread and cheese, and then, without further ado, I was helped into the back of the wagon.

I took a swig of wine as the oxen pulled away and never once looked back at the palace. The place could burn in Hades for all I cared.

Helen was riding in the wagon ahead of mine, staring hate at me from it. I pretended not to notice, as I didn't want her to think I cared, which, by the way, I didn't. She was Egypt's problem now, not mine, damn her. And I'm not sure which pissed her off the most — that she was being returned to her husband or being cut adrift by me. Since both were just peachy with me, I wasn't inclined to ask. As a matter of fact, I never said a single word to her during the trip back to Salt-Pans. Neither did Thonis. After watching her cavort around with the Pharaoh, he figured her for a manipulating bitch, which she was, and wanted no further part of her.

"My god," Thonis declared one evening while watching Helen turn her charms on an ordinary soldier, "has she no shame?"

"None whatsoever," I replied. "You know what she says after sex?"

"What?" Thonis asked.

"Thanks guys!" I answered.

It's the only time I heard Thonis laugh.

And that's about all I remember about the trip back, except that I ran out of wine about half way, which really sucked, but I do recall that we arrived at Salt-Pans around sunset. Looking down on it from a sandy crest less than a league away, the place appeared pretty much like we left it — ugly mud huts surrounding a pristine temple — we could barely make them out in the fading light; it would have been a very welcomed scene too had it not been for the fact that there wasn't a single soul in sight. The place looked totally deserted!

Alarmed, Thonis immediately drew his sword, jumped on his horse and, with our escorting soldiers running along behind him, made a beeline straight for the temple. I scurried down from the wagon and watched them go; my main concern was that Pandarus and our crew had escaped and sailed away with the treasure. As it was, I was half right and half wrong. Just as Thonis and his men were about a hundred cubits away, there was a blood-freezing shout, followed by the whistle of shafts and I watched in horror as several of the soldiers began staggering about the sand with arrows protruding from their bodies. Then, shadowy figures emerged from the surrounding darkness and leaped upon the surviving soldiers like a pack of hungry wolves. For several agonizing moments, men screamed and fought and fell in confusion. I could see Thonis amongst them, slashing viciously at the attackers from his saddle, and then an arrow struck his breast, and another, and another, until he fell to the ground and out of my sight.

For a moment, I was frozen in shock, then, my coward's instinct told me to run and I did. I went running away from the crest, arms raised above my head in terror, screaming at the top of my lungs, "We're fucked! We're fucked! We're all going to die!"

Helen tried to stop me as I ran by, and I'd have slapped her face if I had the time, but I didn't, so I eluded her grasp, and I kept running as fast as my feet could carry me. Unfortunately, they weren't fast enough to outrun a horse. I know this because, soon after that, I was being followed by a man on horseback and the animal kept getting closer and closer until, eventually, I could feel it's warm breath on my back.

"Leave me alone, for pity's sake!" I yelped over my shoulder at the man.

A lot of good that did!

As the horse pulled up more or less abreast of me, the man raised his sword in the air and sent its hilt crashing down on my head. The blow instantly stunned me and sent my body flying to the ground. I lay motionless in the sand, trying to collect my wits while the man dismounted and walked over to me. I was still too dizzy to scream, or squirm, or blubber, when his face suddenly appeared less than a foot away from mine.

"Hello, Paris," he said sarcastically. "Did you have a nice trip?"

It was Pandarus, of course, and once again, I was in his clutches. I shivered involuntarily as I realized it, and I probably would have started crying too if I hadn't been so lightheaded.

"I see you found us a pilot," he said, lifting me up to my feet. "That was damned thoughtful of you. Now we can go home."

He held me as we made our way over to the horse and then he hoisted me up on it; I tottered on the horses back until he swung up behind me and steadied me with his arm. Then we moved slowly back to where Helen and the wagons were. She ran over to greet us when we arrived.

"Oh, Alexander, baby, there you are!" she yelled, running over and hugging my leg.

There didn't seem much point in responding, so I stared down at her in silence, hoping that she would just go away and leave me alone.

Fat chance!

"I should be very, very angry at you," she continued yapping, "but I forgive you. I forgive you! All that matters now is that we are together again. Oh, darling, I love you so much!"

Even though my mind was still in a daze, I knew better than to believe her. I wasn't knocked that stupid. Still, there was nothing I could do about her or my terrible situation except accept them, with a great deal of disappointment, of course. Later, during the voyage back to Troy, when I thought about the two opportunities I had to escape, and the bad things that had kept me from doing so, I almost jumped overboard — but, I reminded myself that Oenone and our child were out there waiting for me to come home. All I had to do was stay alert and wait for another opportunity to come around. Until then, I saw no reason why I shouldn't enjoy myself as much as possible. I did this mainly by enjoying Helen's body as much as possible. I mean, why the Hades not? I figured, since I was stuck with the bitch and all, I should go ahead and get my troubles worth out of her. Wouldn't you? Of course, you would have. So I spent most of the voyage back to Troy below deck, screwing Helen's brains out. And that, by the way, formed the basis of our relationship afterwards. It's like the more problems she caused me, the more I fucked her. I know that sounds sick — and it is — but it's how I maintained my sanity during all the troubles that were yet to come.

Chapter Seven

The room is quiet now.

Helen is gone.

She must have left while I was lost in thought.

I move my leg slightly, and a bolt of pain immediately shoots from my crotch to my brain, and I moan loudly, at which somebody laughs. I open my eyes and see that my sister Cassandra is standing by my bed. Her hair is a mass of tangles and her robe is dirty and disheveled. Her chin is wet from drooling so much. She's disgusting, she's crazy, and she's snickering insolently at my discomfort.

I tell her to fuck off.

She doesn't.

"You're gonna die, you're gonna die, you're gonna die," she teasingly sings over and over again.

God, how I hate her! I've always hated her, mainly because she's been urging folks to kill me ever since we first laid eyes on each other in the Temple of Zeus. Thank god no one ever listened to her. And I think that's why she's so fucking cuckoo now. It must be tough to be an ignored fortuneteller. And I don't mean to sound like I believe she can tell the future because I don't. In my opinion, she's just a damned good guesser. I mean, given my propensity for trouble and all, it's a pretty safe guess that, sooner or later, I'm gonna cause something bad to happen. Agelaus knew it. That's why he warned me not to stay in

Troy. And Cassandra somehow knew it too. That's why she was always warning folks about me and because they didn't heed her warnings, she went off her rocker.

It happened the day we returned from Egypt. We came sailing back into port on a fine, sunny morning. The ship's Aphrodite sail was bellying proudly in the wind, signaling our return, and soon, people began to stream down to the port in order to get a gander at us. By the time we dropped anchor, there were folks everywhere, waving and throwing flowers; merchants, soldiers, fishermen, wives, daughters, officials — the whole of Troy seemed to be celebrating our return. The ship's crew beamed and waved back, enjoying it fully. Aeneas was right, we were hailed as heroes. Somehow or another, all of Troy had heard about our exploits and, just like he predicted, they were downright proud of them. In their eyes, we had avenged all the wrongs the Greeks had done to us and so, there was a tremendous bustle amongst them, and cheering, and celebrating.

And that's precisely when Cassandra went bonkers.

It was just too much for her to handle.

You may recall, when I left, she had stood on the dock warning everybody that I would bring a conflagration back with me, which, you'll agree, is pretty much what I did. But the people of Troy didn't listen to her then and they damned sure weren't listening to her when I returned. They were too busy enjoying the sweet taste of revenge. Little wonder then, as they crowded around me, calling me the Champion of Troy and silly things like that, Cassandra went plumb nuts. And I'm not just talking about a simple nervous breakdown either. Nope, not even close. I'm talking, out of control, mind-blowing, full pledged insanity here. I never thought anything could go as crazy as she did. You have seen it! She got so upset that she ripped off that stupid golden veil she was always wearing, threw it to the ground and started hopping up and down on it all crazy like. Of course, folks who saw her do it naturally thought she was doing some kind of weird celebration dance and several of them actually joined in. It was only after Cassandra started eating the battered, dirty veil that her dancing partners finally wised up enough to call for help. When the authorities arrived a short time later, my sister was still chewing away, and so, it's no great surprise that they carted her off to the loony bin right then and there.

The only surprise is that they didn't haul me away with her because, to be completely honest with you, I went just about as crazy as she did. You see, I got so caught up in the tumultuous welcome that I sorta lost my head and forgot about warning folks of the dangers that lay ahead. I let their adulations and hurrahing get to me and I must have looked pretty crazy, strutting among the crowd proudly, shaking hands with men that would soon be dead, lustfully hugging their future widows and patting their soon-to-be orphans politely on the head. Yep, I was crazy all right, no doubt about that. And when I got to the palace, where things quieted down enough for me to think straight, it was too late. I was officially a national hero and, believe me, once that mantel gets placed on your shoulders, it's awfully hard to take off. Especially when you are as morally weak as I am. And what's worse, I was a hero to my father too.

"Paris, my son!" he welcomed me loudly as I walked into the throne room. "That's my boy! Come in, son, come in! I'm so damned proud of you!"

You know how it feels when your father talks to you like that — your heart melts and you feel closer to him than you've ever felt before and the last thing you want to do is ruin the moment. That's exactly how I felt, that paternal closeness, and since I had never experienced it before with him, I tell you, it was utterly intoxicating, so you'll understand if I didn't tell him the truth.

"I knew you had it in you!" he bellowed. "Good boy! My god! Sacked a Phoenician city, hoodwinked the Egyptians and raided the Greeks! Jolly good show, boy, jolly good show! My other sons certainly can learn a lesson from you!"

They were there too, standing just behind my father — Hector, with his great muscles and piercing, dark eyes; Deiphobus, proud and vain; Polites, trim and athletic — all turning green with envy.

I approached them pretty easy, which shows you how crazy I was, cause, believe me, the closer you get to the crown, the greater the danger becomes. No one knows this better than me, but at the time, I was feeling a little tipsy from all the adulation and wasn't thinking too clearly. I even tripped a bit as I walked.

"My god!" says Deiphobus, "he's drunk again. He can't even walk straight."

I wasn't drunk, of course, I was just overly excited.

"Who cares if he is?" my father immediately retorted. "That's how swashbucklers like him celebrate their victories. Let him drink if he wants, he deserves it. As a matter of fact, let's all drink with him!"

This just keeps getting better and better, thinks I.

And my father called for wine. Then the servants ran through the side doors, up some stairs, into the kitchen, and then back again, bearing several large goblets of wine. They handed us each one, bowed and stepped respectfully away.

"Here's to my brave son Paris!" my father yelled, raising his cup in salutation.

"Here...here," seconded my bothers hesitantly.

We drained our goblets, and my father embraced me, and asked if I had enough wine. I looked at him pretty tough, you know, just like a swashbuckler should, and said, no, goddamnit, I hadn't. So we had another round and another round after that. And then, believe it or not, my father began to weep and insisted on embracing me some more. I, of course, was pretty astonished by this but the wine helped me handle the awkwardness of the moment.

Finally, my father took me by the hand and said, "Paris, my son, you have done me a great service. Not only have you avenged all the wrongs that the Greeks have done to Troy, you have also given me a way to get my sister Hesione back from them. When the Greek envoys demand Helen's return, as I know they will, I will demand they return my sister in exchange."

I don't have to tell you how thrilled I was to hear that. It was certainly the opportunity I had been waiting for. Not only was I getting rid of Helen once and for all, but, since my father was prepared to negotiate with the Greeks, I felt fairly confident a war with them could be avoided. After that, I figured, the road would be open to Oenone, and I'd be hailed as a hero as I took it too. You'll agree that I couldn't have asked for anything better.

So, I puffed out my chest and told him a bunch of rubbish about how glad I was to be of service to him adding, humbly, that I only did what any loving son would do for his father. (Believe me, I can ham it up given half the chance, as there isn't an ounce of shame in me. And I can act brave too, especially if I am standing someplace safe!) Anyway, to continue, I said, oh, sure, it was dangerous and all but the risks were certainly worth it. Troy's honor was at stake and that's what mattered the most. My lone regret, I concluded, was that I only had one life to give for my country.

Ha!

Anyway, when I was done spouting off, my father was absolutely bawling. I swear, I've never saw a grown man, beside myself, of course, blubber so hard. Like father, like son, I guess. Anyway, unfortunately, my brothers didn't buy a word of it though. They just stood there looking down their noses at me warily. So, just to make sure they would never learn the truth from Pandarus and Aeneas, I graciously mentioned my two shipmate's roles, although minor, in the adventure, and asked that they be rewarded richly for their services. My father at once agreed, between sobs, promising that he would restore Pandarus as commander of the Guard and make Aeneas second in command of the Army. He also said he would allow them to keep a portion of the treasury they stole from Menelaus. I accepted for them both, again graciously, figuring that would be enough to shut them up forever.

After that, my father let Troy's nobility enter the room and there was a great deal of bowing and scraping, which I accepted with a martial air, and since I had a license to get drunk, I asked the servants for more wine. They brought it to me by the bucket load and very soon, I got wonderfully tight. That's why I have only a blurred recollection of all the attention and admiration I received afterwards, which, I guess, is just as well, seeing how I didn't deserve an ounce of it.

When I sobered up three days later, I was laying on the cold floor of my house, with my head pounding, and my stomach in torment; to make matters worse, Pandarus was there, alternately laughing at my agony and talking loud enough to make sure my discomfort continued. Where Helen was I don't know. We were separated shortly after coming ashore and I hadn't seen her since. Not that I really cared.

I forced my eyes open and tried to sit up, only to discover that neither one was a very good idea, so I settled back down and decided to wait until the room stopped spinning before attempting to do anything stupid like that again. I laid there listening to Pandarus' voice thinking maybe he'd go away if I ignored him long enough, but he didn't, so, I eventually gave up and decided to crawl under a nearby table for a little peace and quiet. I was halfway under it when I suddenly heard the words Menelaus and Odysseus come out of Pandarus' mouth.

Thinking: this can't be good, I immediately stopped crawling and said, "What?"

"I said, Menelaus and Odysseus are here to negotiate for Helen's return," Pandarus answered. "They arrived this morning. They're staying over at Antenor's house."

Well, that surprised me pretty good, so much so, that I rose up with a start, bumping my head on the table as I did.

I was ready to yell in pain, when I got a grip, or more precisely, Pandarus got a grip on my leg and pulled me out from under the table. I protested, but he turned a deaf ear, until we reached the middle of the room.

"Oh, shut up," he said, releasing my leg, "and understand this — I'm not about to lose a single ounce of gold or my promotion, so don't go thinking you're gonna cut a deal with Menelaus like you tried to do with the Pharaoh. Understand?"

I paused. How best to handle this? Should I tell him about my father's plans? No, my inner voice warned. Let him find out by himself.

"I swear, the thought never crossed my mind," I answered, rubbing the spot where my head had hit the table.

"Good!" Pandarus answered. "See to it you don't cause I'll be watching you."

I didn't like the sound of that, especially since it sounded like the bastard was thinking about hanging around, so I figured it would be a good time to cut ties with him once and for all.

"Keep your damned gold for all I care. Just leave me alone." I said. "As far as I'm concerned, we're even. I got you your old job back and more money to boot, so now, I don't owe you a damned thing."

I paused again for rebuttal, but Pandarus didn't say a thing. He just stood there staring down at me, no doubt, mulling my words over in his pea brain. While he did, I suddenly heard a knock on the door. Thinking a convenient excuse had arrived to end our conversation; I quickly rose up on my elbows and called for the visitor to enter.

The door immediately swung open and in stepped old Antimachus. You might remember that ancient fossil; he's the mayor I bribed to keep the tavern open. Yeah, you know, that crooked old fucker. Anyway, since the tavern had been closed for a while, I was clueless as to why he was there.

"You got my gold?" Antimachus immediately asked.

Thinking that the old coot's brain had finally dried up and he had gone senile, I said, in a very slow manner so he could keep up, "Ah… Antimachus…the tavern's been closed for a while now…and I don't intend to reopen it….so I don't need your services anymore…run along now…and eat your pudding…do… you… understand…me?"

Only Antimachus hadn't been talking to me.

He was talking to Pandarus.

"Yes, I do," Pandarus answered.

Bending down, he started rifling through my pockets, which was downright degrading, but since it wasn't as degrading as being knocked silly, nor anywhere near as painful, I decided not to stop him. Eventually, he discovered that I had two monogrammed bags of gold coins stored in them, which he took without so much as a thank you.

Straightening back up, he added two bags of his own and tossed all four over to where Antimachus was standing. They hit the ground around his feet with a loud jingle.

The old fart greedily snatched them from the floor, opened each one, inspected their contents closely and smiled with satisfaction.

Pandarus grinned back and said, "Just make sure you argue against sending Helen and her treasury back to Sparta and there's twenty more for you."

Antimachus nodded understandably, closed the bags, stuffed them in his pockets, and left.

After he was gone, Pandarus looked down at me and said, "Now we're even."

I was stunned, to say the least, and I didn't know what to say. Neither did my inner voice. So we watched in silence as Pandarus walked out of the house. As the door closed behind him, I shook myself like a dog to clear my head, then I pinched myself, you know, just to convince myself I wasn't dreaming, and then I put my hands behind my head, stared up at a fly on the ceiling and wondered how it could hang upside down for so long without falling on its ass. I could afford to wonder about something so trivial, and to bid my time too, because, for once, events were beyond my control. And the best thing was, I didn't have to worry about how they were going to turn out either. You see, I was completely sure that Antimachus and Pandarus were wasting their time because I was confident that when Menelaus heard my father's terms, he wouldn't hesitate a second agreeing to them. Who wouldn't? I mean, they were only fair. And besides, it was also the smart thing to do. Who would be stupid enough to go to war over a couple of women?

Shows you how dumb I was.

Anyway, the only plan I had was to look as noble as I possibly could through the negotiations, you know, for reputation's sake. That's because I wanted folks to have a high opinion of me as I waved goodbye to them the next morning. So I got up and made my move. First, I packed my bags in anticipation of my journey back home to Oenone, and then, I took a long, warm bath, called for a manicurist and a hair dresser, and punished two bottles of wine while they went to work on me. When I was toasted and pretty enough to go out in public, I threw on my best Babylonian tunic and headed for the palace.

I got there just as the negotiations were about to begin. Since I hadn't been invited, I figured it would be best if I stayed out of the way, and healthier too, given Menelaus' temper and all, so I discreetly slipped into the throne room's balcony, which, except for a curious servant or two, was completely deserted. I sat down far enough from the railing so the people below couldn't see me but close enough so I could peek down at them every now and then.

When I was finally situated, I cautiously leaned over and caught a glimpse of the scene below. I can still see it; Trojan nobles and officials of every kind were crowded together like sardines. You would have needed a royal directory to identify them all. Antenor, Aeneas and Antimachus were standing at the mob's forefront looking like they wanted to slap the snot out of each other. Before them, my father was seated on his big throne rubbing his forehead nervously. Hector sat next to him wearing the same dumb expression on his face that he always wore. Deiphobus was there too, standing just behind Hector's chair, no doubt, annoyed he wasn't sitting in it. Off to the side, Pandarus leaned carelessly against a wall, observing everything and missing nothing. And in the middle of them all, stood Menelaus and Odysseus, very brave and regal.

I had never seen Odysseus before and, let me tell you, he was one strange bird to behold. Short, squat, built like a boxer, he appeared to be anything but a king. If you passed him on the street, you'd swear he was a common blacksmith or, like I just said, a boxer, but if you were able to look him in the eye — which was hard, since he always kept his head lowered — you'd see that he had the sharp eyes of a warrior. And then you'd realize his appearance was just a calculated disguise designed to get you to lower your guard. Odysseus was cunning like that. Make no mistake; Odysseus was as sharp as they came.

Menelaus was at his elbow, wearing a fancy purple robe with double folds and trimmed in gold. A large, gold brooch clasped the folds. I may have run off with his wealth but, by god, he wasn't gonna show it. I couldn't help but be proud of him for that and I wanted to call down to him and say how sorry I was for everything but, of course, I couldn't. Things had gone too far for that. So I bit my lip and leaned back to listen.

Menelaus spoke first.

"Great King Priam," he began, all fancy like, "permit me to get straight to the point. I welcomed your son Alexander into my house as a beloved friend and loyal companion. I trusted him as I would my own brother. And how was my trust repaid? With deceit and robbery! When my back was turned, your son used his grace and sweetness of words to seduce my wife, and when he saw her falter, he forgot his friendship with me, and his royal office, or that he was a guest in my house, and lured her to a nearby island, so his followers could plunder my palace's treasury in her absence."

What a bunch of bullshit! I nearly burst out.

"I come before you now," Menelaus continued, "to ask the return of both my queen and treasury. I beg you to right the wrongs that have been done to me by your son and restore the friendship that has existed between our two kingdoms for so long."

Amen to that, thinks I.

And then it was Odysseus' turn to speak.

Head down, he studied the floor for a moment, as though unsure as how to begin, and then, in his fake country drawl, he said, "Mighty king. I ain't no man fer purdy talk, that's why some folks call me "Noman", so please excuse my backward speech 'cause even though I'm Ithaca's king and all, the plumb truth is, I'm jus a simple farmer that knows more 'bout plowing than he do 'bout speechifying."

See? I told you Odysseus was certainly a man of twists and turns. Simple hayseed, my ass!

"But," Odysseus continued, nodding his head sideways towards Menelaus, "this here man standing next to me is descended from a long line of warrior kinfolk and the truth is that he'd rather die than put up with an insult of any kind. His brother, King Agamemnon of Argo is jus like him too. Why, as we speak, the mighty King is busy herdin' together an army whose number will match the sands on that beach out thar and they won't stop 'till victory is got. So, if'n I were you, I'd give my friend back his queen and treasury, 'cause if'n you don't, I'm purdy sure Troy will be plowed under for it."

Well, that was a bold threat for sure, no doubt about that, and bedlam broke out down below because of it. I listened in horror as the majority of the assembly cried out in anger. Leaning slightly forward, I could see them shouting and shaking their fists at Odysseus. Only a handful of Trojans seemed to be in support of him. They were lead by Antenor, who was well-known Greek lover. It was no secret that he had a large number of business deals and marriage ties with the smelly bastards.

"Friends, Trojans, fellow countrymen," Antenor shouted above the din, "calm yourselves! Can we honestly say that Prince Paris' actions were not insolent and lawless? I think not!"

And that's when papa got really pissed off!

"How dare you!" he barked at Antenor. "How dare you accuse my son of being insolent and lawless! Have you forgotten what the Greeks did to us a mere twenty years ago?"

He stood up and turned to Menelaus and Odysseus, seething; I have never seen him so angry.

"I can't believe my ears!" he snapped at them. "You have no right to complain about the actions of my son and his comrades because it was your countrymen who first attacked us in a time of peace. From our city, they stole our treasury, they also carried off my sister, Hesione, and gave her as a prize to Telamon. And when I sent an envoy to ask for her return, your countrymen laughed at him and treated him rudely. Tell us why we shouldn't do the same to you? Because you claim to have a big army! Do you think that scares us? Trust me, it doesn't. Let your army of sand pebbles come, I say, and watch it be smashed upon Troy's walls!"

That sent the room into pandemonium. I watched wide-eyed as the assembly hurled insults and obscene gestures at Menelaus and Odysseus. How they stood it, was a mystery to me. I'd have fainted for sure. But they just stood there, perfectly composed, acting like they didn't have a care in the world. It was utterly amazing.

When the hubbub died away, my father returned to his throne and, with a contemptuous snort, said, "You shall have Helen and your treasury back on one condition: when you return my sister to Troy and pay for the damage Hercules did to our city."

So there it was. All the cards were finally on the table. I looked down at Menelaus and thought, for god sakes, man, take papa's offer and let's get this thing over with.

I should have been pinning my hopes on Odysseus instead.

He scratched his beard anxiously, you know, kinda like a hick does when he's confused, and said, "Well, now, I dunno, king, ya see, thar's a problem with that; your sister Hesione is a happily married woman. And not only that, she's also Queen of Salamis and she's had herself a Greek son too; mighty Ajax, so I ain't so all fired sure she still fancys comin' back to Troy."

I have to admit, I never thought about that, and, from the surprised look on my father's face, it appeared that he hadn't either. Still, he wasn't about to be deterred, and if anyone knew how to dicker, it was my father.

And that's precisely when everything took a turn for the worse.

Leaning back in his chair, my father scratched his beard to mimic Odysseus, and, in a equally fake country voice, said, "Well, now, Noman, seems we got us one of them thar coincidences, 'cause just last night, Helen was a tellin' me how happy she is to be here in Troy with us all and how much in love she is with my son and how she wishes they were hitched and all. I reckin she doesn't want to return home either."

I don't know who was more shocked, me, Odysseus or Menelaus, although, I believe, the smart money's on me. I swear, my jaw fell open and I nearly toppled over the railing.

So that's where that hussy has been, thinks I, smooching my father's ass! Goddamn her!

I had to bite my knuckles to keep from screaming.

Menelaus didn't have to bite anything. "Damn you!" he screamed at my father. "Marry Helen to Paris, dude, and their honeymoon will be spent watching Troy burn! I swear, my brother and I will not leave one stone in Troy standing if you do!"

And that's when Antimachus finally stepped forward to earn his pay.

"How dare you speak to our king in that manner!" he bellowed. "And how dare you threaten us!" Then he turned to the assembly and yelled, "Trojans, how long are you going to suffer these insults!"

Aeneas was the first to respond, of course, because patriotic dunderheads like him always are.

"Not for long, I tell you!" he shouted. "Apparently, the Greeks think they can return and carry off our women anytime like want! Enough talk! Let them come, I say, cause this time, we'll kill every goddamned Greek that steps foot in our country."

Only Antimachus didn't want to wait that long. He wanted blood right then and there.

"Kill those two!" he screeched, pointing a crooked arthritic finger directly at Menelaus and Odysseus. "Kill them and we'll send their heads back to Agamemnon as our answer!"

There was a general shout of agreement at this, and soldiers started forward, swords drawn, to carry out Antimachus' wishes, but Odysseus kept his head as they approached, no pun intended, and yelled, "We evoke the right of single combat to resolve this issue!"

There was a moment's pause, followed by an exchange of confused looks — and then Menelaus stepped forward and challenged me to open combat, saying that if he killed me, Helen and his treasure would be returned to him, and, if he lost, the Trojans could keep them both.

Now, in case you don't know, a duel between two antagonists was an accepted way of resolving disputes in both Troy and Greece. Not only did it cut down on needless bloodshed, it also saved time and money too, which is pretty cool, I guess. But if you're about a hundred pounds lighter than your opponent and have the courage of a bunny rabbit, then it doesn't seem like such a good idea. I am talking about myself, of course, so it's no surprise that I immediately started crawling towards the balcony's exit seconds after Menelaus issued his challenge.

And I'd have made it too, that is, if Helen hadn't suddenly appeared in it and opened her big fat mouth.

"Oh, Alexander, there you are!" she shouted out with glee. "I've been looking all over the place for you. Oh, darling, I have had the most wonderful time with your family! They are so nice! And they have given me the most beautiful room to stay in, but, baby, I really want to stay with you. Can I move into your house? Oh, please, please, please! Can I? I have some decorating ideas we really must discuss."

The whole time she was talking, I kept nodding my head and rolling my eyes towards the throne room, hoping that the stupid bitch would take a hint and shut the fuck up. Only, she didn't. And everyone down below heard her voice and, what's worse, everything she said to me.

"Paris!" my father immediately yelled at the balcony. "Are you up there?"

"Yes, papa, he is!" Helen answered back all innocent like.

I squeezed my eyes shut and cursed the day I met her.

When I was done cussing, I sighed heavily and reluctantly rose to my feet. Peering slowly over the railing, I saw that every face in the room was looking up at me. I smiled down at them and waved. Of course, I looked damned stupid doing it and not a single face smiled back, especially not Menelaus'.

He glared up at me like a man about to go berserk, his eyes were burning with rage, and for a moment, I thought he'd bound into the balcony and tear me apart with his bare hands. Then he checked himself, and his mind seemed to clear, and in a loud, firm voice, yelled, "Helen, get down here right now! You're coming home with me!"

Helen came forward without any hesitation, frowning sternly, and took hold of my arm. Casting her beautiful eyes down at Menelaus, she shouted, "No! I'm Paris' woman now! We love each other! Now go away and leave us alone!"

I almost fainted. Besides being a big, fat lie, the carelessness and stupidity of it was absolutely mindboggling, as there wasn't the slightest doubt that her words would lead to war, or even worse, my death. I looked at her in complete astonishment and wondered if she was out of her fucking mind.

Menelaus' eyes began to burn again and he yelled, "I'll kill him if you don't come home with me!"

"Ha!" Helen quickly scoffed. "You think Paris is afraid of you! He'll kick your sorry ass if you don't leave right now!" Then, she glanced over at me for confirmation and said, "Won't you, honey?"

I immediately looked down at Menelaus, frantically shook my head no and, in a voice that was three octaves higher than usual, said, "Ahhh...actually...I was hoping we could settle this in a friendly manner...because...ahhh...the truth is..."

"Outside, on the city's plain!" Menelaus angrily interrupted. "To the death, in one hour."

One hour!

Yeah, right!

It took that long just for the palace guards to catch me!

I swear, I ran all over the citadel trying to evade them, but, when you're surrounded by massive walls, all you can do is run around in circles. That's the only reason they were able to catch me, otherwise, believe me, in one hour, out on an open plain, I would have been long gone.

As I struggled against the soldier's attempts to get me ready for the duel, Hector impatiently yelled, "Oh, for god's sake, Paris, be a man!"

I was laying spread eagle on the ground, and a soldier was attached to each of my out-stretched limbs, pinning me down, while another soldier worked hastily to fasten pieces of bronze armor to my body.

"Shut up, you stupid prick!" I shouted back at Hector, kicking at the soldiers as I did, "and tell these men to let me go."

"Come on, Paris, be brave!" he continued. "Do you want the Greeks to think you're a coward?"

"I don't give a shit what they think!" I hollered, twisting about wildly.

"They'll mock us," he said, "and say we sent a pretty boy to fight who doesn't have a pinch of courage."

"What part of 'I don't give a shit' don't you understand, you big, stupid lout!"

That pissed him off. "Listen," he said, "this is your fault. Did you not carry Helen off and allow your followers to raid Sparta's treasury?"

"No, I didn't!" I roared, then, pointing an accusing finger at Pandarus, I shouted, "He did!"

Pandarus laughed and said, "Paris, stop squirming around so my men can suit you up."

"I'm not 'squirming', you evil bastard," I barked, "I'm shaking with fear. Can't you see I'm gonna die?"

That seemed to put a thought in his head. I mean, if I died, he'd be out of a fortune. I'm surprised he didn't think of that earlier.

Turning to a soldier standing behind him, he said, "Sergeant, have the archers man the south wall and bring me my bow."

The sergeant nodded obediently and marched away to carry out his orders.

Turning back to me, Pandarus winked slyly and said, "Don't worry, I've got everything covered."

What he meant by that, I didn't know, or care, as I was too busy feeling sorry for myself. This is totally unfair, I shouted out loud, what have I done to deserve this? All I wanted to do was have a good time and go home. What's wrong with that?

The soldiers laughed. My limbs were fast growing numb from their grasp, and I knew I couldn't resist much longer, and then, the last greave was fastened to my leg, and I was hoisted up, and a golden helmet with long horsehair was plopped down on my head.

I looked through the helmet's narrow eyeholes and panicked. "I can't see a goddamned thing in this stupid bucket!" I protested.

I really couldn't. All I had was a narrow field of vision about four feet wide, which was pretty alarming, mainly because I couldn't see which direction to run in. That didn't stop me from trying to escape though — no surprise there — but after a couple of labored steps, I soon discovered that I could barely move in all that bulky armor. I felt like a fucking turtle. That made it easy for the soldiers to grab me again and wedge my ass into the back of a nearby chariot. I swore at them as they did, and even flailed around some, which caused the chariot to shake a bit. The driver warned me to stop thrashing or the chariot might turn over. I hoped it would, of course, and told him so; adding that he and his chariot could go straight to Hades for all I cared.

"It's your funeral," he answered nonchalantly, whipping the horses forward as he did.

And that's exactly what it felt like as we traveled to the battlefield. All along the way, folks lined the road, waving their hands and scarves, as if to say goodbye and bid me farewell one last time. That's how I took it anyway. And that's how I waved back at them.

It was outside the lower city's south gate that my funeral officially began. There was a big crowd of people already on hand when I pulled up, and soldiers from both sides were standing in orderly ranks on the plain a short distance beyond. Pandarus and his archers were perched upon the wall like a line of crows, while Menelaus, Odysseus, Hector and Deiphobus huddled together in the open space between the two formations of soldiers. God only knows what they were talking about. Maybe they were making bets. If they were, I'd have placed the odds of me winning to be at least a kahbillion to one — Menelaus could have had a heart attack, I guess. Outside of that, I was pretty much fucked.

At the soldier's insistence, I stepped out of the chariot, and cheers immediately broke out from the crowd. I could hear them yelling their fool heads off but I couldn't see a single soul. As a matter of fact, I couldn't see much of anything except the ground and people's feet. That's because I couldn't take a step without my helmet falling over my eyes. Deiphobus alertly noticed this and ran over to me.

"There," he said, fastening the helmet's chinstrap firmly under my jaw, "you're all set, tiger. Go get him!"

He was grinning when he said it and I could tell that he was thoroughly enjoying the pickle I was in, but before I could say anything smart back, or even take a breath, a soldier came up carrying a great big round shield. I watched in horror as he strapped it to my left arm. It was so heavy that I could barely hold the damn thing up. When he was done, another soldier stepped up and handed me a spear. For a moment, I considered dropping the spear and shield to the ground, but since Menelaus was pacing around me like an angry lion, I figured it might be a good idea to hang on to them as they seemed my only hope.

So, there I was, looking like a damned fool, shaking like a leaf, desperately trying not to soil my drawers, when Hector and Odysseus started measuring the space where Menelaus and I were to fight. Back and forth they walked, until the killing field was accurately marked off. Twenty paces, I think, altogether. The idea was for us to stand and throw spears at each other across that allotted distance. First person to die, loses. It was crazy, of course. And when I look back on it now, I can't help but be amazed at the stupid things guys will do for the sake of a woman. Especially for one they've both already screwed. So don't try to tell me we're the smarter sex. Have you ever seen two women fight a duel to the death over a guy? Heck, no. They ain't that stupid.

Anyway, after marking off the ground, Odysseus and my brother placed two lots in a helmet to decide who would get the first throw. Seeing how poorly my day was going, I was counting pretty heavily on coming in second, so, it's not hard to imagine my surprise when my lot suddenly popped out of the helmet. I was like; *finally, something's going my way for once.* But then, I realized that throwing a spear was probably going to be my last act on earth and, since it wasn't at all how I had planned to spend my last moments, I got depressed all over again.

Finally, the moment of truth arrived, and everyone took their places. By that, I mean, everyone got out of the way so that Menelaus and I could commence to kill each other like proper idiots. The crowd went silent and just stood there staring at us. No whispering, no coughing, no nothing. It was downright freaky and I wasn't sure what to do next, that is, until someone, I think it was Pandarus, yelled, "Throw your spear at him, Paris!" And so, there wasn't anything left to do but that. And let me tell you, throwing a spear at someone isn't as easy as it sounds. Believe me, it takes both skill and strength, and unfortunately, I had lots of the former and hardly any of the latter. You see, my spear hit Menelaus' shield dead center and simply bounced off. A loud moan immediately rose up from the crowd as it did. The Greeks, of course, were ecstatic and Menelaus was beside himself with joy. For several moments, he stamped around thanking the gods — and then his eyes fixed on me; lifting his spear, he cocked his arm and, with all his might, sent the deadly missile flying straight at me.

And that's when everything seemed to go in slow motion. As the spear slowly hurtled through space at my chest, I saw my life pass before my eyes, and realized I was about to die over a dumb blonde, and that didn't seem right somehow, so I raised my shield just as the spear was a couple of feet away. It struck the shield like a bolt of lightning, jerking everything back into full speed again. The spear went crashing through the shield with so much force that it actually managed to penetrate my bronze breastplate, and, what's worse, tear a large hole in my expensive, new Babylonian tunic, ruining it completely. But I had no time to worry about the garment just then; I went stumbling backwards, out of control, until my right heel suddenly struck a stone, and I went crashing to the ground. For several seconds, I laid on my back in the dirt, totally witless. And then I heard the crowd cry out a warning and Menelaus bellow with rage. Instinctively, I sat up and saw that he was charging straight at me, screaming wildly, drawing his sword as he ran.

There wasn't time to stand up and run, as a matter of fact, I barely had time to raise my shield before he was upon me. He struck my upraised shield with all his strength, driving it back into me, and the Greeks whooped with glee — and then he hit it over and over again, much like a carpenter hammers a nail, until finally, his sword caught the edge of my shield and sent it flying off of my arm. I watched in horror as it landed several feet away.

"Dude, I've got you now!" Menelaus roared.

I was crawling away on my hands and knees before the last word left his lips. My only hope lay in reaching the shield, so it seemed, and, by god, I'd have made it too, that is, if my arm was three feet longer, because that's as close as I got to the damned thing before Menelaus suddenly planted a foot squarely on top of it. I looked up at him like a trapped rat. He grinned down at me and raised his sword to deliver the death blow.

And that's when I lost it.

"I'm sorry!" I blubbered. "For god's sake, please, Menelaus, don't kill me. I didn't do it. I swear I didn't do it. Can't we just settle this by playing rock, papyrus, scissors? Anything! But please don't kill meeeeeee! Pleeeeaseee!"

A fat lot of good that did!

There was a moment's hush, and his sword flashed down. Then there was a sickening thud on my helmet and my head snapped back. As I fell sideways to the ground, I caught a glimpse of Menelaus' face and was surprised to see that it was contorted with rage. Another quick glance told me why — his sword had splintered on my helmet! The blade was completely gone! I could hardly believe it. And neither could Menelaus.

"Cruel Zeus," he raged, "why are you cheating me of my victory, dude?"

I wasn't about to stick around long enough for Zeus to change his mind. In a flash, I was on my hands and knees again, and crawling away faster than a startled monkey. Unfortunately, it wasn't fast enough, because Menelaus quickly caught up with me again and kicked me to the ground. Then he laughed, leaned down, grabbed the horsehair attached to my helmet, and with amazing strength, started swinging me through the air by it.

Around and around and around and around I went, arms and legs spread out wildly in all directions.

"Whoa!…Whoa!…Whoa!…Whoa!" the crowd chanted in unison each time I completed a full circle of flight.

It was downright embarrassing.

And fucking scary too!

That's because the helmet's chinstrap was biting into my neck like a hangman's noose. I felt certain I was going to be slowly strangled to death, and I've experienced nothing more terrifying before or since. Around and around I went, gulping for air, desperately clawing at the strap, until finally, the suffocating pain in my throat began to spread down to my chest and I felt myself sink into unconsciousness. And, do you know, that's exactly when the chinstrap broke! I swear, it really did! And I immediately went careening off into space. I landed with a heavy thud several cubits away. Menelaus, on the other hand, went spinning out of control into the ranks of his troops, knocking several of them down in the process. When he emerged a second or two later, he was madder than ever and armed with a spear.

And that's when things got totally ridiculous.

Okay, now, as a kid, did you ever play that spinning game? You know, the one where you spin around and around until you can't stand it anymore, and then you try to run in a straight line, only you can't because you're so goddamned dizzy. And everyone stands around laughing at your ass because the only thing you can do is stagger around like a drunken sailor and fall down. Yeah, that one!

Well, that's exactly what Menelaus and I looked like.

So, like I just said, Menelaus was really pissed off. He screamed a curse that split the heavens and ran towards me, waving his spear, but because the idiot was so damned dizzy, he quickly veered off to the side and went crashing into the Trojan line. Laughing heartily, the soldiers checked his progress, righted him, and shoved him back into the arena. He took three confused steps in my direction and promptly fell to the ground. The crowd went into convulsions. And that's when I rose to my feet. My head was spinning so bad that I put my hands out in a feeble attempt to steady myself. For several seconds, I stood there swaying to and fro, until finally, I lost my balance, and started stumbling around haplessly in an effort to keep from falling down. Of course, everyone was just howling at my clumsiness. Then, I caught a glimpse of the south gate, and decided it was time to go home. I was laboring to do so when Menelaus suddenly stood up and began heading in my direction again. He came at me in a very unsteady manner, pointing his spear warily. I shrieked in terror as he approached and wobbled forward as fast as I could, but, unfortunately, for every three steps forward I took, I had to take two sideways, so I didn't get very far before he was close enough to pitch his spear into my back.

Ignoring the danger behind me, I stumbled past the soldiers, past the crowd, the walls of Troy getting steadily closer with every five steps I took. There wasn't a sound from the crowd now. From somewhere close behind, Menelaus cried out for me to stop and die like I man. I ignored him, of course, and kept staggering forward, sobbing with fright.

And that's exactly when I heard the deadly swoosh of an arrow.

And Menelaus cry out in pain.

Turning around quickly, I saw that he had been struck in the stomach with an arrow. He was doubled over in pain and blood was flowing from the wound like a waterfall. I was immediately shocked and dumbfounded. For the life of me, I couldn't figure out what was happening. Searching for an answer, I glanced up at the wall and the first thing I saw was Pandarus standing on top of it, smiling contently, with a bow in his hand.

He looked down at me and winked.

Like he said, he had it covered, and with one shot, he had managed to keep his gold, save my life and start a fucking war.

For a second, I wondered if I should thank him or curse him, but then, the Greeks cried, "Foul!" and they rushed over to protect Menelaus. As they surrounded him with their shields, Odysseus ran up to me and yelled, "You will pay for your treachery! And so will Troy!"

Then, suddenly, from out of nowhere, Aeneas appeared and confronted Odysseus. "If you and your fellow Greeks don't get the fuck out of here," he yelled, "we'll kill every one of you right now! Leave now or die!"

To be honest with you, I didn't pay attention to a single word the two lunatics said. I just stood there staring at them in a daze, unable to believe that I was still alive, or that I was safe. And when it finally dawned on me a moment or two later that I had survived, and I was indeed safe, I began to cry with relief and tears streamed down my cheeks all the way home.

I was still feeling pretty emotional when I walked into my house and so, to calm my nerves, I went straight to the bar and poured myself a tall goblet of wine. I kept pouring and drinking in rapid succession until I was three quarters drunk. After that, I thought about sending for a whore, you know, to help me relax a little more, and then, I realized I was still stuck with the biggest whore of all and, suddenly, I wanted Helen really, really bad. Can you blame me? I mean, hadn't she almost got me killed? Damn straight she had. So why shouldn't she give me some pay back? Heck, in my opinion, she owed me punishment sex. I drank some more wine while I considered the justice of it, and ordered a servant — an old woman oddly named Aphrodite — to run over the palace at once and tell the hussy I was home waiting to be pleasured. I liked the sound of that, mainly because it seemed to put our relationship in its proper perspective.

By the time the servant returned with Helen, I was opening my third bottle of wine and looking for a bigger goblet to pour it in. Ah, thinks I, the hussy's finally here, time for some fun. Then, as I walked across the room to greet her, she suddenly sat down in a chair, wrapped a shawl around her head, and started bawling. Surprised, I immediately stopped in my tracks and stared down at her in disbelief. What does she have to cry about, I wondered, hadn't I been the one almost killed? And what had she been doing while I was out there trying to keep my neck from getting broke? No doubt, doing her nails, I thought. And that's when I got a tad upset.

"What wrong with you?" I cried. "Break a goddamned nail?"

"I am so embarrassed," she confessed. "I would have rather you fought bravely and died, than you having run away and survived. All of Troy thinks you are a coward now."

If she thought I'd be upset by that bit of news, she was in for a big surprise. As you well know, I've always considered myself to be a lover, not a fighter, and if the rest of the world had finally figured that out too, well, good for them.

"So?" I said, with a nonchalant wave of my hand. "Who cares what they think? I'm alive and that's all that matters. So come on baby, let's go upstairs to bed. I want you really bad right now."

"No, I can't," she pouted.

"I'll nibble on your ear," I tempted.

"No," she answered firmly.

"I'll let you be on top," I continued.

"Nope," she replied, shaking her head under the shawl.

"I'll do that thing with my tongue you like," I persisted.

"Okay," she sniffled.

Chapter Eight

"What are your orders today, sir?" a voice asks.

I open my eyes and see that Cassandra is gone. Thank god for that.

Unfortunately, Aeneas has taken her place.

"What are your orders?" he asks again impatiently.

It is a mystery to me why he keeps bothering me. Oh, sure, as the crown prince, technically, I'm still in command of the army and all, but he seems to forget that I am a crown prince with a fucking arrow sticking out of his dick! You'd think he'd know I have far more important things to worry about than his stupid little army. But the fool doesn't. Like I said before, Aeneas was one of those duty-minded bastards who believed in maintaining military decorum all the way to the grave. I can't tell you what a big pain in the ass they are.

"Go away and leave me alone," I answer.

"No can do, sir." Aeneas replies. "The army awaits your orders."

"Oh, for god's sakes, Aeneas, look!" I yell, pointing down to my wound, "I've got so much poison in me it's coming out of my ass!"

"So?" he shrugs, "I've been wounded four times in the last ten years, once seriously in the hip, and at no time did I relinquish my post as second in command of the army."

Exasperated, I roll my eyes to the ceiling and say, "Well, I guess that qualifies you for the army's most wounded soldier award then, doesn't it? Go away and give yourself a fucking medal!"

He doesn't.

"Not till you issue the army's daily orders, sir," he says.

I let out a loud sigh and give in. "Okay," I say, "tell the men to clean their gear and get some rest."

"Their gear is spotless and they are well rested, sir," he quickly answers.

"Tell them to dig some latrines then," I say.

"Dug," he answers.

"Tell them to practice their marching," says I.

"They spent two hours drilling this morning," he says.

"Well, then, have them spend two more hours drilling!" I impatiently counter.

"The army manual says two hours a day is enough," he answers, shaking his head no.

Flabbergasted, I look at him and say, "Okay, general, I give up. What do you suggest the men do?"

"Attack," he answers, without the slightest bit of hesitation.

"Attack?" I ask.

"Attack," he confirms.

"Attack what?" I ask.

"Attack the Greeks," he answers.

I am instantly horrified. I swear, if I ever meet an army general who knows how to do anything but attack, I'm gonna shake his fucking hand.

"No," I say firmly.

"Why not?" he asks.

"Because I said so!" I yell.

I've got enough blood on my hands and don't want to add anymore, so I'll be damned if I'm gonna let the army attack again while I'm in command of it. Still, the army has to do something, I guess, and Aeneas won't go away until he gets his stupid orders.

For several moments, I rack my brain for something harmless the army can do. Aeneas stands by my bed while I think, patiently waiting for an answer. Finally, I come up with an idea. And it's a real humdinger that should keep him out of my hair for days.

"Have the army start developing evacuation plans," I order.

He fidgets around uncomfortably and asks what I mean.

"Have the army start planning for an evacuation," I explain, "you know, in case Troy's walls are breeched by the enemy."

"The Trojan Army does not retreat," he informs me stiffly.

"Make it a fighting withdrawal then," I say, trying to placate him, "you know, buying time so the people of Troy and our sacred objects can get safely away."

The word 'fighting' sparks his interest, as does the chance for glorious sacrifice. What better way for a soldier to die, than while protecting the flight of his people? That hooks him, of course.

"Where will the people escape to?" he asks.

"Oh, I don't know," I say, musing, "maybe Mount Ida?"

He considers this for a moment in silence.

"Hey!" he suddenly erupts. "What about Italy? I hear it's really nice there."

"Yeah, sure, Italy sounds great," I answer. I'll agree to any place on earth if it'll make him go away.

"Okay, then, we'll plan to conduct a fighting withdrawal all the way to Italy," he answers. "And once we're there, we'll build a democracy, and a really big, kick-ass army, and when we're ready, we'll counter-attack the Greeks from the west when they least expect it. The bastards won't know what hit them!"

"What goes around, comes around," I answer with an affirming nod. "Now, go away and work out the details with the rest of the army."

Smiling proudly, he snaps to attention and salutes.

I return his salute and try not to laugh at his silliness.

He turns on his heels and leaves. As he does, I recognize the ceremonial sword I gave him for being the best man at Helen's and my wedding.

That's right, I know it's hard to believe, but Helen and I actually got hitched.

The wedding took place a week or two after my fight with Menelaus. My father wanted to let the Greeks know he wasn't fooling around, so he asked Helen to sign a divorce proclamation, which the hussy was only too happy to do, and, soon afterwards, he made arrangements for us to get married in the palace. Aeneas was named, or rather, assigned, to be my best man because all of my brothers refused to accept the position. Seems I soiled the family name during my duel with Menelaus and they didn't want anything to do with me. Of course, that was just fine and dandy with me. I didn't want to get married anyway and anything preventing the ceremony from happening was nothing but good news to me. In the end though, I had no choice, as Aeneas was ordered by my father to step in and see that I performed my duties in a satisfactory manner, which the idiot did with all the gusto of an army drill instructor. I'll bet no groom has been as thoroughly trained as I was. I shit you not, Aeneas had me reciting my wedding vows so much that I was repeating them back in my sleep.

The wedding itself was a gloomy affair, mainly because the official conducting it died during the ceremony.

And you thought your wedding was a friggin' nightmare!

Mine actually killed someone! I'm not kidding, it really did!

You see, for some strange reason, my father chose Aesacus to preside over the proceedings. You might remember him — he's the fucker who interrupted my mother's dream and was directly responsible for sending my ass out to die on the slopes of Mount Ida. Yeah, that bastard! Anyway, ever since my return, he had fallen from grace, even though a blind man could now see that his warnings about me were pretty much on the mark, especially in light of my marriage to Helen. And I'm sure that's what killed the bastard because he died seconds after pronouncing us man and wife. His eyes just rolled into the back of his head and he keeled over dead before Helen and I could seal the deal with a kiss. Served the fucker right, I felt, and I couldn't help smiling, but his death sure put a damper on the rest of the ceremony though.

After Aesacus' lifeless body was carried away, the guests started drinking themselves silly, you know, kinda like doomed prisoners do before they're executed. That's because, like Aesacus, everyone knew the sort of trouble that was coming to Troy's walls because of the unholy union they had just witnessed and so, they tried their damndest to forget the whole rotten thing had ever happened. They did it by consuming vast amounts of wine. Of course, I got stinking drunk along with them, and, as usual, when I've had too much to drink, I made an embarrassing spectacle of myself.

"I'm sorry," I stumbled around saying. "I'm really, really sorry. You know what? You know what? I'll tell you what. I used to think the world was changed by big things, like floods, volcanoes and earthquakes and shit, but noooooo, it's the little things that changes it, like weddings and whores. Am I right? Huh? Am I right? Damn right, I'm right. That's my point. Point. Point? What are we talking about? Oh, yeah, I'm a sex addict."

Helen, on the other hand, looked happy through it all, no doubt, because she had finally gotten what she wanted and she could care less how much trouble it caused. That's Helen in a nutshell and that's a big reason why I got so damned drunk. Not that I ever really needed a reason to get toasted.

Anyway, my father fawned all over Helen, but when he turned to me, he just frowned and shook his head in disgust. You'll agree that was just a tad bit unjust, but then again, I wasn't walking around the place sportin' a prize pair of knockers either. I'm telling you, sometimes, a pair of juicy breasts makes all the difference in the world when folks decide what's good or bad, and so, no wonder papa was prepared to give Helen the benefit of a doubt. Everyone else was too.

I don't remember much about the honeymoon night as I was pretty much wasted. I think we spent it in the palace, doing it once or twice before I passed out completely. It's just as well I did because I'm pretty sure I would have spent the rest of the night crying if I hadn't.

The next morning, Helen and I were summoned to attend Aesacus' funeral by my father's servants. We got there late, of course, because I was so hung over, and Helen couldn't decide which dress to wear. After we were seated on the back row, I looked around and saw long faces everywhere, much like those at our wedding, and I wondered why the heck there wasn't a wet bar. Believe me, I've never seen a group of people who needed a snort more. This was especially true when my father gave the eulogy. I swear, he droned on and on about the greatness of the Aesacus, until I thought my ears were going to start bleeding, and when my father compared Aesacus to a beautiful sea bird, I needed a drink more than ever. I was on the verge of sneaking away to get one when my little brother Polites, who was in charge of the coastal lookouts, suddenly came running up and announced that the entire Greek army was about to land.

The news scared the shit out of me, as you can imagine, and I immediately had only one thought in mind — self-preservation. I was bounding through the citadel's main gate before the first alarms bells could ring, and, by the time they quit clanging, I found myself sharing a dark closet in my house with a bunch of frightened female servants. Together, we cowered in one of its dark corners, hidden by all the clothing, crying our fool heads off. Helen appeared briefly and ordered us to come out. I threw a shoe at her in response and told her to shut the door and lock it too.

Several moments later, I heard the sounds of muffled footsteps and voices, and then, the closet door opened, and Hector appeared in the doorway. He was fully armed and equipped for battle.

"What the Hades do you think you're doing?" he bellowed down at me.

"Calming the servants," I fessed up.

"Don't lie to me! You goddamned coward!" he shouted. "I can't believe you would shirk your duties when Troy is in so much danger."

Seeing is believing, thinks I, now close the door and go away.

Unable to move me, he pointed his spear at my head and said, "Listen to me, mister, if you think you're gonna hide behind a bunch of women while the men of Troy are fighting to defend our city, well, I can assure you, you'd better think again cause, I swear, if you don't get your ass out here right now and join us, I'll kill you myself."

That moved me.

To think fast anyway!

"Okay, okay!" I answered, throwing my hands up in front of my face. "I'll join you! But let me clean up my armor first and get my bow ready for action. I promise you, when both are ready to go, I'll rush out to join the defense, so go on ahead and I'll catch up with you later."

Much, much later, I planned.

For a moment or two, he stood there staring at me in silence, trying to decide whether or not to believe me, and when it seemed he didn't, Helen suddenly stepped forward and said, "Brother, I wish a whirlwind would have carried me away the day I was born so that none of this would have ever happened. But since it has, I wish that I was married to a man as brave as you. We both know Alexander can't be depended on and never will be. So it's up to you to defend our city against the trouble that my husband and I have wrought."

I swear, it was the smartest thing I ever heard the hussy say, and I was so surprised she said it, that I looked up at her in wonderment. Like I said before, I never knew what was going to come out of her pie hole next.

Hector was surprised too, and since her words were true, that is, most of them were anyway — don't believe that shit about a whirlwind — he lowered his spear and agreed with her, adding, "I cannot stay here to see that Paris keeps his word. I must go to my post and command the city's defenses. So, I urge you to make sure that your husband gets his equipment together as fast as possible and joins me before the fighting starts."

"I will," Helen answered with a solemn nod.

Good luck with that! I thought.

It should be no surprise then, that by the time I got my armor together and left the house, the fighting seemed almost over. At least, that's the way it appeared to me because, from my upstairs window, I could see thousands of Trojan soldiers streaming back into the city's walls just as fast as their feet could carry them. I naturally assumed that they were retreating and the battle was over. Little did I know, they were actually doing something known in military terms as 'regrouping for a counterattack'. Had I known that, believe me, jack, I wouldn't have stepped foot out of my house.

And so, like a danged fool, I set off down the street thinking things were safe enough for me to put in a token appearance. Maybe then, I reasoned, Hector would get off of my back and leave me the fuck alone. That's precisely what I was angling for when I marched up to him and said, "Brother, I'm sorry that I kept you waiting when you were in such a hurry, and I apologize if I have not come as quickly as you wanted me to and also, for missing the battle."

He was standing in the midst of his captains. They were all covered in blood and more than half were wounded in some fashion. In sharp contrast, my armor didn't have a spot on it and my hair was perfectly combed.

Hector looked at me like I had just come from the moon.

Then, he smiled slyly and said, "My good brother, you haven't missed the battle. As a matter of fact, you couldn't have come at a better time. We were just reforming to hit them again. This time we'll crush them for sure, so I'd appreciate it if you would take command of the right flank."

Before I could answer, or faint, or cry, or shit my drawers, or run away, or do any of the things I normally do when I'm suddenly startled, Hector turned to an officer behind me and said, "Captain, please escort my brother over to his position and remain by his side until this action is concluded."

The Captain saluted smartly, took me by the arm and said, "It's an honor to serve by your side, sir. Come now, and allow me to show you your post."

The Captain was one of those rigid military types I had come by Aeneas to hate. I had no doubt that he was brave, dedicated, reckless, resourceful, and therefore, just about the last man I wanted standing by my side in a life or death situation. That's because men like him tend to get in the way when one's running for one's life. Anyway, we had no sooner gotten into position, when the dunderhead turns to the soldiers lined up behind us, starts pumping his spear up and down all crazy like, and shouts, "Brave men of Troy, follow your Prince to victory!"

Of course, that kind of talk only serves to scare the crap out of me.

"For god's sakes, Captain" I pleaded, "will you please stop doing that and shut up!"

"But it motivates the men, sir," he protested, then, he turned to the ranks again and shouted, "Who will follow Prince Paris to the Greek ships?"

To the man, I swear, they raised their spears and shouted, "I will! I will!"

I listened to them yell and thought, what in the name of fuck is going on here? Do any of these guys have a fucking brain in their head? Don't they know they are about to die? Don't they know they are on the edge of the abyss?

But before I could warn the soldiers to step back, or talk sense into them, bugles suddenly sounded the advance, and the ranks surged forward, 2,000 men strong, towards the Greek line. I was swept along with them, having no choice, and, shortly thereafter, as the enemy came into view, I immediately saw that we were on the verge of committing mass suicide. Don't think it's the coward in me talking, when I tell you the Greeks outnumber us five to one, because it ain't. I swear, from of the length of their line alone, I estimate their number to have been at least 10,000 men. All of Greece seemed to be there. And what's more fucked up, that son-of-a-bitch Achilles was out in front of them, roaring at us like an angry lion.

And, let me tell you, I've never known a scarier guy before or since. Achilles was a tall fellow, about a head above everyone else, with broad shoulders, I'd say at least a cubit wide, and heavy, muscular arms, almost as big as his massive thighs, and the thin, well-defined waist of an athlete. He was also a strikingly handsome guy, the type women go goo-goo over — bright blue eyes, straight nose, chiseled cheeks and jaw, full lips, and a long, thick mane of dirty-blond hair — you know, the works, and perhaps most amazing of all, Achilles was only a pubic hair past seventeen years old! But before you go thinking he was someone you wanted your daughter to date, let me tell you something else: Achilles was a homicidal maniac. I'm talking on the order of Hercules here. The fucker lived to kill. Weeks before he landed at Troy, Achilles attacked and burned twenty-three cities to the ground just for practice. And if that ain't crazy enough for you, let me tell you something else: Achilles loved to dress up in women's clothes. Damn sure did! And put on their makeup too! Go figure. And, what's more, he thought his horses, Balius and Xanthus, could talk. I swear, the three of them used to carry on all sorts of imaginary conversations. Weird, ain't it? But here's the real kicker: Achilles was an outright necrophiliac. I'm not kidding! He actually loved to screw dead people! That's probably because he was always surrounded by so many of them.

And do you know what it's like to march towards a psychotic teenager who's not only going to kill you; he's also gonna fuck you too?

It ain't a very pleasant experience, I can assure you.

So, anyway, there I was, trapped between two armies of suicidal fools with no way out. As I trudged along, I racked my brain for a means to escape. Would the Captain listen to me if I pointed out that we were about to die? Probably not; the idiot, all courage and no brains, would no doubt think everything was just peachy. What then? Glancing towards my brother, I hoped that he had weighed the odds and was about to order a retreat. But, his steady, relentless advance towards the enemy soon dashed my hopes. Not once did he pause or falter. No sir, not him. You see, out-numbered or not, Hector was going to attack the Greeks in the only manner he knew how: straight for the heart, without any regard for casualties.

"Be brave, men!" my brother yelled, urging the troops forward. "Stay in formation! Look sharp!"

And that's when it hit me.

Turning around abruptly, I quickly walked back towards the advancing ranks of Trojans.

"Sir, where are you going?" the Captain immediately asked.

"Look how sloppy those ranks look, Captain!" I shouted at him. "They're all out of whack. They're disgraceful."

"But, sir, that's because the ground is so broken," he shouted back. "It's hard for the men to maintain good order here."

I entered the first rank and yelled, "Captain, we must see that the men dress their ranks!"

"But, sir!" he pleaded, "we really need to be out in front of the men, to lead them against the enemy!"

Yeah, right!

I ignored him, of course, and kept walking towards the rear of the formation, shouting as I went, "Dress your ranks men! Dress your ranks! You heard my brother, look sharp now!"

The men gawked at me as if I had lost my mind.

I could care less what they thought, figuring they were all about to die anyway, and so, I kept going until I reached the last rank. From there, I could see Troy's walls and not a soul standing between them and me. Finally, the way was clear for me to escape and, you can bet the house, I didn't hesitate a second to do so. There was only one hitch though: that pesky Captain was still at my elbow.

As I started jogging towards Troy, he screamed, "Where are you going now, sir?"

Thinking fast, I shouted, "To get some water for the men! They're gonna need water. And medics too!"

"But, sir, we have to return to our post!" he pleaded again. "We are almost upon the enemy!"

"All the more reason I should go!" I yelled, waving goodbye.

"But sir!" he protested.

I paused for a moment, looked over my shoulder at him impatiently, and shouted, "You take command while I see to the men's welfare. That's an order, Captain!"

Then I ran away.

I didn't see the Captain again until I had reached the safety of Troy's walls. From atop the battlements, I watched our men charge the Greek lines, yelling their stupid heads off, and as they did, I saw the Captain lead the right flank forward; he was waving his spear over his head, and behind him, the men obediently followed. Just before they reached the Greeks, there was hail of arrows from both sides, and the Captain fell to the ground with an arrow sticking out of his skull. Of course, I felt his death only justified my decision to flee, as I was pretty sure I would have suffered the same fate if I had stayed, and so, I didn't feel the least bit bad about deserting my post.

Unfortunately, my brother didn't feel the same way. Hector was pissed off to the max, for sure, and he was all for court-marshalling my ass for desertion in the face of the enemy or something silly like that. And he would have done it too, if my father hadn't stopped him. You see, my father felt it would hurt the war effort by embarrassing us in front of the Greeks, figuring it would do no good if the Greeks thought any of us were cowards. Of course, I agreed with him, adding that perception was everything. He promptly told me to shut the fuck up and instructed Hector not to place me in charge of anything ever again. That suited me just fine, as you can imagine, and so, after that, I was pretty much on my own during the war. I spent most of it on top of the battlements shooting arrows down at any Greek who had his back turned towards me. Not only was this a healthy way to fight a war, it was also kinda fun picking them off one by one, and besides that, it also gave me a ringside seat to all the action.

I won't bore you with a blow-by-blow account of the war. I'll leave all that up to the historians and bards who don't have anything better to do. Instead, I'll give you my take on things, just so you'll understand how I viewed the whole fiasco. And a fiasco it was, believe me, from start to finish. You see, although Hector's suicidal counterattack failed to push the Greeks back into the sea, it killed just enough of them to give them second thoughts about attacking our city again, and so they retreated back down to the beach where they built a fort of sorts and waited for reinforcements. Why they did this has always been a mystery to me because, by then, we were down to less than a thousand men. The Greeks still had about seven thousand left and I'm pretty sure we'd been toast if they would have launched one more attack. But, for some strange reason, they didn't. All I can say is that the Greeks never seemed to have a clear notion on how to finish us off. Nor did they have much unity either. I mean, Agamemnon always seemed to be in a pissing contest of some sort with his fellow commanders, specifically a general named Palamedes, and that caused the Greeks a great deal of division and confusion. On the other hand, since Hector was pretty much running things for us, our efforts were always united. And, with Hector in charge, that meant only one thing: we were going to attack till it killed us. And it damned near did too. I swear, there wasn't a day that passed without Hector launching some sort of an attack. Sometimes, nights too! I'm telling you, it was the damnedest thing you ever did see. I mean, there we were with a thousand men, more or less, and the Greeks with seven times that, yet, we were the ones attacking and the Greeks were the ones getting besieged. Makes you scratch your head in wonderment, doesn't it? I couldn't believe it either. Anyway, while Hector's tactics gave the Greeks fits, it also whittled our forces down pretty good. Before long, we were down to a mere handful of Trojans. The only thing that saved us was that we kept getting reinforcements from our allies. Besides our close neighbors, far off Abydos, Arisbe, Zeleia, Mysia, Phrygia, Paphlagonia, Maeonia, Caria, and Lycia, to name several, also sent us troops. They'd showed up, Hector would pat them on the shoulder and say, "Thank you for coming to Troy's defense. Good show. Got your equipment together then? Very good! Well, then, let's attack." And that's the last time we'd see any of them.

Speaking of which, how Hector survived as long as he did, still amazes me. I swear, for ten years, there wasn't an attack he didn't plan and personally lead. Not one. It was plumb suicidal, believe me. Even his wife, Andromache, thought so. She was always bitching at him about it. Once, while coming down an empty staircase in the palace, I accidentally overheard one of their spats. They were just below me and out of sight. Hector had just come out of a meeting with his captains, when Andromache suddenly ran up and confronted him.

"Dear husband," she said, "I'm so worried about you! Why do you have to lead every attack? Aren't there other generals who could lead them? What about your brother Deiphobus? Or Polites? Or Aeneas? Surely you can find somebody else to do it. Why do you have to do it all the time?"

"Because if I don't," he answered, "it will look like I avoided battle like a coward."

"Coward?" she quickly countered. "Darling, no one is gonna think you're a coward! You've been fighting non-stop for years now. Folks will understand if you take some time off and get some rest. Come on, baby, put someone else in command and let's go home and relax."

"Nope," he replied, "can't do it."

"But, baby," she continued on in a lower voice, "we haven't made love since this war began. I'm getting really, really lonely, if you know what I mean."

It was an invitation for a delicious round of sex if I ever did hear one, you'll agree, but unfortunately, it was one totally wasted on my stupid brother.

"I'm sorry, honey," he said, "but I can't. I know only one way to command an army and that is to be at its forefront all the time."

"But darling," she pleaded, "what if you are killed? Will you leave me with a longing that will never be satisfied? Who will be left to comfort me after you are gone? Please baby, come home and take me in your arms once again."

"Honey, I'm sorry, but I don't have time," he answered. "Please try to understand. I have to lead the army because if I don't, I fear it will be defeated and then, you might be taken captive and forced to weave at the bidding of a mistress, or made to fetch water by a cruel taskmaster. I am personally leading the army to insure that that day never comes, darling."

And that's when Andromache did the only thing she could do. Seizing Hector by the hand, she led him over to the side of the staircase. I could just see them through the railings and I watched in complete astonishment as she pushed him against the wall, and kissed him passionately, while skillfully negotiating her right hand under his tunic. I let out an astonishing gasp as she did, which, luckily, neither one of them heard, and immediately grasped the railing to steady myself.

"Come on, baby, fuck me right here," Andromache whispered, lifting up her skirt with her left hand.

"Here?" Hector answered, looking around nervously.

"Yes, and hurry up too, before someone comes down the stairs," she replied.

Little did she know, or suspect, that someone was already there, with an erection so hard, it almost made him cross-eyed.

Anyhow, Hector paused for a moment, as if to gather his thoughts, and then he caressed Andromache fondly, and said, "Dear wife, please don't get mad, but a woman shouldn't hurry her man like this. I will make love to you when the time is right. Until then, go home and attend to your duties, your loom, your distaff, and managing our servants, and remember, in a time of war, we all have to make sacrifices."

Meet my brother Hector, folks. The dumbest man on earth!

I almost fainted; I always knew Hector was stupid, but until then, I didn't know how much. Nor did I know just how lonely Andromache was either and as I watched her collapse sobbing into his arms, I couldn't help but feel sorry for her.

Hector held Andromache for several seconds after that, without saying anything more, then he released her and abruptly put his red plumed helmet on his head. That's it! No kiss goodbye or pat on the ass. Nothing! I couldn't believe it! Neither could Andromache. She straightened up in astonishment, adjusted her skirt and immediately ran away. It was the saddest thing I ever saw and I couldn't help but be reminded of Oenone and the hurt I had caused her. I realized it was the same as Andromache's and I cursed the day I left my wife. Of course, I wanted to go home to her more than ever, but, at that point, it was impossible because I was in too deep with Helen, the Greeks, and the Trojans. All I could do at that point was put my head down, grit my teeth, and plow blindly ahead.

And so, the war dragged on, day after day, until finally, both sides had enough and agreed to a truce. And that's the other stupid thing about this war I should tell you. Believe it or not, there were more periods of truces in it than there were periods of fighting. I'm not kidding you, there really were! The first truce occurred after the first month's fighting and lasted about six months. Then, there was another month of fighting, followed by a second truce that lasted for three years. Three fucking years! After that, altogether, I think there was a total of eleven more months fighting and five years worth of truces. Amazing, ain't it? Damn right it is. And that's why this fucking war has lasted ten years. You see, every time it reached a decisive point, a truce would be declared to keep the thing from ending. It was downright crazy. I mean, who ever heard of stopping a war so that one side could recover? See how nuts it was?

And let me tell you something else about this fucked-up war: the most important events occurred during the truces, not during the fighting. Oh, don't get me wrong, there were the usual rounds of combat between champions that were exciting to watch and all, but none of them, with the exception of Hector's death, of course, influenced the direction of the war like the things that occurred during the truces.

For instance, during the first truce, Hector and our cousin, Ajax, actually became close friends. In case you don't know who Ajax is, he was one of the Greek's leading killers, and his mother was my father's sister Hesione, you know, the woman my father wanted to trade Helen for. So, it was kind of weird watching them gallivanting around town like a couple of schoolyard chums. They gave each other gifts of swords and belts and there were even rumors floating around that they had been seen kissing and hugging too, although, I don't believe any of them, giving Hector's sexual naivety. But with tough guys like them, who knows? Maybe that's why Andromache was always so lonely. Anyway, whatever it was, folks had high hopes that their friendship would lead to peace between Troy and Greece, and there were even diplomatic talks in that direction, but Agamemnon quickly made it clear that he and his army hadn't come all the way over from Greece for nothing, or to make new boyfriends, and so, the negotiations were shut down and the fighting resumed.

And during the second truce, a levelheaded Greek commander named Palamedes challenged Agamemnon's authority. Seems that since he had organized the army and oversaw the construction of the camp's fortifications, Palamedes thought he should be in charge of things. Agamemnon, of course, thought otherwise, arguing that his money had largely bankrolled the whole project, and so, the two of them spent most of the ensuing truces lobbying for control of the army. That's why some of the truces lasted so damned long. Most of the time, the Greeks didn't know who was in charge. Eventually, believe it or not, Palamedes won out. When he did, Agamemnon promptly declared that he was packing his bags and going home. No one seemed particularly upset by this, since Agamemnon was such a big pain in the ass, but before the Greeks could throw Agamemnon a going away party, Palamedes wondered too close to our walls one evening and I shot him dead with an arrow. I have to admit it was one of the dumbest things I did during the war, as I'm pretty sure, had Palamedes lived, and Agamemnon departed, a peace could have been negotiated. All I can say is, I didn't know who Palamedes was. And the Greeks were not supposed to approach our walls. And I was drunk. And the soldier I was drinking with bet me I couldn't do it. And Hector had been on my ass all day for shirking my duty. And…well, you get the picture.

Anyway, to move on, during the latest truce, a deadly plague struck the Greek camp and damned near wiped it out. That's because the bastards were packed into the place like sardines and since the Greeks are some of the dirtiest people in the world, the only surprise is that it took almost ten years for a disease to pop up in their dump. The sickness started with their mules and dogs, killing them off completely, and then it focused its attention on the soldiers. Soon, they were dropping like flies. There was dead and dying everywhere, and when the wind blew towards Troy, our nostrils were flooded with the stink of death. I swear, you couldn't walk down the street without gagging your ass off. For nine days the plague raged, and when it was gone, so was three quarters of the Greek army. Of course, it was a perfect time for our army to launch an attack and finish the Greeks off once and for all, but do you know, it was prevented from doing so by Troy's citizenry who were afraid our soldiers would carry the disease back into the city when they returned from the battle. I'm not kidding you, folks were downright hysterical about it. They even stopped our emissaries from offering the Greeks peace, which, I'm sure the sick bastards would have readily accepted, and so, another opportunity was lost to end the war. It was just plain nuts.

But nothing could top the lunacy that happened during the fifth or sixth truce. No, sir, not even close. Because, you see, that's when Achilles actually fell in love with my sister Polyxena and vowed to quit fighting because of it.

Let me repeat that, just in case you fainted: Achilles fell in love with my sister Polyxena and quit the war.

That's right, he actually did.

It happened like this: one peaceful day, during the ninth year of the war, Polyxena, Hector, my father and mother, traveled outside the city's walls to pay respect to the war dead. By that stage, there was a vast cemetery, as you can imagine, where the sports arena used to be and a monument of sorts had been dedicated there to all the Trojans and Greeks who had been fool enough to get themselves killed during the fighting. Since it was considered neutral ground, the cemetery was a popular place for folks from both sides to visit. They'd wander around until they found an urn containing the ashes of someone they knew, then they'd stop and make an offering to the departed soul. It was touching to watch them do so, but, I have to admit, the place gave me the willies, mainly because I considered it to be a testimonial to my stupidity. That's why I never stepped foot in it. Say what you will about me, but I do have a conscience.

You couldn't say that about that son-of-a-bitch Achilles.

I'm not lying when I say he was personally responsible for populating most of the urns in the cemetery. He really was. And he also didn't have any qualms about visiting the place either. As a matter of fact, he enjoyed the heck out of it because each visit provided him with another opportunity to brag about his skills as a serial killer. He'd walk around the urns with a pack of bards in tow, and say, "Oh, yes, this is so and so, a worthy opponent, ha, ha, I stabbed him in the head with my spear, ha, ha." The bards following him would smile broadly and jot down every word he said, and that's why, I think, their description of this war has always been so goddamned gory.

Anyway, on that fateful day, the two groups happened to be in the cemetery at the same time. And, just by coincidence, they also happened to be visiting the urn of a Trojan officer named Demoleon, whom Polyxena had been sweet on and Achilles had killed sometime earlier.

For several moments the two groups stood on opposite sides of Demoleon's urn, staring daggers at one another, until one of the bards, a Chios hack named Homer, whips out his notepad and starts asking questions.

"How did this soldier die?" Homer asked.

"I stabbed him in the temple with my spear," Achilles answered boastfully. "It pierced his helmet, smashed through his skull and spattered his brains all over the place."

I don't have to tell you how well that went over on the Trojan side of the urn.

In the uproar that followed, swords were drawn, challenges were made, and blood would have been spilled for sure if Polyxena hadn't suddenly taken matters into her own hands.

Or, I guess I should say, her own fists.

You see, she walked straight past the urn of her former lover, right up to Achilles, and, I swear to god, she slugged him in the mouth. Bam! Right in the kisser! The bastard never saw it coming and, for a few seconds, it stunned him. He just stood there, eyes wide, gaping down at her in disbelief.

And then, believe it or not, she hit him again! Bam! Just like before!

"Stop that!" Achilles suddenly yelled, raising his arms up to protect himself. "And leave me alone, you crazy bitch!"

Wrong move.

Keyword: bitch.

It made Polyxena go berserk.

She was carrying a bronze sacrificial pot that was decorated with little brass studs. In a flash, she slammed it right up against Achilles' noggin. Wham! I was told that the studs made little indentations in Achilles' forehead. God, how I would have loved to have seen that! Anyway, the blow sent him falling to the ground like a bag of rocks. Then Polyxena stood over him, all five feet, two inches, hundred pounds of her, and started pummeling him over and over again with the pot, real hard — wham! wham! wham! — calling him all sorts of vile names as she did.

"You stupid, goddamned, murdering son-of-a-bitch, lowlife, fucking, scum sucking dog!" she screamed. "I'll teach you to kill one of my lovers and call me a bitch!"

Wham! Wham! Wham!

"Ahhhhhhhh!" Achilles yelled in pain.

The crowd around them was absolutely shocked and paralyzed by the scene. I mean, Polyxena was so small and Achilles was…well…you know what a fucking monster he was.

But that was nothing compared to what happened next.

To everybody's surprise, Achilles suddenly covered his face with his hands and started bawling like a newborn baby. I'm not kidding, he really did! And it's good for Achilles that he did too, because his wailings stopped Polyxena's blows. Otherwise, I'm pretty sure she would have beaten him to a pulp. Then, as she stood there glaring down at him in disgust, Achilles cries suddenly grew into a series of maniacal shrieks and, if that wasn't scary enough, he started tearing at his long blonde hair and kicking the ground violently. Crazy? Damned straight he was. Ask anyone who witnessed it.

Finally, after thrashing about wildly for two or three minutes, he regained control of his senses again, looked up at Polyxena and said, "I'm so sorry! I implore you to forgive me! What can I do to set things right? I swear, anything you ask shall be done!"

I figure there were about a hundred answers to that.

Luckily, my sister had the best one ready.

She immediately stiffened, dropped the battered pot on his chest and said, "Stop fighting in this war."

And, do you know, the crazy bastard instantly agreed!

"I swear," he said with feeling, "from this moment on, I will fight no more forever."

"Good," answered Polyxena. "See that you don't."

"And I swear I will love you forever too," Achilles added.

"I didn't ask for that," Polyxena quickly snapped.

"Will you love me forever?" Achilles asked, wiping the tears from his eyes.

"No," Polyxena replied without any hesitation.

"Why not?" Achilles asked, tears welling up in his eyes again.

She sighed impatiently. "Because you're a lowlife, fucking, scum sucking dog. Understand?"

"I can change," Achilles whimpered.

"Prove it," Polyxena replied.

And, snap, just like that, the mighty Achilles was out of the war. Polyxena had accomplished something in five minutes that the entire Trojan army hadn't been able to do in nine years. Go figure. Anyway, I'm sure Demoleon was laughing in his urn. I know I laughed when I heard the news. And I laughed at Achilles every day after that too. So did everyone else. That's because my sister positively made a fool out of him. She's all the idiot lived for. He gave up everything else —

the war, his Greek comrades, his possessions, hookers, random torture, drinking — everything. And guess what? Even then, my sister wouldn't have anything to do with him! And, here's the really surprising part — Achilles is probably the only man Polyxena ever turned down! That one stumped everyone, including me. But it only seemed to egg Achilles on. He tried all sorts of sickening stuff to win her heart. He played his lyre under her window at night, sent her flowers, wrote her love letters, bought her jewelry, performed feats of strength in her honor, heck, he even asked my father for her hand in marriage. And nothing worked! Polyxena wouldn't give him the time of day. It was downright hilarious to watch.

Eventually, Achilles' Greek friends felt the situation was getting out of hand and decided to step in. First, his buddies Odysseus, Ajax and Phoinix tried to talk some sense into him by appealing to his manhood, telling him that he had become a nervous little weenie and a big embarrassment to the whole damned Greek army. When that didn't work, they tried to reason with him. They told him that Polyxena was just a rich Trojan slut, reminding him that even Thersites, the ugliest bastard in the Greek army, had fucked her, along with most of the Trojan army, and therefore, she wasn't the least bit worthy of his affections. I must admit they weren't far off the mark with that one... well...the first and second parts anyway...but, true or not, none of it did them any good because Achilles took their advice as mere jealousy and remained a whipped man. So, in the end, his friends gave up and went back to their camp. And without its number one champion to lead it, the Greek army refused to attack again.

And that's when my father took advantage of the situation.

If the Greeks didn't like Achilles' infatuation, my dad damned sure did because it presented him with a favorable opportunity to end the war. You see, when Achilles asked him for Polyxena's hand in marriage, my father responded by saying that he would give it on one condition: only if the Greeks would agree to his terms and go the fuck home. Do you see the beauty here? In effect, my pop turned the Greek's mightiest soldier into Troy's foremost ambassador for peace. Crafty ain't it? You should have seen it too: each day, Achilles would walk down to the Greek camp and plead with them to return my aunt and go home. At first, they wondered if he was crazy, and when they figured out he actually was, they laughed at him. That proved to be a huge mistake because Achilles promptly slapped the shit out of a dozen or so of them for failing to take him seriously. After that, they learned to treat him with more respect. They would listen to him thoughtfully, trying hard not to laugh, and when he was done, they'd politely walk him to the gate and tell him they would put his proposals to the men. Of course, they never did, mainly because Agamemnon, Menelaus, and Odysseus and the other leaders had no doubts about how the proposals would be received. The truth is, without Achilles to lead it, the Greek army, what was left of it, would have voted to go home in a heartbeat.

And to be honest with you, I don't believe my father really thought Achilles could pull it off. I think he did it mainly to have fun with Achilles and to embarrass the crap out of the Greeks because, you see, I'm pretty sure he wouldn't have went through with the deal even if Achilles had. I mean, everyone knew what a nut job Achilles and his family were. I mean, his dad Peleus was a well known rapist and his mom, Thetis, was an equally famous baby killer. Would you purposely bond your daughter to folks like that? Of course not! Neither would my father. War or no war, my dad wasn't that stupid.

So, anyway, that's some of the silly shit that made this war such a damned fiasco.

And that was pretty much the situation going into this, the final year of the war. Both sides had seen their armies weakened to a point that a military victory was nothing more than a general's wet dream. Yet, neither side was willing to admit the truth and agree to end the bloody lunacy.

And so, the time was right for a leader to step forward and make them face reality.

A really, really cunning leader.

And you're never gonna believe who that guy was.

Chapter Nine

"Are you dead yet?" a nearby voice asks.

I don't have to open my eyes to see who it is. I know the voice. It belongs to my brother Deiphobus. He's here to see if I am still among the quick cause, if I ain't, he immediately becomes the crown prince, commander of the army, and gets Helen's hand in marriage.

Well, fuck him.

I open my eyes, smile and say, "Would you please ask the maid to bring me some punch? I'm feeling a tad parched right now."

A look of disappointment suddenly appears on his face, which, of course, makes my grin grow larger.

That pisses him off and he feints a lunge at me, causing my body to jerk in response. Immediately, waves of pain sweep over me and I can't help but cry out. As I do, he throws back his head and laughs savagely at my agony.

"Almost," he says with satisfaction, "maybe a few hours more."

"Don't hold your breath," I say, through gritted teeth.

A thought crosses his mind and he says, "Well, then, maybe I should hurry the process along."

I watch in alarm as he walks toward me. There's no doubt what he is thinking of doing. He's gonna push the arrow into me till I am dead. And, the terrible thing is that I am helpless to stop him.

Well, almost.

He stops by the bed, looks at the arrow and then at me, and smiles cruelly.

The sweat is pouring off of me like water, and the pain from my wound is unbearable. He reaches over with one hand and takes hold of the arrow. Immediately, a new wave of pain washes over me and I plead with him to stop.

He shakes his head no, leans down close to my face and whispers, "Time to die, brother."

It's the moment I've been waiting for.

As quick as a cobra's strike, I raise the knife I've been hiding under my blanket and place the blade against his jugular. At the same time, with my other hand, I grab a handful of hair to hold his head in place. It takes all my strength not to faint from the pain caused by these two movements.

He immediately freezes.

"Let go of the arrow," I say firmly.

He hesitates and I push the knife deeper into his neck. Dark red blood runs down the razor sharp blade and drops onto the clean, white sheets below. A single swipe of my hand and my brother's out in the cemetery occupying a new urn. He knows it and so do I. We also both know that I'm just as close to death. All he has to do is push the arrow in a little deeper.

We pause, waiting for the other to give in.

Finally, anger wells up in his eyes and I have no doubt about what he is going to do next.

Frustrated, he lets go of the arrow, lifts his arms up sideways and says, "Fine! You're gonna be dead in a couple of hours anyway."

For a second, I consider killing him. I want to. Bad! But something in the back of my mind tells me that it's not worth it. I mean, he's not taking anything from me that I wouldn't happily give up to anyone. He can be king for all I care. And he can have Helen too. He can have them both and be damned for it, I say. Serves the little reptile right!

I release his hair and he backs quickly away. His hand grips his throat to stop the bleeding and he glares at me with the same anger that forced him to let go of the arrow.

"Don't get me wrong," I say. "I really want to kill you. So you'd better run along now before I change my mind."

For a long moment, we both stare hate at each other until, finally, he sneers and walks out of the room. I immediately heave a sigh of relief and collapse into the bed.

How I found the courage to stand up to Deiphobus, I don't know. I've never known.

But I think it happened shortly after Hector's death.

Looking back on it now, I'm almost amazed as you that I finally grew some balls but I guess it was inevitable. I mean, when you are surrounded by a pack of idiots and escape seems impossible, sometimes there's nothing left to do but summon up enough courage to take charge of the situation and figure a way out of whatever pickle you're in. That's exactly what happened to me.

And surprisingly enough, it wasn't that difficult of a problem to solve. It just took some brains and cunning on my part.

But I'm getting way ahead of myself here, so let me back up a bit and explain how it happened.

Do you remember how crazy in love Achilles was? And that he swore to stay out of the war? And how he became a peace envoy for us? Well, all that changed when his buddy Patroclus died. That's the day my brother Hector thought he was going to win an astonishing victory and end the war. You see, we had just received a large contingent of Thracian reinforcements and, as usual, Hector was chomping at the bit to hurl them at the Greeks, only this time, he did something he never did before — he sent out a spy to locate the weak spots in the Greek defenses. The spy's name was Dolon.

Now, let me tell you a little something about spies — you can't trust 'em farther than you can throw 'em. That's because lying and sneaking around is a virtue to them. They are, without a doubt, the closest thing to me you'll ever care to meet, and I don't have to tell you how untrustworthy I am. And that's the way it was with this guy Dolon. I mean, the man even wore a wolf-skin cloak and weasel-skin cap for god's sakes! Come on! If that wasn't a dead giveaway as to his nature, I don't know what was. So, why Hector trusted this fellow is beyond me, but he did, and when Dolon gets caught sneaking around the Greek camp later that evening, he immediately spills the beans about Hector's plan. And what do you think the Greeks did? Bingo! They immediately attacked the Thracian camp! The poor Thracians never knew what hit them — really, they didn't — because most of the Thracians were fast asleep when the Greeks struck. Pretty soon, as you can imagine, there were dead and dying Thracians all over the place. It all happened so fast and was over with so quickly that Hector didn't hear about it until the Greeks were safely back in their fort.

Now, you'd figure that, with his plan thwarted, Hector would show some common sense and call off the attack. I know I would have and you probably would have too. But not Hector. Without any hesitation, the dunderhead immediately rounded up what was left of the Thracian reinforcements and, just as the sun was beginning to rise, launched the attack. The Greeks were ready for them, of course, and stopped it cold, and what's worse, they counterattacked and drove our forces all the way back to the city's gates.

It's then that the battle reached a crisis, and in every crisis, Hector only knew one thing to do — attack some more. Ordering the seven hundred troopers of our cavalry reserve forward, Hector mounted his horse and led a cavalry charge straight at the Greeks. I was on top of the wall firing arrows down on the Greeks when he did it, so I saw the whole thing, and let me tell you, the charge was simply magnificent. And so was Hector. Folks, my brother might have been dumb and all, but, I swear, I've never seen a braver man. He plunged right in the middle of the advancing Greeks with all the fury of a cornered lion, throwing them into complete disarray, and when the rest of the cavalry joined him, the rout was on. From my perch, I watched the terrified Greeks hotfoot it all the way back to their fort. Hector and his cavalry were tight on their heels the whole time, and there would have been a great slaughter if our horses hadn't been stopped by the wall and moat encircling the Greek camp.

I could see the Greek fortifications from where I stood, and, let me tell you, I wouldn't have attacked them with seven thousand troopers. They were just too well built and defended. Nor was I alone in thinking that. Polydamas, our cavalry's commander, argued against it too. But Hector wouldn't hear any of it, of course. His blood was up by then, so he ordered his troopers to dismount and attack the defenses. Usually, cavalrymen are loath to do something like that, but to their credit, they did and they did it well. Soon, whole sections of the Greeks' defenses were on the verge of collapsing.

And that's when it happened.

That's when Patroclus suddenly appeared wearing Achilles' armor.

Remember when I told you Achilles gave his armor away? Well, Patroclus was the guy he gave it to. Only no one knew that at the time. So everyone, including my brother Hector, naturally thought Achilles had rejoined the fight. Actually, Achilles was in a Trojan bar at the time writing love letters to my sister Polyxena. Anyway, Patroclus might have just as well painted a big red target on his ass, because, he quickly became a mark for any nearby Trojan to throw a rock or spear at. Little wonder then that the air around him quickly became full of all sorts of deadly objects. It was a rock that struck him first, knocking him to the ground. As he struggled to regain his feet, a spear hit him between the shoulders. And that's when Hector jumped in to finish the job. Weakened by his wounds, Patroclus could not resist, and Hector drove a spear through the defenseless man's belly.

Then, everybody sorta freaked out.

You see, instead of continuing to hammer away at the Greeks' defenses, the Trojans suddenly shifted all their efforts over to retrieving Achilles' body and, more specifically, his armor. For some reason, the idiots placed more importance on obtaining these two things than they did on winning the fucking war. Go figure that one out. Even Hector lost his mind. Believe it or not, he actually spent the next ten minutes or so chasing Achilles' two horses all over the place, and when he couldn't catch them, he returned to Patroclus' body and tried to cut the dead man's head off. But, by then, the body was being defended by a whole host of pissed off Greeks, who weren't about to give up their hero's body without a fight, so Hector was forced to turn to his troopers for help. Why he did this, I don't know, because it stopped them from breaking through the Greeks' defenses just when they were on the verge of doing so.

Like I said before, my brother was brave, but he didn't have a fucking brain in his head.

Then he compounded his lunacy by launching a series of fruitless attacks in an effort to recover the body. I'm telling you, it was just plain nuts. Back and forth the battle raged over Patroclus' lifeless body and, at times, I swear, it resembled a gigantic tug-of-war. You should have seen it: Hector would latch hold of Patroclus' leg, drag his body towards Troy, then some Greek would run up, grab hold of Patroclus' arm and drag him back towards their camp. In the meantime, folks were dying all around them. It was a bloody mess, for sure. And for what! Nothing! In the end, both sides became so exhausted that they couldn't fight anymore. One by one, they simply gave up and limped back to their respective corners.

Hector, as usual, was the last Trojan to leave the battlefield. No doubt, he walked off of it believing that he had, at least, managed to kill the great Achilles. So, it's not hard to imagine his surprise, when Achilles suddenly walked past him outside the South Gate. Hector looked like he had just seen a ghost and I daresay, at that moment, my brother knew he was a dead man. I mean, during the battle, he had purposely tried to kill Achilles, and when he thought he had, he boasted about it too, bragging about how he was going to plant Achilles' head on a stake and feed his body to the dogs. Well, everybody and his dog knew how Achilles was gonna take that, so, there was nothing left to do then, but bar the door, close the shutters and wait for Achilles' response.

It wasn't long in coming either.

The next morning, Achilles showed up outside the lower city's west gate, yelling blue bloody murder and challenging Hector to a duel. He was also wearing the blood stained armor he had given to Patroclus so there didn't seem much point telling him the whole thing had been one huge mistake and apologizing for it. I don't even think Polyxena could have calmed him down, although, I thought it was worth a shot and said so. But Hector didn't want Polyxena flashing her tits at the enemy and despite everybody's pleas otherwise, including Polyxena's, my brother remained determined to try conclusions with Achilles.

I don't have to tell you how I felt about that, but I will — it was just plain suicide. Not only was Achilles bigger than Hector, he was also much stronger. And crazier too! The way I saw it, Hector didn't stand a ghost of a chance but after all the bragging he had done the day before, I guess Hector felt he had to go. I felt differently, of course.

"You don't have to go," I told him. "Let Achilles keep raving. He'll get tired of it eventually and go home. Then we'll sic Polyxena on him. But if you go out there right now, he'll tear you to shreds."

"That's nonsense!" Deiphobus suddenly chimed in. "My brother's gonna rip off Achilles' head and shit down his throat!"

I looked at Deiphobus like he had lost his mind and, for a second, wondered what he was up to, but before my brain could formulate an answer, he tugged on Hector's shoulder and said, "Come on, brother, I'll help you get ready for battle."

There were quite a few worried frowns in the crowd as we walked by, but Deiphobus met them with a broad smile, assuring everyone that our brother would prevail and then, after he did, there would be a great victory feast in his honor. Nobody believed him, of course, especially not me, but there was little anyone could do about it.

I did think of something though. And I ain't just being smart here, I really did.

While Hector was busy putting on his armor, and Deiphobus was equally as busy egging him on, I turned to a nearby sergeant and ordered him to go to my house and bring me my bow. You see, I had every intention of killing Achilles before he could murder my brother.

Oh, don't get me wrong; I wasn't going to do it out of brotherly love or anything silly like that. I was just going to do it to save Hector's life and, what's more, I didn't give a crap what folks thought about me afterwards. I mean, my reputation was pretty much shot by then, so, what did I have to lose? Besides, the way I figured it, I was Hector's only hope.

The sergeant nodded at me reluctantly and marched away. I should have chosen a faster man because he still hadn't returned when my brothers and I walked over to the east gate thirty or so minutes later. As the gate opened, I looked around impatiently for the tardy sergeant and heard Deiphobus say to Hector, "I'm going outside with you and hold your spears. When you need one, I'll hand it to you. No matter what happens, brother, I will remain by your side."

Then they walked through the gate together and I clattered up the battlement's stairs, swearing at the sergeant as I went, getting to the top of the wall just as Achilles and Hector confronted each other down below.

For several seconds, they just sort of stared at each other like a couple of divorcing spouses and then, Achilles suddenly spit on the ground, and said, "I heard you were going to cut up my body and feed it to the dogs."

It seemed like an eternity before Hector answered. And when he finally did, I couldn't hear what he said, but whatever he said, it sent Achilles into a rage, and then, after that, all I heard was Achilles' wild shrieks and screams.

While Achilles was busy working himself into a lather, I looked around again and wondered where in Hades that damned sergeant was. Time was running out. Achilles was just below me and an easy target too, I could have hit him between the eyes while standing on my head. All I needed was a weapon to do it with. Frustrated I hadn't one, I slapped the wall and shouted, "Goddamnit, sergeant, where the fuck are you at!"

Hector must have heard me, because he looked up, and when he did, I saw his eyes and instantly knew something was terribly wrong.

His eyes were open wider than I'd ever seen them before, and he had a look on his face that I easily recognized. It was the look of fear. Believe it or not, the great Hector was scared out of his gourd.

And I don't blame my brother for being frightened either. I mean, he wasn't facing any old Tom, Dick or Harry down there. It was the lunatic Achilles, who'd personally destroyed twenty-odd towns, and liked to murder people, and fuck them afterwards, and then brag to his horses about doing both, and who, at that very moment, was only seconds away from exploding.

Seconds!

Now, if that ain't enough to make you pee your pants, I don't know what is!

And that's why, when I looked down at Hector, I didn't see the great warrior I had always known. I saw a frightened brother who knew he was about to be torn to pieces by a homicidal teenager. So, I did the only thing I could think of doing in order to save his life. I leaned over the wall and yelled, "Run, Hector, run!"

And for the first time in our lives, my brother and I were of the same mind.

In a flash, he darted away with surprising speed. He hugged the wall as he ran, and I ran along with him. Achilles just stood there watching us run away in astonishment. It took several seconds for him to recover, and when he did, he bounded after us, hurling insults at my brother's back and laughing wildly. The race was on now and I hoped Hector would stay ahead of Achilles long enough for me to find a bow. Then, I'd plug Achilles for sure, and be damned proud I had. So, I yelled down at Hector to keep running, instructing him to stay close to the wall because I was planning to kill Achilles with an arrow. He agreed, of course, and his mighty legs struck the ground like hammers, keeping him a safe distance in front of Achilles.

And wouldn't you know it — there wasn't a single bow or arrow to be found on the walls of Troy that morning! Nor was that goddamned sergeant anywhere in sight. Believe me, it was enough to make me want to break down and cry. But I kept running, and so did Hector, and so did Achilles. Three times, we ran around the city's walls, me on top, them at the bottom, until finally, we became so exhausted we couldn't complete another lap. And that's when Hector did the only thing he could do — he turned around and faced Achilles. He did it by the west gate, where the race had originally begun, and where, by the way, Deiphobus had spent the whole race casually leaning on one of Hector's spears.

Remain by your side, my ass!

Anyway, Achilles ran up to Hector, breathing heavily and said, "What's wrong, little rabbit, can't find your hidey hole?"

Achilles had a spear in his right hand, and he lifted the point in Hector's direction. To my brother's credit, he didn't flinch, but stood his ground, and said, "Okay, I agree to not run any further and to stand and fight. I only ask one thing from you. I ask that, whoever wins this fight, the winner will not strip the armor from their opponent's body, but will give both to the other side for a proper funeral."

Achilles immediately laughed, flicked the point of his spear menacingly, and shouted, "Don't talk to me of a pact, you low-life dog! It would be like asking a lion to make a pact with a man, or a wolf to make an agreement with a lamb, or an eagle to make a deal with a snake, or a bear to…"

"Okay! Okay! Okay!" Hector suddenly interrupted. "I get it! My god, but you are a long-winded, crazy son-of-bitch! Let's just get this thing over with!"

That, of course, sent Achilles into another tizzy, and he screamed, "I'm gonna gouge out your eyes and skull fuck you!" Then he hurled his massive spear at Hector's face, but my brother ducked it, and the missile flew harmlessly over his head and plunged to the ground fifty cubits away. A heartbeat later, Hector straightened back up and, with all his strength, threw his spear at Achilles. It hit the maniac's shield dead center and, much to everyone's surprise, simply bounced off.

Achilles laughed again and said something ridiculous about his shield being made by Hephaestus, the god of fire. Then he pulled out his sword and charged. As he did, Hector quickly turned to Deiphobus for another spear. Only Deiphobus wasn't there! He had slipped inside the gate during Hector's toss, taking all of my brother's remaining spears with him, and therefore, depriving Hector of his favorite weapon.

And that's when it hit me. Deiphobus had set Hector up to die! That's why he had egged Hector on to fight. That's why he volunteered to hold Hector's spears. And that's why he had deserted him at that critical moment. Deiphobus had planned to put Hector at a disadvantage all along, no doubt, because our brother's death would put Deiphobus one step closer to the throne.

Hector realized he had been betrayed too. I know this because he looked up at me and I saw it on his face. For one or two seconds, we just stared at each other in total bewilderment.

And, folks, that's how Hector spent his last moments on earth — betrayed and bewildered — because, you see, a split second after that, Achilles drove his sword through my brother's throat, killing him instantly.

"Noooooooo!" I immediately screamed in the sudden hush that followed. Then my knees buckled, and I slumped down on the battlement's walkway and began crying. Through the tears, I cursed Achilles and then I cursed Deiphobus. The treacherous bastard had killed our brother just as surely as Achilles had. I slammed my fists into the wall and called Deiphobus every foul name I could think of. When I was finished cussing, I took a deep breath, composed myself the best I could, and headed home.

Tears were still streaming down my face when I got there and so, I wasn't the least bit bothered to discover that the house was deserted. I just wanted to go upstairs, lie down and bury my head in a pillow. As I was trudging up the stairs to do so, I thought I heard a voice, so I paused for a moment to listen. In the silence that followed, I heard the voice again, this time coming out of the bedroom. Thinking it was the maid, or perhaps the butler, I hustled forward to tell whoever it was that I wanted to be left alone for the rest of the day. Opening the bedroom door, I stepped inside and instantly received the second shock of my day.

I'm telling you, it ranked right up there with Deiphobus' treachery!

When I stepped into the room, Helen was bent over the side of the bed, straightening up its ruffled blankets. She was completely naked and when she saw me, she immediately got an expression on her face like her world was about to end. That's because it was. You see, standing on the opposite side of the bed, was the very same sergeant I had sent to get my bow. His tunic was down around his knees and he had been in the act of pulling it up when I opened the door. He stopped when I entered and gaped over at me in surprise. I swear, I've never seen an erection disappear as quickly as his did at that particular moment! Anyway, for I don't know how long, we just stood there staring at each other in complete shock.

And I don't know what stunned me more — that Helen had cheated on me in my own house, or the sergeant had disobeyed my orders, or that both had resulted in the death of my brother, although, looking back on it now, I'd have to say it was the latter, mainly because I got pretty damned upset. I mean, I always knew Helen was a hussy, no surprise there, and I really couldn't blame the sergeant for jumping her beautiful bones — what man wouldn't — so there ain't no other explanation for me getting so pissed off other than the fact that my brother was dead.

And I guess that's also why I lit into the sergeant.

Without warning, I leaped across the room and hit the sergeant squarely in the jaw with my fist. He screamed and fell to the floor, flinging up his hands to protect his face from another blow. He should have been covering up his groin instead, because, that's where I struck next.

Oh, I know, I know, the kick was totally uncalled for, and I ain't proud I did it now, but on the other hand, I can't begin to tell you how good it felt at the time. Believe me, had I known how much kicking the shit out of someone improves your mood, I'd have done it years ago.

Anyway, the sergeant's hands immediately shot down to his balls, and his eyes crossed, and I was just about to kick him again when he had the good sense to curl up into a tight, little ball and faint.

Helen had collapsed on the bed by then and lay there sobbing quietly. For a moment or two, I looked down at her and wondered what she was crying about. God knows, she had so much to be sorry for, but knowing her, I quickly figured it was because I had finally exposed her for what she really was — a fucking harlot. And then, with that in mind, all the other times she had cheated on me came flooding back — Thonis and the Pharaoh — and my rage grew.

Crossing over to her side of the bed, I reached down, grabbed a handful of hair and lifted her up by it. She screamed as I did, but that didn't deter me, and when I could look into her eyes, I said, "Listen to me, you little slut. If you ever cheat on me again, I'll kick you out of the house. Do you understand?"

I must have looked awful frightening when I said it because she shuttered and instantly agreed.

But I didn't stop there.

"From now on," I said, "you will play the dutiful wife. You will tend to our household and see to my every need."

You know, the main ingredients of a good marriage.

"Do you understand?" I shouted.

Once again, she didn't hesitate to agree.

"And you will not sneeze, laugh or sew on that fucking loom of yours without my permission, got that?"

Just so you know, I hated that damned loom. That's because Helen had spent the last ten years weaving a tapestry on it that glorified the war. It seemed more than a little sick to me that Helen would commit to needle and thread all the carnage that she was personally responsible for causing. Goes to shows you how little conscience the big trollop had.

Anyway, Helen shook her head in agreement and continued to sob away. For a moment, I thought about slapping her around a bit, you know, just to show her what would happen if she didn't keep our agreement but I didn't because, you see, for some reason, it suddenly dawned on me that I had a bigger fish to fry.

A fish called Deiphobus.

Pushing Helen forcefully back down on the bed by her hair, I went over to where the sergeant was lying and grabbed his sword. Tucking it firmly into my belt, I stormed out of the house and headed over to the palace.

Okay, now, I know what you are thinking here: my god, Paris, what the heck got into you? Where'd you find the courage?

Well, let me tell you, it's just this simple: I fucking snapped. You see, suddenly, I had had enough of the war, Helen, Troy and all the lunacies that were connected with them and I was determined to end them once and for all. And, more importantly, I didn't care what happened to me when I did. All I cared about was setting things right again. And since I was surrounded by a bunch of incompetent idiots, I figured I was the only one with enough brains to do it, and so, like I said before, I took charge of the situation.

And I guess you could say that's when I grew a pair.

Funny how that works.

But before you go patting me on the back, let me tell you this: I'm truly sorry I didn't show some courage earlier because if I had, I wouldn't have participated in all the folly that had caused this stupid war. Then, maybe, a whole lot of folks would be alive today, and I'd be dead, which, believe me, is preferable to living with the guilt I must bear for the vile slaughter I helped cause. So you won't hear me crowing about how I finally wised up. If you ask me, it was a little too late, and I deserve to be forever damned in Hades for it.

But so should a whole lot of other folks as well.

And that, for the most part, was my state of mind when I stormed into the palace looking for my brother. I found the bastard in the throne room attending an emergency meeting of Troy's elite. They were busy discussing Hector's death and trying to decide what to do about it. Apparently, Achilles was still outside Troy's walls, dragging Hector's lifeless body around the place with his chariot. The spectacle of it had horrified everyone in the room and, as usual, most of them were for launching an immediate attack to avenge Hector's death.

Of course, since they were all so stupid, no one was considering the fact that we were once again down to a handful of troops, or that Achilles was still out there in a berserk rage, or that the city was full of frightened, weeping citizens in need of comfort and reassurance. I listened to the councilors for several seconds and then exploded:

"Oh, for fuck's sakes, attack with what? The army was decimated yesterday in Hector's attack, and with Achilles on a rampage, do you want to throw away what is left of it? I swear, you guys are the stupidest…"

"Well, well, well," Deiphobus suddenly interrupted, all snotty like. "Look who's here. Daddy and I thought you'd…"

That's as far as he got because, without any warning, I kicked him in the balls with my right foot. Who's your daddy now, you treacherous prick? I booted him so hard that I thought I heard his nuts crack. Three of his buddies caught him as he went down, and another one stepped forward to confront me. Immediately, a cry went up from the assembly — shouting that I had gone crazy, that I should be arrested for doing such a sick thing, et cetera, et cetera, and that's when I got really pissed.

So I kicked the guy confronting me in the same manner. And he went down just like Deiphobus did, only this time, no one tried to catch him because the crowd around me was busy yelling and pushing, saying stupid things like, "Who do you think you are!"

There was nothing left to do but wave my sword around and tell them.

"I am the Crown Prince, first in line to the throne and Commander of the Army! And I'll kill the first man who says I ain't!"

The room immediately went silent. They just stood there staring at me with a look of complete consternation on their faces. I'm sure the thought never crossed their mind that I was now the Crown Prince and if it did, I'm just as sure it was one they wanted to ignore. I can't really blame them much for that, given my poor reputation and all, but like it or not, that's the way it was and, by god, that's the way it was gonna be because that's the only way I was gonna get my life back with Oenone.

Anyway, I wasn't sure what was going to happen next, but while I waited for their response, I realized that I didn't know how to use a sword, and I was immediately sorry I never learned. However, I waved it around like I had, hoping my manly brusqueness would convince them not to fuck with me.

It seemed like an eternity before anyone said a word, and then my grieving, tired father stepped forward and said, "Yes, Paris, you are all you said you are and from now on, you will be treated as such."

To be honest with you, my father was so out of his mind with grief over Hector's death, I don't think he was quite aware of what he was saying or agreeing to. Had I been on my toes, I'm pretty sure I could have gotten his permission to hand Helen over to the Greeks but, unfortunately, I didn't think about doing that just then. That's because my mind was almost as jumbled up as his. All I could think of was, well, Paris, old boy, you have done it now and there ain't no way out this time. But to my credit, I shoved the sword back into my belt, threw back my head defiantly, looked straight at the crowd, focused on the matters at hand, and said, "From now on, I'm running things around here, and there ain't going to be another attack until we have an overwhelming force to do it with."

Without waiting for anyone's opinion on the subject, I quickly turned to Antenor and said, "Go to the Greeks and ask for a truce. I'm sure they'll give us one since they are as beat up as we are. After that, send envoys out to our allies and ask them to send us some more troops."

"We've already bled most of our allies dry," he answered, with a helpless shrug.

"Surely there must be someone left." I was fully prepared to sacrifice the lives of complete strangers for my freedom.

Antenor thought about it for a minute or two, running his hand carefully over his beard as he did, and then he nodded and said, "We haven't asked the Ethiopians or Amazons for help yet."

I nodded back and was just about to tell him to go for it when Aeneas impatiently stepped between us and said, "What about Achilles? How long are we going to let him drag Hector's body around our walls?"

Angered by the interruption, I lost my cool and snapped, "Well then, General, put some fucking archers up on the wall and drive him away!"

For a second, Aeneas seemed embarrassed that he hadn't thought about doing that beforehand, and then he gathered himself, snapped to attention, saluted and walked out of the room to carry out my instructions. As I watched him leave, my eyes suddenly fell on Pandarus, who was standing quietly by the door.

Just so you know, Pandarus had spent the war watching it from the citadel's battlements along with the rest of the Imperial Guard. And, what's more, as the Guard's commander, he had made a small fortune accepting bribes from rich families who wished to see their sons sit out the war in a safe place. As a result, the Guard had become almost entirely manned by a bunch of spoiled rich kids whose wartime service consisted mainly of sipping punch and playing cards in the Royal Palace.

Well, all that was about to change. Big time!

"Captain Pandarus!" I shouted, motioning him over to me.

Reluctantly, he walked up and saluted.

"How many men do you have guarding the citadel, captain?" I asked, returning his salute.

"Five hundred," he answered comfortably.

"Five hundred, SIR!" I immediately corrected him.

"Yes, sir," he replied in a more respectful manner. "Five hundred, sir."

"Good, have them reinforce the regular army immediately," I ordered. "I'm sure Aeneas can use them."

A startled gasp immediately swept the room. That's because most of the men standing in it had a son serving in the Guard. Some even had more. Remember that son-of-a bitch Antimachus? You know, the guy Pandarus bribed to kill Menelaus and Odysseus, and the mayor and I had to bribe in order to keep my titty bar open. Well, all three of his sons were serving in the Guard. Amazing ain't it? I mean, Antimachus was all for sending other folks' kids off to die but when it came to his own…well…all I can say is, that's a fucking politician for you!

When the murmur died down, Pandarus glared at me for a quick moment and said, "But, Your Highness, sir, the Imperial Guard is supposed to guard the citadel and protect the royal family."

"Well, they're regular front line troops now, so see to their reassignment," I quickly answered, glaring back, hoping he'd say something smart so I could clap the fuckhead into shackles and throw away the key.

But he didn't, although I'm sure it took everything he had not to punch me in the kisser with his fist. Instead, he bit the bottom of his lip, saluted and turned to leave.

But I wasn't done yet.

Before he could get away, I ordered him to join the regular army as well.

Payback's a bitch, believe me!

He looked back at me, snarled slightly, and saluted again. I returned his salute, fairly offhandedly this time, and told him he could leave. That pissed him off even more, as I hoped it would, and I couldn't keep from smiling as I watched him storm out of the room in a rage.

After Pandarus was gone, I turned to Antenor again and told him to contact the Ethiopians and Amazons as quickly as he possibly could. Promise them anything, I instructed him, just get them here. And then I turned to the councilors and explained again that it was my intention to remain on the defensive until the Army was big enough to smash the Greeks for good. They took it pretty well, I guess, although, from the surprised looks on some of their faces, I could see that they were having a hard time believing I was actually running things.

Realizing this, I said, "Look, I know what you are thinking here and I don't blame you for thinking it. In the past, I was a drunken, selfish coward. I realize that now, and I'm ashamed of it. But the only thing I can do at this point is to make amends for it. And that's what I aim to do. I helped start this fucking war and now, I'm the one who's going to end it. And I'm gonna do it with or without your support, although, I would appreciate your help. And, don't worry, because after this war's over, I swear, I will step down as Crown Prince in favor of anyone my father chooses. I have no desire to rule this kingdom, nor do I think I deserve the right to do so in light of my terrible mistakes and character flaws."

Very smartly said, I think you'll agree, and I meant it too. The last thing I needed was the headache that came with being a king. All I wanted was to end the war, make amends for my sins, and go home to Oenone. I figured it was the only way I could look into her beautiful eyes and smile again.

There was a moment's pause, as everyone digested my words, then Antenor stepped forward, bowed and pledged his support. That opened up the floodgates, I guess you could say, because, after that, one by one, the other men in the room marched up and did the same thing. I have to say, the whole thing astonished me but, nevertheless, I was very relieved and somewhat grateful to have their support.

When that bit of ceremony was over, someone asked about retrieving Hector's body.

Since I hadn't given it much thought, I didn't have an answer readily available.

But my father did.

"Leave that to me," he said in a low, shaky voice. "I will retrieve my son's body."

Without explaining how he was going to do it, he put on his cloak and started making his way through the crowd. It opened up before my father, with men bumping into each other as they struggled to get out of his way. He passed by them silently, head down, so they wouldn't see his tears, and walked out the door. It was one of the saddest things

Chapter Ten

I feel someone lightly touch the tip of my nose with their finger and hear a woman's giggle.

Instantly, I smile and open my eyes.

It's my favorite person in the world right now.

It's my sister Polyxena.

She looks as beautiful as I've ever seen her. That's the wonderful thing about my sister; she just keeps getting better and better. Too bad other folks can't do the same thing.

I smile up at her and she smiles back. As if by magic, the room suddenly seems brighter. Then her eyes wander down to my wound and her face softens with concern, making the room seem dull again.

I want the smile to return, so I say, "Break any hearts lately, beautiful?"

Her eyes return to my face and she smiles again. "No," she pouts, "and I'm not going to either. Not until you get better again."

"Well," I answer, "I might just lay here forever then, just so I can keep you all to myself."

Her eyes light up at that, and she takes my hand. Giving it a little squeeze, she looks me and says, "Ah, you're so sweet."

It's obvious she loves me. And to be honest with you, I feel an affection for her that I have never felt for any woman, including the ones I've wedded and bedded. And it's not because we are brother and sister either, I mean, just look at the bad relationship I have with my other siblings. No, it has more to do with the fact that Polyxena and I are kindred spirits. The reasons for this are simple. We come from the same dysfunctional family and because we do, Polyxena is every bit as lonely and addicted to sex as I am. That's why I understand her better than I do anyone else and that's why I care for her so much.

And you know what?

It's our bond, quite frankly, that ultimately ended this fucking war, cause, you see, without Polyxena's help, I would have never been able to kill that bastard Achilles. And without Achilles out of the way, we'd never have been able to whip the Greeks like we did.

Read that again. Love trumps war.

Kinda sets an interesting precedent, doesn't it?

Here's how it happened: After I wrapped up my meeting with Troy's elite, I walked around the palace trying to figure out a way to kill Achilles. The place was full of soldiers, diplomats, nobility and servants. Not one of them smiled at me. In fact, they kept their distance and stared at me as if I had suddenly lost my mind, which was good, I guess, because it reminded me of the way folks used to look at Achilles after he went bonkers over Polyxena and that's what started me thinking about using my sister to kill the crazy motherfucker. All she had to do, I reasoned, was to lure Achilles someplace close enough for me to get a shot at him with my bow. It seemed an easy enough thing to do and, as you well know, I liked things easy, and more importantly, low risk. So, feeling quite satisfied, I walked into Polyxena's palace apartment to discuss my plan with her.

She had a lavish room that looked more like a gaudy bordello than it did the suite of a royal princess. There were naked statues of men and women everywhere, mood candles, red or pink carpets, red walls with pink trimmings, red or pink cushions, a big red heart-shaped bed, and a large pink couch located near the room's heart-shaped fireplace. The apartment was certainly designed for screwing, alright, which isn't very surprising, given its occupant and all. Anyway, I found my sister sitting on the edge of the bed, crying her eyes out over Hector's death. I immediately sat down next to her and put my arm around her shoulder.

Burying her head into my chest, she cried, "Oh, Paris, isn't it all so terrible? Remember how Hector used to be alive?"

"Yes," I said, pulling her close, "I do."

And for a second I imagined him alive. Standing around Troy with a dumb expression on his face. Then I imagined him dead. Running through the Elysian Fields with the same dumb expression on his face. Poor guy.

Of course, I blamed myself for his death. Not only was I guilty of starting the war that killed my brother, but also now, my bungling and naïveté were responsible for not saving him.

"And I'm sorry I didn't save him," I confessed. "I wish I could have done better."

She wrapped her arms around me and squeezed. "It's not your fault," she said. "There was nothing you could do."

Yes there was, I told her. Then I reiterated in detail how I had attempted to save Hector's life, empathizing, of course, all the things that caused me to blow it. I accused Deiphobus of scheming to kill our brother and I told her about finding Helen and the sergeant in bed together. I even mentioned the look on Hector's face when he died. Everything.

Then I shut up.

After a short pause, she exploded. "Those bastards!" she yelled. "How could they do that to our brother?"

"It's still mostly my fault," I answered.

"No it ain't!" she replied. "You tried to save our brother. Everyone else did their level best to kill him. Those fucking jerks! God, I can't wait to kick their asses!

That's Polyxena for you — angel, nympho, cock teaser, ass kicker. I swear, when she got pissed, lions ran for cover.

"I already kicked their ass," I declared proudly.

"Really?" she asked, shocked.

"Really," I answered. "I kicked Deiphobus in the nuts, stomped the shit out of the sergeant and slapped Helen around a bit."

Okay, I know, the last part about Helen was a stretch, but what the heck; I wanted to show Polyxena I wasn't fucking around.

"Really?" she asked again.

It's always a surprise when a coward shows some guts.

"Really," I answered.

She laughed and then playfully tapped the tip of my nose with her finger and said, "Good for you."

I quickly caught her finger with my hand, squeezed it between my fingers, and said, "That only leaves Achilles and I'm not about to let him get away with Hector's death."

Polyxena was instantly furious again. "I'm glad to hear that," she said. "Do you have something in mind?"

"Yes I do." I quickly answered. "I want to kill the bastard by luring him someplace where I can shoot him with an arrow. And that's where I need your help. I figure since he loves you so much, it'll be easy for you to lure him into the Temple of Apollo where I can get a good shot at him."

Then, I paused for a second to let my words sink in.

But I didn't need to.

Cause Polyxena was already onboard.

"Perfect," she said. "Let's get that motherfucker!"

Well, that settled it; together, my sister and I were gonna make Achilles pay — and pay big time. We spent the rest of the evening drinking and planning the assassination, and then, when the details were worked out to our satisfaction, I kissed her on the forehead and went home. Helen was still lying naked in our bed when I got there — apparently the sergeant had let himself out — and so, staring half-drunk down at her, I wondered if I should punish her in some unreasonable manner or just go to sleep, and for a moment or two, it was touch and go either way, but then she rolled over, opened up her legs to me and I quickly forgot about disciplining her or sleeping altogether. I don't have to tell you what I chose to do instead. Like I said, there's nothing you can do when they shove it in your face.

Anyway, I should, however, tell you about what my father did. You see, while I was busy with Polyxena and Helen, dear old dad was equally as busy trying to get Hector's dead body back from Achilles. I don't really know how he got into the Greek camp. All I know is that, somehow or another, he managed to get inside it without getting his throat cut and, what's even more amazing, he was actually able to enter Achilles' tent and confront the crazy kid himself.

Now, there are several accounts of their encounter and you can believe any one of them you wish, but I have it on good authority from a servant who was there that it went something like this:

Achilles: What are you doing here, old man?

Priam: It's King Priam, damnit, and I've come to get my son's body back from you.

Achilles: Well, you can't have it.

Priam: Why not?

Achilles: Because I am going to have supper with it.

Priam: What?

Achilles: We will be having roast lamb with an avocado salad covered in olive oil. Would you like to join us?

Priam: (quite shocked) No! How can you have supper with my dead son's body?

Achilles: Why not? I've spent most of the day with it and I've kinda grown fond of it, oh, and don't worry, my servants are cleaning it up right now, so it's gonna look very presentable. I also instructed them to dress it in a purple robe. Did your son like the color purple?

Priam: Ah, well, he liked…hey, what a minute! This is sick! You're fucking crazy!

Achilles: Please don't talk to me like that. I hate it when people talk to me that way. Your son's body doesn't talk to me like that. My horses don't talk to me like that. Dead people don't talk to me like that.

Priam: (tactfully) Okay, okay, okay, look, I'm sorry.

Achilles: Apology accepted. Are you sure you don't want to join us for supper then?

Priam: I will in place of my son.

Achilles: Do you promise not to call me crazy anymore?

Priam: I promise.

Achilles: Okay then. Would you like to spend the night with me afterwards? I have an extra cot out on the portico.

Priam: Do I have to?

Achilles: No, but I hate to sleep alone. I was gonna sleep with your son's body, but since you will be taking its place at the dinner table, I figured you'd might want to take its place on the cot also.

Priam: (nervous) We're just gonna sleep, right? I mean, no funny stuff or anything like that.

Achilles: I just want the company.

Priam: (desperate) Can I take my son's body back home in the morning?

Achilles: Sure.

Priam: (reluctantly) All right.

Early the next morning, dad came driving up to the palace in an old wagon. Hector's body was sitting bolt upright on the buckboard beside him, looking as if the two of them had just returned from a Sunday drive. It was a strange sight to behold, believe me, and definitely not for the simple minded, because when my wacko sister Cassandra saw it, she totally flipped out and started running around the city, telling everyone she met that Hector had miraculously returned from the dead. Fortunately, by then, most of Troy's citizens knew what a complete nut job my sister was and so, they didn't listen to her. That, of course, sent her into another frustrated rage and the authorities were forced to arrest her ass all over again. As sis was being hauled off to the loony bin, Polites and I carried Hector's body to his bed. There, we laid him out all proper like, and he looked really splendid, except for his face, which still wore its usual expression of vacant dullness.

Unfortunately, that proved to be way too much for Andromache because she took one look at the Big Guy's mug and promptly went almost insane as Cassandra did. Without any warning, she suddenly screamed, ripped off her robe, jumped on top of my brother's body and started smothering his face with her huge bazoomas. Of course, that was pretty cool to me, since Andromache was so hot and all, but unfortunately, other folks in the room didn't see it the same way, and so, they quickly pulled her off of Hector's corpse and wrapped a blanket around her bare body. After that, she sat down in a chair next to the bed and began wailing loud enough to deafen a harpy. Between screams, she cried, "Husband, you have left me a widow and our small son fatherless! I fear for our future. Who will protect us and our city from the Greeks now that you are gone? Paris? Ha! I doubt it!"

It's not hard to guess how good that made me feel and I started to say something in my defense but she screeched again and said, "Now that your brother's in command of the army, I fear that the city will be razed and overthrown and our women will be carried away to the enemy's ships, I among them, and made to do all sorts of perverted things over and over and over again!"

It was almost like she was countin' pretty heavily on getting captured and raped, so much so, that I quickly glanced around the room to see if she had her bags packed for the event.

"Oh, Hector," she continued, "you died without taking me into your arms one last time and giving me a memory of our lovemaking that might have stayed with me when I am in the arms of some cruel taskmaster!"

I swear, women never cease to amaze me. I mean, there was Hector, deader than dirt, and what was Andromache bellyaching about? Not getting laid! Goes to show you that women are just as shallow as us guys, so don't be fooled into thinking they ain't. It's a lesson I learned the hard way from Helen and that's why I was totally prepared for what happened next.

As Andromache's loud wailings turned into quiet whimpers, I heard footsteps behind me, and, lo and behold, the shallowest slut of them all suddenly appeared.

"Hector," Helen screamed, brushing past me, "dearest of all my brothers-in-law! Your death has broken my heart and I curse the day Paris' lust brought me to these shores. Had I known Paris' passion would cause your death, I never would have invited him into my home."

It was a damned lie, of course, and I wasn't about to stomach it for one moment. Especially, not after the shit she had pulled the day before and so, when she turned around to glare at me disdainfully, I shot her a look that unmistakably said she was treading on thin ice — super-duper thin ice. Well, she got the message, because, as quick as a heartbeat, her whole demeanor changed. Turning back to Hector, she quietly confessed, "But I am to blame as much as your brother is and I only hope you can forgive us for what we have done."

Okay, I admit, it wasn't much, but for Helen, it was a ton, and it's also the only time I ever heard her come close to admitting anything near the truth. Anyway, it was enough to stop me from dragging her out of the room by her hair and kicking her ass out the front door.

"Oh, Hector!" Helen continued to pour it on, "You were always so nice to me. When others were clamoring for me to be returned back to Menelaus, you would not support them."

Shows you just how damned dumb the bastard really was, thinks I.

"And because you didn't, I knew you loved me," she cried. "Therefore my tears flow for you, and for me, because there is no one else in Troy who is kind to me now. Everyone seems to want to do me harm."

The last part was aimed at me, of course. I guess the big trollop just couldn't resist taking one last shot, but it didn't accomplish anything, other than to harden my resolve to make her toe the line, because, you see, I realized, like Andromache, she was only thinking about her own welfare, and so, when she was finished with her little act, I applauded loudly and told her to go home and bring me back a sandwich. To everyone's astonishment, she did.

And I'm glad she did too, because no sooner had I taken a bite out of it when my mother suddenly comes crawling into the room on her hands and knees and starts barking up at me like some kind of hungry dog. Son-of-a-bitch! I thought with surprise. I gotta tell you, it's pretty unnerving to discover that your mother has gone canine but, at least, I had enough sense to lure mom out of the room using the sandwich before she could pee on my leg or do something much more embarrassing. Everyone else just stood there like fools and gawked.

After I had gotten mother safely back to her room and called for a veterinarian, I decided to leave before anyone else could go crazy, so I said goodbye to Hector and set off to settle things with his killer.

It was Polyxena who came up with the most important parts of the plan that we used to kill Achilles with and, since it was, she played a major role in implementing them.

First, she sent Achilles a note that read:

My Dearest Achilles,

I have finally realized you are the man of my dreams and I love you with all my heart. Please meet me outside the east gate, in the Temple of Apollo, around sunset, so that I may give you that love. Please come alone and leave your armor at the door because I want to unleash all my passions on you the second you step inside the door. I hope you can handle it!

Yours forever, Polyxena.

P.S. This is not a trap. XOXOXO.

And then, she put on a tight, V-neck, backless red dress that barely covered the wiggling parts of her body. I'm talking a dress so short that it looked more like a shirt and so deeply cut that you could see the tiny gleaming pearl planted in her belly button. I'm also talking red stockings she fashioned out of fishnets and a pair of red shoes with thin spiky heels she proudly called 'pumps'. Know what I mean here? Heck, I got hot just looking at her and *she was my sister!* Anyway, after that, she stood outside the Temple's door and waited for Achilles to show up. I, on the other hand, went inside and found a good hiding place to ambush the son-of-a-bitch from.

Now, let me tell you a little something about a religious temple; they're awfully relaxing places. I mean, they're cool inside and quiet — except when the priests are busy singing their stupid little hymns — and folks tend to talk to one another in whispers. In short, they're kinda like a bedroom. And that can be awfully bad if you haven't had any rest the night before you visit one. I know this because, having spent most of the previous night screwing Helen's brains out, I no more than got comfortable before I was out like a light.

What can I say?

Anyway, how long I slept, I dunno, but I missed the preliminaries. When I finally woke up, Achilles and Polyxena were wrestling on the floor naked not more than three cubits from my dark, little nook, and from the way the two were knocking nasty, they must have been at it for a while.

Okay, say what you will about Achilles, but, let me tell you, the bastard was one damn fine lover. He hammered steadily away at my sister with all the strength and gusto of a horny bull, causing her to experience one orgasm after another. Powerful orgasms! I'm talking the screaming, body shaking, wet, I-forget-why-I-am-here kind of orgasm. I almost forgot too. But then, in between their bumping and exploding, I suddenly remembered the role I was supposed to play in our little drama.

Noticing that Achilles' back was turned to me, I thought: hello, Paris, ole boy, it's now or never. So, I grabbed my bow, quickly notched it, took aim, and let the arrow fly. It was a perfect shot, hitting Achilles square in the back, right between the shoulder blades.

And then, believe it or not, I swear, the arrow bounced completely off!

Just like it had hit a stone or something impenetrable like that!

I've never seen the likes before in my life!

And I would have been truly amazed had I had the time to be so, but I didn't because, instantly, Achilles was on his feet roaring like an enraged lion. I couldn't run, so there was nothing left to do but notch another arrow and try to get another shot off. Believe me, I can't remember when I've been so scared, which says a lot, and it affected my aim too, because my hands were shaking so bad that I was pointing the arrow down when I released it.

And, do you know, it struck Achilles in the right heel.

Only this time, it didn't bounce off.

It went right in, almost like it was going through a block of cheese.

Go figure.

Achilles looked down at the arrow and appeared to be as surprised as I was, and then he went into a painful stagger. His agonized screams echoed through the temple as he did, sending, I'm sure, any curious priest scurrying out the back door. All this lasted ten or so seconds, I guess, then he dropped to his hands and knees, coughed up some blood and toppled over. He hit the ground with a crash. As he lay sprawled on his left side, his breathing became labored, and then, it suddenly stopped altogether. After that, there wasn't a twitch. The great Achilles was dead. Oddly, enough, he still had a full erection.

I remained in my nook until I was sure Achilles was dead — believe me, jack, I wasn't taking any chances — and when I was, I stepped out of it warily and walked over to where Polyxena was lying. We looked at one another for a moment, quite bewildered, then she smiled broadly, and I pulled her up to me and gave her a big hug.

We couldn't have been happier.

Our brother Hector had been avenged.

And it couldn't have occurred at a more appropriate time because, you see, Achilles died at the exact same moment Hector's body was being consumed by fire on his funeral pyre. I couldn't have planned it any better, you'll agree. And believe me, it sure did perk up everyone's spirits when I walked up to the funeral and tossed Achilles' severed head in the middle of it. It was all over but the shouting after that. The Trojans, of course, were ecstatic. They danced wildly around the streets and, for once, nobody had anything bad to say about me. Who cares if I shamefully ambushed Achilles? The fucker was dead, and that's all that mattered to them. The Greeks, on the other hand, nearly shit their pants because, they knew, as we did, that with their number one champion dead, they were pretty much fucked. I swear, we heard their anguished cries all the way in Troy.

Of course, Aeneas was all for attacking their camp before they had a chance to recover, but I wouldn't hear it.

"Not until reinforcements arrive," I told him sharply.

"But we should strike them when they are leaderless and confused," he replied impatiently. "Now's the perfect time!"

"They're not *that* leaderless or confused yet," I answered.

"Yet?" Aeneas asked, looking a bit puzzled.

"Yeah, yet," says I.

You see, I had another trick up my sleeve. Having watched the Greeks fight so desperately to recover Patroclus' body, I kinda knew what they'd do if I offered them something just as important.

"Send Achilles' body to the Greeks," I instructed Aeneas, "with a message pinned to it saying that we will reward his armor to the Greek who wins a boxing contest held in honor of their fallen hero."

He considered my order for a moment, and then, confused by it, said, "Okay, his body, I understand, but why on earth would you want to give away his armor?"

"Because," I answered, flashing him a sly smile, "I figure they'll kill one another to win it."

And, you know, that's just about what the damned fools did too! For the next couple of days we watched in amusement from Troy's walls as the Greeks beat the bejabbers out of each other trying to win Achilles' famous armor. They did it with so much enthusiasm that their camp was soon full of maimed soldiers. I'm telling you, it was a doctor's worst nightmare. There were thousands of injured Greeks, limping, crawling, and some on litters, all in a disordered mass. There was no one on duty, no watches, no guards, no leadership, no nothing, except one great big brawl smack dab in the middle of the Greek camp and when the fighting was over, only Odysseus and my cousin Ajax were left standing.

And that's when I sent in a delegation to judge the winner.

Only I gave the delegation's leader, a captain named Serestus, special instructions not to have Odysseus and Ajax fight it out with fists, but instead, to judge them solely on their past merits. I guess you could call it a beauty contest of sorts. And it was a rigged contest as well. I also told Serestus not to pick Ajax, no matter what, because, you see, everyone knew he was a better man than Odysseus, and so, by not choosing him, I figured it would drive a wedge between him and Odysseus and thus, divide the whole goddamned Greek army.

Divide and conquer, that was the name of my trick.

And I know what you're thinking here: Since when did you get so damned smart, Paris?

Well, it's like this, when you're a coward like me, your whole survival depends on being clever. Show me a dumb coward, and I'll show you a dead coward. It's just that simple. And since I was in a very dangerous situation, I had to be pretty fucking smart if I was going to get out of it. I can't explain it any better than that. And, besides, I couldn't help looking smart since I was surrounded by so many idiots. I'm telling you, they made a retard look like a fucking genius! So don't go thinking I suddenly got smarter, because I didn't. I was just the only one, Greeks included, with enough brains to figure out how to end this silly war, that's all.

Anyway, as luck would have it, the Greeks weren't eager to see their top two champions beat the crap out of each other either, so, when Serestus offered them an alternative way to settle the contest, they immediately accepted it. Ajax, on the other hand, wasn't overly thrilled because, having already whipped Odysseus' ass once before during the games held to honor Patroclus' death, he had no doubts he could do it again. That explains why Odysseus had such a relieved look on his face when he joined Ajax in the center of the wrestling ring. He wiped the sweat from his brow and shook hands cordially with Ajax. Then he thanked Serestus for his idea and asked the captain to be fair and impartial while judging the contest. Having no intention of doing either, Serestus went straight in.

"Ajax, why are you more deserving of mighty Achilles' armor than Odysseus?" Serestus asked.

Ajax took a deep breath, glared at his opponent for a moment and said, "Odysseus, you think you are so fucking smart, well, your fancy words will do you no good here because everyone present knows you are not my equal in deeds or strength. Who was it that kept the Trojans away from Patroclus' body? Me! I made the Trojans' pay for Patroclus' death, and where were you? Nowhere in sight! That's because you are a goddamned pussy and a weakling. You didn't even want to join this fucking war. Agamemnon and Menelaus had to drag you away from that stinking farm of yours! My ships and I were the first ones to heed the brother's call to arms. They didn't have to come find me. I found them! And it was because of you that we left brave Philoctetes on holy Lemnos after a snake bit him because his painful groans made you feel uncomfortable. Let me tell you something, little man, ten Odysseus' are not equal to one Philoctetes. How much better off would we be if we had left your worthless ass on Lemnos and brought a wounded Philoctetes with us instead! A lot! Because, at least, Philoctetes would have fought! He would have put his ships with mine on the outside of the line where the danger is. Where do you always put yours? In the center, where it is the safest because the enemy's fire cannot reach you there! I have faced fire and the Trojans without fear. You cannot say that. Why, you can't even put Achilles' armor on. It is too big and heavy for your scrawny muscles. Nor can you even pick up his heavy spear! So, quit wasting my time and allow me to reap the reward we both know I deserve."

Instantly, Odysseus' cordiality vanished and his face became flush with anger. "Ajax, you big, stupid lout!" he barked. "If I was as dumb as you, I'd be embarrassed to open my mouth. All you do is blab. You say I am worthless and feeble. I am proud to say that I am better than you in plans and talk, and these are the things that multiply a man's strength. By using skill, quarrymen in the mountains easily cut out a sheer rock that is unbreakable; with their skill, sailors cross the great roaring sea when the waves are high; with their arts, hunters subdue powerful lions. Because you are so damned dumb, you don't realize it's with his mind that man accomplishes everything. Always, in every kind of work and planning, a man with wide knowledge is better than a thoughtless man like you. Hear me now, you big piece of shit, a man's strength is useless and his size comes to nothing if they are not accompanied by a shrewd intelligence. As for Philoctetes, I will go get him. I will sail to Lemnos and bring his ass here. And while I am at it, I will go to Scyros and pick up Achilles' son, Neoptolemus, as well. You see, that's planning for you. That's how you get things done. That's why I am so important to this army. All you have done is stand here and tell everyone how brave you are. That's all you ever do. I have done more planning in the last minute than you have done in the last ten years! And don't accuse me of being a coward either! I have never run in battle. I have always stood my ground, even when facing a multitude of Trojans. They rushed towards me and I made them pay for their foolishness with their lives. As for my ships, I did not draw them into the center because I feared the enemy's power, but so that I could plan things with Agamemnon and Menelaus. And I was not afraid of Hector's spear either. I was one of the first to defend Patroclus' body. I killed far more of the enemy than you did beside his body. And finally, you Trojan half-breed, Achilles and I share the distinction of Zeus' blood, so I'm sure his armor will fit me just fine."

At this, Ajax roared with laughter and said, "Odysseus, I swear, you are the most annoying man in the world! I didn't notice you at work in the fighting around Patroclus' body, nor did any other Greek. When the Trojans were trying to drag his body away, I was the one who stopped them from doing it. Not you. I kept fighting them until they finally gave up. Not you. And when the fighting was over, you were nowhere to be seen. Who among us here can say that Odysseus took part in the fight? Speak up!"

Before anyone could answer, Odysseus said, "Ajax, I don't think I am your inferior in either intelligence or strength, although you are very distinguished. In intelligence, I am vastly your superior; in strength, there may be room for argument, but, regardless of the degree, I can actually say I possess both. You cannot claim that. You might be strong but, I swear, you are dumber than an ox. And the army already has its share of oxen. But there is only one Odysseus!"

Of course, all this was music to Serestus' ears — I'd have given a chest full of gold to have heard it myself — and Serestus knew the Greeks were right where I wanted them. As they looked to him for a decision, I don't suppose there was a man in the Greek camp who commanded more attention than my crafty captain did. He played the thing out perfectly too. Gathering his companions in a tight huddle around him, he appeared to be discussing his decision with them, at least, that's how it looked to the Greeks, but, in reality, he was warning his men to get ready to run because all Hades was fixing to break loose. And then he turned back around to the assembly and released it.

"After careful consideration," Serestus said, "we have decided to award the immortal armor of Achilles to Odysseus!"

Now, I don't know who was surprised more, Ajax, Odysseus or the whole goddamned Greek army, because Odysseus' jaw immediately dropped open, Ajax cursed and the army groaned. Nor do I know how long it went on like that — ten, twenty, thirty seconds maybe — but it lasted long enough for Serestus and his men to safely make their way over to the camp's gate. There, they paused and watched Ajax go plumb bonkers. With a mighty oath, my cousin grabbed Odysseus by his "crisping, red-golden" hair and ripped out enough strands to weave a small wig with. Then he slammed Odysseus to the ground so hard that it knocked the breath out of him. And that's when Serestus and his companions started high-five'n each other. Then, Ajax jumped on top of Odysseus and began hopping up and down on his chest like it was an old mattress or something. It took nearly a dozen Greeks to pull Ajax off and then, with a gasping Odysseus in tow, everyone ran for the safety of the ships. After that, all you could hear was the sound of slamming doors, turning locks and the screams of Ajax.

"Goddamnit!" Ajax cursed. "Odysseus, get back out here so I can cut your lying ass up with my sword!"

You'll agree, I couldn't have hoped for anything better.

"Get out here Odysseus," Ajax shouted, "or so help me, I'll start burning the ships one by one until I smoke your sorry ass out!"

Okay, maybe that would have been a little better.

When Odysseus failed to appear, Ajax grew even more enraged, so much so, that he started running around the camp all wild like. I guess it was then that he went completely mad because, as he ran up to a flock of sheep, he suddenly stopped and started shouting at them as if they were a crowd of humans.

"Odysseus, I see you hiding there amongst those Greeks!" he yelled.

And the frightened sheep went, "Baaaah!"

"Don't try to hide from me, mister!" Ajax screamed.

And the terrified sheep went, "Baaaaaaaaaah!"

"You other Greeks better quit protecting Odysseus and get out of the way or I will kill you too!" Ajax shouted.

And the petrified sheep went, "Baaaaaaaaaaaaaaaaaaah!"

And then, Ajax reached down, picked up one of the nearest sheep, raised it above his head and slammed it to the ground, killing the poor creature instantly.

The astounded sheep didn't make a sound after that. They were too busy running. But it didn't do them any good because, one by one, Ajax caught up with them and finished each off in the same harsh manner. I'm pretty sure the crazy bastard must have thought he was killing Greeks and, at that point, his comrades hiding in the ships probably wished they had let him fight it out with Odysseus instead of listening to Serestus. Never trust a Trojan bearing gifts, I'll bet they whispered to themselves.

Absolutely goddamned right!

Anyway, it was too late. Ajax's mind was too far gone. Kneeling next to a ram he had killed, he suddenly burst into wild laughter and said, "Lie there in the dust, Odysseus, food for the dogs and birds. Not even Achilles' glorious armor could save you from my anger. Lie there, you dog. The wife of your youth will raise no lament over you. She and your son will not embrace in unrestrained sorrow, nor will your parents. You will not satisfy their desire to have you with them as a fine help in their old age. You have fallen far from your native land, and the birds and the dogs will devour you."

Talk about going cuckoo! I'm telling you, Ajax sure set the bar high that day!

And that's when things got even better.

After Ajax was done with the ram, he suddenly seemed to regain his senses. Looking at the dead sheep laying around him, he said, "Poor, poor sheep. I'm so sorry I did this to you. But it was not my fault. My comrades damaged my mind and inflicted on me an evil madness that made me kill you. How I wish my hands had got vengeance on Odysseus and his trouble making heart. He is a man full of mischief, and he has overwhelmed me with ruin. I wish he might suffer in his heart all the pains that the Furies devise for troublemakers. I wish, too, that they will give deadly conflicts to my fellow Greeks and sorrows to make them weep — and to Agamemnon himself. I pray he will not come easily home to the house he longs to reach."

I couldn't agree with him more, of course. Damn the Greeks, for fucking forever! Amen.

"But why, with all my bravery, do I associate with those I loathe?" Ajax continued to lament. "No more deadly Greek army for me, and no more life grown intolerable. The brave man no longer wins the prize, but the inferior man is honored and better liked. Odysseus is honored among the Greeks, and they have completely forgotten me and all that I did and suffered for the Greek Army. Oh, Hector, my love, I'm coming to join you!"

Then, without another word, he suddenly whipped out his sword — the one Hector had given him — and rammed it through his neck. Serestus said the blood gushed out of Ajax's throat with a loud rushing noise. Sounded kinda hokey to me but I didn't question it because I was too busy marveling at everything else he told me. Can you blame me? I mean, for the second time in my life, things had actually gone my way. In the course of a week, without fighting a single battle, I had managed to kill the enemy's two best leaders and throw its army in complete disarray. I was on a roll and I knew it. More importantly, so did everyone else in Troy. For the first time, folks actually started believing in me. I could see it in their faces and hear it in their tone. Even Aeneas quit questioning my orders. All that was wonderful, of course, and I felt slick as chicken shit, but the best thing about my accomplishments was that they helped convince the Amazons and Ethiopians to come to our aid. Success breeds confidence, I guess.

Word of our new allies scared the piss out of the Greeks, of course, and they hastily sent representatives around the Aegean to gather fresh reinforcements before our new friends could arrive. Odysseus was one of those representatives. As you can imagine, he wasn't a very popular man around camp after Ajax's death, so he made himself scarce by sailing off to pick up Philoctetes and Neoptolemus.

Odysseus picked someone else as well, someone who would have more of an impact on me than the other two put together. Well, almost.

Odysseus also picked up Deidameia.

Remember her? You know, the princess from Scyros and the girl I screwed on my father's bed the night Antheus died. Yeah, that chick!

She walked back into my life a month after Ajax's death. It was a quiet evening, not so much because there wasn't anything going on, but because Troy was expectant and hopeful, waiting silently for the climactic battle that would occur when our allies finally arrived. I was in our Army's headquarters, pouring over a stack of intelligence reports from our scouts. It had become a habit of mine to do so, because, mainly, it kept me sober and away from Helen. I also wanted to know as much about the enemy as I possibly could. After I had knocked the stack down by half, a sentry suddenly arrived and reported something to the Sergeant of the Guard.

"The Prince is busy right now," I heard the Sergeant answer, "and he don't have time for no female company. Tell her to go away."

Now, as you can guess, that caught my attention, because, with me, it's all about giving.

"Let the woman in!" I shouted over at the Sergeant.

He immediately snapped to attention and stepped out of the doorway. There was a moment's pause, and then, the figure of a woman walked into the room.

"Hello, Alexander," she said softly.

It was Deidameia, no doubt about that; I recognized her quite easily as she walked into the light from the big lantern that sat on top of my desk. She was just as beautiful as I remembered her and was dressed more for comfort than for romance. I stared up at her as if she was a ghost and, as I did, her eyes slowly began to tear up.

"I'm sorry," she said, wiping the tears away with the back of her hand, "but I've missed you so much."

Now, I don't know about you, but I'm always a bit leery whenever I run into an ex-lover. And it's not just because I usually can't remember their name, although, I have to admit, that's a big part of it. No, it's mainly because of the heartless way I tend to treat women after they have shared my bed and that makes it downright dangerous for me to suddenly bump into one. So, it's no surprise that, when I do, I always ask myself an important survival question: should I stay or run away? In Deidameia's case, the answer to that question was evident in her tears. It was obvious that she was still stupid in love with me, so I decided to stick around and comfort her.

"Deidameia!" I shouted, and then I stood up, ran around the desk, and took her into my arms.

If the Greeks would have suddenly attacked right then, we wouldn't have noticed because I pulled her close and she kissed me passionately. It was a wonderful moment and one that I will always remember. When it was over, I looked into her eyes and told her I missed her too. Of course, it was pure drivel, but that's what a woman wants to hear during a time like that.

"Thank you, baby," she answered, "I needed to hear that."

See?

"What are you doing here?" I asked, kissing her forehead gently.

She sagged heavily against me and said, "I've come to ask for your help."

Okay, when a woman says something like that, especially after ten years of pining after you, there's really only one answer you can give 'em.

"Sure, baby, you can always count on me," I said. "What is it?"

"Well," she said, "I don't know any other way to tell you this except to be frank."

"Go ahead," I gulped.

"Well," she explained, "the Greeks are using my son Neoptolemus as a figurehead to raise the morale of their army and since you are in command of the Trojan army now, I wanted to ask you to protect him from harm."

I leaned back and flashed a surprised look. Up to that point, I had no idea she was the mother of Achilles' kid. None of my intelligence reports had mentioned it.

"You and Achilles," I muttered, "had a son?"

For some strange reason, I felt betrayed.

She buried her head into my chest and said, "A month after you left me on Scyros, Achilles came to our island in order to escape the war. My father gave him permission to hide out in the royal apartments with my sisters and me. He thought Achilles would be safe there."

Safe my ass, thinks I, talk about letting the rooster into the hen house!

"Anyway, before long," she elaborated, "Achilles was wearing our dresses and putting on our makeup."

Astonished, I said, "Oh, you've got to be kidding!"

"No, really, he did," she answered, "and he liked it too. After a while, he actually looked more like a woman than we did. He said he was doing it to further his disguise but my sisters and I knew otherwise. I mean, he was so into it. Soon, ships were arriving from all over bringing him all kinds of dresses and accessories. He had a closet to die for, I'm telling you."

See what a crazy fuck Achilles was? I couldn't help but laugh.

She started sobbing. "Please don't laugh," she said, "because it's not funny. You see, after you left, I got really, really upset. News arrived that you were with Helen, and all of Greece was hunting you, and so I didn't think there was any chance that you would return to me like you promised."

I remembered the promise and immediately felt damned stupid for making it.

"Then, one night," she sobbed, "I got so mad at you that I slipped into Achilles' bed and offered myself to him. He took me, of course, and made me pregnant. There was supposed to be a wedding, but before it could take place, Odysseus arrived with a ship full of women's clothing and weapons, which he used to trick Achilles into revealing his true identity with, and shortly after that, Achilles sailed away with him to join this war. We never got married."

And then, she leaned back, looked deeply in my eyes and said, "Oh, Paris, I'm so sorry. I never stopped loving you. Please protect my son, if not for me, then, for old time's sake."

Now, I have no doubts what Hector would have said, and that fucking Aeneas too. They'd have given her a lecture about a commander's wartime duty or something silly like that. That's because they both had war drums for hearts and marching manuals for brains. But not me! Deep down inside, I was still a lover, not a soldier, and so I decided to give her my standard performance for sticky situations like this.

I paused for a moment, you know, for dramatic effect, and when the scene was set, I pulled her into my arms once again, looked deeply into her beautiful eyes and said, "I love you too, I always have, and don't worry, I promise I'll do everything I can to protect your child."

And immediately after I said those words, a strange thing happened. I realized they were true. I wasn't acting, I actually meant them, especially the love part. Well, kinda. I mean, I certainly felt something strong like that for Deidameia. How could I keep from it? She was, after all, the only woman who really loved me for the shiftless, irresponsible guy I was. All the other women loved me for something else. Oenone loved to change me. Helen, if she ever loved me, which I seriously doubt, only loved me because of what I could do for her. Compared to them, Deidameia was a breath of fresh air. So I couldn't help feeling something strong for her, whatever that something was.

After that, we spent the rest of the night talking. Just talking. Amazing isn't it? Anyway, I don't remember everything we talked about, but I recall telling her how this war really got started and asking her about her son. She told me he was a splitting image of Achilles — god help him — and that he was as sharp as a tack. I made a joke that brains ran in Achilles' family, which cracked us both up, since we knew that wasn't anything near the truth. She also told me about how rambunctious the boy was and that there probably wasn't a tree or mountain on Scyros he hadn't climbed. She talked about her son with such delight that I could easily see she loved him very dearly and I could not help but reflect on how Oenone would probably do much the same thing with our son. Its then, I think, it hit me that I had a son, roughly the same age as Neoptolemus, whom I had never gotten to know and that, naturally, made me feel very, very sad.

Noticing that I had grown quiet, Deidameia asked me if there was something wrong.

"Ah, well," I said, "I just feel bad that I wasn't able to keep my promise to you."

I was fudging a little, of course.

"That's okay, baby," she answered, "I understand now, and maybe after this war is over, we can be together again. I will always love you."

I didn't have the heart to tell her about Oenone and our son. Or that I would be going home to them after the war. So, I gathered her in my arms and kissed her passionately. Then I walked her to the west gate where I did both again, only this time, I knew it was for the last time. Afterwards, we were both too overcome with emotion to say goodbye, so she just sort of nodded and walked away. I can still see her now, her beautiful face in the dawn's light, and remember how my heart broke as I watched her go.

I stood and looked until she disappeared, and then I walked back to the Army's headquarters. I found the place in an uproar which, I guess, was just as well, since I needed something to take my mind off of Deidameia.

"What's going on?" I immediately demanded to know.

"Sir, good news, our allies are near!" the Sergeant answered smartly. "The Amazons have been sighted five leagues north of our city, and the Ethiopians have been seen about ten leagues south of it."

Well, that perked me up right quick, I tell you, and I instantly snapped into command mode.

"Perfect. Send messengers to both armies." I instructed the Sergeant. "Tell them not to come into the city. I don't want the Greeks to know that our allies have arrived. Tell the Amazons to camp on the banks of the Simoeis and tell the Ethiopians to camp on the Scamander. Tell them also that we will be sending supplies and that I will visit their camps before night fall."

The Sergeant nodded his head excitingly as I said it and when I was finished, I looked him in the eyes and shouted, "Go!"

In a flash, he was off, and I followed him through the door yelling for the Army's Quartermaster.

"Where's the Quartermaster?" I screamed. "Get that big fat bean pusher in here!"

Just so you know, and not think me overly rude, Quartermasters always tend to be on the plump side. That's because they are in charge of the Army's food rations. And that's how it should be too, I mean, show me a skinny Quartermaster and I'll show you a hungry army. Fortunately, I had a very good — and fat — Quartermaster, so in calling him that, you see, I was really praising the job he was doing. It's an army thing.

Instantly, a portly captain named Cadmus appeared before me and saluted. "Yes, sir," he said. "What are your orders, sir?"

I saluted back and said, "Send rations out to our allies. You will find the Amazons camped on the Simoeis and the Ethiopians on the Scamander."

"How much should I send, sir?" the quartermaster asked.

"Everything, except for one day's rations for our army," I answered.

"Everything?" he replied, sounding like a starving man hesitant to give up his last biscuit.

"Yes, every goddamned thing," I answered impatiently.

I could see that his feelings were hurt.

"Don't worry, Cadmus," I said, "we'll get more food. I hear there's a bumper crop of wheat in Canaan."

The Captain rolled his eyes and said, "You ever bargained with a Hebrew, sir?"

"No," I answered impatiently, "and I don't intend to either, now get the fuck out of here and carry out your orders, or I'm gonna have you placed on a diet of bread and water."

I was in no mood to fuck around or to have my orders questioned. It's also an army thing.

Terrified, the Quartermaster saluted once again, and turned nervously away, accidentally bumping into Aeneas in the process.

"Hey! Look out, captain!" Aeneas yelled at the clumsy Quartermaster, and then, turning to me quickly, he said, "What's going on?"

Unwilling to stand around and explain my plans to him, I said, "There's no time to explain. Have our horses saddled and get us a cavalry escort."

"Why? Where are we going?" he asked.

"To meet our allies," I answered, running out of the room. "I'll tell you more on the way."

Moments later, I was riding north with a small cavalry escort to welcome the Amazons. As we rode along, I told Aeneas that it was my intention to attack the Greeks the next morning. I was going to lure them out on the city's plain, I explained, and then hit them on the flanks with our allies.

"How are you going to get the Greeks out of their fort?" Aeneas asked.

"Simple," I answered, "we will lead our army against their encampment in the morning and attack their walls, and after awhile, I will signal a withdrawal. The Greeks will see us retreat, think we are beaten and counterattack us."

"Just like they did the day Patroclus died," he replied.

"Yeah, just like then," I said. "And they'll follow us all the way back to Troy. Then we'll turn around, pin them with the reserve cavalry, and signal our allies to attack. The Greeks will be surrounded and destroyed. Then we'll burn their ships, dismantle their camp, and call it a day. "

I have to say my plans made perfectly good sense to me, and probably to you too, but Aeneas was totally confused by them. That's because they had too many working parts for him to understand. He wasn't used to conducting a military operation that consisted of a feint, withdrawal, pin and flank attack. Nor was anyone else, for that matter. You see, up until then, armies would simply line up and slam into each other like a couple of prize fighters, you know, that sort of stupidity. So I guess you can credit me with developing a far better way of fighting — one that almost insured victory. And that's why I was in such a confident fettle when I rode into the Amazon's camp.

Now here's the kicker.

Confident or not, crown prince or not, allied commander or not, you just don't ride into an Amazonian camp unannounced.

That's because they get awfully pissed if you don't call ahead first. It's a woman thing, I guess, because, you see, just like females everywhere, Amazons need time to get dressed up, do their hair and put on their war paint. And if you don't give them time to do that, well then, buster, you're likely to find yourself swinging upside down from a tree limb by a rope.

I know this because that's exactly what we found ourselves doing shortly after we entered the Amazon's camp uninvited. As you can see by now, with me, the fun never stopped. We had no more taken ten steps into the place, when there was a wild rush of women from all sides, and a painful thump, and the next thing I knew, we were swinging from tree branches by our heels. And, buddy, let me tell you, when you are wearing a kilt like we were, and nothing on underneath, hanging upside down can be an awfully embarrassing experience.

And downright dangerous too!

"Hey, I think that bird up there is staring at my dick," a soldier behind me said.

I looked up and saw a big black raven sitting on one of the branches above us. Sure enough, the creature was looking down at us.

"Maybe he thinks it's a big worm or something," another soldier chimed in.

I didn't like the sound of that and neither did the other guys. Almost immediately, we started shouting, "Shoo bird! Shoo! Get out of here! Go away! Get!"

In the middle of our screaming, Aeneas groggily asked, "What's… what's going on?"

He was dangling next to me and had just regained consciousness after being knocked out during the tussle with the Amazons. Apparently, our yelling woke him up.

"Oh, nothing," I snapped, "we've just been hanging around here waiting for you to wake up."

Ignoring my sarcasm, he said, "Why'd the Amazons attack us? I thought they were supposed to be our allies. Where'd they go? What do you think they are going to do with us? And why is that bird staring at my dick?"

"How the fuck do I know?" I angrily replied "Maybe they've switched sides and plan to kill us."

"They went back to their tents after they strung us up," a sergeant behind us answered, "probably to sharpen their knives."

"That bird up there thinks your dick is a worm," a nearby soldier warned.

Then there was another desperate round of 'Shoo bird, go away bird!' which continued unabated until the raven was frightened away by the sounds of approaching footsteps.

Immediately, I started twisting and turning so I could swing around to see who it was. As I struggled to do so, I bumped into Aeneas, which promptly sent him careening into the man next to him, and so on and so on, until we were all thumping into each other like pendulums.

"Stop!" I yelled.

"You stop!" Aeneas screamed back.

"Everybody stop!" a familiar bass voice shouted behind us. "So I can cut you down."

It was Cadmus, the Quartermaster.

And then, presently, all three hundred pounds of him appeared before me.

"Let me guess," he said with a slight smirk, "you didn't ask permission to enter their camp."

"Is that what you are supposed to do?" I quickly asked.

"Yes, sir," he answered, taking out his sword.

"How do you know that?" I asked.

"I do business with the Amazons all that time," he answered, twirling me around so he could cut rope binding my wrist. "That's where the Army gets its saddles from. Amazonian saddles are the best in the world. Those girls love to ride, sir. And they just hate it when anyone barges into their camp without an invite. We'll have to wait here until they get all dolled up and when they're ready, they'll send someone out to fetch us."

I'm gonna promote this fat son-of-a-bitch to general, thinks I.

"Is there anything else I need to know?" I asked.

"Yes, sir, don't stare at their boobs, they don't like that very much either," he said.

Okay, of all the advice I have ever gotten from anyone, I can't think of anything more important, or timely, than Cadmus'. That's because, you see, as a whole, Amazons have to be the most beautiful women in the world. I'm telling you, they beat Spartan women all to Hades. And I'm not just talking beautiful faces or figures here either. I'm also talking beautiful breasts. And I'm just not talking nice breasts. I'm talking big, round, firm garbanzas, you know, the kind that makes a newborn baby's mouth water. So here's the deal: Cadmus' advice probably saved my life because Amazonian women like to sashay around totally topless and, had he not have warned me against it, I'd have gawked at their bouncing breasts like a starving baby. And the Amazons would have strung me up for it too, only this time, probably by my balls. Ouch! But, of course, that didn't stop me from stealing a quick glance here and there, especially when I thought I could safely get away with it.

"That's a beautiful necklace," I said to the Amazon sent out to lead us into camp.

She was a fine, strapping piece — almost as tall as me, dark tanned skin, and as beautiful as Helen. She wore a deerskin kilt about her trim waist, with a short spear in one hand and a sword in her belt. The only other thing she wore, other than some leather sandals, was a necklace of beadwork that hung down between her ample breasts.

"Isn't the necklace beautiful, men?" I asked, hoping they would catch my drift.

They did.

"Yes, yes! Oh, my! Very beautiful! Why, it's the most beautiful necklace I've ever seen! Magnificent! Wonderful! Exquisite!" they eagerly answered.

Of course, we weren't looking at that stupid necklace. We were all zeroed in on her wonderful knockers. And since it was my idea, I guess you could say I was showing my men how to gawk at a woman's goodies without getting caught. Who knew my skills as a pervert would someday save lives?

"Oh, thank you," she answered, seemingly unaware of what we were actually staring at.

"Do all the women of your tribe wear necklaces like that?" I asked.

"Yes, we all do," she innocently replied.

Thank god for that, thinks I.

"I can't wait to see more of them," I said, real nice like.

"Then follow me," she said simply. And she led us into the Amazon's camp.

A crowd of about five thousand topless women met us there and welcomed us with great cheer, which, believe me, was a vast improvement over the reception they gave us earlier. Smiling and waving back gratefully, we followed our guide through the roaring mob and across the camp to where another group of women was standing in a semi-circle. There were thirteen of them altogether, presumably leaders, no doubt, from their regal bearing, and they watched us approach in complete silence, until Cadmus and I stepped into the center of their little assembly.

"Hello, Captain Cadmus," says a nearby beauty.

At that, Cadmus bowed deeply and said, "Hello, Queen Penthesileia, I am honored and pleased to be in your presence once again."

Realizing that I was in the presence of a blueblood, I immediately bowed too, and said, "I am also honored, Your Majesty."

"And who might you be?" Penthesileia asked.

I told her who I was, and there was another loud cheer from the crowd.

Now, I gotta tell you, given my sordid record with women, I never thought it possible that I would ever be cheered by so many women — and topless ones, at that — so I was a little more than sorry when Penthesileia raised her hand to silence them.

"Rise, Prince Alexander," Penthesileia said in the quiet that followed, "and let me embrace you as our ally."

Believe me, jack, she didn't have to ask twice!

In a flash, I was upright and hugging one of the most gorgeous women I had ever laid eyes on.

Penthesileia couldn't have been a day over twenty-five, which, by the way, isn't all that young for an Amazon queen, given the dangerous lifestyle they tend to live. She stood just as tall as me, so I found myself looking directly into a pair of dark, almond eyes. Her skin was tanned golden brown due to its constant exposure to the sun, and her long, straight, hair was as black as a coal and adorned handsomely with eagle feathers. She was dressed much the same as our guide, only her weapons were beautifully adorned in silver and ivory. They were about the only things that set her apart from the others — Amazon queens don't believe in wearing fancy crowns or robes — but one look into her lordly, dark eyes, left me with no doubt I was holding a woman as strong as any male who ever sat on a throne. Strength was written all over, from her beautiful face to her…my god…what a wonderful pair of knockers she had! Let me tell you, I've never seen a better pair of jugs on a woman before or since, and, of course, I couldn't help gawking at them.

"Wow," I said, "those…I mean…that's a really beautiful necklace."

"Thank you," she said, proudly lifting it up so I could get a closer look. "I would give it to you as a present but the tiny leather pouch attached to it contains my umbilical cord and so, its magic would be of no use to you."

My first response was to go, "yuck!", and shy away from the disgusting thing, but since that wouldn't have been very smart, and more than a little dangerous too, I said, "That's okay, great queen, the presence of you and your army are gifts enough."

And since she seemed to be into gift giving, I said, "And please allow me to return the compliment by presenting your people with gifts of food to show how appreciative Troy and I are that the Amazons have come to our aid."

Turning to Cadmus, I said, "How many supply wagons are on their way to this camp, Captain?"

"One hundred, sir," Cadmus answered.

"And what do they contain?" I asked.

"Meats, vegetables, grains and wine," he rattled off like a bookkeeper.

Well, that made the Amazons happy and there was a joyous outburst. That's probably because, for once in their wild nomadic lives, they weren't going to have to run around spearing the local wildlife for an evening meal. And that's just as well, I guess, because the last thing I wanted was for an Amazon hunting party to accidentally bump into a Greek patrol before the next morning's battle could be fought.

Anyway, after the celebration quieted down, Penthesileia smiled and said, "Thank you for the wonderful bounty. You are, indeed, a very thoughtful ally. And a mighty one too! I understand you killed the mighty Achilles single handily. Please tell us how you did it."

That took me aback for a moment or two; I mean, how do you tell an Amazon warrior queen that you ambushed a mighty enemy from behind, in the dark, while he was busy screwing the daylights out of your sister?

Let me give you some advice: you don't.

Instead, you lie your ass off. It's the only way you can maintain her respect.

So, I muttered something silly about engaging Achilles in a single round of combat in front of Apollo's statue, you know, to honor the sun god with a test of strength and courage between two heroes.

How my fellow Trojans, who knew the truth, kept from laughing, I don't know how, but luckily, they didn't, and because they didn't, the Amazons bought my story hook, line and sinker. I'm telling you, those girls are suckers for stories about glory and battle. And that's a good thing to know if you are looking to be their friend and, more importantly, if you want to get laid, because, you see, shortly after I finished telling it, Penthesileia looked at me lustfully and said, "Will you be spending the night with us, great prince?"

Make no mistake, it was an offer for sex if I ever heard one, and I'd have jumped at it too if I didn't have to arrange things with the Ethiopians that very same day. Believe me, sometimes, being a responsible commander of an army, or even a responsible male, can be a gigantic pain in the ass. And it's worse if you're a sex-alcoholic like me. But there was nothing I could do about it, so, I bit my lip and reluctantly apologized to Penthesileia for not being able to spend the night with her.

And that, by the way, was only the second time I ever turned down sex.

Easily two of the most painful moments of my entire misspent life.

"Too bad," Penthesileia answered, all straight forward like, "because I was hoping you would impregnate me. I'm sure a union between two great warriors like us would produce an equally great daughter."

Believe me, it's a warm feeling to be considered prime breeding stock by such a splendid female and I suddenly knew how my prize bull Cronus felt. No wonder the big shit bag always seemed so damned content! Unfortunately, there was nothing this poor little bull could do about it except apologize profusely and try not to cry.

"I'm sorry," I said, "I'm really truly sorry, I can't tell you how sorry I am, but I must visit the Ethiopians to coordinate things with them."

"I understand," she answered with a slight frown, "and so, let us speak no more about it. Come now and tell me about how tomorrow's battle will be fought and the role my Amazons will play in it."

I then went over the details of my battle plan much like I had done with Aeneas, so I won't bore you with them again. The only difference is that Penthesileia seemed to catch on to my strategy much quicker than he did.

"Your plans are innovative and bold, Alexander," she proclaimed when I was done. "And I am confident that they will destroy the Greeks and throw fire upon their ships. You can count on my people to do our part."

Then there was a round of cheers from the surrounding crowd echoing her sentiments, during which, Penthesileia smiled at me and said, "Go now and arrange things with the Ethiopians. We will meet on tomorrow's battlefield and afterwards, when we are victorious, perhaps we can speak of producing a daughter once again."

That was just peachy with me, of course. Well, sorta. I mean, I wasn't all that keen about fathering another kid but, on the other hand, I figured a romp in the hay with Penthesileia was worth running the risk. So I smiled back at her, bowed and said, "Queen Penthesileia, I look forward to having that conversation with you."

She bowed her head in return, and turned away, but as I watched her go, I noticed she couldn't resist turning around to take one last look at me, and when she did, we traded smiles once again. I must admit I was thrilled; I never imagined things would go so well, especially after the poor start we had and all.

As we left the Amazon's camp, Cadmus came up alongside and congratulated me, saying he couldn't have done it better himself, and I promoted him to general on the spot because of the key role he had played in its success. Aeneas accepted Cadmus' promotion coolly, the condescending prick, but I was in too good of a mood to care; the Amazons were staunchly on board, and I rode towards the Ethiopians in high spirits.

We heard the Ethiopians long before we encountered them; the steady drumming of their tom-toms lead us straight to their camp. It was a constant hammering that never varied in pitch or rhythm, just, 'boom...boom...boom', you know, kinda like a heartbeat, only faster, and just about as mesmerizing. All I can say is thank god there wasn't a Greek patrol within earshot that day.

The camp itself was gigantic. Based on the number of tents I saw in it, I'd put the total number of Ethiopians to have been around ten thousand.

Now, you'd think with that many people, their camp would be a disorderly mess, but it wasn't. On the contrary, their camp was well organized into neat little sections they called kraals. There were at least a hundred tents within each kraal; all set the same distance apart. It's like the whole thing had been marked off with a measuring stick or something. Little wonder then, with discipline and organization like that, they were able to march to Troy's aid so quickly.

In the center of their camp, there was a round plaza of sorts, and that's where all the banging was coming from. A row of drummers sat in the middle of the plaza, hammering steadily away on huge drums, while a large group of dancers stomped the ground to dust around them. It was an unusual spectacle to watch because I had never seen people dance in the manner that they did. I'd say they shuffled, more than danced, and as they did, they made sliding motions with their hands that I found to be very amusing. And if that wasn't entertaining enough, every now and then, one of them would fall on the ground and spin around on his back with his legs up in the air, and then he would hop up, and start skipping about wildly. I had never seen the likes before in my life, and it was Cadmus who clued me in.

"They are celebrating their upcoming victory, sir," he said.

"What victory?" I asked.

"Tomorrow's victory," he answered.

I shot him a puzzled look.

He fidgeted about uncomfortably for a second and said, "You see, sir, it's a tribal thing. They know that they will be fighting a major battle tomorrow, and they know that a bunch of them won't survive it, so they are celebrating their victory together while they still can."

You have to admit, it made a lot of sense, and once again, I was impressed by Cadmus' knowledge.

"Why are they dancing so funny?" I asked.

"It's just their style, sir," Cadmus answered. "Plus they're hopped up on Khat."

"Khat?"

"Yes, sir. It's a plant with long green leaves that grows wild in the region. They chew on the leaves throughout the day. It makes them really hyper and excited. They're very fond of it."

I certainly could see why. Khat sure made dancing fun. I mean, they were the dance, the dance was them, and they were all together, goo-goo-g'joob.

"How do you know all this, general?" I asked. "Do you trade with the Ethiopians too?"

"Yes, sir," he answered, "it's where the army gets its leather and hides from. That panther robe you wear all the time came from Ethiopia."

Who knew?

"Is there anything else I need to know?" I asked.

"Yes, sir, eat anything offered to you," he answered.

My stomach didn't like the sound of that, but I decided to accept Cadmus' advice, come what may. I mean, at that point, I'd have eaten monkey balls if that's what it took to gain the support of the Ethiopians, but, I must admit, I wasn't looking forward to it, and so, I rode into their camp with a great deal of gastronomic trepidation.

We entered the encampment looking for Memnon, the Prince of Ethiopia, so we headed towards the camp's main plaza, figuring it was as good a place to find him in as any. Along the way, we passed row upon row of neatly placed tents, and the usual groups of soldiers mingling around them, and several officers too, all of whom greeted us with a welcoming wave and broad smile. We waved back without stopping and rode straight through until we reached the plaza.

It took about ten minutes before any of the dancers noticed our presence, and when they did, they stopped, one by one, partly out of courtesy, partly out of curiosity, until finally, the celebration halted all together. In the silence that ensued, a small boy suddenly appeared, whom I took to be a royal page, and announced that the Prince would appear directly. The boy was followed by a dozen or so shamans, all of whom were wearing weird masks and holding little rattles. They immediately set about raising a ruckus, screaming, "Boogedy-boogedy-boogedy-boooo!"

I listened to their gibberish and watched in complete amazement as they ran about the plaza haphazardly, shaking their rattles wildly, gyrating like madmen, which, in my opinion, they totally were.

"They're driving away evil spirits," Cadmus whispered in my ear, "it's done every time an important meeting takes place. The prince will see us immediately after they are done."

And sure enough, when the shamans finally stopped their silly ranting, the Great Prince of Ethiopia marched proudly into the plaza. And what a man! He stood about a head above the tallest man in our party and was wider by a shoulder than our biggest. He was very powerfully built, with heavily muscled arms and legs, and a chiseled chest partly hidden under a cape of lion skin. His skin was as black as night and his face was…well…almost as handsome as mine. Of course, the last trait immediately caught my attention and upon closer inspection, I couldn't help but notice there we shared a strong resemblance.

"Why does he look almost like..." I quietly whispered to Cadmus.

"You?" he quickly answered.

"Yeah," I replied.

"You don't know?" he asked, almost in disbelief.

I flashed him a look that said I wouldn't have asked if I did.

"Well, sir, you see, ah, well, Memnon's your first cousin," he explained cautiously. "His mother Eos is your father's sister and your aunt."

My head snapped back and eyes immediately went wide with surprise. "What?" I said, "Why didn't my father tell me that?"

Cadmus quickly cast his eyes nervously around to make sure he couldn't be heard and when he was satisfied, he whispered, "It's that whole interracial thing, sir. Your father has never been too proud of the fact that his sister is married to a black guy."

"Ohhhhhhh," says I, finally getting it.

Okay, now, let me tell you something. I'm not prejudice against blacks or any other racial group for that matter. Never have been and never will be. But before you go patting me on the back, let me tell you why. You see, it's not because I possess any high ideals — we both know I don't — it's simply because when you are a lowlife like me, you quickly learn not to go around casting dispersions on other folks just because of their skin color. It just doesn't make sense. So it's totally beyond me why my father would go around believing his black brother-in-law was an embarrassment because, in my opinion, dear old dad's as dumb as they come. If he wasn't, he would have stopped this stupid war a long time ago.

And here's the real kicker: Memnon was ten times sharper than dad.

Figuratively and literally!

"Hey, Captain Cadmus!" Memnon roared. "What language shall we converse in today, Trojan, Ethiopian, Greek, Phoenician, Hebrew or Egyptian? Hey! I just learned a new language. It's called Termit. I'll teach it to you if you want. It'll help with your trading because the people of Termit make some damn fine sword blades. Here, let me show you one."

And, in a flash, he whips out this really enormous sword.

Running his finger along the blade's shiny surface lightly, Memnon said, "It's made out of a new metal called iron and it's ten times stronger and sharper than bronze. It'll slice clean through a bronze shield. I know, because we used these weapons against the Solymi on the way up here and really hacked the shit out of them. The Solymi were sent by the Greeks to intercept us but we sure showed them. Hey! Did you know…"

As you can tell, Memnon was high on Khat and, as a result, was something of a chatty Kathy. Left unchecked, he could talk for hours, moving quickly from subject to subject, until you thought your brain was going to explode. Luckily, Cadmus already knew that.

"My lord," Cadmus interrupted. "If you don't mind, we'll converse in my native tongue because I have a very important guest with me today that I would like you to meet."

And, without further ado, Cadmus introduced me to Memnon.

"Cousin!" shouts Memnon.

And for the second time that day, royalty embraced me.

"Welcome to my camp!" Memnon shouted in my ear while nearly squeezing the breath out of me. "I've heard so much about you!"

Before I could answer or catch my breath, Memnon held me at arm's length, you know, to get a good look at me, and said, "Hey! I know you. You're the guy who won the games I competed in ten years ago when I first visited Troy."

Remembering them and him, I shook my head yes and said that I was.

"Hey! You're really fast!" he said, "Come on, let's race again!"

And, instantly, a big cheer rose from the crowd, making it impossible for me to decline, and attendants rushed forward to remove my armor until finally, I was almost as naked as Memnon was. Then we stood together on a makeshift starting line, and the crowd parted in front of us, and somebody yelled go, and…..

I had the good sense to lose the race on purpose.

"See!" Memnon said, huffing and puffing on the finish line, "I knew I could have beaten you if I hadn't wasted so much energy in the wrestling contest." And then, he said, "Hey! I remember you didn't put up much of a fight during the wrestling event. Did you do that on purpose? Did you conserve your energy for the race?"

I smiled sheepishly, nodded my head and admitted I did.

Memnon smiled back and said, "Well, I'll be! Now that's good strategy."

And that's when I saw my opening.

"I also have an equally good plan to fight the Greeks with, cousin," I said.

"I'll bet you do," Memnon said with a slight chuckle. "Please tell me about it."

And for the third time that day, I outlined my battle plans. Memnon listened carefully to me as I did and, when I was done, he looked at me in wonderment and said, "Cousin, do you realize, with my iron and your brains, we could conquer the world?"

I told him that destroying the Greeks and ending this war would be enough for me.

"Suit yourself," he replied with a shrug. "But it's ours for the taking. Remember that. Hey! Have you eaten yet? I haven't and our race has left me famished. Let's eat! Hey! Have you ever eaten hippo? It's really delicious. Tastes just like pork. Only the chops are bigger. My country is positively swarming with the creatures. Hey! You should visit it when the war is over. Mother would just love to meet you. Hey! We could…"

I never had to say a word during the whole feast that followed. Memnon did all the talking. I did, however, have to taste all sorts of nasty stuff, so when the hippo finally arrived, I was only too happy to gorge myself solely on it. And yes, it really did taste just like pork.

When the banquet was finally over, I thanked Memnon for his hospitality and told him that I had to go so that I could get the Trojan Army ready for tomorrow's battle.

"No, cousin, please stay a while longer," Memnon begged. "We'll drink to tomorrow's victory and get drunk together. Come on, what do you say? Hey! Have you ever tried Khat?"

I could see where that was going.

"No thanks cousin," I answered politely. "I really must return to Troy tonight so I can get the Army ready but, tomorrow, after the battle, we'll celebrate our victory with a big party, I promise."

And that, by the way, is the only time I ever turned down an invitation to get drunk. Ain't it amazing what you can convince yourself to give up in order to accomplish something important? Too bad I didn't learn that earlier in life because, if I had, I'm pretty sure I would have said no to pussy, ass, tits, booze, sex, blow jobs, buttsex, threesomes, foursomes, orgies, gang-bangs, hookers, strippers, sluts, virgins, lesbians, groupies, cheating wives, drunk chicks, porn, dominance role playing, lap dances, frat parties, sorority parties, lingerie parties, happy hours...

Never mind.

I ain't buying it either.

So, anyway, Memnon offered to ride along with us, but since I had heard more than my share of "Hey!" for one day, I declined his offer, explaining that, should we stumble on a Greek patrol on the way back, his presence would be spotted immediately and the enemy would know his army had arrived.

Not wanting to ruin our battle plans, he agreed, and so, we shook hands, and hugged, and hugged again, before finally saying goodbye.

I got back to Troy an hour or two before midnight. Since I had been up the night before with Deidameia, and spent most of the day in the saddle, and hung from a tree limb to boot, I was dead dog tired when I entered the Army's Headquarters and so, my meeting with the Commanders was pretty much short and to the point.

"At sunrise tomorrow," I explained, "we will attack the enemy's camp. Aeneas and I will lead the infantry forward. Polites and the cavalry will remain within the city's walls. Captain, I mean, General Cadmus will command the archers on the battlements. Our infantry attack will be a feint designed to lure the Greeks out of their fortifications and get them on the plain where they can be annihilated. Upon my order, or Aeneas', should I be incapable of giving it, the infantry will retreat after the initial attack on the enemy's walls. Hopefully, the Greeks will leave their camp and pursue us. General Cadmus, when you see our withdrawal, you will send gallopers out to our allies, signaling them to launch their attack. When our infantry gets within bow range of our walls, it will turn about and form ranks. General Cadmus will order the archers to fire when the Greeks are close enough and my brother will hit them with our cavalry. That should be enough to check and hold the Greeks in place long enough for our allies to come up and strike their flanks. The Greeks will be surrounded and destroyed once and for all. After that, we will join forces with our allies and burn the enemy's camp. Does anyone have any questions?"

"Yes, sir," asks Aeneas, "where will you and I position ourselves?"

I don't know if he asked that because he had doubts about my bravery or if he just needed to be told where to stand, but if it was the former, well then, he was in for a great big shock.

I looked him square in the face and said, "We will position ourselves in a chariot that will be located in the infantry's front and center. Captain Pandarus will be holding the chariot's reigns, and together, we will lead the attack."

I figured that since the three of us had started this damned war together, we should end it together, or, at the very least, die together trying. Seemed only fitting.

Aeneas appeared satisfied with my answer; Captain Pandarus, who was standing in the background, didn't seemed as pleased, probably because there wasn't any profit to be made, but I think he appreciated the irony of it because he flashed me a look that clearly said, "Good one!" I ignored his look and him, focusing instead on the task at hand.

"Are there anymore questions?" I asked.

There was none and so, like all commanders do before an important attack, I tried to inspire the men with a final speech. Looking directly into their eyes, I said, "Tomorrow, men, we have a chance of ending this war. All it will take is one more effort on our part and since you are all veterans of many battles, I don't have to tell you what that effort is. I will ask you though, to give that effort, not for me, nor for my father, nor for glory, but for your families, so that they can finally live in peace and happiness once again. Go then, and do your duty for them."

I'll admit, it wasn't the most inspiring speeches of all time, and probably a dancing coach could have done a better job, but I think it was enough to send the men off with a sense of purpose.

And so, that was that. Everything had been set into motion. There was nothing left to do but lie down and try to get a few hours sleep.

Now, most soldiers will tell you that it's damned near impossible to get a good night's sleep before a big battle, and I'm sure they're right for the most part, but, I must tell you that I slept like a baby that night and what's more, I dreamed too.

And what a doozy of a dream it was!

I had no more than shut my eyes when Aphrodite suddenly appeared before me in all her glory. Her face was as beautiful as I remembered, with ruby red lips and rosy red cheeks. Her long blond hair fell past her shoulders in golden curls. She wore a long black dress that was low cut enough to catch a blind man's attention on a dark night and tight enough to seem like a second skin. She stood there appraising me in a very seductive way, which, normally, I would have welcomed with a whoop and a hard-on, but given the next day's activities, I wasn't as thrilled as I might have been.

"What do you want?" I asked all leery like.

"You," she whispered.

"Yeah, sure you do," I snapped. "Well, you can't have me."

"What?" she said, looking totally confused.

"You heard me, doll," I answered. "Now blow. I have a very important day tomorrow and need to get some rest."

"How dare you speak to me like that!" she roared. "I am your patron goddess! I have protected you from harm and made you into what you are today!"

"Oh yeah?" I yelled back, sarcastically. "And what have you made me? Let's take stock, shall we? Hmmmm... let's see...well... for starters, I haven't seen my wife or kid in ten years...and, oh yeah, I helped start a war in which thousands of innocent people have died and...let's see... there seems to be something else missing...what is it?..oh, yes!...AND I'M MARRIED TO THE BIGGEST SLUT IN THE WORLD!"

"Hey, I promised you the love of a beautiful woman!" Aphrodite quickly retorted.

I couldn't help but laugh.

"Is that what you call it?" I asked, smirking. "Love?"

"Yes," she replied.

And that's when I really lost it.

"Well then," I screamed, "you are just as fucked up as she is, aren't you, you stupid, cock-teasing bitch! Fuck, fuck, double fuck, I've had enough! I curse the day I met you and I wish you'd just go away and leave me the fuck alone!"

There was a second or two of silence, in which she stood there blazing with rage, and when she moved towards me, I was scared enough to pull the blanket over my head.

She stopped at the cot's edge, reached down, pulled the blanket from my face and said, "Okay, human, so be it. From this moment on, I will no longer protect you. From here on out, you will be on your own."

I quickly pulled the blanket back over my face and meekly muttered, "Good riddance."

Then, I listened to her stomp her feet, kick the wall and throw something across the room before damning me one last time and disappearing in a brilliant flash of light.

Looking back on it now, I guess I should have hedged my bets and kissed her sacred ass or, even better, screwed it. If I had, maybe I wouldn't be lying here with an arrow sticking out of my dick right now. But on the other hand, who knows what would have happened? I mean, if you believe in that sort of thing, I might have survived the battle without a scratch but, in doing so, some other god would have gotten pissed off I had and I might have been made to wander around the world for years like a tramp before I finally got to go home. Who wants silly shit like that? Certainly not me. So, it's probably better I cut my ties with the gods like I did. Especially since Oenone will be here shortly to patch me up.

Anyway, oddly enough, I slept pretty well after all that, so much so, that I woke up feeling completely refreshed. As I rubbed the sleep out of my eyes, I heard the patter of feet and when my vision cleared, I saw that Cadmus was next to my cot holding a plate of fruit and bacon.

"Good morning, sir," he said, offering me the breakfast.

"Good morning, General" I said, sitting up and taking the plate from him. "What time is it?"

"About an hour before sunrise, sir," he answered.

"Good," I said, over a mouthful of bacon. "Is the Army ready?"

"Yes, sir, every man is in position and knows his duty," he answered.

I smiled and tossed him a piece of bacon. He caught it and immediately stuffed it into his mouth. For a moment or two, he crunched the bacon until it was gone and then he said, "There's nothing left to do but launch the attack."

And that's when alarm bells began rumbling in my stomach. You see, up until that moment, I'd been so busy planning the battle that it never once crossed my mind I'd have to fight in it too.

As I absorbed the dreadful realization that I was probably going to die, I popped a big, purple grape in my mouth and nervously started chewing the shit out of it. Cadmus studied me closely as I did and since there seemed to be something on his mind other than bumming another piece of bacon, I stopped chewing and said "What?"

He lowered his eyes uncomfortably and said, "Ah, nothing, sir. I was just wondering if you were scared, that's all."

I resumed chewing the grape and pondered his question. It was a good grape. It was also a very good question because it made me think about my fear.

Fuck, yeah, I was scared!

But I realized I had to get a grip because the time had come for me to make a stand and set things right. I had been running and hiding for too long.

"I've never been so afraid in my life," I quietly confessed to Cadmus. "Now help me put my armor on."

Chapter Eleven

The sun has almost sat because darkness is starting to engulf my room. Soon, a servant will come in and lower the lamp's flames to a dim glow. Then the shadows that have haunted me all day will disappear and I will finally be alone. Maybe I'll sleep then. Perhaps I'll even dream. But whether or not I do, I'm sure Oenone will be here in the morning.

In anticipation of her arrival, I close my eyes and try to imagine her walking into the room. What will she look like? I wonder. What will she say? What will I say? Will she bring our son? What will I say to him? How will I explain my absence? What color eyes did my son have? Blue, I think. No, wait, maybe they're brown like Oenone's. I don't really recall.

So many questions!

At least, I have all night to think about them.

I shut my eyes and take a deep breath. Suddenly, my nose catches the scent of flour.

That can mean only one thing.

Cadmus!

I immediately glance towards the doorway.

All of Cadmus is standing in it. His body is so wide that it touches both sides of the door's wooden frame. Obviously, the army hasn't started starving yet.

"Hello, General," I say.

"Hello, sir," he answers.

"I was just thinking about you." I say. "Please, come in."

He squeezes through the doorway and approaches my bed. When he gets close enough, I can see that his face is sad, no doubt, because of my bad condition.

"Don't worry," I say, "I'll be okay. I've sent for someone who can heal me. She should be here in the morning."

"Good," he says, trying his best to sound relieved.

"So, what have you been up to?" I ask in an effort to change the subject.

"I've just come from the bakery," he answers. "The army has enough bread left to last three more days."

"Three days," I repeat. "Are you planning to get some more flour?"

"That's why I came by tonight, sir," he says. "I mean, besides to see how you were doing, of course, and give you some good news."

"Give me the good news first," I say. God knows, I can use it.

He nods and says, "The Greeks, what was left of them, pulled out this evening. They're gone, sir. So I guess the war is finally over. And since it is, I guess I should go to Canaan to replenish our grain supplies. After that, I'll probably sail to Ethiopia and drop off Memnon's ashes to his family. Then I'll go to Termit and try to get the army some iron weapons. I should leave tonight since the army's food supplies are so dangerously low."

My ears latch on to the news of the Greek's withdrawal and I am instantly elated.

"They left?" I ask.

"Yes, sir," he answers with a nod. "Their camp appears to be deserted. Aeneas is sending a scouting party out right now to look the place over."

I blink at him in amazement and say, 'Well, that's it then, we won."

"Yes, sir," he says with a broad smile. "You did it."

I smile back and offer him my hand.

As he takes it, I say, "Thank you for your help."

He shakes my hand warmly and says, "It was an honor, sir."

Then he releases it, pats me on the shoulder and turns to leave.

Smiling, I watch him wobble away.

Just before he gets to the door, he pauses for a moment, then turns around and, jokingly, asks me if I am still scared.

"Not anymore," I say.

And I'm not.

Really.

But, believe me, I was plenty scared the morning of the battle, so much so, that I felt like puking up my breakfast and I probably would have too if Cadmus hadn't been there to calm me. I guess he could sense that I was pretty nervous. Funny how fat people always seem to pick up on things like that. Anyway, after I admitted my fear, I felt better and, for some strange reason, that gave me enough courage to face the day.

Looking back on it now, I guess it's all right to be afraid but it's not okay to allow that fear to govern your actions or cause you undo worry. Life's way is too short for that. That's why I'm not scared anymore.

So, anyway, after I checked my gag reflex and strapped my armor on, Cadmus handed me my bow, and together, we walked down to the West Gate. Just outside of it, we found our infantry eager to attack; confidence in my plan was running high amongst the men, I could see it in their eyes and hear it in their voices.

Unfortunately, their confidence didn't extend to me personally.

"You goin' all the way this time?" a battle scarred veteran asked when our eyes met.

He was questioning my bravery because he had, no doubt, been among the soldiers I deserted during the war's first battle.

"Yes," I firmly answered, "I intend to go all the way this time."

The veteran stared at me for a moment with a skeptical look on his scarred face; then, after a few seconds more, his look softened into acceptance, probably because I had been man enough to admit my past cowardice.

"One more attack then," he said.

I nodded in agreement and said, "Yes. Just follow me one more time. That's all I ask. I won't let you down, I swear."

I guess that was enough for him because he immediately turned around and roared an order. Instantly, the ranks opened up and we were surrounded by soldiers.

"The Prince has something to say, men!" the man yelled, "Be still and let him talk!"

I looked around at the men — you never saw so many men eager to fight — and for the second time that morning, my breakfast nearly came up into my throat, but then I swallowed hard and muttered something designed to help keep it down for good. I said, "This is it. For once, we outnumber the enemy. And besides that, we have the element of surprise on our side. There's no doubt then, that this is going to be the war's last battle. All you gotta do is show some courage and then you can go home."

And get this: although I was mainly talking to myself, the men were so motivated by my little speech that a great yell went up and they started beating on their shields all crazy like. But before their enthusiasm could spread to the whole army, the old veteran quickly stepped forward and shouted, "Quiet down! Do you want to wake the Greeks up? Form up your ranks again and be quiet! We'll be at the enemy soon enough and then you can make as much racket as you want! Form up now! Form up!"

They quickly fell back in, impatient as bloodhounds, and I couldn't help marveling how life had brought us together. I mean, they had spent the last ten years bravely fighting the war while I had spent the same amount of time selfishly shirking my duties, and yet, here we were together. It's like both roads led to the same place. Weird isn't it?

Anyway, as I stood there pondering the mysteries of life, Aeneas suddenly appeared to tell me that the infantry was ready to advance and that, if we started now, we would reach the enemy's walls just as the sun was coming up. That caused me to focus on reality again and so I nodded at the men, wished them luck, and quickly followed Aeneas over to our chariot.

Pandarus was standing in the vehicle when we got there, tugging at the reins and swearing at the three horses harnessed to it. I jumped in behind him and he started cussing me too. Since I was trying my damnedest to look brave, I told him to shut up, which pissed him off even more, and he snapped the reins angrily. The horses immediately bounded forward, forcing Aeneas to leap aboard as they did.

About two seconds later, I heard of series of commands on our left and right, and then watched our infantry surge forward. There were about fifteen hundred of them — all that was left after ten years of war — and they marched behind us in grim silence. I could not help but admire them as they did, their ranks were so quiet and orderly, and every face was staring bravely ahead. Of course, Aeneas and Pandarus had seen it all before so their minds were focused elsewhere. While I gawked at the brave little band behind us, they began to argue about where the chariot should be stationed. Aeneas thought we should remain at the forefront of the army, no matter what, while Pandarus thought we should position ourselves behind it when the attack on the enemy's fortifications began.

"There's a ditch in front of the Greek wall, you numbskull," Pandarus shouted at Aeneas.

"So?" Aeneas shouted. "We'll have some men throw a dirt bridge across it."

For once, I agreed with Pandarus.

"Will you two shut up?" I shouted. "When the attack on the walls begins, we will position ourselves behind the army. Pandarus will steer, I will fire arrows at the enemy and Aeneas will defend the chariot from close range attack."

"Don't tell me to shut up or how to fight from a chariot!" Pandarus yelled back at me. "How many battles have you been in, you whiny little shit! This is my forty-second fight. I've killed more men than you are years old."

"Don't talk to him like that!" Aeneas immediately jumped in. "He is the Army's commander and you will treat him with respect!"

What we were still arguing about, I didn't know.

"Oh, fuck you, Aeneas, you gung-ho bastard!" Pandarus shouted. "We wouldn't be here if it wasn't for him!"

I was astounded, to say the least.

"How do you figure that?" I roared. "You two knuckleheads started this war, not me!"

"Don't call me a knucklehead!" Aeneas shouted.

"You just said I'm the army commander! Duh!" I bellowed sarcastically at Aeneas. "I can call you any fucking thing I want!"

"See?" yells Pandarus. "He thinks he's a goddamned king or something!"

"No, I don't!" I screeched.

"Yes, you do!" Aeneas shouted. "You think you're such hot shit with your fancy-dancy strategy."

"Oh, well, excuse me, smart guy," I fired back. "I guess we should have just lined up in broad daylight and flung ourselves on the Greek's camp after they had breakfast and were ready."

"What's wrong with that?" Aeneas shouted.

I looked at him in amazement and yelled, "It gets people killed, you dolt, and settles nothing!"

"Oh, yeah, and what do you think is going to happen today?" Pandarus screamed. "We've got one foot in the grave already riding around in this fucking chariot. And I was going to open up a laundry this week!"

I was just about to tell him what he could do with his stupid laundry when the dark outline of the Greek camp suddenly appeared before us.

"Shhhhhhhhhh!" I quickly said, "We're almost there."

We turned away from each other with lofty distaste and stared at the camp.

"Do you think they're still asleep?" I whispered.

An arrow whizzing past Aeneas' head answered my question.

Apparently, our loud argument had alerted the Greek sentries. God, I remember thinking, why didn't I leave these two idiots at home? If I had, I'm pretty sure, we could have gotten all the way up to the walls without being noticed. That's how quiet and disciplined the soldiers behind us were. Anyway, what was done was done, and a second whizzing arrow quickly convinced me that there was nothing left to do but order the attack.

In one voice, the commanders leading the infantry responded with a loud command to charge, and then hundreds of dark figures went rushing past our chariot. They covered the short distance to the enemy's walls in about ten seconds, screaming like demons as they ran, and when they got there, ladders went up and torches were lit. In the flickering light, I watched our men valiantly climb up the ladders, stabbing and hacking at the defenders above. God, what a jumbled mess it was! Soon men were fighting all over the battlements, waving torches, roaring at the top of their lungs, running, ducking, slashing, clutching, pulling, pushing, cutting each other to bits, falling off the walls, clutching their wounds in pain or dying in silence. It was just plain madness and so totally mesmerizing that I lost all track of time. How long it went on, I don't know. But it must have been awhile because, suddenly, Aeneas was at my elbow, pointing at the rosy-fingered dawn, and asking how much longer the attack should continue.

I looked at the rising sun, then over to Troy's walls, which I could clearly see, and said, "Signal the withdrawal."

He immediately turned to a nearby drummer, who began banging away, and then, moments later, with a loud cry to retreat, the whole Army suddenly turned on its heels and began to rush past us in disorderly mass. They did it so convincingly that I wondered if they were running away for real.

Concerned, I looked over at Aeneas, who instantly read my thoughts and said, "Don't worry, they'll stop."

Then, turning to Pandarus, he calmly said, "We should join them."

The chariot wheeled around quickly and began treading its way through the retreating mob. As it did, I turned around and saw that the Greeks were steaming out of their camp after us like angry hornets. Then, I looked over my shoulder to Troy and saw two groups of riders heading north and south. Knowing that they were on their way to our allies, I looked back at the onrushing Greeks, shook my fist at them and screamed, "That's right, you bastards, come out and get us!"

They couldn't hear me, because, by then, we were out in front of our infantry and out of earshot. But that didn't stop me from hurling more curses at them and I did so until Aeneas finally told me to shut up so that he could reform our infantry.

About twenty cubits from Troy's walls, Aeneas ordered Pandarus to wheel the chariot about, which he promptly did, and while Pandarus struggled to steady the horses, our infantry quickly joined us, forming one long solid rank of shield and spear to our front. I'd say that there were about thirteen hundred of them left, and of that, a good many were wounded in some manner. But they stood their ground nevertheless, glaring at the Greeks like madmen, determined to face an enemy four times their number even if it meant certain death. It was truly an amazing sight.

"Steady, boys," Aeneas said to them coolly. "They'll be in arrow range soon."

I turned to see if the archers on the walls above us were ready and was immediately relieved to see that they were. I also saw Cadmus too, standing in the middle of them, calmly surveying the situation while eating a chicken leg.

"Steady," says Aeneas again.

I looked back at the Greeks; they were almost upon us, barely a hundred cubits away. Odysseus, Menelaus and Agamemnon were in their chariots leading the charge. I could hear them urging their soldiers forward, promising that victory was at hand.

"Steady," repeats Aeneas, over the growing din.

I gaped at the oncoming tide of Greeks and wondered if Aeneas was talking to me personally because, from the looks of things, it appeared that I was the only frightened person on the battlefield at that particular moment. Everyone else seemed perfectly calm. Anyhow, if he was talking to me, he was wasting his breath because I couldn't have run away even if I wanted to. That's because my feet were frozen in fear to the floor of that damned chariot.

"Steady," says Aeneas again.

I'm telling you, I could actually feel the ground shake. The Greeks, all four thousand of them, were a mere twenty cubits away. So close that I could actually see the whites of their hate-filled eyes and, I swear, they all seemed to be looking right at me.

"Steady," goes Aeneas calmly.

I looked up at Cadmus and thought, why don't you give the order to fire, you crazy fat bastard! What are you waiting for? Desert? Fire, fire, fire! For god's sakes, fire! I never wanted to hear someone say that word so badly in my life.

And then, thankfully, I did.

"Fire!" Cadmus bellowed.

Instantly, the sky above us became darkened with five hundred arrows. I followed their flight with my eyes and watch them plunge into the Greek ranks below. Immediately, men went down in a jumbled heap and a loud groan rose up from the Greek Army. Its whole front rank seemed to disintegrate before my eyes. The horses hitched to Odysseus, Menelaus and Agamemnon's chariots were hit too and went down in a tangle of legs and harnesses. All three leaders were thrown to the ground and temporarily stunned. In the confusion that followed, Cadmus released another flight of arrows and, once again, more men and horses fell to the ground. A great cry went up from our soldiers and a nearby captain immediately requested permission to charge.

"Not yet," answered Aeneas. "Wait for our friends."

And then, right on cue, our allies appeared.

They came flooding in from the north and south, and it took me a second to recognize them. The Amazons were wearing dazzling breastplates and helmets with golden plumes, while the Ethiopians were sporting loincloths of antelope tails, armbands of white goat fur and ostrich feathered headdresses. They were attacking, all right, and then I heard a voice shouting nearby, and I looked over at Agamemnon, who was screaming his fool head off, trying desperately to get his men to come to his aid.

And, let me tell you, the look on his face was absolutely priceless! I knew it well: fear.

He was standing near his overturned chariot, urging his men to dress their ranks around him in a voice so shrill with terror that it sounded like a goat being chased by a couple of horny farm boys.

"Come on, men!" he pleaded. "Gather around me and protect your kinggg! Protect your kinggggg, men! Protect your kingggggggg!"

As I listened to his shrieks become more and more desperate, a positively wonderful thought entered my mind, and I quickly notched my bow with an arrow, took aim at the screaming idiot, and fired. The missile plowed into his right forearm. Not one of my better shots, I have to admit, and I was notching up another arrow for a second attempt, when I glanced up to see that Agamemnon was being hustled away to safety by a small group of royal bodyguards.

I watched him disappear into the crowd and thought, well, Agamemnon, you can run but you can't hide, we'll catch up to your ass shortly.

Then there was a joyous yell from our ranks as our allies slammed into the flanks of the Greeks, and I cheered too; I don't think I've ever been happier in my life. I was smiling at Aeneas, clutching my bow victoriously, when I saw him turn to the eager captain and calmly say, "You may launch your attack now, Captain."

Another cheer went up, and our men leapt forward, shoulder to shoulder, and fell upon the Greeks like a pack of hungry lions. The enemy immediately reeled backwards from the onslaught, stumbling over dead comrades, turning and fighting desperately as our men closed in for the kill. I heard the captain yell, "Take no prisoners!" and watched the spears and swords of our men find their marks. In front of me, Odysseus and Menelaus staggered about wildly, hacking and slashing at anything within range. I had a beautiful arrow shot at Menelaus, and could have killed him easily, but couldn't find it within myself to do it, so I did the next best thing by shooting the soldier standing next to him. The man screamed and feebly clawed at the arrow buried in his chest until a nearby Trojan finished him off for good.

Then Troy's West Gate opened up behind us and out of it poured Polites and the troopers of our cavalry reserve. Straight at the enemy they went, three hundred lances altogether, gathering speed with every step they took, Death sweeping forward. Odysseus, Menelaus and about five hundred Greeks were on the verge of breaking away from our infantry when Polites' cavalry smashed into them. Most of the enemy were immediately bowled over and ground into a bloody pulp by the horse's hooves, but Odysseus, Menelaus and a handful of other Greeks somehow or another managed to remain standing. In the confused melee that followed, Odysseus came face to face with Polites. My brother stabbed at him with his lance but Odysseus wrestled the weapon out of his hands and murdered him with it. I immediately turned away painfully and regretted putting Polites in command of the cavalry. When I looked back again, Menelaus and Odysseus were sitting on top of my brother's horse and riding away from the press at breakneck speed.

Immediately, Pandarus snapped the reins angrily and we set off after them. I clung to the side of the chariot, peering through the jumbled mass of men in front of us, trying to keep my eyes on our two fugitives. Menelaus sat behind Odysseus, looking calmly back at us, his helmet gone, his face caked in blood. There were about a hundred or so Greeks running behind them and, when we got close enough, some of these fleeing soldiers turned around and attacked us. From all sides, one after another, they lunged at our chariot, but Aeneas and I fought them off each time they did, leaving a trail of dead Greeks in our wake.

Elsewhere, the battle was almost over. The plain all around us was littered with thousands upon thousands of dead bodies. Here and there, surrounded bands of Greeks still fought in a desperate attempt to get back to the safety of their fortifications. It was into one of these clusters of about three hundred Greeks that Menelaus and Odysseus rode. As we closed in on them, I watched the two dismount and immediately set about organizing the men around them. I could see them shuffling men about here and there, plugging gaps with fresh bodies, shoring up the band's defenses. Their only hope, as I just said, was to fight their way clear. And they might have done it too, if they hadn't chosen to join a band occupying the very center of the battlefield because, you see, it quickly became the focal point for all three armies to attack.

Glancing quickly around, I could see thousands of Trojans, Ethiopians and Amazons approaching from every direction. Pandarus was whipping the horses forward to lead them in, and soon, the chariot was tearing along at breakneck speed. I desperately hung on to its sides, trying not to fall out and bracing myself for the impact that was sure to come.

"Faster!" screamed Aeneas. "Faster! Hit them at full speed! Tear a hole into their ranks!"

"Shut up!" Pandarus shouted back. "Don't tell me how to drive a chariot!"

"There, there!" Aeneas yelled, pointing wildly. "Hit that section of their defenses! It's weakest there!"

"I told you to shut the fuck up!" Pandarus responded angrily.

While I listened to them argue, Memnon suddenly came riding up alongside the chariot and waved at me. He was riding a fine black stallion and wearing an outlandish ostrich plumed bonnet. I swear, the thing was so big, it looked like a gigantic bird was perched on top his head. I stared at it a moment or two, and was just about to say something, when, almost out of the blue, an arrow suddenly buried itself in the middle of my cousin's chest.

"Heyyyyyyyyyyyyyyyyyyyyy!" Memnon immediately screamed.

Instinctively, I ducked, and more arrows whizzed past, and when I came back up, Memnon's horse was galloping rider less beside us. I had only a second to look back, because, just then, the chariot suddenly went careening into the enemy's ranks like a battering ram. After that, everything became a blur of screaming soldiers, flashing blades and raging horses. Luckily, the blur didn't last very long because we were going so fast that we tore straight through the Greek position, punching a large hole into both sides of their defensive ring.

When we wheeled back around to survey the damage we had done, I saw Penthesileia lead about five hundred or so mounted Amazons through the gaps we had created. She was waving her fancy spear and loudly urging her Amazons to follow her. God, what a magnificent sight they were! I'm telling you, those girls hacked to pieces any Greek warrior man enough to stand up to them. I saw Penthesileia drive her lance straight through a burly Greek's body and then turn around and lop off another soldier's head with her sword. The other Amazons swirled around her, creating a deadly vortex of slashing weapons and stomping hooves that soon littered the ground with hundreds of dead and dying Greeks. And, sadly enough, that's what caused Penthesileia's downfall, because, you see, there was so many bodies underfoot that they caused her horse to stumble sideways and fall to the ground. I watched Penthesileia disappear into the struggling mass and gasped. Instantly, the Amazons rushed to her aid but, by the time they cut their way to her side, it was too late. The Greeks had stabbed her to death.

That's war for you, I guess. Don't believe all that gibberish the bards tell you about glory and honor. War's just death waiting to happen, plain and simple. And if you are in the wrong place at the wrong time, or if you take one wrong step, you're gonna die, and there ain't much glory in that. Just ask Memnon and Penthesileia.

Anyway, the Amazons lost their queen and it's a shame too, because the battle was almost over. You see, when Penthesileia went down, contingents of Ethiopians were already attacking the Greek camp. We could see them scaling the walls and fighting on the battlements.

Aeneas looked over at them, and then back at the disintegrating pocket of Greeks in front of us and said, "We'd better join them the attack on the fortifications. There's nothing more we can do here. This action's almost over."

Pandarus shouted at the beasts, snapped the reins and the chariot pulled away.

"Goodbye, Penthesileia," I whispered under my breath as it did. "You were a splendid woman, much too good for the likes of me."

About half way to the Greek fortifications, there was a sudden yell behind us, and I turned around to see that our troops were celebrating the Amazon's victory over the pocket Menelaus and Odysseus had sought refuge in. I naturally assumed the two Greek leaders were dead and felt happy that one was and a little sad about the other. I don't have to tell you which.

There was still more fighting to be done, of course, and on the plain behind us, I could see groups of Trojans, Ethiopians and Amazons heading our way. They came sweeping down the plain, spears on their shoulders, line abreast, led by captains, sergeants or even privates, all seemingly eager to be in on the final kill and, although I didn't have to, I waved them on and so did Aeneas.

"Come on, men!" we shouted. "To the ships! Let's finish them off!"

Up ahead, as I just told you, the attack on the Greek camp was already going full bore. A thousand or so Ethiopians were assaulting the walls using the ladders we had left behind in the morning's attack. Hundreds of black-limbed warriors were already on top of the battlements, hacking and slashing at a handful of Greek soldiers left behind to defend the camp. Below, in front of the gate, there was a tremendous struggle going on as well. I could see armored Greeks, survivors of the morning's battle, desperately trying to beat back the Ethiopians so that they could get inside their fort. The gate was opened slightly to admit them and it was there that Pandarus aimed our chariot.

I gaped at Pandarus and thought, surely the madman doesn't intend to slam our horses into a wooden gate. There's a vast difference between wood and flesh, you know, especially in density, and I was just about to point that scientific fact out to him when I noticed the Ethiopians were getting out of our way and the Greeks...well...when they saw us thundering towards them, their eyes went wild with terror, and to the man, I swear, they turned around and fled through the gate, pushing it wide open in the process. We charged right through it and were immediately followed by a large number of Ethiopians. Once inside, we were instantly met by a hail of arrows from the ships parked on the nearby beach. I swear, every sailor in the Greek navy seemed to be armed with a bow, and they began firing pell-mell into our ranks as we swept by their ships. Their deadly missiles hit all three of our horses and Pandarus too. He jerked back from the reins and fell against me with two arrows sticking out of his chest. I caught him in my arms, and as I struggled against his weight, he looked at me, smiled and said, "See you in Hades, smuck." I wasn't sure how to respond to that and besides, there wasn't time anyway, because the chariot immediately careened over sideways and I was thrown to the ground. For a moment or two, I had a bug's view of the battlefield and saw hundreds of black feet stream past my head, then, for some unknown reason, I stood up and stumbled over to the chariot. Aeneas lay next to it, knocked unconscious or dead, I wasn't sure which. Panduras lay in a pool of blood next to him, undoubtedly, waiting for me in Hades. Ethiopian warriors were swarming all around us, finishing off the Greeks sailors and setting fire to their ships. It's a shame cousin Memnon couldn't have been there to see them do it. He would have been proud of his men for sure.

Anyway, I just stood there taking it all in, feeling quite satisfied that I had risked my neck enough and I would have ended my participation in the battle right then and there if it hadn't been for a woman's scream. It came from across the battlefield and when I looked in its direction, I saw Deidameia, holding Neoptolemus in her arms, running away from a dozen or so Ethiopian soldiers. She was desperately trying to reach the part of camp still being defended by Agamemnon and the tattered remnants of the Greek army. Instantly, without thinking, I grabbed my bow, a handful of arrows, and headed in her direction. Notching the bow as I ran, I got there just as the lead Ethiopian was rearing back to throw his spear at her. Only problem was, as I took aim at the spear chucker, out of the corner of my left eye, I saw that bastard Philoctetes standing a short distance away, getting ready to shoot me with that fucking poison arrow he had gotten from Hercules.

And so, in the space of a heartbeat, I had to make the biggest decision of my life.

Do I save my own life by killing Philoctetes?

Or do I save the life of my ex-girlfriend by killing the Ethiopian?

A real dilemma for anyone with a conscience, you'll agree.

And, given the fact that I never had much of one, I'm pretty sure you're gonna be shocked by what I decided to do.

Believe it or not, I actually shot that damned Ethiopian!

My arrow hit him squarely in the chest, knocking him to the ground, spear and all, and then, two heartbeats later, as I watched Deidameia run safely away, I felt Philoctetes' arrow hit Mr. Happy right between the balls. Immediately, I doubled over in pain and fell to the ground. The remaining Ethiopians whirled around in my direction in search of the man who had just killed their leader. As their eyes settled on me, I managed to raise my hand and point an accusing finger at Philoctetes, hoping it would be enough to persuade them that he was the culprit.

It was.

The Ethiopians glanced over at Philoctetes, and then said something in Ethiopian that can only be interpreted as "Let's get that motherfucker!" because, immediately after that, they charged him in unison, and the last I saw of Philoctetes, he was being chased up the beach by a pack of howling Ethiopians.

Served the cocksucker right and I hope they caught up with him too.

Anyway, as I lay there wriggling in agony, someone suddenly walked up behind me and said, "That was a pretty clever trick."

I was in no mood to thank him for the compliment because my wound was burning like Prometheus' fire and if there's one thing that makes me forget my manners, it's searing pain, so I grimaced and said, "Get me to a doctor, for god's sakes."

"That's gonna be a little hard to do right now, dude," the voice answered.

I immediately froze.

Did he just call me dude? I asked myself. There's only one guy who calls me that and he is…oh, shit…standing right behind me!

It was Menelaus!

I let out a shriek that Panduras probably heard down in Hades, and tried to crawl away, but Menelaus grabbed my collar and began dragging me towards the camp's wall. I clawed helplessly at the earth as he did and said, "I'm sorry, really I am, I'm really sorry, please don't kill meeeee."

"Shut up," he growled. "I'm not going to kill you."

Well, that was a welcomed bit of good news, you'll agree, especially in light of everything, so I did as I was told and choked down my terror.

He propped me up against the wall and said, "Just sit there and chill. I'm sure a surgeon will be along directly after things die down a bit."

I sat there, but, by god, I didn't relax. Instead, I stared up at him in total wonderment. How the fuck did he survive the battle, I asked myself. And then I saw why — he was wearing a Trojan uniform! Somehow or another, during all the confusion, he had managed to swap uniforms with one of our dead officers. And if that wasn't enough, he was also covered in blood and dust, effectively hiding his true identity even more.

He sat down beside me and since we were so tuckered out, we just sort of leaned against one another for support. In front of us, hundreds of warriors, mainly Ethiopians, were running about haphazardly. That's because most of their leaders had been killed and so, there wasn't anyone left to lead them against Agamemnon, who was still holed up at the far end of the camp. Every ship on the beach, except a few on Agamemnon's end, was burning out of control, sending long trails of black smoke up to the heavens.

Menelaus surveyed the terrific scene and said, "Did you plan all this?"

"Yes, I guess I did," I answered, almost apologetically. "Someone had to put an end to this stupid war."

He chuckled slightly and said, "Well, dude, you certainly did that. We're finished. We don't have enough troops left to dig a latrine with."

"Neither do we," I replied softly.

It's difficult to describe how I felt at that moment; it was like a nightmare had finally ended. I felt relieved and happy that it was over, but at the same time, I felt like shit. I just couldn't shake the heavy guilt I felt for starting the awful thing.

So, I blurted, "I'm sorry that it came to this. I tried my best to prevent it."

"I know, dude," he said, all friendly like. "Deidameia told me yesterday."

I looked at him in surprise and said, "Did she tell you about Helen too?"

"Yes," he said, looking me straight in the eyes. "I should have known better to leave you alone with that conniving whore, dude. It's my fault I did and I'm sorry for doing so because it cost me my best friend and caused this war. I hope you can forgive me."

I was so overwhelmed, I wanted to go somewhere and cry my guts out but since I couldn't, I offered him my hand instead. He took it with a sad smile and we crammed all our feelings into that handshake. For I don't know how long, we just sat there pumping our hands up and down emotionally. We were friends again and that was enough to forgive all the bad things that had passed between us.

Then some Trojan stretcher-bearers appeared, and Menelaus immediately called out to them. "This is Prince Alexander of Troy," he yelled, "and he needs urgent medical care! Carry him to a surgeon at once!"

"What about you?" I asked hastily as stretcher-bearers headed our way.

"I'm cool, bro," he answered. "I'll chill here until nightfall, then I'll slide out of this uniform and sneak into our lines. It shouldn't be hard.

And when I get there, I'll tell Deidameia you saved her life and kept your promise."

For a second, I marveled I had finally kept a promise to a female, and then I asked, "What about Helen? What do you want me to do with her?"

"Keep the worthless bitch," he said with a slight shrug. "She's good for nothing."

"Oh, I don't know about that," I said with a faint smile. "I've turned her into a pretty good servant."

"Really?" he said, genuinely surprised.

"Yeah, it's a long story, but I've got her waiting on me hand and foot now," I explained quickly. "All you gotta do is lay the law down to her."

A look crossed his face like he had never thought of doing that before, and then he shook his head disgustingly and said, "I was always such a sucker for her boobs. She'd flash them at me and I'd forgive anything she did."

I started to tell him that it was much the same with me, but the medics arrived and I couldn't. It didn't matter though because I'm pretty sure he already knew it. Heck, anyone who has ever been with Helen knows it. And that's why we allowed her to make fools of us. I understand that now and when I think about how stupid she made us look, I'm not proud of it, but, at least, I feel a small degree of satisfaction knowing that I finally wised up.

And that brings me back to the beginning, back to Oenone.

She'll come and save me because I've wised up enough to deserve a second chance.

You see, I finally realize how special women like Oenone, Deidameia and Polyxena really are. Not to get all lovey-dovey, but when you experience the kind of love they offer, like I did, and compare it to the kind of shit I had to put up with Helen, well, you can't help but see how lucky you are to have had them in your life. And you know what? Their love is good enough for me. I no longer need or want other women in my life. Nor do I want to live life in the fast lane with the likes of Menelaus. From now on, I'll get my kicks decorating a room for Oenone or by watching our son climb beech trees.

So, no worries, Oenone will come, I know she will, because I have finally grown up.

Chapter Twelve

Night has fallen. I'm waiting for the servant to come in and attend to the lamps.

I get Helen instead.

I gaze up at her sullenly. For some reason, she smiles and kisses my forehead. It's the first time she has kissed me in weeks and I can't help but wonder why.

"What was that for?" I ask.

"To make you feel better," she answers.

It'll take more than that, I think.

"And I've also brought you something for the pain," she says, presenting a cup containing a mysterious liquid.

Looking at it cautiously, I ask her what it is, I mean, god knows, the last thing I need to do right now is take a leak.

"Just something I mixed up for you," she says pleasantly. "It'll help you sleep."

I certainly need to do that, so I nod my head okay.

Very gently, she slips a hand under my head and lifts it forward so that I can drink from the cup. As she does, I can smell the perfume she is wearing. Honeydew. It's the fragrance she wears during special occasions. She wore it the night we went to Kranai together and for a second, I wonder why she is wearing it now.

Then my lips touch the side of the cup and I focus on drinking the cool liquid instead. She tilts the cup so the stuff streams past my lips, across my tongue and down my throat. The liquid tastes like wine and bitter nuts. I frown in disgust when it's gone.

"There," she says, "now you'll rest."

She eases my head back down on the pillow and stares down at me, waiting for the drug to take effect.

It does.

As fast as magic, the pain from my wounds starts to dull and for a moment or two, I feel wonderful. I close my eyes and think of Oenone. She'll be here in the morning when I wake up and I think about how lovely she will look and then, I suddenly realize I can't feel my legs anymore. Immediately, I open my eyes and look down at them. They've grown cold and I can't wiggle my toes! Alarmed, I look up at Helen.

"Just relax, honey," she says reassuringly, "and let the drug take effect. It'll all be over in a second."

And it suddenly dawns on me: I've been fucking poisoned!

The bitch is trying to kill me!

I want to choke the shit out of her but my arms and hands won't respond. They've grown cold too. All I can do is lie here and die by degrees.

"Why?" I ask forlornly.

"To put you out of your misery, of course," she says nonchalantly while inspecting her gown closely. Apparently, she wants to look good for my death.

"But Oenone is..." I mutter, my words falling off because my tongue has grown numb too.

Suddenly, the room starts swimming in and out of focus and I close my eyes to make it stop.

In the silence that follows, I hear a man's voice say, "Is he dead yet?"

"Almost," Helen answers.

I open my eyes slightly and see that my brother Deiphobus has entered the room. He is holding Helen in his arms and they are kissing passionately.

Suddenly, all the pieces fall neatly into place. Helen has decided to marry my brother after all, that's why she's wearing honeydew and fussing about her dress. And it's why I am about to die.

I can't say I'm surprised because, with Helen, it's always been more about opportunity than it has ever been about romance. I'm just upset I never saw it coming.

When they finish kissing, Deiphobus leans back and says, "Have you heard, darling? The Greeks left behind a great big wooden horse. It's a tribute to our city and it's so big, we're gonna have to knock down the gate just to get it inside the city."

A wooden horse!

Immediately, my mind flashes back to the Oracle and her prophesy.

"When the Greeks build a horse, the Palladium will no longer preserve Troy and the city will perish in flames," she had said.

Oh, shit!, my mind screams, it's coming true! It's fucking coming true!

Suddenly, I'm not upset anymore.

And with the last bit of my strength, I look up at the future Mister and Missus Extra Crispy and laugh.

The End

T H E   E N D

She did it.